# ANDRE GONZALEZ

# Time Roller

*For my mother, Julie.*

"Don't worry; don't be afraid, ever,
because this is just a ride."

—Bill Hicks

# GET EXCLUSIVE BONUS STORIES!

Connecting with readers is the best part of this job. Releasing a book into the world is a truly frightening moment every time it happens! Hearing your feedback, whether good or bad, goes a long way in shaping future projects and helping me grow as a writer. I also like to take readers behind the scenes on occasion and share what is happening in my wild world of writing. If you're interested, please consider joining my mailing list. If you do, I'll send you four FREE novellas as a thank you!

You can get your content **for free,** by signing up at https://andregonzalez.net/join-newsletter

# Chapter 1

*August 24, 1978*

An ice cube slid down the back of Beverly Tanner's shirt, and she vaulted into the air.

"Dammit, Bobby!" she shouted, wriggling her body and flapping the back of her shirt until the ice fell to its splintered death on the scorching pavement.

Bobby, her fifteen-year-old son, cackled. He gripped his stomach, struggling to keep from falling over as he gasped for breath amid the onslaught of giggles.

"Sorry," he finally said, his voice cracking thanks to puberty. "I had to. It's only ninety degrees today, remember?"

Beverly crossed her arms and shook her head, struggling to keep a grin off her face as she glared at her son. "At least give me a warning next time. It *did* feel nice—I can't deny that."

Bobby hugged his mother's arm. He had a big heart and always found opportunities to make others laugh. A long day under the sun at Miracle Park was no different.

"Well, are you ready to head out for the day?" she asked, knowing they weren't going anywhere yet.

Bobby let out an exaggerated laugh. "Good one. You know where we're going. You said we'd save it for last."

"Of course. My fearless, young daredevil. Why do you insist on riding these roller coasters?"

"You worry too much, Mom. It's the end of summer break. And I want to finish it with a bang."

She had planned this trip away for just the two of them to celebrate the end of a fun summer before Bobby started school in two weeks back in Des Moines. They made the three-hour drive west to spend two days in the new Miracle Park.

The park was nestled in Hilburn, Nebraska, a small town ninety minutes west of Omaha, virtually in the middle of nowhere.

Having found an area of flat land spanning five hundred acres—only yards north of the Platte River—a wealthy businessman named Alexander Carter had bought the land, hoping to create a theme park to rival Disneyland California.

"There it is," Bobby said, his voice dripping with awe, the reflection of all the park's flashing lights in his bulging eyes.

They turned the corner and passed by a carousel filled with shouting children on their left, and an area on the right with the "impossible games" as Beverly liked to call them. Ring toss, milk bottle toss, bean bag toss. *So much unnecessary tossing.*

In front of them stood the main attraction. The roller coaster that put Miracle Park on the map. The Time Roller stood seventy feet tall at its highest peak right before the big drop when the train reached a top speed of forty-five miles per hour.

The wooden roller coaster towered over Hilburn, the all-white paint job making it look like a snow-capped mountain peak for those driving along Highway 30, as was Mr. Carter's intent. Since Hilburn had no existing structures taller than one story, one could see the Time Roller from nearly anywhere in town—along with Miracle Hotel, which stood five levels tall directly next to the theme park.

The Tanner family had stopped in Hilburn on a couple of occasions during summer road trips to visit relatives in Cheyenne. Beverly couldn't remember much about the city outside of Zig Zag Lunchroom, where she insisted they served the world's best chili. They had only seen the sign promoting Miracle Park when they passed through last summer.

*LET YOUR MIRACLES BE GREAT IN THE SUMMER OF '78*, the billboard had read, cartoon images of a Ferris wheel and the Time Roller serving as a colorful way to grab the attention of the unknowing passersby.

Bobby had been so excited that day, so Beverly promised to bring him when it opened.  They had taken Bobby to Cedar Point in Ohio for his tenth birthday, and he had grown obsessed with roller coasters ever since.

The legend of the Time Roller spread like wildfire across the country, its steep drop and electric speeds said to rival only Space Mountain in California, which had just opened the year prior. Rumor spread that a woman had become ill after riding Time Roller, vomiting in her seat, and the ride started again before she had the chance to get off. She returned from the second ride unconscious and was said to have been in a coma for two weeks before waking up without a single memory of what had happened.

"And that sounds fun to you?" Beverly had asked Bobby as they planned the trip at the beginning of the summer.

"Mom," he had said, rolling his eyes in that loving way only teenagers could pull off, "it's probably a made-up story. You know, to get people excited to ride it. I never saw anything about it on the news—even went to the library to see if they had any newspaper clippings. Nothing."

Bobby had an analytical mind. He didn't believe anything told to him without backing it up with his own research at the library. It made parenting him both frustrating and reassuring—his parents weren't exempt from his desire to confirm their claims with evidence.

"Well," Beverly said, "are you going to ride it or stand here and stare at it all night?"

He hadn't looked away, and even stopped in his tracks once the Time Roller had come into clear view, making them both feel like insignificant specks of dust in the vast universe.

A train of cars was currently ascending the majestic hill, riders screaming into the night sky as they enjoyed a bird's-eye view of Hilburn below. A twenty-foot clock stood in front of the ride, the outline and arms glowing a light blue as the arms spun in a constant, counterclockwise rotation.

A girl with glasses and dangling red hair stopped next to Bobby and Beverly, gasping and jumping into the air as she pointed at the roller coaster, pulling her parents and older brother toward the Time Roller. "There it is!" she squealed. "They say you feel like you're waking up in another year once the ride ends. Let's go!"

"I'll never understand the thrill," Beverly said, starting toward the famous roller coaster.

"Don't sound like such an old lady, Mom," Bobby muttered, clearly hoping none of the kids his age heard her while they passed by. "Didn't you ever ride roller coasters when you were a kid?"

"I sure did. It was called The Legend. But it was nothing like this. It was simple. Smaller. This Time Roller is massive. And forty-five miles per hour? No thank you. There's no reason to be going as fast as a car on a theme park ride."

"So you're really not going to ride it with me?" Disappointment slipped into Bobby's voice, and it was almost enough for Beverly to push aside her staunch beliefs—or fear—and just get on the ride. But she couldn't. Just looking at how high Time Roller truly was made her stomach drop to her knees. The thought of her son getting on such a thing was already troubling enough.

"Sorry, love, but I'm not getting on that ride. I've ridden everything else in this park over the last two days—and what's that, thirty rides?—but I have to draw the line here."

Bobby shrugged. "Fine. I guess that's fair."

"Do you want me to stand in line with you?"

Bobby shuddered, as if the question offended him. "Mom. Thank you, but no." He lowered his voice to a whisper. "That's embarrassing."

"But if I was riding it, then it's suddenly okay for me to stand next to you in line?"

"Exactly. Cause you'd be riding it. Not holding my hand to make sure I get on and off the ride without a problem. I'm not a baby anymore."

"I know," Beverly replied, reaching out and ruffling her son's hair. If only she knew what would soon happen, she'd have wrapped him in her arms and pulled him out of the theme park against his will. "You remind me that all the time. Now, go get in line. It looks like the shortest it's been the entire two days we've been here."

And it was. Yesterday, the average wait time was ninety minutes to get on Time Roller, it even got as high as one hundred forty minutes at one point, at least according to the young lady working the entrance. She suggested coming back an hour before the park closed, claiming they told guests a longer wait time than was true to defer them to other rides. "But it's honestly around a thirty-minute wait between seven and eight o'clock," she had whispered to Bobby.

They had gotten caught up with other rides last night and weren't able to get in line. But Beverly promised to build their entire day around doing just that tonight. And here they were at 7:02, less than an hour until the park gates would close. Less than forty minutes until dozens of lives would change forever.

Sometimes you can feel when tragedy is about to strike. The mood shifts. The air becomes heavy and *different.* And that instinct that lies deep within us starts sounding the alarm.

Other times, tragedy comes out of nowhere and steamrolls all the remaining innocence we have. And all you can do is run and pray to all the gods and heavens that you just might make it out in one piece.

Bobby smiled before parting ways with his mother. She watched him go to the ride's entrance and join the end of the line that snaked back and forth about ten rows deep.

*Gonna be awhile,* Beverly thought, looking around for something to kill the time. She spotted a concession stand selling boxes of popcorn and stood in line for five minutes. A couple of benches were in front of the impossible games, and she parked there to enjoy her popcorn. She had a view of Bobby in line, and after another five minutes of eating her snack—she expected more popcorn for the whole two dollars she had to spend—he had moved up a couple of rows.

"So it moves a little faster than other rides," she said, studying the next train of cars climbing the hill. Ten cars, two people in each. Plus, they had two trains going. Considering forty people would get on the ride within every five minutes, Bobby didn't really have much more time to wait. There were maybe one hundred others in front of him.

The salt and butter from the popcorn made Beverly thirsty, so she found the nearest lemonade stand and ordered two cups, one for Bobby when he got off the ride. He could drink it during their walk back to the hotel.

Beverly had kept in decent shape just from maintaining their house in Des Moines. She took a walk through the neighborhood every morning and met with a couple of friends every Friday during the summer to play a match of tennis. None of that prepared her for two days of walking around a park just north of twenty million square feet. Her calves and the soles of her feet burned with exhaustion. Fortunately, their hotel bathroom had a deep bathtub, and she planned to soak in it for at least half an hour when they got back to the room.

After another wait in line, Beverly got the lemonades and returned to the benches, where she found a tired family had occupied them. Two kids of about seven lay across one bench, while the parents sat on the other with their heads hung low, fatigue crawling all over their faces. They left enough space on the end of the bench where Beverly could fit, so she took the spot.

"Long day?" she asked the mother next to her.

The woman looked up, startled as if she hadn't seen Beverly slide into the space next to her. She forced a gentle grin. "That's one way of describing it. This is our third day here. I guess you can say it's been a long *week*."

"Three days?!" Beverly asked. "Bless you. My son and I

are on day two, and we leave tomorrow. I can't even imagine doing this another day."

"We leave tomorrow, as well. I'll give this place credit, though. The kids all slept like logs these past two nights. I suppose tonight'll be the same."

Beverly laughed and wasn't sure why. She had become a little slaphappy and figured hearing her own voice say they were going home tomorrow brought her a giddy type of joy. "*I've* been the one getting quality sleep. God knows how many miles I've been walking each day."

"I heard the average family walks eight miles if they spend an entire day in this park. And I don't doubt it. We're just waiting for my oldest to ride this Time Roller one more time before we head back to our room. He just got in line."

"Oh? Are they riding by themselves? My son is also in line."

"Yeah. He's ridden it four times this week. Came and rode it while we took the little ones to the smaller rides."

This settled Beverly's nerves. "My son's been in line for about twenty minutes now—he might be close to the front. I can go see if he wouldn't mind letting your son ride with him—he's also alone."

The woman waved her off. "It's fine, really. The longer he stands in line, the more time we get to sit here. My husband doesn't even want to stand in line anymore. He's definitely ready to leave this park tomorrow."

The husband nodded silently next to his wife, zoned out like a zombie without a clue.

Beverly laughed. "If you say so. Think I'll go take a peek and see where he is in the line. Excuse me."

She stood up and strolled toward the roller coaster's entrance, craning her neck to see over the zigzag of people standing in line. It took her a minute, but she spotted him once the line moved. "Only one more row to go," she said to herself. "Probably two more rides for him to get on."

Beverly looked back to the bench and saw the woman lying on her husband's shoulder. She'd be doing the same thing right now if her husband had joined them, but he had an important work meeting with "the suits" about a project he had been working on for months.

She didn't want to bother the couple any further and remained waiting at Time Roller's entrance, standing under the archway where the ride's name was spelled out in lightning-bolt lettering.

Across the hordes of people, Bobby happened to look back over his shoulder and locked eyes with his mother, smiling and waving. The anticipation of finally getting to ride this legendary coaster had clearly reached its apex as he stood mere feet away from getting on.

The next train departed, and he shuffled forward, sliding into the line that would be for the second car from the front.

"Just get in the front row," she muttered under her breath. "You've already waited this long."

But she had no way of relaying this message to him, not that it mattered. He was going to have just as much fun regardless of where he sat.

The train that had just finished arrived, and she saw Bobby bouncing in place while he waited for the riders to get off, clearing the way for his seat. It only took a quick thirty seconds for the platform to clear of the prior riders, and Bobby wasted no time as he practically jumped into the second car, fastening the seat belt over his lap.

Beverly hadn't seen such a wide smile on her son's face in

ages. Whatever mystic charm this Time Roller possessed had certainly brought out his inner child in full force. The ride sat two people per cart, but there must not have been any other single riders, as Bobby sat alone.

*I should have just asked if that other boy could ride with him. He shouldn't have to enjoy this experience alone.*

One more glance at her son proved otherwise. His grin reached from ear to ear as the two ride operators made their way down the train, tugging on the seat belts and lap bars to ensure they were properly secured. The employees returned to their post behind the control box and paused for ten seconds before pushing the button to start the ride.

The train jolted forward before smoothing out as it ascended the steep hill. The *click, click, click* of the chain pulling the riders up echoed around this area of the park. It had fallen eerily silent, several guests having already made their way to the exit.

Those on Time Roller remained, the front of the train less than twenty feet from the apex of the towering coaster.

*Click, click, click.*

How that sound would boomerang around her brain like a bat trapped in a cave.

*Click, click, click.*

Less than ten feet from the drop that guaranteed endless thrills. Since Bobby was alone, he leaned over the edge of the car, hands elevated in the air as he readied for the drop, and looked down at the world below him.

Beverly didn't know for sure but believed Bobby had locked eyes with her once more. She probably looked no different from a small ant in the crack of a sidewalk from his viewpoint, but she *felt* something in that moment. Felt her son's eyes on her. Even through the darkness of nightfall, she still made out the whites of his teeth as he grinned way up there in the stratosphere. Oh, how that image would stay burned into her mind until her dying day.

*Click . . . click . . . click . . . CRACK!*

The sound overpowered all the other noise in the park, several heads whipping around to find the source. It could have been a tree trunk snapping before falling over to wreak havoc. Or perhaps an electrical line had gone haywire.

But none of that appeared to be the case, and that's when the screaming began.

To the casual passersby, including those zooming by on the freeway, everything looked perfectly normal within Miracle Park. The Ferris wheel made its rounds. Kids licked ice cream cones while others cried when theirs splattered on the ground. Grumpy parents dragged their exhausted children through the park. Families giggled as they waited in lines. And the park's main attraction, Time Roller, had just started its most recent lap around the roller coaster.

The train went up the hill, just like any roller coaster should. Only those standing directly outside the ride witnessed the horror. Just as the front car was within inches of the top, the haunting crack occurred, and with it, the entire train rolled backwards.

The freefall was faster than the ride's advertised top speed of forty-five miles per hour. In three gut-wrenching seconds, the screams radiating from the roller coaster were of a pitch never heard within an amusement park. Beverly had heard the normal shrieks of delight over the past two days. The joy mixed with fear and a splash of euphoric fun.

Now, there was no joy or fun. Only terror.

The world came to a standstill as the small audience gathered around Time Roller watched as the rear car plummeted to the base of the ride. A blood-chilling screech, likely from the emergency brakes, howled into the night like a werewolf out for blood.

The bumper of the rear car hit the bottom platform at an angle and speed no engineer had ever anticipated. The screeching abruptly stopped like someone had pulled the plug from a jukebox, and the car jammed against the platform.

A couple sat in the rear, eyes wide, mouths even wider, as they braced for the moment of impact. The car in front of them lost no momentum and flattened the couple within a split second.

The rest of the train had come off the tracks, seven other cars suspended vertically in midair, bending and curving at the connection points between each car, hovering over the park like an untamed snake ready to attack.

One rider must have taken a dare to unbuckle their seat belt, as their body soared through the air, landing on top of a funnel cake stand sixty feet away from the ride's entrance.

All the cars separated from each other.

Two landed upright on the paved walkway that led from the ride's exit to the rest of the park. Another two landed nearby, only upside down, and taking out a chain-link fence in the process. One smashed into the other two that were already splintered debris on the platform. Another somehow landed back on the tracks, albeit at a crooked angle. Still, it glided backwards at a much slower rate and gently bumped into the pileup on the platform. The other two spun in violent three-sixties in the air, looking almost acrobatic as they danced around each other. They hit each other and shot in opposite directions, one heading toward Beverly, the other toward the lemonade stand she had gone to just minutes before.

Bobby was in the one that knocked out the lemonade stand like a bulldozer, leaving nothing but splinters of wood from the structure, plastic cups scattered in every direction, napkins floating in the air like feathers falling gracefully to the ground. Beverly saw the other car sailing toward her and dashed out of the way before it could flatten her.

It landed only fifteen feet away from where she had dived, hitting the ground as the metal car dragged along the concrete.

The entire park fell deathly silent. Beverly crawled back to her feet, blood oozing from the scrapes on her elbows and knees. It felt like she had twisted her ankle. Pain shot from the joint with each step as she labored toward the demolished lemonade stand.

"Someone do something!" she shouted to everyone stand-ing around.

No one moved. Mouths hung agape, eyes bounced in every direction. No one knew *what* to do. Where to start.

The blood splatters everywhere looked black under the moonlight, except for on the roller coaster. The crimson stood in sharp contrast against the white-painted wood. Some-where in the distance, sirens wailed. The police department was only two miles north of the park, in the center of town.

Beverly dragged herself toward the rubble, a harsh gnawing tearing away at her insides. She knew what she'd find but had no choice. If there was even the slimmest of chances he was still breathing, she needed to get him out of the debris.

Groups of people ran to the scene, others fled.

"He's alive!" a voice shouted from behind.

Beverly whipped her head around to a group of four people

running to the car that had nearly landed on her. Two boys were in it, one lying lifelessly over the edge, another moving his blood-smeared head from left to right.

Seeing this gave Beverly hope as she continued toward Bobby. She reached the mound his car had created and started lifting the tall shards of wood, tossing them aside until she saw the blue paint of the car.

"Bobby!" she screamed, and now people were running in various directions, some crashing into each other as they didn't know who to go help. A husband and wife rushed to Beverly's side and helped her lift the remaining wood. "Please, God, let him be alive," she begged to whatever power would listen.

First, she saw his arm, snapped into a ninety-degree angle at the midpoint of his forearm. Blood streaked over his skin like rivers splitting in three directions. The last piece of wood was removed by the couple, revealing Bobby's head cocked back, eyes open and staring lifelessly at the sky above.

Those eyes never blinked. A breeze ruffled the spots of hair that weren't caked down with blood, but nothing else on him moved.

"My sweet boy," Beverly whispered, caressing her son's head in her hands, tears falling from her face onto his forehead. The lights from Time Roller's sign reflected in his eyes.

Beverly stepped back, tremors overtaking her body, and shrieked to the heavens.

# Chapter 2



*Present Day*

Arielle took the last bite of her mac-and-cheese burger and pushed the plate back. "That was…" she said through heavy chewing that ended with a sharp gulp, "incredible."

Felix laughed from across the table. "Noted. I can make that on our next mission, if you'd like."

"You can make *this*?"

Felix gazed at her empty plate with an *are-you-kidding-me?* look. "It's just fried mac on top of a burger. Not exactly a groundbreaking creation."

"We'll see if you can make it up to this same quality."

Felix, who was in the middle of sipping his Coke through a straw, snorted at this comment, soda spouting out of his nose. "Same quality? Arielle, we're at the Cheesecake Factory for God's sake. Half their shit comes in frozen, and they just whip it all together. I can make this same burger from scratch, and it will blow your mind. Most people use their time travel to go back and do silly things. I go back and take lessons from some of the best chefs to ever walk this planet—Bourdain, Robuchon, and Boiardi, to name a few."

"You *met* Anthony Bourdain?!"

"Not directly. But I took a group class he taught in Houston on one of his book tours. Think it was in 2003."

Arielle shook her head. "You crack me up."

"What? You don't seem like the type to go back to see a concert or sporting event."

Arielle laughed. She had only told Selena about the hundreds of lives she had lived upon receiving her Juice. The lives that rounded out her entire persona today. Before any of the glory of her rise to the top-ranked Angel position, Arielle was merely a somber, broken CIA agent trying to find her footing in life after a madman massacred her family. Those hundreds of lives she'd lived not only made her, they *saved* her.

The Cheesecake Factory wasn't the place to go into these details with Felix. "I've gone back to see concerts. Don't act like you're above that kind of stuff. You've definitely gone back to old sporting events."

"Only once, actually. I don't really have a desire to see sporting events when I already know the outcome."

"What did you go watch?"

"Just a random Yankees game in 1927. They're considered the best baseball team ever, and I wanted to see if Babe Ruth was really everything he's hyped up to be."

"And?"

"And he hit two home runs that game. Even threw out a runner at home all the way from the right field wall. So yes, his legend is very much real. And what concert did you go back to see?"

"Ritchie Valens. My parents both adored him. There's a box somewhere in storage that has all of his vinyls. Probably in mint condition. I remember every Friday night they'd have their own little dance party in our basement. Dad would make seven and sevens and always had Cokes for me and my brother. They started with the faster songs to break a sweat, but the night always ended with Ritchie. 'La Bamba' and 'Come On, Let's Go,' then they'd end with a slow dance to 'We Belong Together.' I can close my eyes and see them swaying back and forth like they were the only two people in the world."

They sat in silence, Arielle's eyes glossy with a thin layer of tears.

"Wow," Felix finally said. "Everything you do in your life has so much *purpose* behind it. Even something as mindless—well, what I *thought* was mindless—as a concert, carries so much weight."

Arielle shrugged. "I've been that way ever since the shooting. Once I realized life can end at any moment, and that we don't really control our fate, all I can do is make sure every day has a purpose. Time is a resource, and we have less of it each time we take a breath. Why would I want to waste a single second of what I consider the most precious resource we have?"

Felix grabbed a slice of bread before leaning back in his seat. "I can appreciate all that, but Arielle, you need to slow down. You're constantly at it. You're going to cut your life short because you never rest. Take a vacation to unplug. You can even travel back in time to take it. That way, you only use ten minutes of your actual life. And after a vacation, you need to come up with some hobbies. As long as it has no relation to our work. I've been reading a lot about mental health lately, and we need to take care of our minds, especially because of how much death we witness on the missions."

Arielle had killed dozens of bad people during her time as an Angel. No matter how much these evil men and women deserved it, taking a life *did* weigh on her conscience. Add the other random casualties of the mission work, and Arielle had probably seen a couple hundred people take their last breaths.

"And what do you do?" she asked.

"I have video games and TV shows. I'll binge both during my time off. That's exactly what I've been doing these past couple of weeks. I just finished *Better Call Saul*—I highly recommend it."

"I couldn't tell you the last time I watched an entire TV series."

"I know, maybe sitting still for a few hours is too much to ask of you. Your hobbies don't have to be that way. Go hiking, backpack through Europe, jump out of an airplane."

Arielle grinned. "I've always wanted to sky dive."

"See. The time off between missions isn't going anywhere. If your idea of relaxation is falling through the sky, then make those arrangements. What have you been doing, anyway?"

"Some work, but not as much as you'd think. I've read a couple books, rearranged furniture in my basement."

Felix shook his head. "Are you still going out with Javonte?"

"Yeah, but I'm thinking about calling things off."

"Why?"

"We have plenty of fun together. It just feels like something is missing."

"Is he just another shallow athlete?"

"Actually, no. He's brilliant. Very business focused. Almost seems like football is his side hobby. He's always looking for new opportunities, and even started a new foundation to sponsor football teams at some of the lower-income high schools in Denver. He's an incredible person, but something isn't clicking."

"The spark?"

Arielle shrugged. "Who knows?"

"Not me." Felix laughed. "I know nothing about sparks—I'm just quoting things I hear in movies."

"Watching a lot of rom-coms?"

"Well, sure, but I watch everything."

"Well then, what am I supposed to do? It feels like a waste to let a good man like Javonte go for no good reason."

"Well, what's the real reason? Without thinking about it, what's the first thing you'd change about your relationship?"

Arielle looked up for a second, climbing into her thoughts. "We'd be able to spend more time together."

"Interesting. So your main issue has nothing to actually do with *him*."

"I guess I never thought of it that way. Both of our schedules are so busy. I've only gone out twice with him in the two weeks since our last mission ended. And now football season is around the corner, so it'll be even less."

"So he's the right person at the wrong time. That sucks."

Felix never held back the truth.

Arielle hadn't considered this logic during her heated conversations with herself about the state of her relationship with the running back.

"Right person at the wrong time," she repeated. "That pretty much sums up my love life since college."

"Maybe this seems too obvious, but just talk to him. Let him know where you stand. His response will tell you everything you need to know."

"Selena did mention that a while ago. I dread those tough conversations, but it might be time."

"Speaking of, have you heard from her at all? Sorry for

changing the subject, but I sent her a text last week, and she never responded."

"She went to New York to visit her mother. I talked to her yesterday. She said they've been pretty busy venturing around the city. But she'll be on the red-eye flight tonight to come back to Denver. We have our meeting with the commander tomorrow."

"I know. How kind of him to set it for eight o'clock. I'm sure Selena will be a joy in the morning."

They had both learned after a few missions that Selena could be rather horrendous when she didn't get a full night's sleep. Odd for someone who loved to stay out partying on the weekends. A late flight into Denver only guaranteed she'd be a groggy mess in Commander Briar's office.

"She'll be fine as long as she's not buying everyone on the plane shots."

"She wasn't able to get a flight from the Road Runners?"

"No. Now that everyone is getting more time off between missions, the organization's planes are all booked up."

"Wow, talk about first-world problems."

They shared a laugh while their server brought their bill. Felix whipped out his card to pay on the kiosk on the table.

"I've been wanting to talk to you about something," Arielle said.

Felix finished paying and looked up. "Is something wrong?"

"Not at all. Quite the opposite. You've been proving yourself more capable than your role. I've seen it, and I know the leadership team sees it, too. Commander Briar might ask you about working in the field."

Felix shook his head. "Pass. That isn't for me. I've seen what you go through. No thanks."

"First off, no one is going to pressure you into it. If you really don't want to do it, that's fine. But you should at least hear them out."

"What could they possibly say? I'm sure it pays more money, but that's hardly a concern. I'm already set for life. If they think I care about status, or climbing the ranks, they're wrong. My work is fun. It gives me purpose."

"And that's great. None of that would change. They build teams around your strengths and fill in the weaknesses. You could lead your own team one day, and you'd still focus on the spying and technology aspect of missions. You'd have a combat specialist like me assigned to your team, and you'd get to call the shots."

"But that's not something I'm concerned with. I enjoy working for you. Everything runs smoothly because you make it that way. I'm in the perfect scenario right now."

"Our team won't last forever. The needs of the Road Runners are constantly changing. Eventually, we'll get split up and go our own ways."

"Do you know something?" Felix asked, leaning forward to study Arielle.

"No. Meeting with Commander Briar is the only time I ever hear things like that, and he's mentioned nothing of this matter. I've just been paying attention to how things are going within the Road Runners, and more specifically, the Angels. Some people climb the ranks and get re-assigned. That won't happen to our team anytime soon, but it will eventually. Selena is coming into her own form. You are, too, even if you won't admit it. With some combat training, you could become better than I ever was."

Felix laughed. "Good one."

"I'm serious, Felix. You can do things I can't. You're a deeper thinker than I am. Really, the only area I am more skilled than you is combat, driving, and experience."

"It's really nice of you to talk me up, but I'm telling you I'm perfectly content. If you're trying to motivate someone, save it for Selena."

"I'll be having this same conversation with her. I just want you to be prepared for this possibility. My guess is two to four more years working together. That's still a lot of missions to come, but eventually you and Selena will outgrow this team and lead your own."

"If you say so. Shall we leave this fine establishment now? Apparently, I need to get to bed early tonight. I wonder what our next mission will be?"

# Chapter 3

Across the country, Selena Nicole sat in a French restaurant with her mother, two hours before she needed to head to the airport for her flight home.

"When will you come visit me in Denver?" Selena asked.

"You tell me. When is the best time of year to go?" Her mother poked around her *coq au vin*.

"I'd say May or September."

"Well, it's already August, so I'll plan a trip out in May. Unless you want me to come for Christmas?"

"I don't know what I'm doing yet. Dad asked me to visit him for Thanksgiving or Christmas. I just need to decide which one I'll do."

"Thanksgiving is easier. Fewer people traveling out of the country. Paris is beautiful at that time of year, too. They decorate all over the city for Christmas by then."

"That settles it. I'll see if I can get off work for a month. Spend a couple weeks in Paris, then fly here to New York and spend some time with you over Christmas."

"A month off from work? I swear, the more you talk about your job, the less real it sounds."

"It's plenty real—just flexible. I can work from anywhere

in the world if I need to."

Selena had told her mother she took an account executive job for a consulting firm while she continued her pursuit of landing an acting gig. Her mother questioned why she didn't go back to Los Angeles or New York if she was truly serious about acting. While Denver was a growing city, it had virtually no market for up-and-coming actors. Denver provided the "job" she needed, and many talent scouts accepted virtual auditions, so it didn't matter where she worked, as she could always fly out for in-person auditions.

Her mom accepted the story, and Selena knew she'd never spend the time looking it all up to see if it was true.

"If you say so," her mom said. "And are you sure about two weeks with your father? How much of that time will you actually get to spend with him?"

Selena heard the disgust in her mother's voice. Even fifteen years after their divorce, she still never refused the opportunity to take a jab at her ex-husband.

"Mom, I've told you. He's not like that anymore. I'll probably be with him the whole time."

"Him and his whore?"

"Mom!"

Her mother burst into laughter. "I'm kidding. I'm sure she's a nice lady."

Selena knew her mom wasn't actually kidding. "Chantal has been with Dad for like four years now. She's been warm and welcoming every time I visit."

"Well, she sounds just lovely," her mom replied sarcastically.

"And what's going on with you? Every time I've tried asking, you always change the subject. No more of that. I'm getting ready to head home, so you can't keep avoiding the topic."

Her mom tossed her hands in the air. "What do you want me to say? I'm fifty and single in New York City. I've dated some men, but nothing has come of it. You don't need to worry about me—I'm fine."

Selena knew that was a lie. As a child, she had overheard her mother crying on the phone one night to a friend shortly after the divorce papers were signed. Her mother had confessed her fear of ending up alone for the rest of her life. *Dying* alone. Those words, and the palpable fear from that night, had clung to Selena's conscience ever since.

Selena reached across the table and grabbed her mother's hand in a gentle caress. "You know, Mom, it doesn't have to be this way. I know you don't want to hear it, but maybe you should move away from New York. Get a fresh start somewhere else. This city is a shitshow for any single person. Go somewhere more laid back with less drama."

"Let me guess. Denver?"

"I'm not even saying that. Denver is an option, but why not somewhere even smaller? You can live in the suburbs, maybe even move upstate right here in New York."

Her mom laughed. "Live upstate? What do those people even do for fun? Stare out their window and watch the leaves change? I could never—"

"Yes, that's exactly what they do. With the person they love. They sit in their house and enjoy their life *together*. Sure, they don't go to some new fancy restaurant opening every week, or Broadway once a month, but they have each other. Is that not what you want?"

"When did you get so wise about love? Is there something—or some*one*—you're not telling me about?"

"Not at all. I'm like you, Mom. I go out every weekend and have a blast. But that's the phase of life I'm in. I still understand the importance of eventually finding someone I can build a life with, but I don't know what that will even look like."

"Are you calling me old?" her mother asked, winking across the table.

Selena laughed. "No, Mom, you're not old. You're just in a new phase of life, and I don't think you're fully seeing the bigger picture."

Her mother placed her free hand on top of Selena's. "No, I am. I'm just a gal torn between the two lives I want. I suppose something will eventually force me to choose. For now, I'm fine. Trust me when I tell you that."

"Okay."

"Now, shall we go get some dessert? Amorino is doing two-for-one scoops of gelato all week."

"Deal."

They paid their bill and stepped back outside to Eighth Avenue, starting toward the gelato shop three blocks away. A man sat on an upturned bucket beneath a lamppost, playing smooth jazz from a saxophone. The instrument's case lay open in front of him, so Selena tossed him ten dollars.

"Can I just say how proud I am of you," her mother said. "You grew up around a lot of wealth and had to deal with an intercontinental divorce at such a young age. Your life could have gone so many directions because of all that, yet here you are. Normal. Humble. Twice the woman I could have ever dreamt of being."

"Mom, stop."

"No, I mean it. I live in this city. I can see the ugly side of humanity after a quick stroll down any block. Greedy people. Envious people. Selfish, inconsiderate assholes. Some days, it feels like those are the only people living in New York. You have a big heart. Your top priority might be yourself, but that doesn't mean everything else falls to the wayside."

"I've been surrounding myself with some really good people. I have two friends I work with who just mean the world to me. The three of us couldn't be any more different from each other, but somehow it all works. We spend a lot of time together. We make each other better, not just in work, but in our personal lives."

Her mother grinned widely. "I love to hear that. Hang on to those friends. I had some like that, but friendships don't always last. They require just as much work as a romantic relationship. If these are friends from work, make sure you stay friends after you're done working together."

Selena had never considered that future possibility, and the thought sent swirls of angst into her stomach.

"I will. We all put in the effort."

"Good. And most importantly, once these friends of yours start getting into serious relationships, or start having kids, make sure you're there through all of it. That's how you become more than friends. Be a family for each other."

"How did you know my friends aren't already in those situations?"

"Because you said you spend a lot of time together. That wouldn't be the case if those other things were true. So I'm telling you now, prepare for it, and be ready to adjust your friendships to work around the busy lives you'll all eventually have. You still have to keep your friendship a priority—be selfish about it, if you need."

"Thanks, Mom."

As they walked, Selena intertwined her arm with her mother's, leaning her head on her shoulder. The city bustled as it always did, and Selena missed it. She perfectly understood the appeal, and her mother's struggle to step away from the chaotic lifestyle.

Selena was leaving tonight, however. And she couldn't wait to get back to her friends.

# Chapter 4

They gathered in Commander Briar's office the next morning, Selena halfway done with her second cup of coffee.

She let out an exaggerated yawn, stretching her hands high above her head.

"Long night?" Felix asked.

"Shouldn't have been, but I got stuck sitting behind a fucking baby. And yes, they cried for just about the entire flight. So if you don't mind, I'll be going home after this meeting and sleeping until my body wakes me up."

Arielle giggled. "But you don't want to jump straight into the mission? Me and Felix are ready to roll."

Selena stuck up her middle finger just as Commander Briar stepped in.

"Wow," he said, grinning as he crossed the room to his desk, sitting in the throne-like chair. "Flipping each other off before the mission even starts. Not a good sign."

"It's nothing personal," Selena said. "Arielle knows that."

"Just another day with Selena," Arielle confirmed, and they all shared a laugh. "Is everything okay, Commander?"

Just as their meeting was to begin at eight, Commander Briar had stepped out of his office for what ended up being twenty minutes.

"Yes, everything's fine. We have a special guest in town today. I'll bring her in when we're done talking so you can meet her. But let's discuss missions first. Selena, I understand you were injured on the last one, and that's not something I take lightly. What could have gone differently to prevent that incident?"

Selena touched her face where she had been pistol-whipped, the wounds having cleared up and, fortunately, leaving no scars behind.

"It was a freak occurrence. The past, most likely. Honestly, it's my own fault. I wasn't paying attention to my surroundings."

"Bull!" Arielle cried. "It was *not* your fault. It was mine and Felix's for not stopping him sooner."

"You couldn't have known what that man was going to do," Selena said. "Besides, the past was already working its magic, locking you out of the building. And you still got in. Honestly, Commander, give these two a medal or something. They sprinted up thirty flights of steps, and if they had been even ten seconds slower, I might not be sitting here right now. I don't think I ever properly thanked you two."

Arielle shook her head as silence blanketed the office. "You don't ever need to thank us. You would've done the same. It's what we do."

"She's right," Felix added. "Our instincts took over as soon as we saw Raj arrive at the parking garage on the last mission. It was nothing."

"It sounds like everything worked out," Commander Briar said, standing and circling behind his chair. "But how can we improve? There has to be something."

He pulled out a thick file and dropped it on his desk before sitting back down.

"We *had* the building access," Arielle said. "But we had already given it back. This was literally the night we were finishing the mission and ready to return to the present. The only thing we could have tried was shooting Raj before he went up the elevator, but that wasn't something I was willing to risk. Cameras all over that garage, one murder already in the books. It would have been reckless."

"But that's still what happened," Commander Briar said. "You still ended up killing him, and it would have been on camera had he not already stopped the video footage. Maybe next time, just take the shot."

While he had plenty of harsh experiences with the past, Commander Briar never had to work missions like the Angels. This frustrated Arielle, yet she didn't say anything to their organization leader about this.

"I'll consider it," Arielle said.

"Very well. And I encourage all three of you to think of how you can be better prepared for these types of scenarios on future missions. That's all I ask. And if you need anything at all, just let us know."

"Thank you, Commander," Felix said.

"I don't want to beat a dead horse," the commander continued. "Shall we talk about the next mission?"

A knot formed in Arielle's gut. It always did right before learning where she would be off to next. "Let's hear it."

Commander Briar flipped open the file and sifted through the contents, pushing forward a grainy colored photo of an amusement park. "This is Miracle Park. On August 24, 1978, the pull cord on their biggest roller coaster, the Time Roller, snapped while pulling a train of riders up the initial drop. Five people died, and thirteen were injured. Only two out of the twenty riders walked away unharmed. This incident was horrific, and eventually saw the park shut down."

"So it was done on purpose?" Arielle asked.

"We have reason to believe it was. The authorities investigated the matter at the time and deemed it an accident, but our team wasn't so sure. Our scout team hangs around the locals after tragedies—it's actually an effective way to get leads and different perspectives. A lot of locals believed an environmentalist was involved in some capacity." The commander pushed forward another photo, this one showing a young woman with short, wavy hair, big round glasses, and a charming smile as she leaned against a tree trunk. "This is Willow West. She had been clashing with the park's owner ever since it opened, claiming the park was polluting the town's drinking water and air. She often led protests outside the park, discouraging people from going in. All she wanted was for the park to get shut down. Authorities searched her home but found no evidence she was tied to the tragedy."

"Willow," Selena said with a slight laugh. "She even looks like a hippie. Her parents must be so proud."

"She's not the only suspect. Several employees at the park were disgruntled. Now, most of them were teenagers, so it's highly unlikely they would be capable of pulling off a stunt like this, but we need to cover our bases."

"So the owner was a real piece of work, then?" Selena asked.

Commander Briar nodded and pulled out another photo, this one of a heavyset man dressed in a gray suit, one hand holding his lapel, the other with a lit cigar pinched between his fat fingers. "Meet Alexander Carter. A businessman who came from money and wanted nothing more than to open his own version of Disneyland in the Midwest."

"Is he considered a suspect?" Arielle asked.

"No. He had nothing to gain from this tragedy. In fact, his life pretty much spiraled after all this happened. Sabotaging his own park makes no sense, and everyone from our scouting team agrees he truly was hellbent on making the park the best attraction in the country. But he treated his employees like shit, which might be the root cause of this awful event."

"So, what is our mission, exactly?" Arielle asked.

Commander Briar smiled and crossed his arms. "Now this one was quite the argument. Half of our team wanted it to be informative—find out what really happened, and if it was an accident or not. The other half wanted you to prevent those riders from getting on the roller coaster—save the lives and call it a day."

"But we can't prevent honest accidents," Arielle said.

"Precisely. So without us knowing for sure if it was an accident or not, this mission will be informative." Commander Briar closed the file, leaned forward, and lowered his voice. "Between the four of us, if you find out this was done on purpose, you have my full blessing to intervene and stop it. But only if it's safe."

"Well," Felix said. "It already sounds like we're not dealing with bad guys with guns, so I'm at peace with whatever we have to do."

"Don't be so sure. Just because nothing of the sort happened during the original timeline doesn't mean that will be the case once you start poking around. Alexander Carter was hungry for money and power—those are the people you have to watch out for the most."

"When are you expecting us to start?" Arielle asked.

"Within the next five days. This report is already plenty thorough about the people you'll be encountering and the town. Hilburn, Nebraska. Have any of you ever been?"

They looked around at each other and shook their heads.

"I didn't think so," the commander said. "This small town is only known for this tragedy. You can blow by it on the interstate and not even realize it. Alexander Carter grew up traveling with his father for his oil-related business trips back and forth from Dallas to Sioux Falls, and they always stopped in Hilburn for the night. I guess he became kind of attached to the memories. The park is still standing—been abandoned for forty-five years now. Word is you can sneak into it. It's on the outskirts of town."

"Why haven't they torn it down?"

"Like I said, it's a small town. No one there has the type of money to buy the land, or even demolish the damn thing. The millionaires who have stopped by to look at it don't see the value of opening a park in the middle of nowhere—even though it was running pretty lucrative for Alexander Carter. No one wants to take on the risk, or deal with the publicity that might come with opening a new business on those grounds. So . . . it just sits there, falling apart piece by piece."

"I bet it's so creepy," Selena said. "I can't wait."

"You're nuts," Arielle said. "We're not going to walk around that abandoned park."

"Actually," Commander Briar said, "our team is suggesting you stop there in the present day first. You'll be able to explore the layout of the park and get familiar with where everything is. Everything is in the exact spot as when you'll be traveling back to 1978."

"I don't understand," Arielle responded. "It's just an amusement park. I'm sure it takes a day to study the map and learn the layout."

"For the park, yes, that's probably true. But you'll want to learn the behind-the-scenes locations around the park. Where are the offices? Are there secret ways to get into them? Where do the employees hang out on their breaks? That's where the gossip will happen. Who makes the schedule? Where is it kept? This is all information that will apply to the mission. Take the time to learn the park. It even had a hotel on the grounds for guests to stay. Even though the park hadn't grown to the size of Disneyland yet, Mr. Carter owned enough of the land to make that happen. You have plenty of ground to cover."

"Understood."

"Now, are there any questions?"

After a few moments silence, Felix replied, "No, sir."

"Great. If you'll excuse us, I need a word in private with Arielle. Best of luck on this next mission."

# Chapter 5

Arielle watched as Felix closed the door behind him and Selena.

"How are you doing?" Commander Briar asked, his tone shifting from professional to one of a caring father figure.

"What do you mean, Commander?" Arielle asked, her heart rate suddenly spiking. Was she in trouble for something? Did the commander have terrible news to deliver?

"Just in general. How's life? Are you still happy in your role as an Angel?"

Arielle scrunched her face. "I'm doing pretty good. Still trying to get a grip on all this extra time off between missions. Overall, I'm happy and loving my role. What is this all about?"

"Good. I just wanted to check in. I don't know how much you follow the news of our time travel world, but it's getting wild out there."

"I'll admit I barely keep up with the news unless there's a major headline."

"That's probably for the best. I like to think the Road Runners are just going through some growing pains, but I'm not so sure. It's been an adjustment to this time of peace. Our organization was started to stop the Revolution from taking over the world. Fifty years of that. Every recruit during that time joined knowing the risks and objectives. And that made life simple. It unified every single member against our common enemy. Now that we no longer have that enemy, people are letting loose."

"What's going on, Commander?" From his tone, she could tell he was stressed.

He let out a chuckle. "Our members are taking chances they shouldn't be. The number of people in our prisons has spiked dramatically in the last couple of months."

"I've only heard of the prisons—always thought they were myths."

"Oh, they're real, and spread throughout time."

"Are people using time travel for evil?"

"I wish—that's a lot easier to address. No, unfortunately, we've had many incidents where our members have shared our secrets with regular people. Some instances have been blatant, like people telling their neighbors and *showing* them how it all works. Others have been more discreet—operating fortune-telling businesses, things of that nature. It's almost as if people are bored and unsure what to do with themselves."

"And why do you want to discuss this with me?"

"Changes are coming, I'm afraid. Elections for a new commander are in six months, which means campaigning will begin in three months. And now that we're in a time of peace, it's not like before, when people would run for office based on their strategy for taking down the Revolution. Now, people have ideas. *Dangerous* ideas."

"We're not becoming the next Revolution, are we?" The thought sent a shudder down Arielle's spine. Everyone had rejoiced when Chris Speidel, the former leader of the

Revolution, was eliminated from the world. Good beat evil, and that's how she imagined their small corner of the universe would remain.

"I don't see that happening, but it could eventually lead that way. Some candidates want to find a way to co-exist with the regular folks of the world—more than we already do. One man was actually running a time travel agency. Regular people would walk into his office, pay him $5,000 for the chance to go back and revisit their past, and he let them go on their merry way afterward. He at least threatened death to anyone who shared this secret, but how sturdy is that?"

"A time travel business? Why?"

Commander Briar shrugged. "I'm afraid we grew too quickly for our own good. Toward the end of the war, Commander Strike basically approved a flood of new recruits. She saw the end in sight and just wanted as many bodies on the ground as she could get. No interviews, no background checks. We're talking tens of thousands of people who went on to recruit their families and friends. Now we're paying the price. We have the Bylaws, but not enough people to enforce them. We've always had teams monitor all time travel activity—kind of like air traffic control—but we're outnumbered. This combination of factors is going to soon snowball out of control."

"What are we doing about it?"

"The clock is ticking on my term. There's only so much I can push through. For starters, I've ceased all recruiting. Second, I'm working with a team to create an academy for new time travelers. There are lots of details to figure out, but the goal is to have a school for adults who are recruited, and a separate school for children who are born into this life. This will teach everyone the history of our organization, ways to recognize when time travel is being abused, and just an overall sense of what makes a standout Road Runner. These academies will also help guide our members into fields where they are interested in growing their careers."

"That's a genius idea. Brings a lot of much needed structure."

"I know. Sadly, not everyone feels the same. You'll see some candidates bring up this topic and tear it down as brainwashing. Indoctrination."

Arielle rolled her eyes. "Let me guess, the people opposed to a system of education are right here in the U.S. of A."

Commander Briar grinned. "At least we have all of North America, and a majority of our other countries are on board for the schooling system. But we all know who likes to shout the loudest. It will be a hot topic on the campaign trail."

"Are there candidates who support it?"

"Of course. And I've been meeting with a few to give my endorsements. One is here today, and I thought you'd like to meet her." Commander Briar whipped out his phone, pressed two keys, and waited ten seconds. "Elijah, you can send her in now. Thank you."

The commander hung up the phone and rose from his seat.

Arielle, no clue what was happening, looked over her shoulder as the door swung open.

A woman of six feet in height strolled into the office. Her blonde hair flowed freely halfway down her back, piercing blue eyes scanning the room.

Arielle's eyes bulged as she slowly stood, mouth hanging open.

"Arielle," Commander Briar said. "I'd like you to meet

Stella Robbins—"

"I know who you are," Arielle said, her limbs suddenly trembling. "The Cut-throat Canuck. You're a legend."

Stella laughed politely, grinning wide. "Oh, please. I'm nothing of the sort."

"With all due respect, Ms. Robbins, you're wrong. You shattered every glass ceiling. And did it with a smile. I haven't been in time travel all that long, but I've read all of your books. They've helped me become who I am as an Angel."

Stella blushed. "Maybe we can make some of those books required reading in these schools Commander Briar wants to build."

"They absolutely should be. *Time is Killing Me* is one of the best books I've ever read—time traveler or not."

"Oh, dear, you really are being too kind. But thank you. If you ask me, you're the legend. Not even I had a run as impressive as yours."

Arielle could die right here in Commander Briar's office and be content with how her life played out. Getting called a legend by her idol felt as real as walking on clouds.

Stella Robbins was the first woman to join the Angel Runners. The first to successfully complete a mission. And in a matter of three months on the job, became the first woman to reach the top-ranked position. She had joined in 1984 when the organization was still mainly dominated by men. And while the Road Runners had no prohibitions against women, Stella carved her own path to success, writing all about her trials and tribulations in the aforementioned book.

When Arielle had joined the Angels, one of her trainers suggested she read *Time is Killing Me.* She did, and never looked back. That book had sparked Arielle's desire to live out different lives in the past—something Stella had done, but not nearly on the same scale as Arielle.

"I thought you'd like to meet Stella," Commander Briar said. "She's in town to meet with me about an endorsement for the commandership."

Arielle, who hadn't realized she had been shaking Stella's hand for the past twenty seconds, looked her straight in those sky-blue eyes. "You're running for commander?! You totally have my vote."

Stella placed her free hand on Arielle's shoulder. "Thank you, dear. But this meeting is more to get a feel for things. Nothing is official yet."

"I was just telling Arielle about how bleak the future is looking for us," the commander said.

"Don't listen to any of that negativity," Stella said, shooting a wink at the commander. "Martin Briar is known as many things, but an optimist is not one of them. Let me guess, all doom and gloom?"

Arielle nodded. "Sort of."

"I don't see it that way. All I see is opportunity ahead for our group. Sure, there are some questionable things going on, but why not explore all the options? Road Runners are creative and innovative. Opening a time travel-related business is obviously a risk we don't need, but what if we implement controls on it and add it as another income stream? We mustn't be so closed-minded. The academy is a brilliant idea, one I think the next commander would be wise to implement and invest in. Our scientists are already looking at ways to make time travel even easier."

"How so?" Arielle asked, sitting back down but staying at the front of her seat.

"Imagine a life with no more Juice."

"Hey now," Commander Briar interrupted. "I just oversaw the completion of our newest lab that makes Juice."

"And we're grateful for it. Juice isn't going away any time soon. But that lab will also be the brains for our future. Teams will look for time portals around the world. Some of our scientists have started research on creating watches and clocks that will allow you to travel back and forth through time. The Book of Time contains centuries of information about how to properly execute time travel. Our ancestors were well ahead of their time, but they couldn't have imagined the type of technology we have today. There is so much we can refine. Imagine traveling back and speaking to your past self without your head exploding."

"Is this all for real, Commander?" Arielle asked.

He nodded hesitantly. "It is. The Book of Time possesses many secrets from the past."

"As does that vial of blood," Stella added.

"Excuse me?" Arielle gasped. "I thought the blood from the Keeper of Time was disposed."

Commander Briar pursed his lips. "We only said that. We didn't want anyone thinking it still exists—too dangerous for myself and the entire organization."

"But it *does* exist, and it's still dangerous."

Commander Briar raised a hand. "I know what you're thinking. It can't be accessed easily. The vial is locked in a private safe and requires two keys to unlock it. I have one, and for security reasons, I won't share who has the other. Rest assured, it's impossible for this vial to fall into the wrong hands."

"Many of us want Commander Briar to be the Keeper of

Time after his term ends," Stella said.

"And I still believe no such role should exist," the commander said. "I will continue to push for the destruction of this vial until my last day in office, but the Council feels it's irresponsible to end something that has been around for centuries."

"Does it really make you invincible?" Arielle asked. "And let you travel through time by simply thinking about it."

"Yes and yes, among many other things. It's too much power for one person to wield. Those days are behind us, and if they ever take out the vial, I hope it's long after I'm buried."

"To be fair," Stella said, "I don't think anyone else should have it. Commander Briar has earned the right to become the Keeper of Time, and if he doesn't, then so be it."

Commander Briar stood from his seat, lips white from how tightly he had them pursed. "That's enough of this topic. Stella, we have business to discuss. Arielle, thank you for everything. I look forward to seeing how your next mission goes. Now, if you'll excuse us."

Arielle nodded, stood up, and shook hands with the commander and Stella.

"It really was a dream come true to meet you," she said to the former top-ranked Angel.

"Good luck out there, Arielle. I'm always cheering for you."

# Chapter 6

Later that night, Arielle's doorbell chimed. Selena had been over before, but it was a quick visit before they headed out for a night on the town. Felix had never been over. Now that she thought about it, Arielle had never actually hosted anyone in her home. Her grandmother didn't travel anymore, leaving no one else to visit.

Arielle hurried down the stairs and rushed through the foyer to open the door. "Hey guys!"

Selena had a wide grin, while Felix was looking all over the place.

"Are you kidding me?" Felix asked. "I thought for sure Selena was pranking me when she told me to drive here. You live in a mansion on top of a hill."

"Come in, you two," Arielle said, stepping aside.

Felix entered with the same amazement on his face. "Look at this place. You have a Frida Kahlo painting?! Is it an original?"

The painting hung above the stairwell, depicting the face of the young artist on a deer's body with several arrows lodged into its torso.

"Yes, it's the original," Arielle said.

Felix's eyes bulged even wider. "How? That has to cost at least ten million dollars. Maybe even double."

Arielle shrugged. "I don't remember what I ended up paying. The entire house was done by a home decorator. She took care of all the details."

"Arielle, I had no idea you lived like this. No wonder you invite no one over. But if you don't mind me asking, *why?* It's just not you. Why did you get such a big place with all this fancy stuff?"

Arielle laughed. "Honestly, I hate moving. I wanted to buy my forever home and be done with it. Now I never have to move again. I like to think I'll have a family someday and won't always be alone. Until then, I don't mind the quiet."

"I would've never guessed. You're so humble. I mean, we all have a ton of money from the Road Runners, but few people use it like this. Impressive taste."

"Thank you. I've been enjoying it more now that we get all these days off."

Felix scoffed. "I sure as hell wouldn't leave this place if I lived here. Do you have a swimming pool out back?"

"As a matter of fact, yes. Pool and basketball court in the backyard. Sauna in the basement. You're both welcome any time. Selena, did you get some sleep? You look much more alive."

Selena nodded. "About seven hours. I needed it *bad*. Feeling much more like myself now."

"Glad to hear. Shall we get started? I think the pizza will be here in another hour."

"You ordered pizza?" Felix asked. "You probably have the most incredible kitchen in the world, and you ordered pizza?"

"Felix, snap out of it," Selena said. "You're being worse

than that night Arielle met Javonte at the club. Stop making a fool of yourself. We get it, you *love* to cook. But the rest of us are normal."

"You're normal, Felix," Arielle said. "I just didn't feel like cooking tonight."

"Well, if you ever want me to come over and cook," Felix said. "I can absolutely *throw down* in a place like this."

They all shared a laugh.

"I'll keep that in mind," Arielle said. "Now, shall we head to my office?"

They followed Arielle up the stairs, Felix stopping to admire *El Venado Herido*—The Wounded Deer.

"Why did you choose this painting?" he asked. "Just curious."

"She gave me a few options for which art to hang here. This one just called to me. Khalo lived a life in constant physical pain, yet she powered through to become the greatest Mexican artist of all time. Look at the deer. If the arrows weren't in its body, you'd think it was perfectly strong and healthy. Even her face looks calm and under control. She has nine arrows in her body yet is completely unbothered. My pain might not be physical, but I relate to this image on so many levels."

Arielle continued to the landing at the top of the stairs, not wanting to get emotional—just like Kahlo in the painting.

They followed her into the first door on the left of a long hallway. Three TV screens hung on the main wall. Two love seats were nestled in the corners next to the door. In the middle of the room stood Arielle's desk, a keyboard and mouse the lone objects atop the polished mahogany.

"Wait," Felix said. "Those three massive screens are your computer monitors?"

"Yes."

Felix shook his head. "Who are you? Dr. Evil?"

Arielle laughed. "The office was actually the only room my decorator didn't touch. I left it up to the Road Runners to set up how I needed."

"Okay, Arielle Lucila. I see how it is. Can't even share the goods with your friend who *worships* this stuff."

"I can put you in touch with the guy who set this all up. You're more than welcome to copy my office. Can we finally get to business, please?"

The shift in Arielle's tone forced Felix and Selena to sit down in the love seats.

Arielle sat behind her desk and fired up the massive monitors. The first one showed a map of Hilburn, Nebraska. The second showed a portrait of Alexander Carter. And the third had the picture of Miracle Park they had seen in Commander Briar's office.

"Alright," Arielle said. "Hilburn is the smallest town we've ever done a mission in. We won't have the luxury of a big city to help hide what we're up to, so we'll need to use some discretion. It's not so small that every resident knows each other, but it's close. Population is 20,000. It's very much a blue-collar type of people. They work hard and enjoy relaxing weekends with neighbors and friends. Lots of activities around town during the summer months, which is when we'll be arriving. Felix, you'll need to finalize where we're going to live. We need to blend in. The north side of town has a community college. There is a neighborhood two miles south of the college where, I presume, students live. Our roles will be three cousins who moved to Hilburn from Denver."

"To go to a community college?" Selena asked. "That story

doesn't make sense."

"To us. Let's say we wanted to get away from the big city. Not to stereotype, but most of these people likely hate big cities, even though their idea of a big city is Omaha ninety minutes east. They'll appreciate a shared disdain for the city life, so we need to play off that."

"Okay, but we should still try to keep to ourselves?"

"Of course, but it's going to be harder because of how small the town is. I'd say we need to focus more on not having a set routine. Don't eat at the same restaurants or visit the same bars."

"And what job am I doing?" Selena asked.

Arielle smiled and pointed to the picture of Miracle Park. "You're going to work at the park, of course. We need you to learn as much about Alexander Carter as possible. Felix, you'll be bugging his house and office to start."

"Got it," Felix said, pulling a notepad and pen out of his pocket. "And for communication, it's going to be a challenge. The 1970s had those big radios, so I'm not sure how we can each get one *and* be discreet. We'll have no way of reaching each other besides the pay phones set up around town."

Arielle nodded. "I've already highlighted all the payphone locations on our map. There are six spread through Miracle Park, plus three more outside of it. Selena, you'll need to call one of us at home if anything comes up. And I'm sorry to say this will be one of those missions you can't bring your cell phone."

Both Arielle and Felix glanced at Selena, knowing what that sort of news did to her. She licked her lips before pinching the bottom one under her teeth and nodded calmly. "Lovely. At least it's only six weeks, right?"

"Correct. Six weeks is all we'll need. It sounds like there is always a job opening at the park because so many people hate working for Carter and quit. Commander Briar was right, though. We'll need to explore as much as we can in the present day. I'd like to fly out there tomorrow morning. We'll be going into Omaha and making the drive west to Hilburn. A day at the park should be enough to get familiar, and then we'll make the jump back in time."

"Weapons?" Felix asked.

"Small pistols for all of us. I've still got some throwing knives. I think that's all we need. We're not expecting life-threatening danger on this mission, but we still need some level of protection. I can bring down Carter with my bare hands if it comes to it."

"I expect nothing less." Felix finished scribbling a note before looking up. "So, what's our strategy?"

Arielle stood up and shot a finger toward the monitor showing Alexander Carter. "That man, though not responsible, is the source of this incident—assuming it was done intentionally. We will find out everything we can about him, but more importantly, those who interact with him. People hate him. In fact, most people in town hate him. He rolled into this peaceful town with all his money and opened a park that is actually drawing a lot of tourists. Many fear Hilburn will grow into a big city. He built this park and hotel, and now people don't blow by on the freeway. They're stopping and staying. He even bought the town's newspaper, and the locals fear he can push whatever narrative he pleases to get his way."

"There are surely locals who love him," Felix said.

"Yes. The city government. The tax revenue from the park

is unlike anything Hilburn has seen. Their new budget allows them to take on so many more projects for the town. They're the last people who want to see the park get shut down."

"So we have Carter, his park, the government, and newspaper on one side. And everyone else on the other?"

"Basically, yes. There are exceptions to both sides, but overall, that's a fair assessment."

"So if there is a suspect, it can literally be any disgruntled resident in town, not necessarily an employee."

"Correct. But we will start with employees. They'll have the most direct reasons for wanting revenge against old Alex."

"And what about that hippie chick Commander Briar was talking about?" Selena asked.

"Willow West. While Selena is getting acquainted with the staff at the park, I'll be following Willow and any other leads on the outside. I suspect there will be a lot of moving parts, so Felix, be ready for me to call upon you."

He offered a tight-lipped grin. "I suppose I won't have much to do aside from monitoring Carter."

"I know. I'll probably have you start simple, like chatting with locals to get a feel for what they think about the park and its future. There's always a hint that can be picked up from those conversations. People love to gossip, especially in these smaller towns."

"Anything beats having to pretend I'm a superhero. I don't enjoy talking to people, but I'll take it."

"You'll do fine. Now, we'll be jumping back to July 10, 1978. I'm accounting for a couple of weeks for Selena to get hired and start working, though it might move much faster than that. For those days, until she gets hired, the three of us will spread across town and start learning what we can."

"Are we going to have a day to enjoy the park?" Felix asked. "Or can we only look at it for six weeks and dream?"

Arielle shot him a questioning look.

"What?" he asked, tossing his hands in the air. "I love theme parks. This sounds like one I would have definitely visited if it never shut down."

"Are you going to ride Time Roller?"

"Well, duh. It's still going to be safe once we arrive."

"I suppose we can spend a few hours in the park on one of those early weekends. They say Saturdays and Sundays are when Willow liked to march around with her signs and megaphone, and I'd like to see her in action."

"Oh great," Selena said. "So we get to be yelled at by an authentic hippie from the Seventies."

"You should take her some vegan bacon from the future," Felix said. "That'll blow her mind."

They all laughed, knowing Felix's disgust for fake meat.

"Well then," Arielle said. "Are we ready to leave tomorrow morning?"

# Chapter 7

They rolled into Hilburn, Nebraska, the following day, minutes after noon had struck. Felix had made all the arrangements for their house and transportation. They rented an SUV from the airport in Omaha and drove the hour and a half west to Hilburn, cruising into the laid-back town on a quiet autumn afternoon.

They took Highway 30 into town, which became 23rd Street and cut through the heart of Hilburn. Everything the residents needed could be found on this three-mile stretch of road. Restaurants, pharmacies, doctors' offices, grocery stores, and tons of fast-food joints.

"It's not that small," Selena said. "We've already passed a Walmart a mile back."

Felix laughed. "Yeah? You ready to move out here? I'm sure the nightlife is bustling."

"If by bustling, you mean everything closes at nine, then you'd be correct," Arielle said, adding her own laughter.

"They have an airport here," Selena said, looking out the passenger-side window in the backseat. "Could have saved us this boring ass drive."

"Oh, I know, but we were never flying into Hilburn. Could

you imagine the gossip that would start if our private jet flew into this little town? We'd have eyes on us the moment we stepped off the plane. Not so much in Omaha."

"That's fair," Selena said. "Are we going straight to the park?"

"Actually, no. I'm starving, aren't you guys?"

"Well, yes," Felix said. "Why wasn't there any food on the flight? That's my favorite part of each trip, and now I feel robbed of that experience."

"You'll be fine," Arielle said. "I told them not to worry about getting all that food together for such a short flight. By the time anything had been cooked, we'd have had about twenty minutes to scarf it down. Besides, I want to ask some locals what they remember about this tragedy. Keep in mind, it was only forty-five years ago, so anyone fifty-five and older will probably have memories of the dreaded Time Roller. Kids are in school, so I imagine most people out and about right now are retired. They'll definitely remember how everything unfolded."

"Right there," Felix said, pointing out his window ahead. "Definitely a local restaurant."

Sandwiched between a Wendy's and McDonald's stood a small brick building with a plum-colored sign hanging over the entrance.

"Stack-n-Steak Family Restaurant," Arielle said, slowing down and turning into the parking lot. The north side of the lot had a strip mall with Valentino's Italian Buffet and an urgent care center serving as the bookends for the half-dozen businesses in between. Three pickup trucks were parked outside the restaurant, all covered with an array of bumper stickers—American flags, Confederate Flags, I Back the Boys in Blue.

"I think this is as local as we can find," Selena said.

"Well, let's check it out." Arielle parked the SUV in front of the entrance and killed the engine.

They filed into the restaurant to a room filled with four-person tables stretching to the back wall, each one with table covers matching the same plum as the sign outside.

"Good afternoon, folks," said an older woman who stepped out from a side door to the kitchen. "Just the three of you?"

"Yes, ma'am," Arielle said, spotting three men sitting at a table in the back corner, each wearing trucker's hats that looked one size too small for their meaty heads. Empty plates lay scattered on their table, cups half full of soda in front of each man.

"Take a seat wherever you'd like," the woman said, waving her arm to the entire floor.

Arielle led the way to a table in the center of the dining room, pushing the napkin dispenser and bottle of ketchup to the center. Selena took the seat next to her, and Felix sat across from them.

"Can I get some drinks started for y'all?" the woman asked.

"I'll have a water," Arielle said. Selena and Felix ordered a water and Coke.

"These prices are incredible," Felix said, scanning the menu. "Steaks are the only things over ten dollars, and even those are under twenty."

"And you know it's fresh," Selena added. "We drove past about two hundred cows on the way here."

The woman returned to the table with their drinks. She had short gray hair done in a perm and wide glasses sitting on the perch of her nose. An apron with flower designs was slung over her potbelly, and she reached into the front pocket to pull out her notepad.

"Have you decided what you'd like to eat?" she asked.

The three looked around and nodded before placing their orders.

Once the woman stepped away, Selena said, "So, are you going to ask those guys back there what they know about Miracle Park?"

Arielle looked over her shoulder, scrunching her face. "I'm not sure they're old enough. Early forties, I'd say. Would've been babies when that all went down. Now, our server, she's definitely old enough. We'll see what she knows."

On cue, the woman stepped out from the kitchen, and Arielle waved her over. "Excuse me, ma'am."

"Yes, dear, did you forget something?"

"Actually, no. I had a question. See, my cousins and I arrived in town a few days ago. We're starting the new semester at Central Community College."

"Oh? My grandson graduated from CCC just last year. Great school. Where are y'all from?"

"Denver," Arielle said. "We needed to get out of the big city. I think small-town life is more for us."

A grin touched the woman's lips. "Well, that's something you don't hear too often. Welcome to Hilburn. I know you'll enjoy everything our fine city has to offer."

"Yes, we're excited. But we're new to town and still learning where everything is. We noticed the old amusement park down by the river. Is it going through some sort of renovation?"

The woman threw her head back and laughed. "Oh, I'm sorry, you three. That park has been closed since '78, and it's never coming back."

"Oh," Arielle said, feigning surprise. "Why is it still there after so many years?"

"That's a long story, but I'll summarize it as best I can. It all happened in 1978. I was the age you all look to be right now. There was a terrible accident. The big roller coaster—the one you can see from just about anywhere in town—broke down in the middle of a ride and killed five people. Thirteen others were seriously injured but survived."

"Oh my goodness," Selena said, placing a hand to her mouth, never shy to deliver a performance.

"Yes, it was ugly, and the park was permanently shut down after it closed for the summer. It's unfortunate that it took such a tragedy for that to happen, but most of us were happy to see it closed. See, the owner, Mr. Carter, was a nasty man. The park was one thing—stirred up a lot of noise during its construction. No one here wanted a tourist attraction like that, bringing all the city folk from Omaha every summer. Trashy people. They'd come into town and litter all over the place. Trashed our restaurants and movie theater, especially on the weekends. And worse, they treated us all like we're dumb. I can tell you, some of the smartest people live in this town. But since we like to have a simple life, we get treated like second-class citizens from the big city dwellers. Since we don't live the way they expect, they pretend we're only here to serve them. Still goes on today, but thankfully not nearly as much as when that awful park was open."

"You said the owner was a bad man. How so?"

The woman shuddered, as if a spirit had just brushed a finger down her spine. "Mr. Carter was the worst. For punishment, he'd lock employees in closets, refuse them their lunch breaks, or *any* breaks. He always tried to short paychecks, and when someone asked about it, his payroll staff would take weeks, sometimes months, to rectify the matter. He treated staff like they were his slaves. No humanity in that man. Not an ounce."

"And what happened to that roller coaster was an accident?"

The woman shrugged. "*I* believe it was, but there's lots of theories. Conspiracy theories, you could say. Many think someone sabotaged the ride so the park would get shut down, but I don't believe someone from this town could do such a horrific thing. Not in Hilburn, no ma'am."

"Whatever happened to the owner?"

"Financially speaking, he got what he deserved. Lawsuits left and right. He had a ton of money, power, and influence, but he couldn't hide from the lawsuits. He lost in court and had to pay out millions of dollars in settlements and court fees. It bankrupted him, and he fled town. He stuck around until 1980, living in the penthouse of that fancy hotel he built. No one knows when he left—we just stopped seeing him. His car was gone, and the park was locked up. Good riddance is all I can say."

"Wow," Arielle said, taking a swig of the coffee that was already cooling. "That's an incredible story. How do you know so much?"

"Oh, dear, it's because I worked at the park."

# Chapter 8

Their server was Mary Pickett, and she was more than their server. She owned the diner, having bought it from the prior owners back in 1992. In her early seventies, she debated putting the place back up for sale and retiring, but claimed she wouldn't know what to do with all that free time. Her son, Casey, owned and operated Casey's Diner three blocks further east and considered the prospects of buying his mother's restaurant.

Arielle didn't care about any of this and wanted more information about Alexander Carter and the evening from hell in Miracle Park.

But Mary seemed reluctant to keep speaking on the matter. Even all these years later, the older woman still suffered from the trauma of what she had witnessed that night. Just like Arielle didn't care to discuss the mass shooting that took her family weeks before Christmas. She couldn't press Mary to do the same, so they had left with full bellies and a big thank you in the form of a one-hundred-dollar tip.

"I can't believe the first restaurant we stop at and it's someone who worked at the park," Selena said. "What are the odds?"

"Small town," Arielle said. "Just small enough for something like that to happen. We're definitely going to see her in the past."

They drove down the rest of 23rd Street, passing more fast food, a buffet, and the Hilburn Fire Department, before turning on 45th Avenue to head north. They arrived at their house five minutes later, Arielle parking along the sidewalk.

The real estate team had to travel back and purchase the first house they could find for sale. It was in a neighborhood three miles north of Miracle Park, on a block of cookie-cutter homes that all had the same perfectly manicured lawns. They pulled up to the ranch-style house.

"This is it," she said. "Seems like a quiet neighborhood. Long lawns, so we're not really too close to the neighbors."

"Where the hell are we?" Selena asked. "This is the most vanilla street block I've ever been on. How is anyone supposed to know which house is theirs? They all look the same."

And they did. As far as they could see, every house had a bottom half of brick exterior with off-white siding above. Even the layouts were similar: wide windows revealing a living room to the left of the front door, kitchen to the right, two-car garage next to that.

"Felix, what's the deal with our cars in the past?" Arielle asked.

"They said two will be parked in the garage, and the third in the driveway."

Being the corner house, the driveway stretched far and wide, able to fit another four cars if needed.

A mail carrier strolled down the sidewalk, whistling tunes as sweat streamed down his face, earphones blocking out the world around him.

"This neighborhood seriously seems like one out of those older movies," Selena said. "The kind where everyone gets along, and they leave the doors unlocked just so the neighbors can come and go as they please."

"I'm sure it's going to be even more like that once we jump back into the past," Arielle said. "Shall we drop off our stuff inside before heading to the park? Then we can come back and jump to 1978 to get started."

"Let's roll," Felix said, the first to step out of the car. They gathered their luggage from the trunk and trudged up the walkway to the front door, where Felix pulled out a key and jiggled it into the lock.

They stepped into the home, pleased to find a simple layout. A short hallway led to the back side of the house, forking into a perpendicular hallway that led to one bathroom, two bedrooms, and the dining room, which was adjoined to the kitchen. A patio door in the dining room led out to a massive backyard, plush green grass running the length of the property, a twelve-by-twelve tool shed standing along the back fence serving as the property's border. Fifty yards beyond the chain-link was a playground on Gerrard Park. A couple of high schoolers who must have ditched class swayed back and forth on the swing set.

"Cute little spot," Selena said.

"I could totally live somewhere like this," Felix said. "Middle of nowhere, but still part of a society. Great food. Peaceful neighbors—I'm assuming."

"Can't wait to see how outdated everything will feel once we go back. I pray there is no shag carpet—just seeing that could make me vomit."

"Well, let's hope it's all over your room . . . and bathroom."

Selena socked Felix in the arm, earning a raucous laugh.

"Enough you two," Arielle snapped. "Two bedrooms up here for me and Selena. I'm assuming you want the basement to yourself, Felix?"

"Duh," he replied. "It makes me feel more like a spy when I can do my sneaky surveillance from a basement."

"Whatever you say. Let's drop our things off in the living room and head out."

A couple of minutes later, they were piling back into the SUV and started their seven-minute drive to the park.

"Get familiar with this drive, Selena," Arielle said. "You'll be making it every day once you start working at the park."

"Oh, joy," she replied, leaning her head against the window as they zipped through a mostly residential route before reaching the highway that took them south to the park.

They turned onto Eighth Street and drove past Pawnee Park, home to tennis courts, and the football and baseball fields used by Hilburn High School. The road forked, and they took it south, circling around the sports fields and disappearing behind a thick stand of trees that seemed to block them out from the rest of the world. They followed the road to a massive, abandoned parking lot, the gray asphalt gleaming like white sand under the afternoon sun.

The back of the parking lot was at least a mile from Miracle Park's front gate. They crept through the parking lot, potholes and cracks scattered about. Once closer, the old hotel came into view.

"The Miracle Hotel," Felix said, reading the sign hanging sideways off the building's facade.

The hotel had a beige exterior, chunks of paint missing, windows shattered, and the building appeared to tilt slightly to the west.

"I bet it was stunning when it was open," Arielle said. "Sounds like Carter really loved the finer things in life, and if he lived there, you know he made it his own."

"We're not going in there, are we?" Felix asked. "Looks like the whole place is about to fall apart."

Arielle shrugged. "Eventually. We'll look and see how safe it seems. We're not even in the past, so there won't be any need to tiptoe around."

They reached the park entrance, stopping the car in the drop-off lane.  "Let's check this place out," Arielle said, turning off the engine and rushing out, nearly tripping as she ran to the park gates.

A folding security gate stretched across the pathway, a rusty padlock hanging from the thick chains wrapped through the slots. Felix and Selena followed, and they looked up at the top of the gate. Above it, a long sign ran the length of the entry walkway: *WELCOME TO MIRACLE PARK! WHERE MIRACLES COME TRUE!*

Decades of weather and sunshine faded the words to the point of nearly blending in with the sign that was now a light brown.

"It's only ten feet high," Felix said.  "We can hop this easily."

Arielle stopped and looked over her shoulder. "We can't just hop over the front gate. That will seem too obvious."

"Obvious to who? The birds in the trees?"

"He's right," Selena said. "We haven't seen a single person since we turned off the highway. That park we passed was empty, and this place is tucked away so no one has to think about it. I doubt locals ever come here, except for maybe the anniversary of the accident."

"Maybe an occasional tourist," Felix added. "There are some weirdos fascinated by visiting sites of tragedy."

"Sounds like something you'd do," Selena said.

Felix grinned. "Sure. I used to. Since becoming an Angel and working all these missions, it's sort of lost its luster. That's beside the point. We're here to explore the park. We can either hop this fence—which I'd consider trespassing, or we can break the padlock—which is probably breaking and entering. I suppose we could walk around to find another entry point, but I'm sure it's going to be locked up the same way."

"We're already parked in front of the damn park," Selena said. "Might as well go in. If anyone comes looking for us, I'm sure we can get away without being caught."

"Alright," Arielle said. "So trespassing it is."

She stepped forward and reached up, gripping the gate as she planted her foot in one of the lower slots to elevate herself. The gate wobbled furiously once she reached the top and threw one leg over to cradle it. For a moment, she thought the whole gate might collapse under her weight, but it held sturdy.

"Just take your time on the way down," Felix instructed, hands already grasping where he planned to climb. Selena had already started further down the gate.

Halfway down, Arielle hopped off the gate and dusted off her clothes while she waited for Felix and Selena. The entrance led through a covered strip of concession stands and booths that once hosted park employees to help guide visitors to their areas of interest.

"This place looks like the end of the world," Selena said.

"You're right," Felix said. "Popcorn buckets on the ground. Trash cans full after all these years. Look, there's even a sweater on the chair behind the guest relations booth."

He pointed to it, and something about that lone blue sweater sent chills down Arielle's back. It really looked like someone had barged into the park in 1978 and kicked everyone out in the middle of whatever they were doing. Only to never return.

A couple of mice dashed across the pathway, running into a tipped-over paper cup for shelter.

"It blows my mind all of this is still here," Selena said. "Like it hasn't even been cleaned. Do you think there are still bloodstains on the roller coaster?"

They continued through the entryway and stepped back outside on the other end, the pathways to the amusement park branching out in three different directions.

"It's possible," Felix said. "But something like bloodstains has probably washed away after all this time. Rain, snow, sunlight over forty-five years. I highly doubt anything looks like how it did the day this place shut down."

"Let's hope," Arielle said. "Time Roller is in the back of the park, right where Carter wanted it so people could see it from the highway."

They crept through the park, passing old rides and attractions. The Ferris wheel stood in front of them, the higher gondolas swaying in the breeze. A couple of gondolas had fallen off the ride like apples from a tree, their remains a pile on the ground. Weeds sprouted through several cracks in the pavement, and some rides had bushes growing around them. A smaller roller coaster likely meant for children had two trains on the track, stopped at the bottom of the first drop, bird shit covering the ride like someone had attacked it with a paintball gun.

"It looks like people probably snuck in here after Carter left town," Felix said. "Had the park to themselves. I bet that was fun."

"Yeah, until you're riding the Ferris wheel and take a final plunge to your death," Selena said.

"I doubt anyone was on it when that happened. It's clearly not safe anymore, not that this place even has power running to it."

"Don't worry," Arielle said. "You'll get your turn riding everything once we go back in time. I want to go to the roller coaster last. Which way do you think the offices are?"

"No need to wonder," Felix said. A map of the park stood in front of them behind a cracked, plastic protective case. The kiosk that sheltered the map had two drawers stuffed with the paper maps visitors once used to navigate the park. He shuffled up and pulled out three maps. "They're a little faded, but still clear enough to see."

He handed them out, and they all flipped them open, heads buried like explorers searching for ancient ruins.

"Looks like the offices are on the right-hand path," Arielle said. "About halfway between us and the back of the park."

"Makes sense," Selena said. "The offices are right next to the walkway connecting the park to the hotel."

"Let's head over."

Arielle led the way, cruising confidently down the pathway, weaving through tipped-over trash cans long scavenged by the critters that once had a field day in the abandoned park.

They reached the office, a beaten building off the path to their right, complete with missing doors and windows.

"People probably broke into the offices looking for money," Arielle said.

They stepped through the open doorway into what was

once a lobby for park guests. Two hallways broke in opposite directions from the lobby. Signage hung above each. The hall to the right led to restrooms, First-Aid, and guest services. The hall to the left only had "Executive Offices" on its sign.

"Let's check out the offices," Arielle said, starting down the hall.

They passed an old time clock on the wall, the rack of time cards next to it still filled with the stamps from each time the employees punched in and out.

Felix stopped and studied it. "Looks like September fifth was the last day of time stamps. That was a couple of weeks after the accident."

"Interesting," Selena said. "Is Mary's card on there?"

"Sure is. Mary Pickett." Felix held up the card for a moment before putting it back into place.

Selena shivered like a gust of cold had just washed over her. "That's so weird. Don't you think?"

"I'm definitely getting strange vibes from this place."

Arielle had kept walking down the hallway and called for them to catch up. She was three doors down at the end of the hall.

"Here it is," she said, tapping on the door's glass window with *MR. CARTER* spelled out in black lettering. She pulled open the door, and they shuffled into the office. "Surprised this door never got busted down."

A lone desk sat under the window overlooking the hotel. Three chairs had been pushed toward the back wall; a leather couch next to those was blocking closet doors. Holes peppered the walls, like someone had taken a hammer and tried to perform their own demolition. Chunks of cotton poured out of gashes in the couch's leather. A small trash bin stood next to the desk, black and charred inside.

"Honestly," Arielle said. "I'm surprised there isn't more damage done here. This man was hated by so many. Obviously, a couple of people thought to come in here and vandalize what they could. I'm sure it was therapeutic. Looks like they even tried to start a fire in the trash can."

Arielle would have done the same thing if given the opportunity. Nicholas Robert Fenton had taken her entire family, and she'd have loved to spend an hour destroying his prison cell, if not the man himself. Some days, the prospect of revenge tasted so sweet in her mouth it was unbearable. Meeting Mary at the restaurant earlier and learning that Alexander Carter had fled Hilburn without any true justice stirred up all those emotions Arielle had learned to keep in check over the years. Paying settlements didn't bring back the dead. It didn't numb the pain. It changed nothing.

And Arielle knew this. She had received seventy-five thousand dollars in a settlement from the mall where the shooting had occurred. That money went straight into her savings account, where she hadn't touched it since. She couldn't, in good faith, spend that money. It wasn't exactly dirty money, but she didn't understand its purpose. Was she supposed to take a lavish vacation in remembrance of her parents and brother? She'd still return to their gravestones after the fact. She considered donating it to a foundation that fought gun violence, but that cause was going nowhere quickly, just like the Time Roller had in 1978.

"Let's look in the desk," Arielle said, snapping out of her daydream.

Selena obliged and slid over to Carter's desk, pulling open the top drawer. "Pencils, stapler, notepads. Not much else."

She closed the drawer and opened the next one, jumping back with a shriek.

Arielle whipped out her gun by reflex, but lowered it once Selena started laughing.

"What is it?" Arielle asked in her most serious tone.

"Sorry," Selena replied. "It's shit. Someone *shit* in the desk."

"That's disgusting," Felix said, shaking his head as he took a step back, no longer interested in examining the desk.

Arielle grinned. "That is nasty, but I can't say I'm surprised. I thought someone might've done that on top of the desk. Inside the second drawer . . . that's just savagery."

They all burst into laughter as Selena stepped forward and raised her foot to push the shitty drawer closed with the tip of her shoe.

"Is it . . . fresh?" Felix asked, a sour expression washing over his face.

"Not fresh. Definitely old. Looked like little white pebbles."

"Alright, that's enough," Arielle interjected. "There's nothing of importance in here. Mostly, we just needed to know how to get in and out. Felix, you'll need to bug this office when we jump back in time. In fact, let's bug every office in this building. We'll want to hear what the staff is saying, perhaps even more than Carter."

"I've already scouted the building. It has doors at the end of each hallway, so three entryways. I don't see any security cameras, so as long as I can get in after hours, I can take my time bugging every room."

"Perfect. That won't be a problem once Selena has employee access. Now, let's go check out this roller coaster and head back to the house. The sooner we can jump, the sooner we get started on the mission."

# Chapter 9

"It doesn't look as big as I thought," Selena said, arms crossed as the three Angels stood in front of Time Roller.

"Of course not," Felix said. "It was only big for its time. We grew up with massive roller coasters made of steel that go over 300 feet high. Back then, all they had were these wooden coasters, and there was only so much you could do with them."

"I guess. I still expected more."

"It's also not in its peak shape," Arielle said. "Look at that ivy growing all over it. I wouldn't be surprised if the whole thing comes crashing down in the next few years."

"It seems like parts of it already have," Felix said, pointing to a portion of the track that was missing.

"Well," Selena said. "Should we examine it?"

"We can take a closer look," Arielle replied. "But I'm not sure we should touch anything. Who knows what people have done to this over all these years."

"Looks like they came back for a memorial," Felix said, pointing toward the towering clock that had once welcomed guests to the roller coaster. At the base of the clock lay a scatter of five white crosses, names of the victims written on each. Tattered stuffed animals lay in ruins, their cotton guts spilling out, probably due to birds seeking fresh materials for nests.

"It doesn't look like this memorial has been touched in years," Arielle said, stepping up to the mound of items. She squatted down and picked up an old teddy bear, one eye missing, but otherwise in decent shape. She looked at the roller coaster before closing her eyes and tried to imagine the day of horror. Bodies and shrapnel soaring through the air. Happiness turning into terror in a split second. She prayed it was an accident and not something done intentionally. If that was the case, the person responsible still wandered freely, never having to pay the consequences.

Felix had wandered to the platform where riders boarded the coaster. Selena stayed back with Arielle, unable to look away from the five crosses that signified lives lost.

"Do we even know about the victims?" she asked.

Arielle nodded. "Their information is in the mission report. Of the five who died, two were from out of town. Three were locals."

"Are any of the people who survived the ride still alive and living here today?"

"Yes. And I know what you're thinking, but we won't get any relevant information from those people. They're the survivors. Whatever logical ideas they have about the topic are buried beneath layers of trauma. They won't know anything about who might have done it, or even why. They'll only regurgitate what they've heard from the news. Nothing different from what's in our mission report. No need for us to stir up their emotions when we won't get anything out of it."

Selena remained silent, and they both watched as Felix returned to them.

"Anything to report?" Arielle asked him.

"No. Just a roller coaster that has been abandoned like everything else in this park. I saw a clump of the yellow crime scene tape they used while investigating. It was all bunched up under the tracks."

"I figured as much. Not much to see here. We got what we need. Let's head back to the house."

* * *

The drive home was silent. Seeing the park, the roller coaster, and the makeshift memorial draped melancholy over their mood.

"Two kids died on that ride," Selena said once they turned into their neighborhood. "Fifteen and twelve years old. Makes me absolutely sick."

"Me too," Felix said. "If someone actually got away with this, we're going to make it right. Do you agree, Arielle?"

"One thing at a time," she replied. "I'm just as distraught as you two, but we can't jump to conclusions. All we can do is follow the facts and decide from there. This is an observational mission, and we must remember that."

"Bullshit!" Selena barked from the backseat. "Commander Briar said we can do whatever we feel is necessary."

"And we will," Arielle replied calmly. "I just don't want us getting ahead of ourselves. I'm not going to speculate and make plans for this and that. One day at a time. One *fact* at a time. We should only make our next decision based on the prior happening. Dwelling on the future only creates a bias in our minds. If we're desperate to bring justice to a perpetrator, then we'll bend the facts to make it so. That's when mistakes happen, and the truth can slip right through the cracks."

They pulled up to their house, the sun inching closer to the horizon. Arielle parked in the driveway and turned off the car. "For what it's worth," she said, "yes, we will bring justice to the person responsible should the opportunity present itself. But get that out of your mind right now. We need tunnel vision to complete the next task. And right now, that means going inside that house and jumping to 1978."

She stepped out without another word and trudged to the front door, drawing one final deep breath from the present day's air. Felix followed and unlocked the door for them.

"Does anyone need anything else before we jump back?" Arielle asked as she led them into the living room where their luggage stood in a pile together.

"We should be all set," Felix said. "I've got our clothing for 1978—extra bell bottoms for Selena—cash, and ID's."

"Good. Leave all modern technology behind. Cell phones won't work. Laptops won't work. You get the idea."

Selena pulled her phone out of her pocket and looked at it with the longing gaze someone might have before saying goodbye to a loved one.

"All I have is the bugging equipment that *will* work in 1978," Felix said. "I can't lie. I'm sort of excited about the challenge of doing this mission with virtually none of the tools we're used to having."

"Good for you," Selena muttered under her breath.

"We'll be just fine," Arielle said. "I've done plenty of missions like this. Even gone back centuries where you can't bring a single item with you. Now *that's* a challenge. Grab your luggage and take out your Juice."

They obliged, each of them wheeling their luggage to a spot in front of the couches and sitting down. Arielle pulled out her flask of Juice, a solid stainless steel one no bigger than a playing card, and unscrewed the lid. Felix and Selena did the same.

Arielle swirled the Juice around, looking into the tiny black hole, and thought back to what Stella had said about the future of time travel. She had been sipping this mystical Juice since she first joined the Road Runners. Everyone had. There was no other way to travel through time. Only the mad scientists who spent their entire lives inside laboratories understood the physics and chemistry of how it all worked. And now they wanted to find other, simpler ways to time travel. Not that taking a sip of Juice required any effort from the time traveler, but creating the stuff was surely complex and time-consuming.

"Remember," Arielle said, raising her flask to eye level, "stay focused on the next thing. Don't worry about what happens later. One day at a time, okay?"

Selena nodded.

"One day at a time," Felix repeated.

"July 10, 1978," Arielle said.

Felix and Selena repeated the date, and they all took a sip of their Juice, bracing for the familiar rumble that accompanied the free-falling sensation as their minds, bodies, and souls disobeyed the rules of time and ventured into the past.

# Chapter 10



*July 10, 1978*

The three Angels woke up on the same couch, luggage in hand, forty-five years earlier.

"Shag carpet!" Felix cried, running his shoes over the thick texture.

The aesthetics of the house had changed entirely.

"Oh dear God," Selena muttered. "Why? Were people on so many drugs in the Seventies that they lost any sense of taste?"

The shag carpet was a golden color. Two zebra-print bean bag chairs nestled in the corner of the living room. The textured dry wall had been replaced by wood paneling in every direction they looked. A television no bigger than fourteen inches sat atop a dresser, complete with dials to navigate the channels and volume.

"Why is everything so *yellow*?" Selena asked, disgusted. "It seriously looks like twenty bottles of mustard exploded in here."

Arielle laughed. "Dare we check out the rest of the house?"

Selena crossed her arms. "I'm a bit horrified and not sure I want to, if I'm being completely honest."

"Kitchen first," Felix said, jumping off the couch, the lone furniture from their future. "But first, gotta lose these shoes. Would hate to stomp all over this beautiful shag."

He kicked his sneakers and socks off, running his toes through the furry carpet. Selena made a heaving gesture, and they weren't sure if she was being serious or not.

Felix hurried to the kitchen, stopping in the doorway. "Oh my."

Arielle followed and saw the kitchen with its patterned linoleum flooring, vinyl tablecloth, and horrendous wallpaper with floral designs.

A machine as big as a microwave sat on the counter. "Is that a coffeemaker?" Arielle asked, squinting as if it couldn't be.

"It sure is."

Selena appeared behind them. "Surprisingly, the kitchen doesn't look as bad as the rest of the house. It's ugly, don't get me wrong, but at least it doesn't feel like I'm walking on a living animal."

"Cooking in here should be interesting," Felix said. "But I'll be fine."

"We need to make sure the cars are in order," Arielle said.

"Good call. Let's have a look."

Felix pivoted and led them to the garage door, pulling it open and stepping through to flick on the light. Three fluorescent bulbs hung from the garage's ceiling, buzzing as they revealed the cars below.

Felix pulled out his notepad from his back pocket and flipped through it until landing on his notes for the mission. "A '77 Chevy Impala and Ford LTD. That means the Cadillac DeVille should be in the driveway."

He slapped the button on the wall, setting the garage door

into motion. The evening sunlight spilled through before they saw the light brown Cadillac waiting on the pavement.

"All is here," Felix said with a satisfied grin.

"These cars are hideous," Selena said with a giggle. "I don't know whether to laugh or cry."

"I'm going to laugh," Felix said. "The queen of cool is going to look anything *but* cool driving around town in any of these cars."

Selena rolled her eyes. "I guess it's fine, since my job isn't all that glamorous. Why are older cars such tanks? These things look like they could take a serious beating and come out in one piece."

"I definitely prefer that," Arielle said. "Especially in a small town like this. I doubt we'll need to race around too often, if at all. I already noticed the drivers are pretty laid back and in no rush. And that was in 2023. I'm sure now they're even more relaxed."

"Hello!" a woman called out from across the street, waving from her front porch.

"Oh shit," Selena said, rolling her eyes.

"Be nice," Arielle muttered, smiling and waving back. "And watch your slang. Remember, it's 1978, speak as neutrally as you can."

"Groovy," Felix said with a wink and a giggle, earning a signature eye roll from Selena.

The woman strolled down her pathway and hurried across the street, cradling a plastic container under one arm like a football.

"Hi there, new neighbors!" the woman said once she reached their sidewalk. The three stepped out of their garage and met her in the middle of the driveway.

"Good evening, ma'am," Arielle said.

"I made the mistake of chatting with your movers a couple of weeks ago. I thought they were the ones moving in, but they told me otherwise. Is it all three of you living here?"

"Yes," Felix said, stepping forward and sticking out his hand. "My name is Felix, and these are my cousins, Arielle and Selena."

"Three cousins living together? You never hear of that. Bless you three for being so close. What brings you to Hilburn?"

"We're going to school at CCC," Felix explained. "So you probably won't see us much during the week."

"Oh, college kids? How lovely."

The woman couldn't have been older than thirty, but Arielle thought she spoke like a fifty-year-old housewife.

"That we are," Felix said. "But don't worry, we're not the rowdy kind. You won't see any parties at our house."

"He's right," Selena said. "We're all business and no fun. Ever."

She clapped Felix on the back while offering a fake grin.

"Well, that's great. I brought you some cookies I made this morning as a little welcome gift. My name is Linda, by the way. Linda Patterson."

She handed over the container of cookies, and Felix grabbed it with pleasure.

"Thank you so much, Linda. That really is thoughtful."

*Is Felix flirting right now?* Arielle thought, having never heard his current tone. It heightened in pitch, and he hadn't looked away from Linda since she stepped foot on their property.

Linda had a natural radiance of joy and gentleness, and

apparently, that charm was working on Felix.

"Do you live by yourself?" Felix asked, earning a hard smack from Arielle.

"Felix," she said through gritted teeth. "That's not something you come out and ask."

Linda waved it off. "It's completely fine. I'm by myself most of the time. Military wife. My husband is a flight engineer for the Air Force, so is out of town pretty much every week. We could have lived in Bellevue—that's where the base is—but I wanted to stay in Hilburn. Born and raised."

"Good to know," Felix replied. "We'll need recommendations for places to eat and things to do."

"I'm always open to an invitation," Linda said, eyes locked with Felix's.

"Alright," Arielle said, desperately needing to change the subject. "We were about to head down to Miracle Park to see what all the talk is about."

"How fun!" Linda cried. "I try to go once a month. Mr. Carter is on to something with that park of his. It just might be better than Disneyland one day. I can't say for sure because I've never been to Disney, but I've seen the pictures. I won't spoil the fun, though. You should go see for yourself. I'll let you to it. If you need anything at all, just come on over and ask. I'm happy to help."

"It was a pleasure meeting you," Felix said, sticking out his hand once more. Arielle and Selena followed suit, and the three watched Linda venture back to her house.

Once she disappeared through her front door, Selena said, "Need a cold shower, Felix?"

Arielle laughed. "Seriously."

"What?" Felix asked, blushing.

"You like Linda," Selena said. "You didn't even try hiding it."

"I was just being friendly."

"Asking her if she's home alone all day."

"That's *not* what I asked."

"It's what you implied. It's fine. You could use a little romance in your life, but I don't think a married woman is your best option. The deck is already stacked against you, my friend. Try elsewhere."

"Oh my God, you two. No. I'm not going to make any moves on Linda. Inappropriate. We're on a mission."

"Yeah," Arielle said. "Nice jab earlier, Selena. I'll make sure you have *zero* fun during these next few weeks. Just the way you like, apparently."

"I was only acting," Selena replied.

"Of course you were. It sounded like plenty of truth in your voice."

"I'll take that as a compliment. That's literally the goal of acting—to convey the emotions of a situation. Now, are we really going to the Park?"

"Of course, we need to submit a job application for you."

Selena crossed her arms. "And you're sure you don't want to join me this time? We made such good co-workers on the last mission."

"We hardly saw each other at work."

"Exactly."

"Enough bickering," Felix said. "Let's take the Caddy and go."

"Wow," Selena said, taking a step back. "I think I like romantic Felix. He's direct about what he wants and lays down the hammer."

Felix only shook his head, cheeks still flushed a light shade of pink.

He disappeared inside for a few seconds before returning with the car keys. He stopped at the keypad on the garage and punched in the combination to close the door.

"Are you going to unlock the car?" Selena asked, standing next to the driver-side door.

"Believe it or not, Selena," he said, "but these older cars didn't have remote controls for the locks."

Felix shuffled over and inserted the key into the driver's door to unlock it.

"No need for all the sass," Selena said, climbing into the backseat. "I already have to deal with not having my own door. I'm going to feel like a prisoner back here. Trapped!"

Felix slipped behind the wheel and fired up the engine while Arielle settled into the passenger seat. "Alright. Miracle Park, here we come."

# Chapter 11

Since it was already six o'clock by the time they arrived at Miracle Park, they had little traffic and no trouble finding a parking spot. They only had two hours to explore. The park closed at eight on weeknights, and ten on weekends.

"Looks a little different from the last time," Felix said as he parked the car in the third row from the entrance.

"I guess it's a bit livelier," Selena said as they piled out of the car and walked to the front gates. *Anything beats that haunted amusement park we visited before.*

Shrieks carried from deep inside the park, likely from riders on Time Roller. Everything was open and illuminated. A window to the right of the entrance had a sign that read *Get tickets here.*

"Did you get the correct cash for this era?" Arielle asked Felix in a hushed tone.

"Of course. That's my job. I've got a couple thousand to last us the mission. Should be plenty, but I can always make a trip to Omaha if we need more."

"Right. Thank you. Part of my brain still worries about those little details. I guess because I worked solo for so many years. Who knows if it will ever go away."

"I understand."

They followed Felix to the ticket window, where the prices showed the admission only cost five dollars, three dollars if entering after five o'clock.

Felix paid the nine dollars, and they were through the main gates within a minute. The guest relations booth was no longer deserted. Instead, a young man stood front and center, waving maps in the air, shouting, "Welcome to Miracle Park! May your day be as miraculous as you are!"

Selena rolled her eyes. *Gag!*

The scent of popcorn, pretzels, and cotton candy filled the covered area. A couple of boys were deep into a game of Space Invaders on an arcade machine next to the restrooms.

"Well," Arielle said. "Shall we head to the offices and get Selena a job?"

She didn't wait for a response and pushed through the crowded pavilion, strolling confidently down the sidewalk they had just explored earlier today, in their present time.

Several groups of teenagers scampered around the park, lips bright blue or red from snow cones. The couples held hands awkwardly, and those with more tenacity weren't too shy to find a hidden corner to exchange saliva for a few moments. There were plenty of families unwinding from a long day at the park and college kids enjoying the summer evening before their lives would soon return to classrooms and homework.

The lines for rides weren't too long, and Selena knew the temptation was swelling for Felix to get on one.

They reached the office building, pleased to find all the windows in place and sparkly clean. Arielle held open the door for Selena and Felix to pass through, entering the lobby blasting air conditioning to the point it felt unnaturally cold.

A young woman sat behind the front desk, chomping on gum and blowing big pink bubbles over and over. A notebook sat open on the desk in front of her, and she scanned it up and down with a pencil in hand.

Arielle looked at Selena and nodded toward the desk.

Selena cleared her throat and stepped forward. "Excuse me?"

The woman closed her notebook, but not before Selena saw the doodles of hearts with initials inside them. "Hello, how can I help make your day more miraculous?" She spoke with the enthusiasm of a monotone professor giving a lecture for the hundredth time.

"I was hoping to apply for a job," Selena said, eyebrows arched. "Are there any openings?"

The woman leaned back, and they saw the nametag clipped to her thin sweater—Mary. Selena felt Felix growing antsy from interacting with the same woman they had just met in their present day, and nudged him in the side.

Mary looked Selena up and down, as if judging if she had what it took to work in a place like Miracle Park. "We have job openings. What kind of work are you interested in?"

"Well, I'm not sure. Just moved here and am looking for full-time work. I have lots of work experience in different fields."

"Hospitality?"

Selena shook her head. "I'd prefer to work in the park instead of the hotel."

"Too bad. We have lots of jobs in the hotel, but we have plenty to choose from here in the park. Why don't you take a seat and I'll call our recruiter. She'll ask you a few questions and can find the right job for you."

Without waiting for a response, Mary picked up her phone and spun the rotary dialer. "Hey," she said in a lowered voice into the phone. "I got a lady here looking for a job . . . no, not for the hotel. Okay." Mary hung up. "She'll be out in a couple of minutes. Help yourself to anything in the fridge."

She pointed to a mini fridge in the corner next to the doors.

"Thank you," Selena said, stepping back to sit down in the chairs lining the walls.

Arielle and Felix sat on each side of her and leaned their heads in.

"So, you're having an interview right now?" Felix asked.

"That's what it seems like," Selena replied, eyes glancing over to the executive hallway. "A bit unorthodox, but I guess it's fine."

"It's perfect," Arielle said. "Imagine if we already have your job lined up tonight. Even if you don't start working this week, it's one less thing we have to worry about. You can help track down some other leads until you start your job."

"Well, I'm gonna go ride something," Felix said, jumping out of his seat. "Beats sitting in this ice box."

Arielle whipped her hand out to grab Felix on the forearm. "You're not going to ride Time Roller, are you?"

Felix scrunched his face in confusion. "Absolutely not. You think I'm crazy?" He chuckled, shaking his head as he strolled out of the office.

The sound of high heels clopping along the floor echoed around them, and they followed the sound to a middle-aged woman strutting down the executive hallway they had just explored hours earlier.

"Hello," the woman said. She wore a sky-blue pantsuit with gaudy jewelry on her wrists and fingers. "I understand you're looking for employment, is that right?" Her big brown eyes jumped across the three Angels, not sure who she was directing her question to.

Selena stood up. "Yes, ma'am. Just me. My name is Selena Nicole."

The woman stuck out a hand to shake. "Grazella Kerr. If you'd come with me, we can have a quick chat. Your friends are welcome to wait here or go enjoy some rides. Monday is our slowest day of the week, so you'll never see the lines as short as they are now." Grazella spoke with purpose and intensity, cut from the same cloth as Arielle.

Selena rarely felt intimidated by others, especially non-time travelers, but something about Grazella's energy suggested she was not a woman to be fucked with. Grazella seemed unafraid to plant those high heels on the necks of whoever got in her way.

"Good to know," Arielle said from behind. "Thank you."

Grazella spun around and started down the hallway, and Selena trailed behind after realizing she wasn't waiting for her. She looked back to see Arielle and Felix step out of the office building. *Lucky bastards get to go have fun while I interview with the Queen of Miracle Park.*

She followed Grazella into the office directly next to Alexander Carter's, craning her neck for a quick view into the owner's workspace and finding it empty with the lights off. *Big boss leaves work early, of course.*

Grazella's office matched her outfit more than her personality. Bright green walls. Potted plants and flowers in each corner of the room. And an immaculate mahogany desk cleared of any trace of work. Grazella circled her desk and sat down in her chair, pulling open a drawer to retrieve a three-ring binder stuffed with papers and color coordinated labels.

"So, Ms. Nicole, are you from Hilburn originally?" Grazella asked, eyes glued to the binder as she flipped through the pages with ferocity.

"No, ma'am. I'm from Denver, Colorado. My cousins and I came out to attend college at CCC."

This caught Grazella's attention, causing her to look up and frown. "You left a big city to come to a *community* college in a small Nebraska town?"

Selena never bought this part of the story herself, but still had to play it off. "Yes, ma'am. We wanted somewhere a little more laid back."

"That's one of the craziest things I've ever heard, and I mean no offense. Attending CCC is the ultimate goal for a lot of these Hilburn locals. It's literally the highlight of their lives. And with many of them being the first of their families to go to college, that's great. But you . . . you could have gone to any school in the country. It seems to me you're doing yourself a disservice."

"I take it you're not from Hilburn."

"Oh God no," Grazella replied, appalled that someone used Hilburn and her own name in the same sentence. "I'm from Philly."

"If you don't mind me asking, why did you come to Hilburn then?"

Grazella grinned, crossed her arms, and leaned back in her seat. She licked her lips before speaking. "You're not scared of me, are you?"

Selena shook her head.

Grazella nodded and narrowed her eyes. "I like you already. Most people come into my office and are shaking the whole time.  My boss says I give off intense vibes.  I told him I don't give a shit. To answer your question, though, I came to Hilburn because it's going to become a big city. A lot of these hicks don't want it to happen, but it's out of their control. You probably hear a lot of chatter about this park, and all of it's true."

In just a few seconds, Selena understood the type of woman she was interviewing with. Grazella was basically a corporate version of Arielle Lucila, perhaps a bit more unhinged, but the same no-nonsense approach. Luckily, Selena had worked with Arielle enough to know how she functioned.  Though neither Arielle nor Grazella would ever admit it, they loved to have their egos stroked.

"I can see why people think you're intimidating," Selena said.  "But I know you're just a woman in a man's world trying to make a name for herself. If you don't hold yourself to high standards, then who will?"

Grazella raised both hands in the air and slammed them down onto the desk.  "Exactly!  I didn't get to this position by taking it easy on people—especially the men. They act all macho but are more sensitive than a teenage girl who just got dumped at the school dance. Give a lady constructive feedback and she improves herself.  Give a man that same feedback and he goes whining to every other man he knows. Pathetic! Someone has to hold these men in check, and that's a role I'm comfortable filling. Is your mother a strong woman?"

"My mom is the greatest woman I know.  Single mother most of my life."

Grazella tossed her hands in the air again, thankfully not slamming them this time. "God bless the single mothers of the world.  They are the strongest people to ever exist.  I'd take them to battle over anyone else. Explains a lot about you, sitting there all self-assured. I like you. Now, tell me, why do you want to work here?"

"Well, it's like you said. I've heard a lot about this place, and it seems like an incredible opportunity to work here."

"Mary said you don't want to work in the hotel. Is that true?"

"I'd prefer to start in the park, at least for the rest of the summer. That way I can get a feel for everything this place offers."

"You think big. We need that. And if that's what you want to do, then I can make that happen. I could really use someone like you to run things in the hotel, but I respect your wish to start in the park. Only a couple months left in our busy season anyway, then we can transition you to the hotel. And get you a big pay raise."

"Thank you, Ms. Kerr."

"Call me Grazella. Only the owner prefers all that formal last name shit. Guy is so full of himself, he literally introduces himself as Mr. Carter. I'd bet seventy percent of the staff here don't know his first name. I call him Alex all the time, just to piss him off."

Grazella laughed at herself.

"I've heard a lot of mixed things about Mr. Carter," Selena said.

"Oh, he's an asshole. A cheap, misogynist piece of work."

"How did you get to your position if he doesn't like women?"

Grazella grinned, a malicious expression like she had made a deal with the devil. "Hard work always speaks for itself. For a business-minded man like Alex, results can't be ignored. I started as an accountant. Gutted the numbers. Let him know where money was being wasted and where more money could be made. He implemented my suggestions, and all of a sudden, business boomed. We constantly clash with each other. Two intense personalities. We both grew up with businessmen fathers—my dad ran a bank in Philly. Plus, I call him out all the time when he's out of line. He's never had someone like that in his life, and I think he hates it most days. But part of him loves it—I just know."

"And the job turnover is high because of him?"

"Sure is. Feels like all I do some weeks is interview for the same positions over and over. I've told him to snap out of it, but he won't listen. He actually tried firing me a few months ago."

"Tried?"

Grazella laughed. "He *did* fire me. But I didn't leave. That's not how Grazella Kerr leaves a job. I reminded him this place would be a disaster without me, then told him to fuck off. And that was the end of it. He came into my office the next morning and talked business like nothing had happened the night before. Such a coward."

"That's incredible."

Grazella shrugged and rolled her eyes. Now Selena thought Grazella was an odd mix of both Arielle and herself. She had Arielle's intense work ethic and Selena's general disdain for people's bullshit.

"I've carved out a life for myself here in this little town. I just wish there was more to do. Enough about all of that. What job do you want? I have a shift supervisor opening I think would be perfect. You'd get to walk around the park all day and make sure things are running smoothly. It's a notch below our team leads, but you'd work directly with them. Best way to explain it is the team leads make the schedules, and you would enforce them. You can yell at the employees if you wish, totally up to you. Mostly high-schoolers and college kids. They need to build some character."

"If that's the job that lets me learn the park the best, then I'll take it."

"It absolutely does. You'll be involved with everything from rides and concessions, all the way down to the custodial team. There won't be a facet of the park you won't learn about."

Selena's chest fluttered with joy. This was precisely the opportunity they needed to complete the mission.

"I only have one question before we can make this official," Grazella said, crossing her hands and leaning forward. "When can you start?"

# Chapter 12

*July 12, 1978*

The three had spent Tuesday exploring Hilburn. They had a list of potential suspects and found their houses, just in case they'd need to follow up later on. They found the important things—gas stations, grocery stores, pharmacies. Their day of fun ended at a diner a mile east of Miracle Park called Dusters.

On Wednesday, Selena was off to her first day of work. Arielle and Felix stayed home with the mission file scattered across the kitchen table as they made preparations for the coming days. A mechanical engineer from the Road Runners was scheduled to meet them at Miracle Park, after hours, for a thorough inspection of Time Roller. Their mission could come to a halt if the engineer found the ride to be faulty so soon before the tragedy. That would explain away any thoughts of tampering or malfeasance.

For now, they had a list of names for Selena to learn more about at her new job, plus others they needed to investigate directly, starting with Alexander Carter.

"We need to bug his office and residence," Arielle said.

"The office should be pretty easy," Felix replied. "I can

even do that tomorrow night while we're at the park meeting the engineer. His apartment is at the top of the hotel, though, so I'm not sure how to even go about that. We'd obviously need to access it during the day while he's working, but it's going to be incredibly risky since he can wander back to his apartment whenever he wants. It's only a five-minute walk from his office to the hotel lobby."

"What if we reserved a room there? And request to stay as high in the building as we can—I'm assuming he has the penthouse suite."

"He does, and that might work. That at least gets us into the building without suspicion. I might just need you to stand guard outside and let me know if he's entering the hotel. I got some radios that should have enough range to cover the hotel and park, but not much beyond that."

"And you won't have issues getting in and out?"

Felix chortled. "Please. This is 1978. Hotels don't have those fancy keypads on the doors. It's a basic lock and bolt. Nothing my lockpick can't handle."

"Okay. I'll call the hotel and book us a room for tomorrow. Hopefully, we can check in early so you can bug his apartment, then we might as well just stay there overnight since we'll be meeting the engineer."

"Works for me."

"Done deal." Arielle crossed an item off her checklist. "Willow West. We need to bug her house."

"I'm not sure we can. You saw the situation there."

"We still don't know entirely what that was. It could have been a small gathering, or the remnants from a party the night before. "

When they had driven by Willow's house on Tuesday, they

found a small one-level home with six different cars parked in the driveway and along the front sidewalk.

"Or a lot of people live there," Felix said, rubbing his forehead. "It was the middle of a Tuesday afternoon. That many cars there? C'mon, let's not kid ourselves."

"It's not even a big house, though. No way more than four people live there."

"We've seen crazier things. I won't rule it out. We need more surveillance to be sure, but before that, we need to know if that's even worth our time. Is she really a suspect?"

Arielle grinned. "I'd say she's our number one target. Listen to this. Carter had her arrested seven times this year for trespassing—basically twice a month since the park's been open. She spends pretty much every weekend outside of the park with her megaphone barking at people to stay out. There were three reports of her and Carter getting into vicious shouting matches right there in front of the main entrance. Carter has made threats to hang her alive, and she shot right back, promising to hang him by his balls the day the park gets shut down. Willow has a rotating group of people who protest with her. Three of them have also been arrested for trespassing in the hotel. I guess they camped outside of Carter's apartment door. One even handcuffed themselves to an exposed pipe in the elevator lobby outside the penthouse suite. This group Willow has amassed is pretty intense."

Felix shook his head. "You'd never expect that kind of thing in a small town like this. Why exactly is she so hellbent on shutting down the park? There has to be more than pollution concerns."

"All the notes suggest she's a staunch environmentalist. I guess she actually succeeded three years ago. A lumber company was suspected of burning their waste materials in the middle of the night and dumping the ashes into Lake Babcock on the north side of town. She actually got hired by the company and went undercover to expose this happening. She got pictures and video, sent copies to the local press and authorities. That lumber company is no longer operating, and she's ridden that confidence all the way to Miracle Park, where I assume she wants to do the same thing."

Felix's eyebrows shot up in amusement. "She did all that on her own? Sounds like she could work on our team pulling those kinds of stunts. I'm sure Selena wouldn't mind *not* having to work undercover at all these odd jobs."

"Pass. We already have Selena, our loose cannon. And if you ask me, this lady is a bit of a nut job."

Felix snickered. "That seems to be a trend with our missions. We've been getting all the crazies lately."

"No shit. Commander Briar is just testing us. I'm sure of it. And we'll meet that challenge. We already have our primary suspect, and once Carter is bugged, we should be set to figure this mess out."

"What are we honestly trying to gain from listening to Carter? We know he didn't sabotage his own park. Sounds like he loves that place more than life itself."

"He does. I want to learn about everyone he encounters. Assuming this was an intentional crime, it wouldn't have been done by some random person passing through town. There is a reason behind it, and it harmed Carter's business. We have Willow and the disgruntled employees at the top of the list, but what if there are others we're not aware of? Old friends. Bitter family. Business associates he's pissed off. Remember, this guy pushes people around. Uses them as pawns to get what he wants. We'll find plenty of people who would love to see the park fail just for the pleasure of watching Carter struggle."

A knock banged on their front door, Felix and Arielle immediately locking eyes. He shrugged before Arielle rose from her seat, grabbing her pistol from the kitchen counter and slipping it into the holster hiding beneath her loose-fitted blouse.

Their door had no peephole, so Arielle poked her head into the living room to look out the window, letting out a sigh. "It's your girlfriend."

"What?" Felix stood up, not sure what that was supposed to mean.

Arielle pulled open the front door to reveal their neighbor, Linda. She wore a long, flowing sundress, and had applied some makeup to her face that softened the tone of her skin.

"Good afternoon, Arielle," Linda said. "How are you today?"

"I'm good, Linda. Is everything okay?"

"Everything is wonderful. I was on my daily walk around the neighborhood and thought I'd drop by again. You three were on your way out the other day, and it felt like we got cut short."

"How kind of you. Just me and Felix are here today. Selena is at work at Miracle Park."

"Say it ain't so! She got a job at the park? That's wonderful news."

Felix shuffled up behind Arielle. His heart beat a little faster at the sight of Linda. She seemed to glow in their doorway.

"Why, hello there, Felix," Linda said with a wide smile. She brushed her hair behind her ears, eyes blinking too rapidly.

"Hi, Linda," Felix said bashfully, trying to avoid eye contact. "Beautiful."

"Excuse me?"

Felix cleared his throat, his cheeks flushing to a soft shade of pink. "It's a beautiful day."

*What the hell is wrong with me?* he wondered. It had been a couple years since Felix felt any sort of spark between him and a woman. *She's married, and I'm a time traveler from the future. Just remember that.*

Linda giggled playfully. "It sure is. Wouldn't mind some company for the rest of my walk, if you're interested."

"I'm rather busy right now," Arielle said.

"Oh," Linda said, eyes bouncing between the two people from forty-plus years in the future. "I meant Felix."

"I'm sorry," Arielle said, taking a step back to allow Felix to move forward.

"I wish I could," he said. "But we're sort of in the middle of something. Maybe another time?"

He wanted to ask for a rain check but wasn't sure if that term was common in 1978.

"Of course," Linda said, shaking her head. "I shouldn't have just come and interrupted your day. My apologies."

"No need. We're still unpacking and getting our matters squared away. Need to look for a job."

Felix took another step forward to fill more of the doorframe. They had no boxes from their supposed move, and couldn't risk being called out by their neighbor, who apparently kept tabs on their house.

Linda nodded. "I understand. You know where to find me. Y'all have a good rest of the day. We'll talk soon."

She offered one final, tight-lipped grin before turning

around and heading back home across the street. Felix watched her hips sway as she walked and could no longer lie to himself. Linda had some kind of hold on him.

He closed the door and bolted it shut, turning around to find Arielle with her arms crossed, eyebrows cocked. "You know what this is, right?"

"What? It's nothing. She's a married woman, and I'm leaving here in six weeks. Nothing *can* happen."

"Oh, but that's where you're wrong. Something *will* happen. It's only a matter of time. This is the past already setting things in motion."

"Arielle, you can't jump to conclusions. You blame the past for literally anything that happens."

"You're right." She uncrossed her arms and rubbed her forehead. "I'm sure Linda goes around to all of her neighbors, asking them to join her on a walk."

"For all we know, she does."

"Bull. She wants to jump your bones. I knew that look in her eyes the second I saw it."

"You're too extreme."

"No. I'm experienced. You know how many missions I've done. Do you really think this is the first time the past has tried pushing back by using lust? It's not. Many Angels have fallen victim to this trap, so forgive me for refusing to stand by and watch you make the same mistake."

"Mistake? Arielle, are you even paying attention? I'm standing right here. Not out there with her. You don't have to remind me we're on a mission. I know how to maintain my concentration. I thought you'd have a little more faith in me by now, but apparently not."

"Would you have gone with her had I not been here?"

Felix gulped. "I . . . I don't know. Maybe. I could use some air."

"Exactly. That walk would have turned into an invitation for a glass of lemonade at her house. Then she steps away for a moment to 'freshen up' and comes back naked. What would you do then? Just because you're a time traveler doesn't make you any less human."

"That sounds like a pretty specific scenario."

"Because I've been on the receiving end of it. I'm telling you, these things happen all the time. If you can see it coming before it gets to that point, it only works out for the better. I'm not saying we need to be mean to Linda, but this is already twice in three days she's wandered over here uninvited. What if she does that in the middle of something important?"

Felix nodded in agreement. "Okay. I see what you mean. Tunnel vision."

"Tunnel vision is correct. We need to do our best to avoid Linda. Even if there wasn't this sexual tension, she seems like a lonely person. And since she's close to our age, she probably wants to hang out with us. I feel for her. She's not in the wrong, but we're here for one thing only. Just promise to always keep that in the front of your mind."

"Okay," Felix said, saliva pooling in his mouth at the mere thought of Linda standing nude in her kitchen. "I promise."

# Chapter 13

*July 13, 1978*

Arielle and Felix pulled into the Miracle Hotel parking lot at noon sharp. It was adjoined to the much bigger lot for the amusement park next door.

Selena had arrived at the park for her second day of work four hours earlier. Her first day had been entirely dedicated to reading the park's handbook, maps, A–Z guide, and any other piece of literature they could put in front of her.

Today, while she ventured back for more, Arielle and Felix had an eventful afternoon planned in the Miracle Hotel. They each packed a duffel bag for a one-night stay, and their plan was to meet the mechanical engineer at 11:30 p.m.

They strode into the hotel lobby, mesmerized by the luxury. A towering water fountain stood in the center. It had three layers of stone, large letters etched in the bottom one that read: *Be the miracle the world needs.*

The floor and counters were made of marble. Gaudy chandeliers dangled from the ceiling, and soft jazz played through the speakers at a most comforting level.

"Feels more like a fancy Vegas hotel instead of some amusement park off the side of a highway," Felix said under his breath as they approached the front desk.

"It definitely feels out of place," Arielle replied.

The teller at the check-in desk greeted them with a warm smile. A tall, scrawny man with an unusually large Adam's apple protruding from his throat. "Good afternoon, folks. I hope your day has been miraculous. How may I help you?"

Arielle was ready to vomit thanks to all the wordplay with "miracle."

"Hello, we're here to check in," she said. "Room should be under Lucila."

The man slipped on a pair of glasses, then pulled a cigarette out of the drawer beneath his desk. He popped it into his mouth and lit the tip in a swift motion that suggested he had done that same move hundreds of times. A hotel ledger sat open in front of him, and he brushed his finger up and down the page until spotting Arielle's name. "Ah, okay. Mr. and Mrs. Lucila?"

"We're not married," she said. "We're cousins."

The man's eyelids fluttered. "Apologies, madam. How will you be paying today?"

"Cash." Arielle nodded for Felix to come over, and he pulled out his wallet to retrieve the needed cash. "Is the penthouse accessible?"

"I'm afraid not. It's currently being used as a private residence. You will be in a suite on the floor just below it, though. Room 402. And that will be forty-five dollars for the one-night stay."

Felix pulled out a fifty-dollar bill from the stash he had received from the Road Runners before the mission.

"Thank you," the man said, raising the bill to the light to make sure it was real. "As guests of the hotel, you will receive a twenty-five percent discount off the admission price to the park, plus one free soda per guest. There is an envelope in your room with your vouchers for those offers. Checkout will be at ten o'clock tomorrow morning. We'll have a breakfast buffet for three dollars per person in the dining room just around the corner from here. Any questions?"

"No, sir, you've been very helpful," Arielle said.

"The pleasure is mine. Here are two room keys. Please return them here to the front desk upon checking out. Should you need anything during your stay, just pick up the phone in your room and dial zero." He slid two brass keys across the desk. They were so shiny, Arielle thought they might have been fake.

"Thank you again."

The man nodded before taking a long drag on his cigarette, and they turned around to head to the elevator lobby across the way.

"Floor four?" Felix asked, pushing the button to call the elevator.

"Yep. Fifth floor is the penthouse."

They stood in silence until the doors parted and they stepped in.

"Did that guy really just light up a cigarette while checking us in?" Felix asked, his voice that of a giddy child.

Arielle chuckled. "It's totally normal. People smoked everywhere back in these days. So don't get surprised by that. Pretty sure they even smoke in hospitals."

"Absurd." Felix pushed the button to take them to the fourth floor and enjoyed the smooth sounds of classic elevator music.

The doors parted and revealed a long hallway running in

both directions.

"We're in 402," Arielle said, starting to the left. Patterned carpeting covered the hallway floor while the walls were covered with loud, yellow wallpaper. "I think Carter tries too hard to make this place fancier than it needs to be."

"You can say that again."

They reached their door, and Arielle unlocked it, stepping inside with wide eyes.

"This will do," she said, tossing her duffel bag on the floor next to the kitchen counter. The suite had a common room with a dining table and two couches facing a large, boxy TV stand, complete with a VCR and VHS movies stuffed into the shelves. Plenty of natural light shone through the several windows, splashing onto the deep blue carpet—not shag, thankfully. The wallpaper had designs of trees to match the plants standing in each corner of the room. A fireplace with a marble mantel crackled as tiny flames whipped around behind a steel curtain.

"This place is awesome," Felix said, mouth hanging open as he joined Arielle in the center of the room. "Are those our bedrooms?"

He nodded to the two doors facing each other, one next to the fireplace, the other behind the couches.

"I believe so," Arielle said, moving toward the one by the fireplace. She pushed the door open to a find a bedroom and adjoining bathroom of similar decor. "I'll take this room. It has a view overlooking the park."

"Sure, take the one with the better view," Felix shouted from the other bedroom. "I get the marvelous view of the parking lot."

Arielle laughed, returning to the common room where Felix

joined a minute later. She sat down on the gold couch and crossed her legs. "So, what's the plan? Are you wanting to try right now?"

"I'm hesitant to do anything right now," Felix said, taking a seat on the other couch. "It's the lunch hour. I figure if Carter is going to return to his apartment during a workday, it would definitely be at this time. Maybe I'm wrong. What do you think?"

"Makes sense. We also don't know what time he takes lunch. Could be early or late, and I don't want to waste time sitting around here only to get delayed later on."

"Think Selena knows?"

"I doubt. It's only her second day. I don't see why she would already know a detail like what time Carter takes his lunch."

"Maybe we can track her down in the park and have her see if he's in his office. She might actually be on her lunch break right now."

"You're trying too hard," Arielle said, brushing her hair behind her ear. "We're already here, Felix. We don't need to go to the park. All we have to do is head up one level and knock on his door. If he answers, we play it off like we're lost hotel guests looking for the swimming pool or something. And if he doesn't answer, I'll head straight downstairs and will keep an eye out for him."

"And we're positive he would come through the main entrance?"

"I didn't see any other way unless he was to walk around the entire building to use a side entrance. Even then, he'd still have to walk *by* the main entrance where I'd see him."

"Okay. It sounds like a good enough plan. Let me grab my stuff."

Felix jumped off the couch and scurried into his room, returning a minute later with two radios in hand.

"Did you not get anything else?" Arielle asked.

He handed Arielle her radio, clipped his to his belt, then patted his pockets. "Everything I need is in here. One lockpick and two bugging devices. It just occurred to me, would we be able to rent a room for the rest of the stay? That would make life much easier."

"How so?" Arielle lifted the hem of her shirt to clip the radio to her utility belt.

"These older bugs need to connect to a receiver. And their range is only one hundred yards."

"And what have you normally done?"

"I usually have to find a bush where I can hide the receiver and come back every day or two to change the tapes. We can probably get away with three days at most."

Arielle sighed. "I don't think reserving a room for six weeks is the best way to go. We need to keep a low profile, and that is something far from normal. Who would stay six weeks in this hotel? And coincidentally disappear as soon as this tragedy happens." She shook her head and stood up, circling to the window overlooking the hotel's parking lot.

"Well, a bush it is," Felix said, joining Arielle at the window. "My only worry is a place like this probably gets landscaped once a week. I'd hate for one of those workers to find the receiver."

Arielle nodded. "What about the parking lot?"

Felix followed her stare to the sea of cars below. "If you're talking about that lot, yes, it's in range. What are you thinking?"

Arielle turned around and clasped her hands in front of her

stomach. "We have three cars, but do we really need three cars at every single moment? Selena's sits here all day while she's at work. And you'll need to set up two receivers, right?"

"Yes. One for the bugs in here, and another for the ones I'll plant in his office."

"Okay. Instead of having to find two hiding places for those, what if they sat in Selena's car during her shifts? Then one of us can drive down here when she gets off work to swap the receivers into another car that will stay in the lot overnight."

"That's a lot of back and forth."

Arielle tossed her hands up. "Not really. It's only a seven-minute drive, and this way, you might as well swap the tapes daily. It's a little tedious, but add it all up and it's only thirty minutes out of our day to make the two round trips. We wouldn't even need to come with Selena in the mornings. We could show up shortly after her and move the receivers."

Felix pursed his lips and looked at the ceiling, brow furrowed in heavy thought as he played out driving routes and schedules. "Okay, it'll be worth a try. Safer than any other options, I suppose. I don't like the idea of leaving a car there all the time. That might draw unwanted attention."

"Great. We'll hang around Selena's car toward the end of her shift to let her know the plan. Maybe she'll want to just stay here overnight. It's not like these couches are uncomfortable for her to sleep on."

"I'll let you have that conversation," Felix said. "Not sure how the little princess will respond to sleeping on a couch. I can just hear her already, complaining about not getting her beauty rest."

They shared a quick laugh before Arielle led them out of the suite. Being at the end of the long hallway, they were next to the stairwell. "Let's go this way," she said, pushing the door open. The lighting was soft, and the clanging of the heavy door shutting echoed madly around them. The stairs twisted in a square-like pattern, and Felix followed Arielle up two short flights until they reached the next door with the letter P painted onto the steel surface.

"This is it," Arielle whispered. "Stay quiet."

She pulled on the door to find it locked.

"Relax," Felix said. "This door shouldn't lead directly into the penthouse——no bolt lock. Step aside." Felix reached into his pocket. In a swift motion, he inserted his lockpick and turned it until hearing the ultimate *click!* "We're in."

Felix pulled down on the door's handle and swung it open to a small space that resembled the hotel's hallways.

"What the hell is this?" Arielle asked as they stepped in, the space big enough to fit one more person. Another door waited in front of them.

"It's like a mantrap, but not really meant for that purpose. It's an extra layer of security between the general public and the penthouse," Felix said. "It was *possible* this door might have led directly into it."

"And you didn't want to knock in case?"

Felix shrugged. "I didn't think that was the case. Had it been, this door would have more than one lock on it. In fact, we might have been gated off from even accessing this part of the hotel."

"So, this other door goes into his penthouse?" Arielle asked.

"Exactly. Two locks, see? The main entryway is from the elevator shaft, but the penthouse still needs a fire escape route to a stairwell. I'd bet this door leads to the back of one of the bedrooms."

"And you think it's safe to break in from here?"

"Doesn't make a difference to me. I think this is actually better, knowing there are two ways in and out. This one is discreet. Not even a camera in this room, like the main entryway probably has."

Felix gestured towards the corners of the ceiling where no cameras were mounted. He balled his fist and knocked hard on the door, the sound bouncing around the four walls that seemed to close in on them.

"Why so loud?" Arielle asked in a soft whisper.

"If he's on the other side of the penthouse, it will be difficult for him to hear."

Arielle nodded, and Felix grew more confident now they had found this secret room. Thirty seconds passed with no one coming to answer the door, so he knocked again even harder.

They waited a minute before Felix jammed the lockpick into the doorknob. "Turn on your radio to channel sixteen and head downstairs. I'm going in."

# Chapter 14

While Arielle flew down the stairs to get outside the hotel as fast as possible, Felix stepped into Alexander Carter's penthouse suite.

*Guest bedroom?* Felix wondered. He had been correct about where the door led. It was a bedroom, but not one that appeared to have been used. A bed was pushed into the corner of the room, boxes and bags piled atop it. The closet doors were missing, showing a rack full of suits belonging to a rather large man. A lone dresser stood against the opposite wall as the only furniture in the room. The drapes were drawn shut, making the room dark and cool enough for a peaceful nap in the middle of this scorching afternoon.

Felix held his breath for twenty seconds to allow complete silence.

*No one's in here,* he thought, tiptoeing forward. The door leading out of the bedroom was wide open, the sunlight from the rest of the suite splashing into what looked to be a hallway.

He approached the doorway and stuck his head out, looking left to a dead end, a painted portrait of a heavy-set man hanging on the wall. Felix thought it must have been Carter's father. He looked right to find the rest of the hallway, two doors on opposite walls facing each other.

*Find his bedroom and office and get out.*

Felix stepped into the hallway and suddenly wished he had brought a weapon. Just in case. Arielle was standing guard, but what if Carter was walking over at the exact moment Arielle was running down the stairs? It would have taken precise, coincidental timing, but crazier things had happened when dealing with the past.

Apparently, Carter didn't subject himself to the trends of 1978, as his suite had hardwood floors. A long rug stretched from the bedroom door all the way to the opposite end.

He stepped out of the room and used the rug to his advantage. His years of stealth training taught him to always take advantage of soft flooring when it was available, so he took slow, cautious steps down the hallway, ready to adjust his weight in case he stepped on an old, creaky floorboard.

Felix reached the next door, which was also open, and found it was a bathroom. He crossed the hall to the other side and saw a laundry room.

*Of course everything is on the other side,* Felix thought. *Got in here easy enough, so I can't complain too much.*

The hallway ended and turned around a sharp corner. Felix poked his head around the wall and saw open space—living room, kitchen, dining area. Beyond all that was another corner that presumably turned into another hallway.

Felix's heart hammered against his ribs. He needed to leave the comfort this hallway provided and would be out in the open for a few seconds if he wanted to cross to the other side.

*What if Carter was already in here and is napping in his room? Or even on the couch in the living room. If he sees me, all he has to do is make a quick phone call and there will be hordes of security looking for me.*

The suite remained silent, and Felix figured a man weighing over 300 pounds probably snored during sleep.  Still not a single sound in the penthouse, except for Felix's racing thoughts.

*Just plant the bugs and get out.*

Felix nodded to himself and stepped out from the corner, walking deadly silent and craning his neck to see the abandoned living room. Carter had a massive black couch, a coffee table covered in business and amusement park magazines. An empty coffee mug remained on the table next to the stack of magazines.

*He likes to read magazines while sipping on his morning coffee,* Felix noted, filing the information away in case they needed it later.

Across from the living room was the kitchen. Dirty dishes, mainly cereal bowls, made a small mountain in both sides of the sink. Takeout boxes were scattered across the countertop. Empty bottles of soda, beer, and wine all fought for space in the overflowing trash can.

*Poor guy doesn't know how to cook for himself,* Felix thought. *Or clean, apparently. Is housekeeping not allowed up here?*

He shook his head, appalled anyone could go through life without the beautiful skill of cooking. The thought made him want to make a five-course meal whenever they returned to their house.

Next to the kitchen was a short hallway leading to a set of double-doors, white with sparkling gold doorknobs.

*The main entrance.*

Having seen enough, Felix sprinted across the common area, screeching to a halt once he reached the other hallway, gasping for air. He laughed at himself, unsure why he was so nervous when he *knew* nobody was home. Something internal kept urging him that something was wrong, but he had seen no cameras within the penthouse, and had no actual reason to believe he would get caught. He patted the radio for reassurance. Besides, all that stuff about gut feelings was a sham. Felix believed in data and science. Nothing else.

This second hallway was nearly identical to the first. Different pictures hung on the walls, but the doors were all open. Carter obviously lived by himself, considering his lack of desire to keep any of the rooms private.

Three doors lined the hallway just the same, and Felix rushed to the first two, eliminating the bathroom as a point of interest and entering the room across from it.

The drapes were open, revealing a bright study. The desk sat directly under the window, a clear view overlooking Carter's masterpiece of an amusement park next door. Felix shuffled to the window and saw guests moving about the park, appearing like little ants in the distance. A ride had just begun on Time Roller, the train sitting atop the first hill before vanishing downward in a flash.

Chills ran up Felix's spine. Carter could have been sitting at this very desk when the accident happened. What a disgusting feeling that might have been.

He grabbed his radio and held it to his face. "Arielle, how's it going out there?"

The radio crackled to life. "Coast is clear," she replied. "No sign of AC."

"Didn't realize we're using code names."

"AC is hardly a code name. Everything okay in there?"

"I'm in his office, just wanted to make sure I'm still in the clear."

"Get back to it. I'll let you know if I see anything."

Felix put the radio back on his waistband and continued examining the room. The desk had papers and files scattered in the middle, pens and paperclips in every other direction. A soft humming came from beneath the desk, so Felix crouched to find a miniature cigar humidor filled with at least three dozen different cigars. Expensive cigars.

He drew in a deep breath and smelled the faint scent of cigar smoke likely embedded into the grains of the walls. It reminded him of his grandfather, whose house always smelled the same way. He had only visited him a handful of times in Colombia, but the memories remained etched into his nose for eternity.

Hearing the confirmation from Arielle relaxed Felix. He was tempted to look through the papers and desk drawers, but doing so could alter the past. His job had long been to get in, plant bugs, and get out. While working with his new team on the last few missions, he had discovered that he could accomplish more beyond his primary tasks. But taking something from Carter's desk, no matter how irrelevant it might seem on the surface, could alter the threads of time against them.

He desperately wanted a cigar as a treat for a job well done, and maybe if everything went smoothly, he'd swipe one on his way out. Taking a cigar from an extensive collection surely wouldn't alter the past's plan to preserve itself.

Planting a bug only took a minute, but the hardest part for Felix was finding the perfect spot. It needed to be somewhere that would pick up sound clearly. Not too far from the source, which he presumed to be Carter's desk. But it couldn't be somewhere Carter might accidentally stumble upon. Hiding one on the desk was too risky. The lamp on the corner had to be manually turned on, causing too much regular contact.

The bookshelf along the back wall didn't have as many books as he hoped. One shelf had a group of trophies, which were from all walks of Alexander Carter's life. First place in a sixth-grade spelling bee. Another for the eleventh grade. Three more trophies stood eight inches tall in the shape of a cup with handlebars on the sides. Businessman of the Year awards for 1974, 1975, and 1976.

*Hell of a run*, Felix thought, wondering who had given out those awards. Nothing was inscribed on the trophies aside from the years and Carter's name, and Felix wondered if the shrewd businessman had made them for himself. Cobwebs filled the cups, and Felix had found the perfect place to plant the office bug. Even if Carter liked to look at these trophies, it didn't appear he had touched them in at least a year.

Felix lifted the trophy nearest Carter's desk with precision, sure not to smudge the dust covering the shelf. The miniature microphone he pulled from his pocket was the size of a half-dollar coin, and he stuck it to the inside wall of the trophy. Having it in there would create a slight echo on the receiving end, but any word Carter spoke in this room would still come through clearly enough.

He replaced the trophy with the same caution as he had taken it down, lining up the edges of the base with the outline in the dust. He had already tested the connection to the receiver in his bedroom below.

Felix grabbed his radio again. "First bug planted. On to the bedroom."

"Copy that," Arielle said. "Still no sign of AC."

Felix hurried out of the room and down the hallway to the last remaining door, stepping into what was Carter's bedroom. The bed was unmade, revealing silk sheets. Three pill bottles stood on the nightstand, and Felix inspected them. Carter had pills for high blood pressure, high cholesterol, and insomnia.

"He's a heart attack waiting to happen," Felix whispered to himself.

Judging by the mess in the bedroom, Felix figured Carter spent plenty of time in here. Clothes lay in heaps across the floor. A stack of Playboy magazines stood three feet tall in the corner next to the closet, complete with a bottle of hand lotion and a box of tissues on top. An ashtray filled to the brim sat next to the pill bottles.

*For having all the money in the world, this guy sure is trying to kill himself quickly.*

Felix figured he could have hidden the bug just about anywhere, so he checked behind the nightstand, where a phone rested on the receiver. Dust bunnies gathered on the floor in the gap between the wall and nightstand. Felix reached back and stuck the second bug to the back of the nightstand, poking at it to make sure it remained securely in place.

"Second bug planted," he said into the radio. "Anything else I should do while I'm up here?"

Felix wanted nothing more than to clean the dishes and take out the trash. That mess brewing in the kitchen was tempting his sanity.

"No. That's all we need."

The radio fell silent, so Felix clipped it back onto his waistband before heading out of the bedroom. Satisfied with his work, he slipped into the office and crouched down to the cigar humidor, pulling open the door. The sweet scent of Caribbean tobacco wafted to his nose and took him back to those visits to his grandparents' house once more. Saliva pooled in his mouth as he debated which cigar to take.

Then, a loud creak came from down the hallway as the penthouse's front door swung open.

# Chapter 15

Felix closed the humidor and stood up, legs frozen as he looked around. The sound of a hoarse cough came from the living room, followed by heavy footsteps.

*He's here?! What the fuck, Arielle?!*

Felix spun around. He couldn't risk stepping out into the hallway, not knowing which way Carter might go. Felix forced his now trembling legs to move. The office had a closet, but four boxes blocked it. He tried to focus his hearing on what Carter was doing, but the concert his drumming heart was playing made it too difficult.

*Shit, just hide.*

His only viable options were under the desk or behind the door. The desk was hardly a hiding spot, so he took long, soft steps toward the office door and slid behind it, getting as close to the doorframe as he could.

"Everything good?" Arielle asked from the radio.

Felix's heart stopped, every blood cell in his veins came to a screeching halt.

"Hello?" Carter called out from the living room. "Is someone there?"

*Shit, shit, shit.*

Felix reached back and twisted the dial to turn off the radio, fighting to keep his breathing silent. He had a one-inch gap to see between the door and its frame, a clear view of Carter's desk.

The footsteps sounded as if they were making circles in the living room.

*Did he move on from it?* Felix wondered, knowing it was highly unlikely. In contrast to the silent penthouse, Arielle's voice might as well have come through a rock concert's speaker system.

The footsteps started toward the hallway, slow and careful. "Is anyone in here?" Carter shouted. "I have a gun."

Tears streamed down Felix's face. Was this how it all ended? He'd heard plenty of horror stories of Angels losing their lives on missions, but none had been cowering behind a door. Would he go down in their odd little history as a coward? He hadn't brought his gun because not only did he hate carrying it, he had Arielle on the outside standing guard. How could Carter have gotten past without her noticing?

He could have already been in the hotel. Maybe he was never at the amusement park and had meetings in one of the hotel's conference rooms. How could they have been so careless to not cover all the details, especially dealing with the most powerful man in Hilburn?

*I'm okay,* Felix told himself. *I know how to fight. One punch can knock him out, or at least get the gun out of his hand. Then I can run like hell. He has zero chance of catching me.*

"I have a gun, and I'm not afraid to use it!" Carter shouted, only ten feet away from his office door. Felix could hear the slight Texas drawl in his voice, followed by Carter cocking his gun.

*Handgun*, Felix noted, making three hundred different plans for how to escape this situation. *I can stay in here and hope he only pokes his head in. What reason does he have to actually check behind the doors? It's the middle of the day, I can wait it out. He needs to go back to work at some point.*

Felix looked through the gap and saw Carter's pistol being held up by his pudgy hand, aiming into the office. Adrenaline burst through Felix, his vision and fingertips pulsing in sync.

The gun whipped around as Carter continued down the hallway. Felix could only see a slim portion of the hallway through the gap, but it was enough to see Carter going toward his bedroom.

"Come out with your hands up and no one has to get hurt," Carter grumbled, frustration growing thick in his tone.

*Did this door creak when I moved it?* Felix thought, not having a clue. His mind had been too much in a panic to notice such a detail. *If he's in his bedroom, I can make it across to the spare room and emergency exit faster than him.*

"Don't fuck with me, whoever you are!" Carter shouted, and that was all Felix needed to hear. Carter was certainly inside his bedroom and out of sight of the hallway.

Felix pushed the door enough to slip out and shuffled around it, first poking his head into the hallway to confirm it was clear. Felix broke into a sprint away from the office. His pounding footsteps surely gave him away, but he was much too fast for it to matter.

"Hey!" Carter barked, his own heavy thuds rumbling down the hallway. Felix reached the other hallway, and just as he turned the corner, Carter's gun fired. The bullet whizzed inches behind Felix and splintered the wall. Felix had no time to even look over his shoulder, keeping his eyes focused on the spare bedroom.

"I'll kill you, you son of a bitch!" Carter shouted, firing another round that just missed the painting of his father at the end of the hallway. By the time that bullet planted into the wall, Felix was already in the back of the spare bedroom, pushing open the emergency exit door.

He slammed it shut behind him and burst through the door to the stairwell, flying down the steps at a dangerous speed. The door to the fourth floor waited, and he flung it open.

"God dammit!" Carter shouted from above, his voice echoing through the stairwell.

Felix didn't think the hotel's owner had any interest in continuing this pursuit on foot, but couldn't wait around to see. He fumbled with the room key as he yanked it out of his pocket, struggling to get it into the keyhole when a firm hand grasped him on the wrist.

"Fuck!" Felix screamed, jumping back and taking a wild swing that missed Arielle's face by eight inches.

Arielle plucked the key out of Felix's grip and wiggled it into the keyhole with a calming precision, pushing the door open and pulling Felix inside with her. She closed the door and twisted the bolt into place.

"What the hell is going on?" she demanded.

Felix struggled to catch his breath, hands planted on his quivering knees as he huffed and puffed, shaking his head. "I . . . could ask . . . the same . . . question."

"You never responded to me on the radio, so I got worried. Thought I'd come check here first. Maybe you came back to the room and turned off your radio without telling me."

Felix regained enough of his composure to speak more clearly. "Carter walked in while I was still in his office."

"WHAT?!" Arielle's hands shot to the sides of her head. "That's impossible. I was outside the hotel the entire time. Didn't look away once from any person who walked over from the park."

"Well, he got into the hotel and all the way to his suite. He either had another way in or was never at the park to begin with."

Arielle paced circles around their common room, head down and arms crossed. "That doesn't make any sense. I mean, yes, it's *possible*, but how unlikely is all that? He could have been away and returned. From where I was sitting, I had no view of the parking lot. He could have parked and slipped in through another entrance. I'm sorry, Felix. I made assumptions, and it almost cost us. Did he see you?"

"Just the back of me. He was walking around with a gun, and I made it out while he was in his bedroom. He shot at me a couple times, but I was running way too fast."

"He shot at you? Shit." Arielle pursed her lips. "That definitely didn't happen in the original timeline. I wonder how this will change things going forward."

"You think it will throw off the rest of the mission?" Felix felt like he might vomit. It wasn't his fault how things played out—although, he could have foregone trying to sneak a cigar and already have been out of the penthouse when Carter arrived. The thought would eat at him for the rest of the mission. They'd all have to be wary of the past throwing up obstacles thanks to this blunder. And what did he have to show for it? A couple of dodged bullets. And no damned cigar.

"It could go either way," Arielle said. "And it all depends how Carter reacts. Let's say he thinks Willow West broke into his apartment. That will absolutely change everything going forward. He might have more harsh reactions toward her on those days of protest. Maybe he completely snaps and kills her. Then what?"

"I'm so sorry, Arielle. I didn't want—"

"Nope. This isn't your fault. You were doing your job. Carter slipped through the cracks, quite literally, it seems."

"But what if I had approached it differently? Then maybe we wouldn't be in this situation."

"Oh, Felix. Don't dwell on things like that. You were trapped and escaped at the first opportunity you saw fit. I wouldn't have played it any differently."

"I could have waited."

Arielle jerked her head from side to side. "Waited? For how long? What if he took a half day and stayed home the rest of the night? You think hiding for twelve hours is a good idea? The longer you're in a place, the more likely you are to get caught. Escaping is the only option, and it must happen as soon as possible. Don't you remember getting stuck under Jake Kennedy's bed? You got lucky that time, but that could have turned into an ugly situation had you waited it out."

"Don't remind me."

"All I'm saying is not to beat yourself up over this. The future of the mission is a little unstable, but I think everything will be fine. If he saw the back of you, then he should at least have been able to tell that you're a man. That eliminates any suspicion he might have toward Willow. Best-case scenario, he'll think it was some random burglar who got away. And with nothing missing, he won't need very much time to get over it."

"Yeah, except he might buy more guns and have extra security."

Arielle shrugged. "Then let him. We have no reason to go anywhere near his precious penthouse for the rest of the mission. You did what we needed. It's done."

Felix had grown an appreciation for Arielle's ability to take a step back and consider the big picture. It settled his nerves. His two bugs were in Carter's apartment, but would there be an investigation of any sort? Maybe some police officers would have a quick look around, but nothing extensive since there was no actual robbery. Certainly nothing that warranted them looking inside the trophies in the office or behind the bedroom nightstand.

"Okay," Felix said. "You're right."

"Try to move on," Arielle replied, finally stopping her pacing and sitting on the couch. "You need a short memory in this business. Relax for the rest of the afternoon, because tonight we're right back at it."

# Chapter 16

The three Angels gathered outside the Miracle Hotel at eleven o'clock that night. They had enjoyed dinner together earlier in the hotel's bar and grill and watched as the waves of visitors lined up at the check-in desk for their weekend of fun.

Selena had caught them up on another thrilling day sitting in a conference room learning the ins and outs of Miracle Park. They promised she'd train in the actual park on Friday. Felix filled her in on the drama earlier in the afternoon, and Selena vowed to ask around for information about Carter and how he went from building to building, because she had definitely seen him walking down the office hallway earlier that morning.

A group of smokers huddled around the trashcan outside the hotel's main entrance, laughing and blowing plumes into the night sky. Arielle turned her back to them and spread her arms around Selena and Felix to form a tight huddle.

"Okay, it's time to head over," Arielle said. "Selena, what can you tell us about park security?"

"There are only two guards who stay overnight. They each make a round every hour, staggered thirty minutes apart." Selena paused while a group of drunk college kids stumbled past them into the hotel. "They only walk on the main pathways unless they find something to investigate. From what I've seen, Time Roller is pretty far from the main path. So if we're meeting the engineer on the platform, we should be out of sight from the guards. Won't be hard to hide under the platform, either. At least while the guards pass. With the route they use, we should see the guards passing by Time Roller at 11:25 and 11:55."

"Okay, good," Arielle said. "We're planning to meet the engineer at Time Roller at 11:30. When is the best time for us to sneak in?"

Selena checked her watch. "Right now. It's 11:04. They have started their round and will walk in the opposite direction from the west entrance. That gate is even safer to climb over since there is less lighting compared to the main entrance."

"How is this engineer meeting us?" Felix asked.

"Time travel," Arielle said. "He's going to Time Roller in his present day and will be jumping back to us at exactly 11:30. Let's head over."

Arielle stepped back to break up their huddle, looking over both shoulders to make sure no one was paying them any attention. She gave a quick nod and led them down the walkway toward the park. Three hundred feet separated the hotel's entrance and the park's west entrance.

They passed a bench where two older teenage girls sat, one crying into the other's shoulder about "that motherfucker Jason." They didn't appear to notice the three time travelers strolling by.

When they arrived at the gate, Felix examined the padlock chained around it. "I can just pick this, you know," he said, reaching into his pocket.

"Not necessary," Arielle said, waving him off. "We can't risk leaving any evidence behind. If they think the park was broken into, they'll just increase security, and we don't know yet how many times we plan on coming back here in the middle of the night." She rolled up her sleeve to check her watch. "It's 11:08 now. Are we still good to hop over?"

"Yes," Selena said with a slow nod. "Once we're over, follow the path straight, then take the first right once it forks into three different directions. That will take us directly to Time Roller."

"You sure know the park well for not having walked around it," Felix said with a soft chuckle.

"I've been staring at the map for three days. I know the place like it's my house now. Plus, I've done some laps around the park on my breaks. That's actually how I met one of the guards who spilled the details of what they do."

"And you timed how long it takes to walk that complete lap?" Arielle asked.

"Sure did."

"Perfect. Now you're thinking like an Angel. Dare I say you're ready for more field work?"

"Dare I say absolutely not? You know, not everyone wants to be like Arielle Lucila, right?"

"It's true," Felix said. "There have been people reaching out to ask how I got into this role on your team. They love the appeal of getting to work on meaningful missions without enduring the same risks as a lead spy or assassin."

"I understand," Arielle said. "Just poking some fun."

"I'm sure," Selena snapped back. "Enough yammering. Let's go."

They returned to the gate and watched Arielle grab the top

crossbar, pulling herself up and over the gate, hopping off effortlessly on the other side.

"Easy peasy," she said. "Who's next?"

Selena stepped forward and followed the same movements as Arielle. "C'mon, Felix."

He sighed before scaling the gate, the task much easier thanks to his height.

"Alright," Arielle said. "Everyone stay quiet and take soft steps. We can't draw any attention to ourselves. If we see a guard, hide behind something as quickly as you can. Selena, why don't you lead the way."

Selena nodded and pushed past Arielle to start down the park's main pathway. The park was just as abandoned as it had been when they visited it in 2023, only this time everything was still in one piece and could be operated with the flick of a switch.

The three practically tiptoed down the path, following Selena as she turned right and eventually led them to the entrance of Time Roller. The towering clock had its lights off, but they could still make out the arms spinning in opposite directions.

"See," Selena whispered. "The guards won't go into the ride from here. The platform is at least seventy-five feet away. We should be in the clear."

She led them down the ride's exit lane that disappeared behind a couple of trees and bushes. Arielle thought the park somehow felt more haunted in the middle of this night compared to their last visit when it had actually been a deserted property. Maybe it was the black energy radiating from the roller coaster that would soon alter so many lives.

They reached the platform at 11:21, and all ducked behind

the trains to remain out of sight from the main walkway.

Exactly four minutes later, they saw the security guard's flashlight beaming in every direction as he strolled along.

"Clockwork," Selena whispered.

Arielle figured Carter ran a strict business. Considering the high turnover, employees were likely fired for not doing any portion of their job correctly. If that guard didn't start his hourly round at exactly eleven o'clock, he might as well not show up for work the following day.

It only took another minute before he was out of sight, leaving the Angels alone. They stood up, no longer worried.

"Do we know who this engineer is?" Felix asked.

"All I know is he's from Portland, Oregon. He's coming from the year 2033, and his name is Yokota Hachigoro."

"That's a bad-ass name," Selena said.

"I don't think I've ever seen someone physically time travel," Felix said. "Is he just going to appear in front of us out of thin air?"

"Yes," Arielle said. "That's all it is."

On cue, a slight tremor came from the ground, followed by a quick flash behind them, like a photographer had just snapped a picture.

The silhouette of a man appeared by the ride's exit gate.

"Good evening, folks," he said, shuffling forward. The man was of average height and significantly thin, with jet-black hair slicked to the side.

"Hello," Arielle greeted, meeting him with a handshake. "Are you Yokota?"

"Were you expecting someone else to poof into your existence tonight?" Yokota asked, grabbing his stomach as he cackled with delight.

Arielle couldn't help but laugh. "Well, no."

"I'm just kidding with you, of course," Yokota said. "That joke gets a laugh about half the time, so why not?"

"Very good," Arielle said, her lips spread into a grin. Yokota arrived with much more laid-back energy than she had expected. When she thought of a time-traveling mechanical engineer, she imagined someone a bit more academic. Yokota wore simple jeans and a T-shirt to complement his stand-up comedian vibe. "Welcome to 1978 and Miracle Park. Do you get a lot of missions like this one?"

Yokota smiled as he recounted his past. "Actually, this is my first time examining a roller coaster—at least on official Road Runner business. Mostly, I travel throughout time to investigate mechanical explosions. Also, lots of elevators and escalator accidents. I studied designing roller coasters in college, but apparently the Road Runners don't want to open their own theme park." He giggled, his eyelids fluttering as he looked to the top of Time Roller. "I think a time-traveling theme park could be a lot of fun. The possibilities are endless."

Arielle thought back to what Commander Briar had said about the future of the Road Runners, where many wanted to invest in time-travel themed businesses. Perhaps an amusement park wasn't as much of a stretch as Yokota thought.

"Well, we're happy to have you. These are my teammates, Selena and Felix."

They all shook hands, Yokota offering a brief bow toward each of them.

"You'll be even happier if I find this ride is an accident waiting to happen," he said. "Then you can all go home. Mission complete!"

"That would be nice," Selena said, putting her hands on her hips as she drew in a deep breath of the night air.

"Well, let's take a little look," Yokota said.

"Did you not need any tools?" Felix asked.

Yokota had arrived with nothing besides the clothes on his back. "Oh shoot! I left my toolbox in the future! Hate when that happens." He shook his head, genuinely disappointed in himself. Then he burst into more cheery laughter.

The three Angels exchanged a glance, wondering if this guy was for real.

"I'm messing with you," Yokota said, getting himself under control. "I don't need tools. Just a flashlight for an examination." He reached into his back pocket and pulled out a flashlight, holding it in front of his face for all to see, like a proud magician pulling flowers out of his sleeve.

Selena giggled and took a few steps in the opposite direction.

"You're too funny, Yokota," Arielle said, unable to keep a grin off her face.

"I try," he replied, clicking on the flashlight. "My job is very boring. I have to make it interesting. The look on your faces is all I need. If I can make an assassin laugh, then I must be on to something. Enough with the jokes, though. Let me get to work."

As suddenly as he had arrived, Yokota spun around and hustled to the short flight of steps that went beneath the platform, throwing open the gate with a sign that read *DANGER: ONLY STAFF CAN PASS THIS BARRIER.*

The three Angels remained on top of the platform, looking at each other.

"Do we need to go down there with him?" Felix asked in a hushed tone.

Arielle shrugged. "I don't think so. Not really anything we can do unless he asks for help."

They heard him whistling a tune below, the glow from the flashlight bouncing around every few seconds. He stayed down there for ten minutes, talking to himself with random lines of, "There you are. How did you get there? Beautiful!"

They snickered each time he said something and had no way of telling how things were going based on his choice of words. He banged on things, but nothing that made enough noise to grab the attention of the guards. At one point, he climbed up the roller coaster's hill, continuing his conversation with himself.

By the time Yokota returned to the platform, his hair was matted to his forehead with sweat. He wiped it away with his sleeve. "Do you want the bad news first?" he asked.

Considering his personality, Arielle wondered if there was actually bad news or if he was setting up another joke.

"Bad news should always be first," Selena said.

"I like you," Yokota said. "You seem very honest. Anyway, the bad news is that your mission is not over."

"So the ride is fine?" Arielle asked.

"The ride is fine. Which is the good news."

"And why is that good news?"

"Well, good news, because you can still stop the accident from happening."

Arielle wasn't smiling anymore. *I think this guy has a bad understanding of good versus bad news.*

"So, there isn't a single thing wrong with this ride?" Felix asked.

"None at all," Yokota said with a proud smile. "From what I read about the incident, the only thing that could have made the roller coaster fall backwards is a bad pull cable. That is what the authorities found broken during their investigation. The cable on this ride is perfect. The only way for it to break in the next month would be if someone destroyed it."

"How do you even go about that?" Felix asked. "Those cords are made of steel and are, what, two inches thick?"

"Someone did his research," Yokota said, stepping forward to slap Felix on the shoulder. "You are right. However, bolt cutters could do the trick. It would take some time, I'd say about four hours, for someone to fray the cable enough where it could snap under pressure."

"I don't understand," Arielle said. "The accident happened at night. Almost before the park closed. Surely there wasn't someone under the platform all day cutting away at the cord."

"I agree. That's not likely. It would require precision and an advanced understanding of roller coaster mechanics. Whoever did it probably came the night before and cut through enough of the cord to make it weak. That doesn't mean it would snap right away, but each time the cord pulled up another train, more pressure was applied to it. If the cable was already frayed, each ride would cause a little more damage until it eventually couldn't handle any more and snapped."

Yokota held out two fists and made the motion of snapping a stick in half. His nonchalance sent chills up Arielle's back. But he was simply doing his job and leaning on his experience to make a sound explanation.

"So we need to find someone who has some serious knowledge about roller coasters?" Selena asked, her eyes boring into Yokota's.

"Definitely. If someone cut too much, the ride might have not even made it up for the first trip of the day. No accident.

Cut too little, and there is no saying how long it might take to eventually snap. Could be months, or even push into the next year. If we are to believe this was done on purpose, the perpetrator would want to see results immediately. The cable is in perfect condition as of tonight, so no one has started on it yet."

They stood in silence for a few seconds. An airplane soared overhead while traffic hummed along the nearby highway.

"Well, thank you," Arielle said. "I guess this gives us a place to start once we dig into the suspects. No idea who might have mechanical engineering knowledge."

"You're very welcome," Yokota said, clasping his hands and bowing to Arielle. "Always happy to help in any way I can."

"Is there anything else we should know before you leave?"

"I don't believe so. This seems like a pretty straightforward case of sabotage. I wish you three the best of luck in stopping it."

# Chapter 17



*July 20, 1978*

Nothing of substance had developed over the following week. Felix and Arielle had started their daily routines of coming to the hotel parking lot to swap out the bugging devices' receivers.  Felix listened at home during the days and had yet to hear anything of relevance from Carter's private phone calls and office meetings. He confirmed, however, that Carter came as advertised. The cut-throat park owner had fired one employee earlier in the week for being ten minutes late from their lunch break, showering them with insults before having them escorted out of the park.

Selena knew the young man who had been fired, Shawn Blackburn. She had worked with him once during her training hour operating the carousel.

Arielle had used her days tailing Willow West and trying to learn more about her house. To her dismay, it seemed to be true several people lived there. Someone was always home, making it impossible for them to sneak in and bug the place.

Today, however, none of that mattered. Selena sat outside on her lunch break, enjoying a cloudy day that kept the temperature under ninety degrees for the first time all week.

Monday had started her week full of hands-on training. She learned the rotations both for ride operators and concession workers as they moved throughout the park in set shifts. Unlike other amusement parks, Carter believed workers stayed more engaged with constant changes of scenery. One hour at each ride, then time to rotate. Same for the concession stands. The whole thing seemed chaotic as Selena tried to follow, but she understood the value.

Each day of training started with the team lead for ride operations, Joy Gillespie.

Park employees were forced to park their vehicles at the hotel lot and make the walk over, to ensure guests of Miracle Park always had spots available.

"Company policy," Joy had said with an eye roll. She had met Selena in the lot for her first day, leaning against the back of her Chevy Vega and smoking a cigarette to pass the time.

After that first day, they met at the time clock in the morning, where Joy took a roll call from the time cards of everyone who had already punched in for the day. If someone was missing, she had to make adjustments to the rotation, print out two dozen copies of the new schedule, then deliver one to each ride in the park.

"Fortunately, I don't have to do this too often," she had said on Wednesday morning once she found two people had called out for the day. "If you call out, you might as well pack up your locker. Remember that."

As she spent more time with Joy during the week, Selena found she was Carter's enforcer within the park grounds. She knew every rule and violation, like she had written them herself. Yet part of her seemed to resent the more obscure rules, like employees needing to clock out during bathroom breaks. "If you're on the other side of the park and have to pee," she had said with a roll of her dark brown eyes, "you have to walk all the way to the office to punch out and use the bathroom there. Then punch back in and walk all the way back. It's an epic waste of time."

Selena thought of this while she took a bite out of her Miraculous Nachos. She had never worked in a job like this before and was even more grateful for that fact. For the sake of the mission, however, she needed to take the rules seriously and always clocked in from her lunch break three minutes before she was due.

Her break had twenty-five minutes remaining as she sat at one of the three tables stationed behind the park's office building. Employees hid out here for smoke and lunch breaks and were often shouted at by Carter if he passed by on his way back to the hotel.

"Smoke breaks," she had heard him mumble on Tuesday when such an episode happened. "Do I pay you scum bags to smoke all day?!" he had shouted at a trio of employees who had actually clocked out ten minutes earlier. He promptly stuffed his lit cigar back into his mouth and kept trudging to the hotel.

Carter's anger went unchecked, and part of Selena wondered if the man could murder someone. His disgruntled voice and constantly irritated facial expressions made him seem on the verge of choking someone to death if they played their cards wrong. Selena noticed how no one ever said a single word in response to Carter's shouting outbursts, and she would treat the situation the same way on her lucky day.

*He's just a giant ball of anger,* Selena thought. *A greedy glutton who only cares about himself and his bank account.*

While the first ten minutes of her lunch break had been peaceful, the rest of it would not be. Two concession workers had taken a seat at the table next to Selena, giggling as they whispered under their breath to each other while pulling their lunches out of brown paper bags. The two looked like sisters, prompting Selena to wonder what Arielle was doing today.

Muffled shouting boomed from the office building's back door, and the two sisters perked up immediately, rotating their bodies to face the door. They must have worked at the park long enough to know that initial shout meant plenty more was coming, and they wanted to enjoy the show.

Selena stuffed more nachos into her mouth, wanting to look as innocent as possible if Carter came barreling out of the building.

"It's best to blend into the background when you see him," Joy had told her. "Regardless of his mood."

*Let these sisters take the risk for being nosy*, Selena thought. *I'm just enjoying my lunch. Nothing to see here.*

The shouting continued, and this time another voice shouted back. A woman's voice. The back-and-forth continued for another twenty seconds before the noise grew louder and clearer.

Joy burst out of the back door, fists balled, and jaw clenched. Selena stood up, about to ask if everything was okay, then promptly sat back down.

Alexander Carter flung the door open, sending it crashing into the wall with a violent rattle that might have shattered the glass had he pushed it any harder.

"Where the hell are you going?!" Carter growled, his face and neck bright red. He wore a black bowler hat on the back of his crown, revealing a handful of scraggly gray hairs near his forehead.

Joy stopped like she had run into a wall, then vehemently pivoted around, cocking a finger at Carter. "I'm going back to work," she said through gritted teeth. "Someone has to keep this park running."

"You better watch that tone, young lady," Carter snapped back. "Or else."

"Or else what?!" Joy shouted, throwing her hands in the air. "Are you going to fire me like everyone else? Good luck having anything get done correctly without me here."

"Correctly?" Carter howled, spit flying from his mouth. "A guest sat down in a puddle of vomit on our most popular ride. You call that a good job?"

The sisters stood up from the table and shuffled back behind Selena, who kept her gaze on her nachos, watching the argument from the side of her eye. Both Carter and Joy had their fists clenched, looking like two street fighters ready to brawl.

"I know you need to blame someone," Joy said, calming her tone, but unable to hide the disgust. "But I was on the other side of the park. I can't be everywhere at once. Maybe if you stopped firing people every day, we could have staff that actually knows what to do when something like this happens."

Carter unclenched a fist and jammed his stubby finger two inches away from Joy's face. "You don't tell me how to run my fucking park. EVER!" His body jolted as he shouted. He lowered his voice. "One more word out of you and you're done. Now, go fix the situation on Time Roller and get the fuck out of my face."

The two held a spiteful stare down for thirty seconds. Selena could see the dials spinning frantically in Joy's mind, passing up the hundreds of different things she wanted to say back to Carter.

Eventually, Carter snorted, tugged on the lapels of his suit jacket, and stomped back into the office building.

Tears welled in Joy's eyes as she turned around and started on the path toward Time Roller. She passed Selena sitting at the table, staring at the ground to avoid eye contact, and muttered under her breath, "I'll get that fat motherfucker back."

# Chapter 18

*July 21, 1978*

Arielle planned to check on Willow on Friday morning but received a phone call while getting dressed. Selena had been asked to cover a morning shift and begrudgingly went into work at eight o'clock.

The phone rang at 8:15, and Arielle snapped it off the hook, knowing only the three of them knew the phone number.

"You need to get down here right now," Selena said, panting for breath. "Protesters everywhere."

"Why are you breathing so hard?" Arielle asked, hurrying to finish brushing her hair.

"Dammit, Arielle, because I had to run from the hotel parking lot. I could hear the protesters from the lot and sprinted over to the office to call you."

"Is Willow there?"

"I don't know. I'd assume so. Just get down here. There's like thirty people with signs right outside the park entrance."

"Okay, on my way."

Arielle hung up and ran downstairs, footsteps thudding on purpose to get Felix's attention in the basement.

"Felix!" she shouted. "Let's go!"

Being the first to go to sleep, Felix was usually the first one awake in the mornings. He had yet to cook one of the grand breakfasts as he had done on other missions, and Arielle knew the matter of his parents moving to New York City was weighing heavily on his mind. Having them so far away from his native San Francisco had stirred up angst ever since they had announced it. His work so far had been up to par, but outside of that, Felix hadn't been much himself.

"Two minutes!" he shouted from the basement, and she could hear him scampering around below, uttering inaudible words under his breath.

Exactly two minutes later, he barreled up the stairs, dark bags under his eyes.

"Is everything okay, Felix?" Arielle asked.

"Yeah," he said, pulling his backpack snug over one shoulder. "I'm fine."

"Change of plans this morning." Arielle shuffled toward the inside garage door, where they kept the car keys on a hook next to the chain lock.

Felix trailed behind, grabbing a banana when they passed through the kitchen. "Oh. Are we not going to the park?"

"We are." Arielle pulled the door open and slapped the button to open the garage. "But we're staying there. Selena just called and said there are a bunch of protesters outside the park entrance. We need to get into that mix and see what's going on. Make some connections. Maybe we can get close enough to Willow to get invited to her house."

She continued into the garage and hopped into her car, firing up the engine while Felix ran to keep up.

"Was that your plan all along?" he asked once they pulled out of the garage.

"Actually, no. But it just occurred to me last night. It's worth a shot, and one we need to take. Because so far, we're not making any ground on potential suspects."

Felix nodded as he unpeeled his banana and started eating.

"You sure you're fine?" Arielle said as they made their way through town, passing the Earl May Garden Center where Willow worked.

"I'm fine," Felix said with some annoyance. "Let's get to work."

His tone suggested he was *not* fine and had no interest in discussing it. Arielle would pick up the matter later. Instead, she turned on the radio and they listened to "How Deep Is Your Love" by The Bee Gees, a pleasant change of pace from the disco that seemed to play every time they were in the car.

Once the song ended, they were pulling into Miracle Park's main lot. "We'll go change the receivers later," Arielle said after parking and turning off the engine. "We need to check out this protest first."

Felix nodded silently and stepped out of the car. Arielle followed, and they instantly heard the shouting from the group at the entrance.

"They really show up for this," Felix commented as they started on the walkway. The protesters were still fifty yards ahead of them.

"Willow must have a way with people," Arielle said. "Clearly she can attract followers who believe in her."

Selena had said thirty people were marching around outside the gates when she called, but it looked closer to fifty now. People waved signs in the air. Many read: *DIRTY WATER IS NOT A MIRACLE.* Others said: *POLLUTED DRINKING WATER IS VIOLENCE.*

The people walked in a coordinated circle, waving their signs and chanting, "Miracle must go! Miracle must go!"

In the middle of the circle, standing on top of a flipped-over milk crate, was Willow West. Her sign leaned against the crate below her feet, and Arielle caught brief glances of it through the constant flow of legs strolling around. Her sign was specific and didn't hold back: PROTECT HILBURN FROM ALEX CARTER!

She held a megaphone, scuffed and battered, and shouted into it. "Illnesses are up by fifty-seven percent since Miracle Park opened. E. coli and salmonella infections are through the roof! Not only is this park polluting our air, they are destroying our town's water supply. And guess what?"

"WHAT?!" the group of protesters shouted in return.

"No one is doing a thing about it," Willow continued.

Several park guests walked right past the protest and entered the park, but many others stopped to see what was going on. Arielle and Felix joined this group, stepping within three feet of the marching protesters who remained in constant motion.

Willow smiled, revealing a mouth full of small teeth and large gums. The crowd around them kept growing, and she fed off increasing energy, raising a fist into the sky. "It's all of us against Miracle Park. I've called the city. I've talked with the water department and have shown them all the facts. Nearly every doctor in Hilburn has signed my petitions. They universally agree the rise of issues we are seeing are due to water-borne illnesses. I've shared this information with the city council. They did nothing. I sent it all the way to Lincoln for our state representatives to review. Those requests have been ignored. I call the governor's office every single day, and no one calls me back."

The group started booing, as did some spectators.

"All we can do," Willow continued, "is keep up this fight ourselves. The more we expose the truth, the more pressure we apply to our good-for-nothing authorities to do something! Thank you all for another huge turnout. You're all beautiful. I love you!"

Willow hopped off the crate, and someone from the group rushed toward her with a boombox over his shoulder. Willow pushed a button and cranked the volume dial, the sounds of Bob Marley's "Get Up, Stand Up" blasting through the air.

The crowd cheered with delight at the song, a handful of bystanders now joining the protest, entering the huddle and filling out signs of their own.

"Is the water situation really this bad?" Felix muttered under his breath. "Because I've been drinking it."

Arielle shrugged. "I have no idea. But if this many people showed up today, I suspect they might actually be on to something. I'd love to look at these numbers she's referring to and see how legit all of it is."

"Then get in line and talk to her," Felix said, nodding to the line of four people that had formed to speak with the protest's organizer.

"Might as well," Arielle said. She had a pair of sunglasses clipped on the front of her shirt, so she slid them on. "Can't be too careful. Don't want to her to recognize me later on."

"Good call. I'm going to hang around and eavesdrop on the conversations. Maybe I'll hear something helpful."

Arielle nodded before spinning around to join the line, which was already down to three people.

All three just wanted a quick word with Willow, thanking

her for her work and relentless approach to keeping attention on the cause. She thanked them in return and encouraged them to fill out signs and join the group.

Once it was Arielle's turn, she stepped forward with a wide grin on her face and offered as friendly a wave as she could.

"Hello," Arielle said, extending her hand. "You're Willow, right?"

"Yes, I am," Willow replied in a giddy tone. "And what's your name?"

"I'm Arielle, and I'm new to town. This is my first time coming to the park, but I wasn't aware of anything you just talked about. Is the park really polluting that bad?"

Willow nodded along while Arielle spoke, keeping a straight face as she listened intently. "Yes, they are, and it might be worse than we thought," Willow said, standing tall and crossing her arms. "See, it all started with the added air pollution. People don't realize the climate effects an amusement park has on an area. It wasn't all that bad when they first opened, but the numbers don't lie. The spike in illnesses started two months after the park opened and has remained at the same level ever since."

"I see. And really, no one is helping?"

Willow shook her head and kicked toward her shadow on the ground. "We're on our own. See, this dictator Alex Carter—I call him Alex instead of Alexander because he hates it—he owns more than this park. He owns the *Hilburn Herald*, and that is our only source of local news in this town. I've submitted my stories to them, but they're never going to publish them. It goes against his own cause."

"A dictator, huh? Seems extreme to say."

Willow giggled and shook her head. "I wish it was. What

else do you call some rich man coming into town, opening this park, buying the newspaper, and buying every government worker and city official he can? Whoever he donates money to wins their elections. I don't have proof of it, but I'm pretty sure he's paid off the water department. They should obviously want to hear about problems with drinking water, but they just give me lip service, always saying they're going to check things out. But they never do."

The protesters had taken a break and were talking among themselves. Every couple of minutes, one of them would pass by and pat Willow on the back or shoulder, muttering "Great work" to not disturb her conversation with Arielle.

Willow was looking around, apparently growing bored. Arielle needed to keep her engaged.

"I'm interested in joining your cause," Arielle said. "Like I said, I just moved to Hilburn, so I can be a regular at these types of events."

Willow's eyes narrowed on Arielle. "I'll have to get back to you on that."

"Fair enough. I am curious, though. What's the goal here? To get the water department to actually come look and force *Alex* to clean up his act?"

Willow threw her head back and laughed. "Oh, not at all. We need that man removed from our town. He is an absolute cancer on Hilburn. Only good thing he's done is provide jobs—minimum wage, I might add—but at what cost? I've never met a person who worked for him that has anything remotely kind to say. No. He's bad for this town in so many ways."

"How do you think you can drive him out of town? Surely it won't be easy if he owns anyone that can hurt him."

"We have to get this park closed down." Willow raised her hands to gesture at the park behind her. "If this goes, he has nothing left. Of everything he has, this is his pride and joy. I believe he cares more about the park than his own fortune. If he's willing to risk it all, then we need to be prepared to do the same. We need to close this park down, no matter what it takes."

Willow's tone had shifted from jolly to one bordering on evil. Cunning. The words sent chills up Arielle's back. Was this really the person responsible for sending all those people to their death?

"God dammit!" a voice grumbled, and everyone looked up to see Alexander Carter stomping from the front gates, hands once again balled into fists. Someone cut off the music. "Is that you again, West?" he shouted. "Get the hell off my property!"

Everyone in the group looked from Carter to Willow, like spectators at a tennis match.

Willow winked at Arielle. "One moment, please."

She walked off, and her group of protesters moved apart to let her through as she strolled right up to Carter, meeting him directly outside the circle of people that was now a glob of bodies.

"I have the right to be here," Willow said calmly, crossing her arms and leaning to one side. She raised her eyebrows in a manner that asked, *And what are you going to do about it?*

"The hell you do," Carter replied. "Show me your permit."

"Gladly," Willow said with a devilish smirk, reaching into her pants pocket and pulling out a folded piece of paper. She spread it open and held it up for Carter to see.

He squinted while he read, finally shaking his head.

"They're not supposed to allow any more protests on my property. All of you must leave now!"

Spit flew out of Carter's lips as he screamed at everyone. No one budged.

"What's the matter, *Alex*?" Willow asked. "Your puppets in the permits department aren't listening to you?"

Carter's face turned a deep red, and Arielle thought his head just might explode if he didn't take a deep breath. "You don't call me that," he said through gritted teeth.

"What's that, *Alex*?" Willow asked, that smirk going nowhere. "You don't like it when I call you the name only your mommy could use? Why don't you crawl into your tower and cry about it?"

Carter looked like he'd been holding his breath through this entire exchange. Even the back of his neck was beet red.

"Get the fuck out of my face before I call the police," Carter snarled, taking another step forward and jamming his pudgy finger into Willow's shoulder.

Four members from the group took a step forward together in unison as Willow lost her balance for a split second. She raised a hand to calm them. "You just assaulted me," Willow said calmly. "Call your cops. You'll be the one going to jail."

"That was *not* assault," Carter said, almost in a laugh.

"I saw assault," one man said from the group of four ready to protect Willow.

"Yep, me, too," said another.

This prompted Carter to take three steps back. He noticed the huddle of guests watching this encounter and addressed them. "Nothing to see here, folks. Our park is beautiful and fun. And we certainly do *not* pollute this fine town of Hilburn. Head inside and have a miraculous time."

"Just don't drink the water!" Willow shouted over Carter's voice.

Carter spun back around, pointing at Willow, but keeping his distance. "I've just about had enough of you."

"Ooooooh," Willow teased back. "I'm shaking in my boots."

Everyone in the vicinity laughed, prompting Carter to storm off, muttering every curse word he could think of under his breath.

Once he disappeared back through the park's gate, the crowd around Willow erupted with applause. "We're getting to him, Willow!" one supporter shouted. "Keep your foot on the gas. He can't handle it!"

More cheering, then the boombox returned.

Willow keeping the pressure on Carter is exactly what Arielle wanted to see. Maybe she was capable of pulling off the stunt that eventually closed down Miracle Park, but Arielle wanted to see for herself. If Willow was capable of such a vicious crime that involved killing innocent people, Arielle had to be the first to know.

# Chapter 19

Arielle and Felix waited another thirty minutes while the crowd dissipated, then headed next door to swap out the receivers.

"Can we listen to these here?" Arielle asked as they hurried down the walkway toward the hotel. "Or do we need to take the tapes home?"

"Either way works," Felix said.

"Good. Let's listen to the office feed for the past fifteen minutes. I'm sure he's made a phone call or two already. If he really has half the town in his pocket, he had to have reached out to someone about the protest."

Arielle broke into a jog.

*I hate when she does this,* Felix thought, shaking his head, then forcing his legs to move faster. He may cover more ground with each stride, but Arielle ran with the energy of a track star on cocaine. After twenty feet of jogging, she had broken into a full sprint.

They had left Felix's car in the hotel lot overnight and reached it in less than two minutes. Felix gasped for breath as he jammed the key into the lock and swung open the door. He circled to the trunk and unlocked it, looking around before lifting the door upward and pulling out one of the receiver boxes.

It was slightly smaller than the boombox they had seen earlier, and even looked similar, with a cassette deck for recording the audio feed. Felix closed the trunk and rushed into the car with the receiver, handing it to Arielle, who had settled into the passenger seat.

She examined it, but Felix knew she had no idea how to use it.

"If we rewind right now," he said, "we risk losing anything that happens from now until we're done."

"I understand," Arielle replied, licking her lips as she stared at the receiver in deep thought. "Let's wait a few minutes then, just in case he's still on a phone call in his office."

"Glad we sprinted over here so you could make that decision," Felix said, shooting a fake, flat smile across the car.

Arielle laughed. "Classic Felix, always complaining about the exercise portion, despite being in as good of shape as any of us."

Felix kept a straight face. "I exercise for my health, not to run summer morning sprints with you."

"*Pobrecita*," Arielle said, smacking Felix on the shoulder with a hearty laugh.

He laughed back, shaking his head and rubbing his shoulder. "Let's give it a try," he said, nodding to the receiver.

"Alright." Arielle pushed it forward on her lap. "What do I do?"

Felix stuck the car key into the ignition and fired up the engine. "Eject the cassette tape. We'll need to listen to it through the car speakers."

Arielle did as instructed, sliding the cassette into the deck below the dashboard with a definitive *snap!*

Felix took it from there, rewinding the tape for a quick five seconds before releasing his finger from the panel. He turned the volume dial up, and they listened to the white noise of silence for the next two minutes.

"Give it a couple more minutes," Felix said. "The good news is the wiretap on his office phone has been working, so we should get to hear both sides of the conversation if he makes a call."

"You never told me you tapped his phone line."

"Yeah. He has a setup that made it easy, with an incredibly low risk of being caught. I've listened to a few of his calls, but they've all been business-related. Nothing exciting."

A crackle came through the speakers, followed by a sharp thud that must have been the sound of his office door slamming shut. They heard inaudible grumbling and heavy wheezing.

"It's him," Arielle whispered, like she was afraid they might blow their cover if she spoke in a regular tone.

Felix nodded, mind snapping into focus. He held up a finger for Arielle to remain silent.

They heard the creak of a chair as Carter presumably sat down. Fifteen seconds of silence followed, then the sound of a dial tone boomed throughout the car. Felix winced and turned down the volume to a more reasonable level.

The line rang twice before a man answered on the other end. "Hilburn City Clerk, how can I help you?"

"Dustin, you son of a bitch!" Carter's voice shouted, making Arielle and Felix recoil as the sound blasted out of the speakers.

Felix lowered the volume once more.

"Mr. Carter," the man replied, his voice instantly on edge.

"How can I help you?"

"You can help me by not allowing any more of these fucking protests at my park. Willow West. Again? How many times do I have to tell you to reject her requests?"

"Well, Mr. Carter, we've done what we can. We've actually rejected more than we've approved. She submits permit requests almost daily."

"I don't see why that's my problem. Reject them all!"

"Mr. Carter, it's not that simple. She has threatened legal action against the city. Says we're violating her first amendment rights. Instead of dealing with a drawn-out court case, we approve one of her requests every now and then. And we give her as little notice as possible. For this one today, we only informed her yesterday morning of her approval. This should help ensure few people show up."

"It's a goddamned *zoo* outside of my park right now," Carter growled. "More and more people each time she shows up with all her fucking signs. How much more do I need to give you to make sure this doesn't keep happening? I'm losing business with all these distractions."

"Mr. Carter, I assure you, this isn't a matter of money. The city's legal team insists we grant her one permit each month to keep us from going to a trial."

"I have lawyers, and they're not afraid of anything. If the city needs to borrow them, you can have them. Just make these damned protests stop."

The man, Dustin, laughed under his breath. "That's not how any of this works, Mr. Carter. Trust me when I tell you we are making this as difficult as we can for Ms. West. Technically, she doesn't even need to request a permit to protest outside of Miracle Park. The city's five percent stake leaves it classified as public property. But she doesn't know that, and still goes through the permit application process."

Arielle and Felix exchanged looks upon hearing this valuable information.

"Fuck the five percent!" Carter screamed. "You people are holding me by my balls with that five percent. Way too much control over what I can do with *my* private business."

"We're always here to support you, Mr. Carter." Dustin's voice had become irritated, like this was a weekly disturbance he personally had to deal with.

"Do better or be ready to pay the price!" Carter shouted, ending the phone call by slamming the receiver on the hook.

The recording returned to a static white noise for a few seconds before cutting to complete silence.

"That's where the tape ends," Felix said. "If he made any other calls, we missed it."

"I think we've heard enough," Arielle said. "Willow wasn't lying. Carter has at least one contact in the city. Dustin from the city clerk's office. We'll need to research and see who that is exactly."

"One thing's for sure," Felix said. "Willow is definitely on to something."

"Absolutely. And beyond that, there *is* something going on that Carter doesn't want everyone to know about. Pollution seems most likely. Willow seems very focused. I don't see her grasping for straws or fudging the truth to fit some agenda. It may have been our first impression of both Willow and Carter, but I'd have to believe her over him."

Felix ejected the cassette and returned it to the receiver. "That's fine and all, but can we tie the Time Roller tragedy to Willow in time?"

"Willow is absolutely involved, but I highly doubt she personally cuts the pull cable. Did you see those four guys ready to pound Carter into the ground after he poked her?"

"Yeah, that was impressive."

"I agree. Willow has a following. They care about her. They believe in her. And that means they'll do just about anything she asks of them. I hope it doesn't come to it, but we may have to wait until the night before to know what's going on."

"I can't handle another close call."

Arielle shrugged. "It's the nature of what we do. No mission we get is ever going to be simple. Just remember that. For now, the best we can do is keep digging into Willow and Carter and these accusations of pollution. Maybe something will turn up that we can use ahead of the accident."

"Let's hope," Felix said, his tone becoming reflective. "I don't like the path we're heading down. We can't get tangled between these two sides. I'm afraid it's going to turn messy and violent."

# Chapter 20

After spending the next forty minutes getting the receivers situated, then tracking down Selena in the park—they had to enter through the side entrance to avoid Willow and her gang from seeing them go in—Arielle and Felix hit the road to drive to Hilburn's municipal building.

They had located Selena to tell her to look for any evidence surrounding potential pollution being committed by Miracle Park. They had a brief discussion about the plausible options, mainly of how the trash was being disposed.

Selena agreed to learn more about the custodial team's process, then griped about working under the beating sun all day. Arielle bought her a cold lemonade, and they wished her a better rest of her day.

Once they left the park, Arielle was on a mission to find Dustin from the city clerk's office.

"Do you have a plan?" Felix asked as he drove them through town. They left the receivers in Arielle's car at the hotel lot.

"Not for this one," Arielle said, staring into space, trying to think up a solid way to meet Dustin once they arrived. "We're going to walk in there and ask to apply for a permit for a peaceful assembly. Hopefully that allows us to meet this

Dustin person. If not, we'll need to figure something out on the spot."

"And if we do meet him?" Felix asked, an eyebrow raised.

"That's where I'm torn. Who do you think he's more afraid of? Carter or Willow?"

Felix chewed on this question and didn't answer until they reached the next red light. "I'd have to say Carter. He has the pull around town, and it sounds like he has already paid off this Dustin character."

"That's true, but Willow is making his life hell with her constant requests for permits. While he may not fear her like Carter, I'm sure he dreads hearing her name or seeing her face."

"What's our angle?" Felix asked. The light turned green, and he continued along Eighth Street, turning north onto Twenty-Fifth Avenue.

"We need to know who Dustin is, and what exactly he does around here. He's involved with both Carter and Willow, but we need to understand whose side he's really on."

Felix pursed his lips, licking them before speaking. "I think we should pose as people on Carter's side. The fear factor alone should put Dustin on edge and more willing to talk. I could see him being more dismissive if we said we're with Willow."

Arielle rubbed her forehead. It was rare she got headaches, but she felt the early signs of one coming on. Maybe it was the heat—it was ninety-six degrees today, and she'd only had a single bottle of water so far. But she suspected it was more of a credit to the mission. What Felix had said earlier at the park was correct. They were getting in the middle of two sides of a war, with leaders willing to hold nothing back in their pursuit of victory. "I suppose both options have their advantages and disadvantages," she said, taking off her sunglasses to rub her eyes. "We can try posing as Carter's team. Money talks, and that's what he's known for."

Felix turned right onto Fourteenth Street and pulled into one of the open diagonal parking spaces in front of a brick building with a generic sign that read *Hilburn City Clerk.*

The intersection of Fourteenth Street and Twenty-Fifth Avenue served as the center of a four-block radius that was home to all of Hilburn's government buildings. The southeast corner had the city council chambers and library. A one-room courthouse stood on the southwest corner. The northeast had their main areas of interest: city clerk, building permits, and the water department. Another block down from there was the police station. All the buildings looked the same with their brick exterior and simple signage, except for the courthouse, which had a statue of George Washington directly outside its front doors. George stood tall and upright, the quote on the base reading, *The best and only safe road to honor, glory, and true dignity is justice.*

"This is us," Felix said as he killed the engine.

Arielle noticed him admiring the cherry-red Oldsmobile Cutlass parked next to them. She figured if Felix ever turned evil, the worst thing he'd probably do was travel back in time to steal vintage cars and sports memorabilia to bring back to the future. Not even to resell, just to collect.

"Follow my lead," Arielle said, stepping out of the car first. The heat was dry, and the light breeze seemed to make it worse, swirling the hot air around and making her head spin. *I should have pushed this to tomorrow,* she thought, starting toward the city clerk's entrance.

A couple of teenagers sat on a bench in front of the building, holding hands and sipping from tall glass bottles of Coke under the shade. They looked peaceful, and Arielle couldn't recall the last time she had a moment to just sit down and do absolutely nothing. They weren't even speaking, simply enjoying each other's presence. Young love was so beautiful every time Arielle saw it. It lacked the pressure of adult romance, where everyone had an agenda and baggage. Jobs, dreams, plans for kids, in-laws. All of that shit made love more complicated than it needed to be. It strained relationships. Arielle once had that young, carefree love with Kevin Fletcher. What hurt the most was knowing he was still out there, shooting up drugs on a park bench somewhere in California, his life forever in shambles. Did he even remember what they once had?

"Arielle?" Felix asked. She had stopped at the office door, hand on the pullbar as she watched the teenagers.

Arielle cleared her throat. "Sorry. Let's go."

Felix looked from her to the couple, puzzled, before following her into the building.

The Hilburn city clerk was given a small office space. They walked into a lobby no bigger than the kitchen at their house. Five chairs lined the wall facing the reception desk. A woman in her early thirties sat behind the desk, batting her green eyes at Felix from behind a pair of bright red cat-eye glasses that matched her lipstick. She chomped a piece of gum like a horse gnawing on hay.

"Afternoon," she said. "How can I help you?"

Felix looked at Arielle, who stepped forward. "Yes, good afternoon. We were hoping to plan a protest and heard we might need a permit. Is this the place to apply?"

The woman cocked her head down to look over the top of her frames. "A protest? For what? You're not with Crazy Willow, are you?"

"Crazy Willow?" Arielle asked, scrunching her face to feign confusion. Apparently, Willow was a celebrity around Hilburn.

"I didn't think so," the woman continued, scanning Arielle from head to toe with a judgmental eye. "You don't look the part. Fill out this form." She reached into a drawer under her desk, leaving Arielle and Felix a five-second window to exchange a look of confidence before she sat up and slid a sheet of paper over.

Arielle stepped up to examine the form, catching a whiff of the woman's floral-scented perfume. "Oh," she said, picking up the paper. "I thought we'd get to meet with Dustin about this. I had spoken with him on the phone last week."

The woman lowered her head again, her gaze burning into Arielle. After an eternity of awkward silence, she held up a finger, picked up the phone on her desk, and pressed three buttons. While the phone rang in her ear, her stare returned to Felix, and her stern expression softened into one of admiration. "I have a couple here to see you," she said into the phone. "Said they spoke to you before about a protest."

Arielle's heartbeat sped up as her lie was fully out in the world.

"Okay," the woman said, then hung up. "Mr. Nash will be out shortly to take you back. Have a seat until then." She gestured to the chairs across from her desk.

"Thank you," Arielle said, shuffling backward to sit down.

They waited for only three minutes, and the woman enjoyed each second, stealing glimpses of Felix every moment she could. Arielle looked over to her partner and realized he had no clue any of this was going on.

*I guess he could have any lady in this town,* Arielle thought, watching Felix stare mindlessly at the wall. From what she had seen in their couple of weeks in town, there weren't many men with tall, muscular bodies outside of the high school athletes. Felix could probably win Mr. Hilburn every year for the next decade by simply showing up. His obliviousness surely made the women want him even more.

Footsteps clopped from the short hallway that connected to the lobby, and they both looked up to see a man strolling along, head held high with a wide grin smacked on his freckled face. He had thick red hair slicked to the side and wore a flannel shirt tucked into a pair of khakis, sleeves rolled up to his elbow.

"Hello, folks," he greeted, sticking out a hand as he approached. His voice was gentle, nothing like the intimidated one they had heard from the recorded phone call with Carter. "Dustin Nash, city clerk. How may I be of assistance?"

Arielle and Felix stood up and took turns shaking his hands. "Hello, Mr. Nash," Arielle said. "We were hoping for a word in private about a gathering we're trying to organize."

"Absolutely," he said, his tone remaining upbeat. "Let's head into my office." Dustin spun around and waved them over. The woman behind the desk kept her eyes glued to Felix as they left the lobby.

They shuffled down the hallway that had only three doors, turning into the first one on the right. Dustin's office had an oak desk in the back corner of the room, his chair against the only window overlooking a courtyard shared by the three city buildings on this section of the block. Two more chairs waited in front of his desk, and he gestured for Arielle and Felix to sit down as he settled into his seat.

"Alice mentioned we've spoken on the phone," Dustin said, scratching his chin. Two framed pictures of Dustin with a sandy-haired woman and a young girl no older than three stood on the edge of his desk. He examined them while he spoke. "Could you remind me what this is about?"

Arielle felt Felix's eyes burning into the side of her face, waiting for her next move.

"That was actually a lie, Mr. Nash," Arielle said, holding her gaze on Dustin.

"I'm sorry?" Dustin asked, leaning forward and blinking rapidly. "I don't understand."

"We're actually here regarding Alexander Carter."

She let the words hang and process in the city clerk's mind. Once they did, he frowned and leaned back, crossing his arms. "No," he said, all cheeriness gone from his voice. "We're not doing this here, and he knows that."

"Doing what?" Arielle asked.

Dustin scoffed and shook his head, reaching out for his phone. "Unbelievable," he muttered under his breath.

Arielle stood up and smacked Dustin's hand, forcing the phone to clatter on the desk. He recoiled, shaking his hand like he had just touched a hot stovetop.

"What the hell do you think you're doing?" Dustin cried, still rubbing the back of his hand where Arielle had struck. "Of all the things Carter can be charged for, you really want to add assaulting a city official to the list?"

"Who were you going to call just now?" Arielle asked, leaning onto the desk and placing the phone back on its hook.

"The police," Dustin said matter-of-factly. "I told Carter if he comes into the office one more time, I'm turning him in. And having him send his goons counts just the same in my book."

Dustin's eyes kept jumping to the phone. He wanted to place that call so desperately.

"Hold on a second," Felix said, raising his hand. He stood up to join Arielle and looked down upon Dustin. "I think we can help each other here. My partner didn't make it very clear. We're not here on behalf of Mr. Carter, she said we're here *regarding* him. Let's all cool down and start over."

*What the hell are you doing, Felix?* Arielle thought, looking at him to figure out just that. His eyes locked with Dustin's for a few seconds before he looked at her and nodded, holding out his arm toward her chair.

She sat down slowly, still ready to pounce if Dustin reached for the phone again.

"Who are you people?" Dustin asked, nearly whispering. He had leaned back in his seat and nervously ran his fingers along the edge of his desk. "You're not from around here, are you?"

"We're not," Felix said, finally sitting down. He had taken control of the room, and Arielle still had no idea what his angle was. All she could do was trust him. "We're private investigators looking into some of Mr. Carter's business dealings. There have been some serious accusations against him and Miracle Park."

"Private investigators?" Dustin asked. "Who's behind this?"

"We're not at liberty to share that information," Felix said. "We're just on the hunt for answers and understand that Mr. Carter may be paying off government officials here in Hilburn. Your office is one that's of interest."

Dustin gulped and started looking around his office. "I don't know what you're talking about," he said, eyes returning to the family pictures.

Felix leaned forward and spoke in a hushed tone. "Look, Mr. Nash, we're not here for you. If you've done anything illegal, we don't care. We're just trying to paint a big picture of what Alexander Carter is involved in. Our goal is to pin everything on Carter and let him take the fall. You don't need to worry about losing your job or going to jail. We will not list your name on any reports."

Arielle nodded along to hammer down Dustin's confidence in them.

Felix sat back and tossed his hands in the air. "That said, we want to know everything you can tell us. Let's start with a simple question—yes or no. Has Alexander Carter ever paid you to do favors on his behalf?"

Dustin kept swallowing mouthfuls of spit, avoiding eye contact with the two Angels in front of him. Once more, his eyes fell on the phone.

"Mr. Nash," Felix said sternly. "I can promise you we don't intend to harm you, but my colleague here can turn you inside out with her bare hands. So I suggest you talk and stop looking at that phone."

Arielle whipped her head around to look at Felix, but he only glared ahead at Dustin, who seemed to have shrunk in his seat. *Since when do you shake down someone like this?* If Felix now had this interrogation tool in his arsenal, their team just took a major step forward.

"And if you call anyone after we leave here," Arielle said, joining in the fun. "We'll know. Like my partner has said, we have no interest in getting you into any sort of trouble. We just need some help. And if it's Carter you're worried about, don't be. He has no idea who we are, or that we're even here in town looking into him."

Dustin considered this and ran through every potential outcome in his head while he looked back and forth between the two time travelers in front of him. He nodded slowly to himself. "Okay, I'll talk."

With those three words, all the tension fled the room.

"Thank you," Arielle said. "Now, what is the payment arrangement between yourself and Carter?"

Dustin rubbed his nose, clearly distraught by the whole situation. "He pays me two thousand dollars a month for matters involving permits around Hilburn."

"Two thousand dollars a month?!" Felix gasped. "That's certainly more than you make here."

Dustin nodded, shame taking over his face. "It is, but what can I do?" His eyes fell on the family picture. "I have a little girl I want to send to college one day, and all this money goes into that fund. I know I'm selling my soul to the devil, but it's for a good reason."

"Settle down," Arielle said, raising an open hand. "We're not the morality police. You do what you need. That's a cute little girl. I don't blame you one bit for wanting to make her life as best as can be. Now, tell us what exactly Carter gets for this exorbitant fee he pays you."

Dustin gathered himself and propped his elbows on his desk. "Quite a bit, actually. I helped expedite his permits for the building of Miracle Park. He needed others for the newspaper. And he's said he plans to open more businesses in town. I guess I'm more of his retainer for permits. I also deny permits for protests—he gets a ton of people wanting to protest him, both at the park and the newspaper."

"Willow West?" Felix asked.

Dustin nodded. "You've done your research. Willow leads all the protests at the park, and gets others from her group to protest the newspaper."

"We're aware of the park protests," Arielle said, scrunching her face. "But haven't heard about the newspaper. What are those about?"

"They claim the newspaper is biased and violates the first amendment by regularly denying publication of op-ed pieces from Hilburn citizens. It's a silly cause and doesn't get nearly the same traction as Miracle Park."

"Who files for the protests at the newspaper?" Felix asked.

"Her name is Lisa Bartlett. I believe she lives with Willow."

Felix whipped out a notepad and wrote the name down.

"And for the park," Arielle continued. "Is there any truth to the accusations about pollution?"

Dustin shrugged and grinned, a sign he was relieved to speak an honest truth. "I have no idea. I've heard so many mixed facts—I'm not sure anyone knows for certain."

Felix scratched his head and drew a deep inhale. "Okay. Nevermind all that. If Carter is paying you, there have to be others. Who are they?"

Dustin shifted in his seat and looked around the room.

*He knows, but doesn't want to say,* Arielle thought. "Dustin," she said. "Same rules apply. We have no interest in bringing down anyone who has been paid off by Carter. We only want him."

Dustin shook his head. "I can't rat out my friends. I have to draw the line somewhere."

Arielle pursed her lips as she glared across the desk. Felix was now watching her for their next move. "Okay. Meet us in the middle. You don't need to give us any specific names. But let us know which city departments Carter has under his control."

Dustin sighed relief, slowly nodding as he stared at his family pictures. "I can do that. But I suppose a fairer question is what department has Carter *not* paid off?"

"It's that bad?" Felix asked.

"Absolutely. His hands are in the police department, water, sewage, city council, parks and recreation. We suspect he owns the mayor, too, but that's never been confirmed."

"We?" Arielle asked, watching Felix scribble notes.

"Those of us who know about each other like to talk," Dustin said, scratching his head. "See, there have been horror stories about what happens if you don't follow through with Carter's requests. Mainly people losing their jobs, but sometimes it's a lesser punishment like a suspension or job probation."

"I see, and what are some departments that's happened to?"

Dustin drew a deep breath and blew the air out of his mouth. "Mainly the police and water department. I don't know the reasoning behind any of it, but it was definitely for not complying with Carter's requests."

Arielle and Felix exchanged a glance and nodded at each other. "It sounds like we have to spend some time looking at these other city departments," Arielle said. "You've been a big help today, Mr. Nash, and your assistance will not go unrewarded."

"What is that supposed to mean?" Dustin asked, frowning.

"You're a good man, Mr. Nash. And we're good people, too, even if you don't believe it based on this initial meeting. Our job is to stop bad people from doing bad things. We have a lot of resources, and I'm happy to send some your way if you'd agree to be a point of contact for us moving forward for the rest of our time here in Hilburn."

"I don't understand," Dustin said, brow furrowed as he looked between Arielle and Felix. "You're also going to pay me? I'm getting paid from both sides of this matter? What am I, like a double agent?"

Arielle laughed. "Definitely not. In the coming months, your stream of income from Carter will end. If you can help us during our investigation here, we'll make it worth your while. Would hate for you to talk yourself out of a steady stream of income. I can get you cash for a year's worth of Carter's payments, but I need two things in return: your silence and any information you can provide as we need. This could end up being our last visit with you, or we may be here once a week. I don't know." Arielle shrugged as she watched the dials turning in Dustin's mind.

He folded his hands against his chest and leaned back, squinting at Arielle. "You're going to pay me twenty-four thousand dollars for all that?"

Arielle nodded. "We can have the cash delivered within a week. It will be discreet, and we can meet you wherever you'd like."

Dustin jumped out of his seat and extended a hand across the table to Arielle. "Deal."

Arielle shook his hand with a satisfied smile. "Thank you, Mr. Nash. And just to be clear, we will know if you tell *anyone* about our deal—and yes, that includes your wife."

She said this in a grave tone and watched as the brief joy he had experienced vanished from his face.

"Understood," he said.

# Chapter 21



July 23, 1978

On Sunday night, Arielle and Selena left Felix after having an early dinner together. Felix had apparently been in a better mood, as he offered to cook them a feast of bacon-wrapped pork tenderloins, mashed potatoes, and grilled asparagus. It was their first lavish meal on the mission, and all three agreed they wanted more before they left.

The two hopped into Selena's car and started for Miracle Park, each dressed in one of Selena's Miracle Park uniforms—khaki pants with a branded navy polo. It was 7:30, and the park closed at 8 p.m. on Sundays. Selena had asked around the park custodial staff for information on the trash pickup schedule. They collected trash on a varied schedule depending on how many visitors came through the gates. What Selena counted on, however, was the final round of trash collecting the staff did once the park closed.

One employee she had spoken with, an acne-infested teenager by the name of George Johnston, told her they all gathered the trash at the end of the night for a team lead or manager to take to the dumpster behind the building.

Selena had ventured across every inch of Miracle Park and

had never seen a dumpster.

"What do you think we'll find tonight?" Arielle asked while driving through town on a quiet, lazy night.

"Who knows?" Selena said. "I doubt it will be anything exciting, like you're hoping. I'm sure there's a dumpster somewhere I'm just not aware of. It might even be over by the hotel. I never go over there aside from parking my car."

"And you weren't able to find out any other information about the park's trash collections? Hilburn only has two trash companies."

"No. I don't get many opportunities to go into our offices and look up that kind of info. Even if I did, it would seem strange for me to ask about such a thing. My role is overlooking rides and concessions. The custodial team is under Park Services—they're a separate, independent team."

"Who runs that team?"

"Nicholas McLaughlin. He's the head of Park Services."

Arielle nodded, putting the name to memory. They would need to look him up for any potential connections to Carter outside of Miracle Park.

"Felix told me something in confidence yesterday," Selena said, her tone suggesting a change of topic. "Can you promise not to tell?"

Arielle smirked. "Okay? What's up?"

"He said you offered the city clerk twenty-four thousand dollars for what he believes is nothing."

Arielle burst into laughter as she pulled up to a red light, turning to look at Selena with her mouth hanging open. "Are you serious? Why didn't he ask me about it? He was with me when it happened? We drove home right after I made that offer, and he didn't say a thing."

"He thought it seemed like a waste of money and didn't want to question you directly."

The light turned green, and Arielle shook her head while driving forward. "Wow. Well, he's correct about it *seeming* like a waste of money, but it's not. I doubt we'll actually need to use that city clerk again while we're here, but the man is a talker. If I didn't pay him off, half the town would know about us by now. Even Carter might have found out we're looking into him."

"But we're not even really looking into *him*. We just want to know who his enemies are."

"Yes, but we can't have anyone complicate that. This city clerk proved plenty helpful, but I couldn't trust him. So I offered him some money, bundled it with a threat, and now we should be good for the rest of the mission. We'll eventually need to talk to people from other departments, and if they're already on edge because the city clerk goes blabbering about the two people who came into his office, then we're just wasting our time. People will have time to make up lies or come up with reasons they can't talk to us. I didn't pay off the clerk for his help. I paid him so we can continue our work without any roadblocks."

"Another lesson out of the book of Arielle Lucila," Selena said, shaking her head. They had entered the park's main lot and Arielle slowed down as they crept toward the entrance.

"Slow night," Arielle said as she parked in a space directly next to the cluster of Disabled Parking spots. "You sure you'll be able to get me in?"

Selena tilted her head to the side and rolled her eyes. "Are you doubting me again? It's Sunday night—the slowest part of the week. There is only one supervisor and one team lead to cover the entire park from six to eight. They'll be making their final rounds through the park before closing all the rides down."

"That reminds me," Arielle said. "Did you ever find out how Carter got into his suite that day Felix was in there?"

Selena grinned. "You'll see the path he takes tonight. Runs along the back of the main walkway.  And he has a rear entrance to the hotel with a private elevator that takes him directly to the penthouse. I hate to say it, but you never had a chance of spotting him."

"Son of a bitch," Arielle said, shaking her head.

"No point worrying about it now.  Let's focus on tonight. The staff won't be anywhere near the side entrance, so we can slip in through there. If anyone happens to question you, just say it was your first day and you've been training with me."

"I'll avoid everyone I can," Arielle said. "You forget, I have plenty of stealth skills."

"Of course you do," Selena said sarcastically. "Let's head in."

Arielle followed Selena around to the side entrance. They passed a handful of people making their way out of the park for the night. Long purple clouds painted the orange sky. An hour of sunlight remained.  Shrieking from inside the park echoed around them, the distant rumble of Time Roller taking guests for the ride of their lives.

The side entrance had four lanes for park guests to enter, but Selena moved past those and disappeared around the corner where another gate waited out of sight, a sign hanging from it that said *EMPLOYEES ONLY*.

Selena pulled a key from her pocket and jiggled it in the lock until the door swung open.

"Wait a minute," Arielle said. "All employees have a key to get in?"

"No," Selena said, closing the gate behind them as they stepped into the park, pulling it to make sure the lock latched. "Shift supervisors and above get keys. We unlock this gate in the morning so all the staff can enter. Otherwise, they're expected to enter through the main gates if their shift starts in the middle of the day."

"Interesting. Would you be able to get a list of names of everyone who has a key?"

"I can put something unofficial together. I can't truly know who actually has a key in their possession, but I know, mostly, who *should*."

"That would be perfect." Arielle followed Selena, who started walking deeper into the park. They were in a low-traffic area, behind a building that housed restrooms. Bushes lined the fence, a few flowers standing out in the dusk. "I'm going to have Felix compile a database of all the potential suspects. I'd say anyone who has a key to the park should be on that list."

Selena held up her hands. "I swear I'm innocent."

They shared a laugh as they came out of the pathway, where the park hummed with more activity. Arielle checked her watch. "Ten more minutes until the park closes."

On cue, a crackling voice announced exactly that over the park's speakers. What remained of the Sunday night crowd was an entirely different demographic than Arielle had seen compared to her other visits. Lots of couples out on date night. Few kids and families. Just people of all ages, walking with their hands intertwined or arms over each other's shoulders.

Arielle could practically breathe in the romance that seemed to cling to the air. And it made her sick to her core. It seemed impossible for her to escape the scenes of love over the past few days. The playful, giggling couples sharing ice cream cones and staring deep into each other's eyes. Even the lights from the park's attractions combined with the soothing voice of Dean Martin singing in the background made Arielle's head spin. Why was the universe shoving romance into her face at every opportunity?

She jerked her head free of the thoughts before Kevin worked his way into her mind. Selena led them toward the majestic Time Roller, and the sight sent a knot of angst into her stomach that she felt every time she laid eyes on the death ride.

"Where are we going?" Arielle asked.

"To the back," Selena said, not slowing down. "That kid told me they take the trash to a dumpster in the back. So we might as well start our search there."

They passed Time Roller and stepped onto a narrow path that curved along the back of the roller coaster. The Platte River flowed a quarter mile away, the dusk sky reflecting off the currently calm waters.

The fence running along the park's perimeter returned to sight as they strode down the path, cutting them off. Selena took a sharp turn to the right, leading them into the darkness beneath a row of towering trees.

"You've explored all of this?" Arielle asked in a lowered voice.

"Oh yeah," Selena said proudly. "This park is massive, and I figured I should know all the ways in and out to help the mission. Here is the secret door very few know about."

Selena walked up to a gate and pushed it open.

"It's not even locked?" Arielle asked, eyes protruding in shock.

"For what? You can really only access it from here. Look."

Selena stepped through the gate, and Arielle followed as they stepped from pavement onto dirt.

"Wow," Arielle said, soaking in their surroundings. A short field separated them from the freeway five-hundred feet away. Cars rode on a stretch of bridge above the portion of the Platte River that twisted back toward the park. The Miracle Hotel towered in the distance to the east.

"We're on the backside of the park," Selena explained. "Again, only a select few know about this place. It's mainly used by team leads as a hideout. Sometimes you just need to get away from Carter. The teenagers come back here to smoke and feel each other up. Let me tell you, some days it's like walking through a wall of hormones in this place."

Arielle laughed. "This is great and all, but why did you bring us here?"

Selena nodded in the hotel's direction. Arielle took another two steps forward to see around the bushes impeding her view. "See that building between the park and hotel? That's my best guess for where they are taking trash."

A building the size of a two-car garage stood in the shadows of the pending nightfall.

"What is that place?" Arielle asked. "I've walked back and forth from the hotel to the park and have never seen it."

"That's because it's further back from that walkway than it looks from here. When you're on that path between the park and hotel, the sides are lined with trees, bushes, and exotic flowers. If you were to push through all that, you'd find that building. It's used by the grounds crew. I've only walked up to it once. Place was locked and I couldn't see through the windows—they were filthy and covered in dust."

"How many ways are there to get there?"

"Three, from what I can tell. You can walk there from here, from the backside of the hotel, or by pushing through the shrubbery from the path between the two."

Arielle checked her watch again. "It's eight o'clock."

Selena nodded. "They'll have already started gathering the trash—probably got a head start because of the slower day. If we're going to see any action, I'd imagine it will be in about thirty minutes. Let's get comfortable."

Selena walked further out, and Arielle didn't like the sen- sation. It felt like they were out in the open for anyone to see. But there was no one around, unless they were hiding in the foliage or watching from their hotel window. Still, it was too dark to even see Arielle and Selena from such a distance.

Selena settled on a rock three feet in width, sitting down and planting her elbows into her knees. Sure enough, a pile of cigarette butts lay scattered on the ground in front of the rock.

"Everything okay?" Arielle asked as she sat down next to Selena.

"Yeah, why do you ask?" Selena kept her gaze on the ground.

"Just checking. I feel like we haven't seen you much on this mission. You're always here. Then we get a couple hours in the evening, and that's it."

Selena looked up. "I'm fine. Just powering through. This town is so boring, and not having any technology is just torture. I figure the faster we can finish this mission, the sooner I can get back to real life."

Arielle laughed under her breath. "Will you be totally honest if I ask you something?"

Selena arched her eyebrows as she looked over her shoulder to meet Arielle's piercing gaze. "Okay."

Arielle had been wanting to ask Selena this question since they first met, but it had taken them time to develop trust in each other. And now, it felt like they were the only two people in the world. "Do you like being an Angel?"

Selena's eyes fluttered at the question. "Of course. Why would you ask that?"

Arielle shifted on the rock, swinging her legs around so her body could face Selena. "I've met a lot of Angels, and every one of them is so energized by their work and missions. Being an Angel is very much a part of their identity. They would die happy as long as it was during a mission for the Angels. I don't get that sense at all from you."

Selena furrowed her brow while fighting off a smile. She looked at the sky, considering her next words. "I know what you mean, and you're absolutely right. Being an Angel is not some badge of honor for me. That may sound messed up to say, but it's just how I feel."

"How can that be? You've done so many missions and your work is incredible. I find it hard to believe you can perform at such a high level having no true passion."

Selena shook her head, her hair whipping around like a flag in the wind. "I *do* have passion. It's just not for being an Angel. For me, it's all about acting. It's all I've ever wanted to do in my life. I'm also a realist. Making it big in Hollywood is like winning the lottery. There are actors out there who bust their ass every single day and never get discovered by anyone meaningful. To make a living from acting is the exception, not the rule. So when the Angels recruited me, and offered me a six-figure salary to act on these missions, I couldn't pass that up."

"But it's not enough?" Arielle asked. "You're getting paid to do what you love. And you make a positive difference in people's lives."

Selena scooted closer to Arielle, their shoulders touching. "And that's great, but it's not what I wanted with my acting career. See, people like to make fun of entertainers of all sorts—athletes, actors, musicians, you name it. And yes, some of these celebrities are so far removed from the realities of our society that it's sickening. But what would our world be without movies, music, sports? Even books. Every single person has to unwind somehow. Imagine going home after a long day of work and only having the wall to stare at. People would lose their minds, and our society would collapse even more than it already has. Stan Lee understood the importance of escapism and built an empire from it. Don't you have a movie or TV show you turn to when you need that bit of comfort in your life?"

Arielle nodded and slid an arm over Selena's shoulder. "Yes. I used to watch the George Lopez Show all the time after my family died. It made me laugh, but their whole dynamic reminded me of my family. I still watch some episodes from time to time."

"See," Selena said, leaning her head back on Arielle's arm, looking at the sky where darkness was overtaking the orange glow. "If all that cast and crew never existed, what would you have? You'll carry that show with you for the rest of your life. It's a part of you now because of what you associate with it.

*That's* the difference I want to make in the world. One where people can actually know it was me who helped them through a tough time."

Arielle stood up from the rock, keeping one foot planted on it so she could lean on her knee. "Well, I'm glad I know where you stand on things. I'll do whatever I can to make sure you get your shot in Hollywood . . . I may have some connections out there."

Selena stood up and threw her arms around Arielle in a bear hug. "Thank you."

In the distance, Arielle saw figures moving in the shadows by the building. She pulled back from Selena and looked her square in the eyes. "We gotta get going."

# Chapter 22

Selena led them down the dirt path toward the grounds crew maintenance building. As she had predicted, the first signs of movement came just a couple of minutes after 8:30. They had the advantage of darkness thanks to nightfall. The only lights along this rear side of the property were those coming from the building they hurried toward. Windows lined the upper walls, a piercing white light glowing from all sides. A lone, orange light shone over the building's back door.

Selena and Arielle had been about five-hundred feet from the building when they left their perch on the rock and were closing in as they crouched low, moving through the night. Cicadas buzzed from the treetops, frogs croaked from the nearby riverbank, and the two Angels slowed to a near crawl to prevent the sound of crunching gravel beneath their feet from traveling toward the maintenance building.

Selena ducked behind a tree trunk to their right, taking them off the path for a moment, where they gathered their breath. She let out a hoarse laugh, a thick layer of sweat forming across her forehead on this humid night. "After all I just told you about wanting to be an actress. I'm out here snooping around. Ain't that some bullshit?"

Arielle giggled quietly under her breath. "I guess you just need to *act* like you're being a spy. Think of it that way."

Selena shook her head. "So, what's our plan from here? Are we trying to see what's going on inside the building?"

"Of course. All the windows along the sides and back are too high for us to see through. You said the ones in the front are lower?"

"They are, but last time I was there, I couldn't see through them because of how dirty they were."

The moving silhouettes they had seen a few minutes ago had both come out of the back door to stand around for a moment before returning inside. At least, that was how matters appeared from a distance.

Selena's stomach twisted into knots. The only way to see what was happening inside the building was by walking straight up to the front door. Arielle seemed completely unfazed by the prospect, and that eased some of the tension for Selena.

"Can you think of any reasons for you to be at the maintenance building at this time of night?" Arielle asked. She leaned around the tree trunk for a better view of their target destination.

"There's not really *any* reason for me to be at that building," Selena said, nervously picking pieces of bark off the tree trunk. "I suppose I could always say I'm looking for someone in particular, but that team has no obligation to answer to me. They're a bit stuck up that way, like they're above the rest of the park staff because they never have to interact directly with the guests."

"We'll have to try." Arielle leaned against the tree and searched for Selena's gaze through the shadows. "Let's walk right up to that front door and see what we find. If anyone spots us, we'll tell them we're looking for . . . was his name George?"

Selena nodded. "George Johnston."

"Perfect. It's not like we're random strangers. You do work at the park, so it shouldn't be some mind-boggling catastrophe if you get spotted."

*You don't know this place like I do,* Selena thought. In just a couple of weeks, she had already witnessed the workplace politics of Miracle Park. They drew clear lines for who should interact with whom. The grounds crew had an unshakable brotherhood and seemed to never catch any heat from Carter. That George had shared any details with Selena was a miracle in itself.

"Okay," Selena said. "Let's go."

Arielle stepped out from behind the tree, and they continued down the makeshift path one long, delicate step at a time.

A minute later they stood directly at the rear of the building, still out of sight from anyone who might wander out the back door. Arielle led the way and nodded to her right. They advanced along the side, the muffled sounds of raised voices carrying from within.

Once they reached the front corner, Arielle halted and put up a hand while she peered around the front of the building. She pressed her back against the wall and spun her head to look at Selena. "Do you smell something?"

Adrenaline had been gushing through Selena's veins like a burst pipe, leaving her unaware of any odors in the air. She drew a deep breath not only to relax herself, but to smell whatever Arielle was talking about. "Is that a campfire?" Selena whispered.

"Not a campfire, but something is burning," Arielle said, looking upward for any signs of smoke.

Selena joined her but saw nothing.

Arielle peeked back around the corner and waved Selena to follow her as she started toward the front door. A similar orange light from the back door hung above the front, the glow revealing no one in proximity.

Arielle shuffled along the front of the building to the front doors, where she crouched below the windows. Selena tried to keep up, thighs burning from walking in such an awkward position for so long.

The windows were covered in a black powdery substance, thick enough to make them opaque. Yet, they could still see a flickering glimmer of orange light from within.

"The fire's in there," Arielle whispered. "And that's not dirt on the windows. It's soot."

Selena rose enough to attempt another look through the glass. She felt dumb for not realizing it was soot the last time she was out here. But the black substance was the furthest thing from her mind. Why would the windows have a thick layer of soot? The pieces of the puzzle were falling into place now.

"Are they burning something on purpose?" Selena asked, partly knowing the answer. "Or do we need to call for help?"

Arielle shook her head. "No, it's intentional. The windows tell the whole story. They do this on a regular basis. I think this is where all the trash goes. Let's get away from the front door."

Arielle pivoted around and motioned for Selena to go back the way they had come from. They remained in the shadows on the side of the building, where no one could spot them unless they had a flashlight.

"Okay, let's think this through," Arielle said. "They bring the trash into this building and burn it every day. Why? That's so much trash."

Selena sat on the ground, back against the wall, wishing for a light breeze to cool them off. "You don't understand Carter. He is so cheap. Everyone starts at minimum wage, and from what I've gathered, every raise has been argued over—and given only to those who last more than one season. Why pay for a trash service to come collect everything when you can have people already on your payroll take care of it?"

"That seems like an absurd reason to burn trash," Arielle said, sliding down the wall to sit next to Selena. "To me, paying a trash service is just a normal expense for running a business. What a silly way to cut corners, but I suppose there aren't really other motives. I doubt Carter *wants* to pollute the sky for fun. I'm not sure what he gets out of that."

"I'm telling you," Selena said sharply, "it's all about the money with him. Nothing else matters to that man. Bring as much money in, and send out as little as possible. They should just change the park's slogan to that. I saw for myself the other day. He stopped at a concession stand, scooped all the ice cream out of the machine's drip tray—you know, where the excess falls off when making a cone—and determined it three cones worth of waste. He deducted one dollar from the employee's paycheck for that. I've acted in a ton of roles on these missions, many for greedy men like Carter, but I've never seen anything like that. He's truly on another level."

Arielle shook her head before cocking it upward to look at the sky. "I don't know how he gets away with so much. I suppose it is 1978—there might not even be regulations against burning your own trash."

"Even if there are," Selena said, "who's going to enforce them? You said he's paid off everyone in town."

Before Arielle could respond, the back door swung open with an aggressive clatter, startling the two Angels to their feet. Laughter and voices carried from the back of the building, and Selena's entire body tensed up.

"Load 'em up, boys," a deep voice called.

Multiple engines roared in the silent night.

"What the hell is going on?" Selena asked, her heart trying to beat its way out of her head.

Arielle placed a calming hand on her back while she craned her neck. "I don't know. We need to move closer. Are you feeling fast today?"

Selena never lacked confidence in her speed, but in this moment, her legs felt limp with fear. "I'm good," she said, Arielle already starting toward the back of the building.

The engines idled, puttering clouds of exhaust that circled the maintenance building. Arielle reached the end of the wall first, Selena crawling on her knees to stay low and out of sight. She peered around the corner.

Three ATVs with attached utility trailers were backed up against the open door. The orange light glowed above the scene, revealing a huddle of three men standing to the side, three others on each of the ATVs.

"Small haul tonight," one of the standing men said, reviewing a clipboard in his grip. "Should only be one trip."

Two other men waddled out of the back door, a fifty-five-gallon barrel held between them. Veins bulged from their necks, their jaws clenched as they hoisted the barrel onto the trailer. They disappeared back inside the building and returned thirty seconds later with a second barrel.

Arielle pulled Selena back and whispered into her ear. "Those barrels are homemade incinerators. They're definitely burning the trash in those."

"And they're taking them to the river to dump them?" Selena asked, her stomach twisting into knots. The situation was growing more disgusting with each passing moment.

"They must be," Arielle said. "Everything is making sense now. If we go back on the path toward the park, is there any way to get closer to the river?"

Selena shrugged. "I don't know. I've never gone that far out."

"That's fine. I wanted to get closer, but we'll probably see enough from here."

And so they watched for the next ten minutes while those same two men loaded twelve different barrels across the three trailers. All while the other three men stood by and watched with their arms crossed, smoking cigarettes, and howling laughter into the night sky.

Once the barrels were loaded, the man with the clipboard stepped forward and slapped the side of the nearest barrel. "Good shit tonight, fellas. Y'all good to dump these and call it a night. We'll start closing up in here."

Without another word, the two barrel loaders hopped onto the trailers just as the drivers kicked them back into gear and sped off, headlights revealing a dirt road leading all the way to the river ahead.

The three men flicked their cigarette butts and filed back inside. In the distance, the roaring engines from the ATVs had dulled, nearly inaudible. Three sets of headlights had indeed stopped at the riverbank, and they could only see the silhouettes moving around, dragging the barrels toward the water and tipping them to empty the contents.

"Jackpot," Arielle said. "There's our water pollution. It's all true. Let's get back home and figure out what's next."

# Chapter 23

July 27, 1978

It took Felix a few days to compile the database of all the people with motives to see Miracle Park shut down, along with those potentially taking money from Alexander Carter to protect it.

The list had one hundred and twenty-seven names on it. People from all corners of Hilburn, Nebraska.

Selena had suggested they inform Willow West of where and how she could get proof of the burnt trash dumping taking place behind the park. "Let her do our dirty work," she had said, suggesting Willow would take pictures and bring them to the attention of anyone who might listen. At least with pictures, she'd have solid proof and couldn't be ignored as easily.

Arielle considered this a good idea but wanted a better understanding of all the moving parts of this riddle. Willow could give the pictures to the wrong person and lose them forever. This wasn't the age of having digital copies of everything, and it cost good money to print multiple copies.

Besides, they needed a believable reason to just give this information to Willow. Arielle had only chatted with her once.

She might not even remember her. They could always leave an anonymous note in her mailbox, but how serious would Willow take that? And Arielle didn't want to put Willow in the line of danger by snooping around where she shouldn't be. It was against their ethics as Angels, plus Willow was a suspect in her own right.

"We need to look at the water company," Arielle said as they gathered around Felix's desk in their basement. He had papers splayed out across the desk, floor, and walls. Each with handwritten notes about different persons of interest. "I think a simple approach is warranted, considering how many suspects we have. We know the park is definitely polluting the town's drinking water. Willow has protested against this, and plenty of people believe her. That leaves the water department as the link in the middle. They would be the ones to investigate any claims and can also make claims go away."

"For the right price," Felix added.

"Exactly. And you think we should start at the top?"

Felix nodded, standing up and plucking a sheet of paper off the wall. "Yes. Now, I have limited information to base my theories, but Carter paid off the city clerk. There is no one higher in that department. For a man of his stature, I don't think he'd dare waste his time paying off someone who can be overruled by someone else. If he's buying city officials, he needs to buy the ones that have actual control. That leaves us with Terrance Copeland, the president and highest-ranking member of the Hilburn Water Department. We don't have pictures of anyone, so I don't know what he looks like. But we know where to find him. I located his home address, and we already know where he works."

Felix handed the sheet over to Arielle and watched her study it for a couple of minutes.

"Are you going to shake him down like you did that poor city clerk?" Felix asked, shooting a quick wink at Selena.

Arielle scoffed. "That was not a shakedown, and you know it. Dustin is on our side, even if he doesn't realize it. But for this water guy, yes, we might need to play dirty. I'd imagine he's even more loyal to Carter because he's probably receiving more money—his role is much more important in the grand scheme of things."

Felix shook his head. "That still doesn't make sense. Something bigger has to be at play. If this was truly about saving money, then Carter would just pay a trash service instead of forking out hundreds of thousands of dollars to these city officials. For someone as frugal as he is, the numbers aren't adding up."

Selena cleared her throat. "I've heard rumors about expansion projects for Miracle Park. Not sure how true any of it is, but could that be a factor?"

Arielle scratched her head. "I figured from the moment we heard how much he paid the city clerk, this was about more than even the park. Multiple people have mentioned Carter wants to own the entire city. But why? And why pollute the drinking water of the city he has to drink himself?"

"I'm sure we'll figure that all out in due time," Felix said, returning to the wall of notes. "For now, we can only follow one thread at a time."

"Well, let's get to it," Arielle said, pivoting around to start back up the stairs. "Who's coming with me?"

Selena and Felix exchanged a glance, Felix's gut wrenching with the anxiety that seemed to always accompany his joining Arielle in the field.

"I'm not going," Selena said. "This is a small town. I have to stay in my role, and there's no reason for me to be visiting the president of the water department."

"She's right," Arielle said over her shoulder. "Felix, you're coming with me."

* * *

They arrived at the home of Terrance Copeland fifteen minutes later, just after seven o'clock.

"Is this really where a city official lives?" Felix asked, eyes wide as they looked at the first tri-level home they had seen since arriving in Hilburn. They had pulled into the neighborhood called Christopher's Cove, a recent development built around a horseshoe-shaped lake. They had already constructed over fifty homes, all appearing to be occupied, judging by the indoor lights glowing around the block.

"I think this is where anyone with money lives in this city," Arielle said. "I'm surprised Carter doesn't have a place out here."

"Ha! Why pay a mortgage when you can live at your place of business?" Felix crossed his arms and shook his head. "See, I'm getting the gist of Mr. Carter—seems pretty straightforward."

"I think the real question is why is the president of the water department living here?" Arielle turned off the engine. "I suppose he could afford it if he pinched his pennies, but that doesn't appear to be the case." She nodded to the car in the driveway.

Felix examined it from a distance. "No penny pinching here. That's a 1976 Lincoln Continental, in addition to a convertible Mercedes. Both are luxury cars in these days. Mr. Copeland has serious money, but from where? Has to be Carter."

"Well, no shit. We know that much." Arielle chuckled. "I was thinking on the drive over, we need to play this differently than our encounter with the clerk. Let's claim to be working for Carter, and we'll say we're here because he has concerns about the protesters. Wants to make sure everything is safe from the side of the water department."

Felix felt the blood drain from his stomach. He hated pretending to be something he wasn't, and dreaded it even more when he had to pose as a powerful, intimidating persona. Sweat trickled down both sides of his face. Even though the sun was beginning its descent, the night still hovered around eighty-five degrees.

"Are we sure this is smart to do at his house?" Felix asked, gawking at the perfectly manicured front lawn.

"Of course. By us showing up randomly, and stating we're here on behalf of Carter, it tells Copeland we're legit. Why else would we know where he lives, unless Carter told us?"

A ball of spit formed in Felix's throat, and he forced it down. "I don't know. I just feel like we're playing with fire. There's always the chance Copeland talks to Carter about our visit. Then what?"

Arielle shrugged. "I'm not concerned. You forget the era we're in. Our faces aren't going to be captured on a Ring doorbell or some basic home security system. We have a lot more leeway. Unless Copeland takes a picture of us, how will he explain our presence to Carter? Besides, it doesn't appear Carter actually has people like the ones we're posing as. We're not in any actual danger. Do you think he's going to hunt us down himself? He wouldn't even know where to start."

Felix's face soured. He didn't like the thought of anyone hunting them down, especially a powerful man with unlimited funding.

"Just trust me, okay," Arielle said after Felix didn't respond, reaching over to place a hand on his shoulder. It comforted him in a way he didn't expect. Arielle's calming demeanor really could shine through in the most random of moments.

"Okay," Felix said, licking his lips with a rather dry tongue. "Let's go."

Arielle squeezed his shoulder before letting go and stepping out of the car. Felix joined her outside and drew in a deep breath of fresh air. The earthy aroma from the nearby lake filled his lungs. Crickets chirped their summer tunes, and further down the block, a group of pre-teens prepared for a friendly neighborhood game of hide-and-seek.

"Confidence is everything," Arielle said, starting up the paved pathway to the house's front door. "C'mon."

A couple of elm trees stood on both sides of the pathway, a tire swing hanging from one, plastic pink flamingos decorating the lawn in front of the other.

*Quite the middle class, middle America vibe going on here,* Felix thought, trudging along behind Arielle.

She strolled right up to the door and knocked on it with a heavy fist, taking a step back and crossing her hands in front of her stomach. Felix joined by her side but couldn't stop looking around the neighborhood. He really had enjoyed their stay in Hilburn and was delighted to find this more affluent neighborhood existed. He'd have to do more research on the city, but it was quietly moving up his list of potential places to move to.

The front door swung open, a tall, skinny Black man appearing in the doorway. His eyes studied them with a hesitant curiosity.

"Good evening, Mr. Copeland," Arielle said, and Felix heard all the confidence in the world in her voice. They didn't even know for certain they had the right house, but she just went for it all the same.

"Yes?" Copeland replied, arching an eyebrow as he looked Arielle up and down. "Can I help you with something?"

"Yes, sir, we are here on behalf of Mr. Carter and were hoping to discuss a pressing matter."

Arielle never broke eye contact, staring deep into the depths of the water department's president.

Copeland gulped, looked around the neighborhood, then rubbed his forehead in frustration. "Okay. My family is finishing dinner. Can you meet me in the backyard?" He nodded toward the side of the house. The neighborhood had no fences, just sprawling grass that connected everyone's lawns to one another.

"Yes, sir," Arielle said, nodding toward Copeland. "We'll meet you there."

Copeland offered an uncertain smile before stepping back and closing the door.

"Let's go," Arielle whispered, gesturing for Felix to walk to the side of the house.

"Are you sure about this?" he asked under his breath.

"Don't start your paranoia," Arielle snapped back. "Did you not see the way he reacted when I mentioned Carter's name? It was an obvious sign of obligation. He *wanted* to turn us away, but you don't turn away Alexander Carter. . . not when he let's you afford a nice big house like this."

"I feel like we're intruding. That's all."

They continued toward the backyard, passing a set of old patio furniture piled along the side of the house. The backyard was even more extravagant than the front. Two aspens stood a perfect ten feet apart, a hammock dangling between them. The newer patio set—that had rightfully replaced the old one—had a round black, wire table with six matching chairs tucked underneath. A firepit made from stones stood between the patio and the hammock, providing warmth no matter where you wanted to lounge around.

The back door slid open, and Copeland stepped out, having slipped into a pair of sandals. He grabbed a pair of glasses from his shirt pocket and pushed them up the bridge of his crooked nose.

"Let's have a seat," he said, gesturing to the table and pulling out a chair for himself. Arielle and Felix followed suit while Copeland crossed his hands on the table. "What were your names?" he asked, his voice sounding more confident than when he had opened the front door.

"Felix and Arielle," Felix said, realizing he hadn't spoken a word since they'd begun interacting with Copeland. "We work for Mr. Carter, and he's asked us to visit you this evening."

Arielle nodded, then added, "It's an urgent matter, Mr. Copeland, or we wouldn't have disturbed you at home."

Copeland waved them off. "It's fine, honestly. I prefer discussing these matters here instead of at my office."

"Certainly," Arielle said with an appreciative nod toward their host. "We won't be long, but Mr. Carter has asked us to check in with you regarding matters at the water department. He's growing increasingly worried about that Willow girl and her protests."

Copeland frowned and shook his head. "She just doesn't go away. As much of a pest as she is, Mr. Carter has nothing to worry about. She files a complaint at least once a week to my department, but we ignore those now. As long as she doesn't get her hands on concrete evidence, she has no case against the town's water supply."

Felix shifted in his seat and leaned forward. "She was shouting numbers at her last protest outside of Miracle Park. Numbers about increasing illnesses in Hilburn. We were at the protest—watching from a distance, of course—but people seemed to believe everything she said."

Copeland chuckled. "People will believe anything you tell them. Do you think any of those people did any additional research into the numbers? Willow could have made up any statistic and passed it on to them as truth. She's smarter than most people in this city, and she knows it. She uses that to her advantage and manipulates people into joining her cause."

"So, the numbers are false?" Arielle asked.

Copeland shrugged. "I have direct connections with the city's health department. Yes, there has been an increase in illnesses, but it's much smaller than what I'm sure Willow is telling everyone. Let me guess, she made it sound all doom and gloom?"

Felix nodded. "She's directly blaming the drinking water on the increase of hospitalizations for stomach-related matters. On the surface, it makes sense."

"Of course," Copeland said, leaning back and crossing his arms. "The truth is, we don't know where the illnesses are coming from. My family and I drink the same tap water as the rest of the city. None of us has gotten sick, and the water looks the same as it always has. Whatever Mr. Carter is dumping into the river is his business. We have one of the best filtration systems in the state, and it can definitely keep our water clean."

*That's what you think now,* Felix thought. *You don't even realize the millions of cancerous particles floating around in the water—and the air.*

He thought back to Arielle's story about the dozens of bags of trash they simply set on fire, presumably every day. Food containers, used tissues, and dirty diapers were just a few things Felix imagined getting torched in their homemade incinerators, all to burn into the ash getting dumped into the river feeding the town's water supply. *Think I'll only have bottled water the rest of our stay.*

"Dustin is working to get Willow off our backs," Arielle said. "But there's only so much he can do. Is there anyone else you can think of who might help us with this matter?"

Copeland ran a finger along the pattern of the wire table, eyes narrowed while he considered the question. "I can't think of anyone else. Dustin keeps Willow away as much as he can, and I make sure no one looks into the accusations against the water department. Mr. Carter had assured me since day one that whatever he's doing will always remain out of sight from the public eye. As long as that stays true, he has nothing to worry about. We have him covered here."

Arielle nodded while Felix balled a fist under the table. People put their faith and trust into their local government for matters as simple as clean drinking water. Yet, this sad excuse of a city official only looked the other way while a con man poisoned his town's water. All for the sake of money to afford this lavish lifestyle.

Arielle must have sensed his underlying rage because she kicked Felix in his shin under the table. "Thank you for your time, Mr. Copeland. We will relay this information back to Mr. Carter. Can he call you if he has any more questions?"

Copeland stood up, joints cracking and popping, "Of course. I always appreciate our conversations. Just assure him everything is fine. He has nothing to worry about."

# Chapter 24

July 31, 1978

Over the weekend, Arielle presented a new strategy to the team of Angels. She believed the tragedy involving Time Roller had to stem from someone's hatred toward Alexander Carter. Willow West was the primary suspect, yet they couldn't find an opportunity to bug her house thanks to a carousel of different visitors and roommates always being present.

"It has to be Willow," Arielle had said. "However, I'm getting the sense there are other crimes going on. Felix was right about Carter having an ulterior motive, aside from saving money. We know how much he's paying the city clerk, and it was plenty obvious he is paying Copeland even more. All that money is to cover something up, which makes me wonder if there are other people involved with Carter who shouldn't be. When this much money is being thrown around to corrupt city officials, it opens up so many more possibilities. If Carter misses a payment, who can't afford to have that happen? Are there collectors out there who would sabotage Carter?"

It seemed possible after the recent discussions they'd had with Copeland and Dustin. Arielle assigned Felix the task of bugging the homes and offices of Terrance Copeland and

Dustin Nash for this new week ahead, all while she planned to infiltrate Willow's inner circle. "We're going to inflict change from within," she explained. "I'm going to provide Willow with everything we've learned about Miracle Park and their trash disposal. I have no doubt she'll raise hell for the city officials involved in the coverup. She'll apply more pressure than we ever could."

While Arielle headed out to find Willow on Monday morning, Selena returned to work for the start of her next week in paradise.

She arrived just like any other day and punched in at the time clock in the main office building. Since she worked the earliest shift starting at 7:30, the office was usually empty. She peered down the hallway and saw Carter's door closed, but the lights on. He rarely came to the park this early, not usually strolling over until closer to nine. Not wanting to chance a verbal assault, Selena left the office building and found her team lead, Joy, sitting at the tables on the side of the building. Having worked with Joy for just over a week, Selena had already noticed she never wore the same outfit—something everyone else on the park staff seemed to do with their basic uniforms. At the very least, Joy picked different colors of polos to wear.

*She must have some fashion sense. Maybe I can relate to her on that topic.*

But she didn't have that opportunity now. Tears flowed from Joy's eyes as she glared furiously at her water bottle on the table.

Selena came to an abrupt stop, not wanting to interrupt, but the squeak from her sneakers was enough to draw Joy's attention.

Joy sniffled but didn't bother wiping the stream of tears off her cheeks. Her bloodshot eyes moved gradually from the water bottle to Selena. "Good morning," she croaked, promptly clearing her throat.

"Oh, hey, Joy," Selena said, wishing she could turn around. Silence hung between them for several seconds before Selena spoke again. "Is . . . everything okay?"

Joy kept taking long, dragged-out blinks, like she might doze off to sleep any moment. "Everything is wonderful," she said, the sarcasm not lost in translation.

"Do you want to talk about it?" Selena asked, taking an unsure step forward.

Joy looked Selena up and down and wrinkled her nose.

"I probably shouldn't," Joy said. "But what the hell? Come sit down."

Joy shuffled over to allow Selena the space to sit next to her on the table's bench. With a moment of hesitation—mainly for not wanting to get seen sitting around by Carter—Selena threw caution to the wind and sat down.

"What's going on?" she asked.

Joy kept her gaze focused on her water bottle, and Selena noticed purple marks on Joy's forearm, four next to each other in the pattern of fingers.

Joy glanced over at Selena and followed her stare to those markings. She pursed her lips to the point they turned white. "Battle marks," she said, letting out a long exhale and shaking her head.

Selena's stomach churned at the sight of the bruises. She spoke just above a whisper. "Joy, who did this to you? Are you in an abusive relationship?"

Joy examined the marks on her arm like she had just noticed

them for the first time, then her lips spread into a maniac grin, followed by an uncontrollable fit of mad laughter. "Yeah. I'm in an abusive relationship alright. With the god damn devil."

Her face snapped back into form as fresh tears oozed, the moist trails glistening in the morning sunlight. "Joy," Selena said, reaching out a hand to caress her team lead on the shoulder. "You can get out of this. I can help you."

Joy jerked her head from side to side. "If it was only that simple. This isn't some abusive boyfriend or anything like that—no, no, no. I'm single and live alone."

Selena frowned. "I don't understand. Who did this then?"

Joy looked over her shoulder and nodded toward the office building.

"Carter?!" Selena gasped in a whisper.

Joy held up her pointer finger to her lips to tell Selena to hush. She whispered in response. "Don't use any names when we're in the park. He asked me to come in early for a meeting today. Turns out there were issues with one of the rides at closing last night, and he got a bit angry."

"You weren't even working last night," Selena said. "How could he blame you?"

"That man will blame whoever he can."

"That doesn't make this okay. We can report him, you know. There are laws against this."

Joy snickered and shook her head, taking one look over her shoulder to ensure they were still alone. "There are no laws that apply to that man in there. You're sorely mistaken if you believe otherwise. I'm fine, really. I'm just going to finish out the summer and disappear from this town forever."

Selena thought of her real life—her Real Time—decades in the future from this exact moment. The screams of those women abused over the years, who forever held their traumatic secrets close to their hearts, echoed in her mind, weighing down on her conscience. She needed to remember this was a different time where not everything was so clear cut.

"You deserve better than this," Selena said, rubbing her hand up and down Joy's back.

Joy shrugged, blinking away some tears. "Perhaps I don't," she said in a deflated tone. "Maybe I'm a magnet for this sort of thing. Maybe it's even my destiny. My dad beat me and my siblings when we were kids. I've had two abusive boyfriends—not physical, but verbal, if it even matters. It's like they've primed me to work for Alexander Carter my whole life. A verbally and physically abusive boss with all the power in town."

Joy snorted away the mucus forming in her nose, closed her eyes, and planted her head on the table. Her shoulders trembled while she cried some more.

"Joy," Selena said, "there are options. You don't have to put up with this. It's not ideal, but why not find a different job?"

Joy raised her head back up, a tinge of evil swimming behind her eyes. "I'm not quitting. All I wanted was to work at Miracle Park this summer. It's prestigious. And I actually love my job. I enjoy every aspect of the work itself. It's just . . . *him.* If he didn't exist, I just might call this my dream job. Instead of a dream, it's hell every day."

"No job is worth taking a beating," Selena said, removing her hand from Joy's back. "Swallow your pride and move on. He doesn't win if you leave. *You* lose by staying. Clearly."

Joy giggled, the sound making Selena uneasy. "I don't

expect you to understand, but I'm not leaving this job. I've put way too much work in this summer to just walk away from it. I can make it to the end of the year—I'll just have to avoid him at all costs."

"And what if he calls you into a meeting again? You can't just blow that off—he'll fire you."

Joy threw her head back and laughed. "Look, I know you're still new, so may not have everything figured out yet. Yes, he fires a ton of people, but haven't you noticed he never fires those who actually keep this place running? Even through all the disagreements and shouting, he knows who is important for the bottom line. I'm one of those people."

Selena stood up, growing infuriated with the whole situation. She jabbed a finger into Joy's chest, startling her out of her seat. "You *are* important to this place, but that doesn't justify you accepting this treatment."

Joy glared at Selena, fists balled up at her sides as she took a step forward.

Selena put up her hand as a stop sign. "I highly recommend you don't take a swing at me. That doesn't end well for you."

Joy pursed her lips, her mud-colored eyes boring into Selena. She drew a deep breath and blew the exhale directly into Selena's face. Joy nodded and took a step back, crossing her hands in front of her waist. "You're right, and I apologize. You're only trying to help. Once again, I let that fat, greedy pig get the best of me. So thank you."

"For what, exactly?" Selena asked, stuffing her hands into her pockets. Even after three weeks on the mission, she still reached for the phantom cell phone in her pocket at least once an hour.

"For calming me down." Joy returned to her seat and picked

a chip of paint off the table's surface. "You walked in to quite the situation this morning. Can't say I would've handled it as well as you. But your calmness is just what I needed because I was talking myself into going back into that office and putting my hands around that bastard's throat. And let me tell you, there is *nothing* I'd rather do than squeeze that throat until the sun goes down."

Joy laughed again, like she was the only one who understood the joke.

"Well, we can't do that now," Selena said in the best playful voice she could muster.

"Of course not," Joy said, drumming her finger on the table. "I have complete faith he'll get what he deserves in due time. All we need is a little patience."

# Chapter 25

Across town, Arielle had a change of heart. She couldn't drag Willow into this matter. While it seemed convenient to hand over valuable information to Willow and let her run loose, that was too much tinkering with the past for Arielle's comfort.

That simple act could set into motion a chain of events that might unravel the entire mission before their eyes. Besides, Willow was far from being cleared as a suspect herself. Their interactions with Willow needed to remain minimal and intentional.

Arielle had stayed home and waited for Felix to finish getting ready for the day. They planned to head back to Copeland's house for what would hopefully be a successful bugging. The water department's president was guaranteed to be away during the workday—they just needed to get lucky and hope Mrs. Copeland had somewhere to be with the kids.

And they were in luck.

Arielle and Felix parked two houses down the block on the opposite side of the street from the Copeland residence. Arielle had her binoculars to watch the house from a distance.

A typical summer morning graced the neighborhood of Christopher's Cove—landscaping trucks lined the sidewalks, groups of men grabbing lawn mowers, weed whackers, and various sprays from the truck bed. A handful of elderly couples went for a casual stroll around the block, stopping at the lake for a peaceful view and to feed the ducks chunks of bread.

"It's gonna be hard if all these people are out," Felix said. "It's a pretty busy neighborhood."

"We have nothing to worry about," Arielle said, lowering her binoculars from the young brother and sister practicing on their roller skates at the far end of the block. "Most of these people will be back in their houses by ten o'clock. Gets too hot."

It was already a few minutes past nine when Arielle pointed this out, and they watched as everyone retreated to their homes over the next hour. Felix took their time together to thank Arielle for changing her approach with Willow. He agreed it was too risky to essentially have her working on the mission without realizing it. He feared her involvement could speed up the sabotaging of Time Roller and catch the Angels off guard. They had their target date and couldn't risk having it change based on their own actions.

At five minutes before ten o'clock, they watched the Copeland garage door slide open. Mrs. Copeland wore a flowing summer dress and sun hat. A boy and a girl, around ten and eight from what Arielle could tell through the binoculars, were dressed in swimwear. The boy had a beach bag full of towels slung over his shoulder and tossed it onto the passenger seat as he settled into the back with his sister.

"We're in business," Arielle said. "Looks like they'll be gone for at least a couple hours."

"All I need is ten minutes," Felix said with a wide grin.

Arielle arched an eyebrow. "Why do you seem so giddy about

breaking into this guy's house? Normally, you're having a panic attack just before."

Felix chuckled. "Well, yes, I still have my usual nerves. But this one is meaningful to me. Mission aside, Terrance Copeland is doing horrible things. People are getting sick now, but a lot aren't. Those who aren't will keep drinking the water, and eventually they're going to develop cancers and who knows what else. This whole town can get wiped out because Copeland wants a few extra dollars to line his bank account with. It's just wrong and I can't wait to see him taken down."

Arielle heard the passion in Felix's voice. They had dealt with sex traffickers, murderers, and bank robbers. Yet, a city official holding a town's drinking water hostage set him off.

"That's fine and all," Arielle said. "But remember, that's not part of our mission at all."

Felix shrugged. "Oh well, I'm gonna pull an Arielle Lucila and take the matter into my hands. Shoot first and ask questions later, right?"

The car with Mrs. Copeland and her children pulled out of the garage. Arielle sighed. "I never shoot first. Don't get that confused. I take matters into my own hands, yes, and I respect your enthusiasm for this matter. As long as your mission work is done, I won't be getting in your way. Do whatever you see fit with this Copeland matter. Just don't jeopardize anything regarding our reason for being here."

Felix nodded, eyes following the Copelands as they disappeared from sight. "That sounds fair to me. For the record, I'm not actually planning on doing anything. I'm just hoping our work on the mission will bring the whole thing crashing down. Hopefully, it'll be more than Carter who takes the fall.

He seems like a rat. I'm sure once he's exposed, he'll throw everyone under the bus. Shall we head over?"

They scanned the neighborhood once more. A few of the elderly residents were still making their way back home or tending to their gardens, but none of the Copelands' direct neighbors were outside.

"Let's go," Arielle said, pushing open her door.

Felix slipped on a pair of sunglasses before following her down the sidewalk. They blended in just fine, looking like any of the other couples out for their morning walk. Any curious neighbors peering out their windows wouldn't notice the holstered gun hiding under Arielle's baggy shirt. Felix had a small tote bag slung over his shoulder, but nothing that warranted suspicion.

They reached the front of the house and exchanged nods. There had been no other cars in the garage, and the house was dark inside. "Let's go through the back," Arielle whispered, and started down the same path they had taken last time to the backyard.

What they hadn't noticed during their last visit was the dirt path that crossed behind each property on this side of the block. The path split every backyard from the lake and provided a scenic view of the water for anyone out for a stroll. A couple of canoes floated in the distance but were much too far to pay them any attention.

"I'll hang back," Arielle said. "Go in through the back door and do what you need." She paused and studied a tool shed at the opposite end of the yard, nodding to it. "I'm gonna snoop around there once you're inside. Won't hurt."

"Did you bring the radios?" Felix asked, taking a quick peek into his bag.

"Nope. We won't need them. Just work quickly. If anyone walks on this path, I'll talk them away."

"Deal. Wish me luck."

Arielle grinned. "I wouldn't dare. You don't need it."

Felix smirked before turning away and starting toward the back door. Arielle drifted out toward the dirt path, looking both ways for any potential neighbors wandering around. The coast was clear except for a couple of geese waddling down the pathway. The canoes in the lake had drifted even further away.

Arielle looked over her shoulder and saw Felix slipping through the back door, closing it gently behind him. She started for the shed; its gray siding faded from the constant abuse by the sun. Otherwise, it stood in great shape, the lone door ajar.

*Must not have anything valuable if they don't even lock it.*

Arielle swung the door open, the hinges creaking in the quiet morning. A handful of moths fluttered out of the shed, Arielle waving them off as she stepped inside. The shed was ten-by-ten, with hooks mounted to the walls, shelves on the right side, a table on the left.

The hooks held various tools—saws, levelers, garden hoses. The shelves had the bigger ones—leaf blowers, a shop vac, bags of grass seed and fertilizer.

Arielle had to push a lawn mower out of her way to get deeper into the shed. A thin layer of dirt covered nearly every object in the shed, as was the case with thoroughly used yard tools.

Everything had this natural dust except the pair of bolt cutters lying on the table. They even had the tag still taped around one handlebar.

*Why does he have a set of brand-new bolt cutters?*

Yokota had mentioned all someone would need to wear down the pull cable on the roller coaster was a few hours and a pair of bolt cutters.

The tool sat on the table and seemed to glow like it had been sent from the heavens. Various junk surrounded the tool on the table—a box of magazines, an old six-pack of beer bottles, and a shoebox filled with packs of cigarettes.

*Copeland definitely comes out here for his alone time*, Arielle thought, wanting to pick up the bolt cutters but not wanting to risk tampering with potential evidence. Was this the tool responsible for derailing Time Roller and destroying all those innocent lives? Bolt cutters had a distinct purpose—to cut through heavy-duty metal. The timing of this discovery was most questionable. They were less than four weeks away from Time Roller flying off the rails, and here was a tool, brand new amid everything else used, in the possession of a man involved with the corrupt activity of Alexander Carter.

*But why would Copeland want to destroy the roller coaster? What does he gain from that?*

Arielle mulled over this question for the next five minutes, unable to break her trance from the bolt cutters, like they had some sort of hold over her.

She couldn't come up with any viable reasons Copeland would sabotage Miracle Park. If anyone in town had the most to gain from Carter's success, it was Copeland. He owed his entire lavish life to the conniving businessman. If Carter left town, the payments would stop. Copeland wouldn't be able to maintain his family's existing lifestyle off his water department salary.

Could Copeland be working with someone else? Did someone steal his bolt cutters to commit the act of wearing down the pull cable? They left the shed door open, after all, and anyone passing by on the trail could swoop in for a quick second and have a plethora of free tools at their disposal.

A knock came from the door behind Arielle, causing her to jump and spin around, hand immediately grabbing the grip of her pistol. Felix appeared in the doorway, hands raised.

"Simmer down there," he said, eyes wide with fear.

"Christ, Felix," Arielle gasped, catching the breath she had momentarily lost. "You can't just sneak up on a person like that."

Felix laughed. "I knocked. What else did you want me to do?"

Arielle waved him off. "Don't worry about it. I was just deep in thought. I have a lot on my mind."

"Is everything okay?" he asked, concern slipping into his voice.

"I've been a bit out of it this mission. Found out my grandma is having some health issues. We can discuss that another time. I found something. Look."

She pointed at the bolt cutters and saw the wheels immediately begin turning in Felix's mind.

"That's not what I think it is," he replied, eyes glued to the tool. "Is it?"

Arielle crossed her arms and paced in a small circle. "It could be. I can't make the connection between Copeland and a closed-down Miracle Park. But there it is . . . a brand-new bolt cutter."

"Well, his house is now fully bugged. Maybe we'll find something out."

"That was fast." Arielle was still shaken up, her eyes

bouncing around the backyard behind Felix.

"Was a straightforward job for once. Let's get out of here. I hate lingering once the job is done."

He turned and stepped out of the shed, Arielle taking one more mental picture of the bolt cutters before following him out.

# Chapter 26

The rest of the week passed in a blur with little excitement. After plenty of discussion, the Angels grew comfortable narrowing their list of potential suspects down to three. Upon finding the bolt cutters in Copeland's shed, Felix believed the water department's president needed to be followed. He volunteered to sit outside of Copeland's house each night to listen to the live feed of activity coming from within. He only needed to be parked within a three-hundred-foot radius and chose a different house on the block each night to camp in front of.

Selena felt Joy needed additional tailing after she expressed her faith that Carter would 'get what he deserves.'

"She has an obvious motive," Selena had explained. While they agreed that much was true, they wanted more to justify following Joy. She was far from the only employee who hated Carter. They could easily find another dozen people who shared the same sentiments as Joy Gillespie. Selena vowed to get closer to Joy but was finding it difficult after their moment of bonding on Monday morning.

Joy liked to slip away once she got involved in a conversation with Selena, using excuses around the park. If she could only get her talking outside of work, they might uncover something useful.

And for Arielle, her entire focus was on Willow West. She had spent the weekdays dropping by the plant nursery where Willow worked, hiding behind shelves or pretending to browse different plants.

She never understood how some people could fill their entire home with plants and treat them like pets. Arielle had lived by herself for years and hadn't once entertained the thought of bringing so much as a single flower home. Once you start talking to plants, you might as well check yourself into the nearest loony bin. She believed this firmly and avoided any such possibility.

Despite being hated by the entire Hilburn government, Willow was a rather normal, contributing member of society. She took pride in her work, offering top-notch customer service to anyone needing help. Her patience and grace when helping the elderly guests with their laundry list of questions made Arielle wonder if she really had it in her to sabotage Time Roller.

Arielle had even witnessed Willow scoop up a spider with her bare hands to keep it from getting squashed on the nursery's main walkway. Who would save a spider, then turn around and kill humans?

*Maybe she didn't mean to kill anyone,* Arielle considered. *Maybe she had a different plan entirely. And that plan...derailed.*

As much as Willow spent her time on the weekends sticking it to "the man," she addressed her boss, an older gentleman by the name of Wayne, with the respect and gratitude you'd expect of a subordinate worker bee.

Following Willow after work proved just as boring as spending the days inside the nursery.  She always stopped at the grocery store to pick up whatever she planned to cook for dinner—lots of chicken and veggies—before continuing home and parking next to the other half dozen cars lining her block. She'd then disappear inside, and Arielle watched through the living room window while Willow sat back on the couch with her friends and passed around a bong for ten minutes. Most days, the skunk-like stench carried to Arielle's car, the scent taking her back home to present-day Denver.

On Friday morning, now twenty days away from the tragedy, Arielle pulled up to the house two lots down from Willow's—just as she had done every day this week—and was surprised to find her not getting into her car at 7:45. Willow had so far proven prompt with her daily routine, so Arielle naturally grew concerned when the young activist hadn't shown her face by 8:30.

The curtains were drawn, but Arielle could still see the shadows of people moving around within the house.

*Not working today?*

Another forty-five minutes passed when Willow finally stepped out of the front door, not dressed in her work uniform, which was a yellow polo shirt with the Earl May Garden Center emblem on the front, and their cheesy slogan on the back: *Gardening reflects your heart.*

Instead, Willow wore a pair of raggedy jeans and a white tank top, a daisy sticking out from the hairband pulling back her wavy brown locks.

*That's the real Willow,* Arielle thought, watching as she trudged to her car parked on the sidewalk, Bohemian purse slung over one shoulder.

Willow slipped behind the wheel of her light blue Volkswagen Beetle, and drove off, not going anywhere near the direction of her work.

Arielle followed her through town until they ended up in familiar territory. Willow parked her car in one of the visitor spots outside the Hilburn Water Department. She sat in the car for five minutes before stepping out, but when she did, others came crawling out from their cars, which were already parked, some around the corner of the building. They looked like an intrusion of cockroaches flocking to a trail of bread crumbs in an abandoned house.

Arielle wasn't one to stereotype any group of people, but she was having a hard time telling apart any of these dozen hippies. She only knew Willow because she was somehow the only one not wearing a pair of sunglasses.

One of her colleagues had a stack of signs and started handing them out to everyone else in the group. Willow chatted with a couple others, keeping her arms crossed as she shifted her weight from one leg to the other. Over the next twenty minutes, more cars pulled up and more people ambled over from somewhere around the block.

*Well, this is the surprise I didn't know I needed,* Arielle thought as the group swelled to north of thirty people. *A protest at the water department less than three weeks away from someone sabotaging Miracle Park.*

Arielle had parked on the opposite side of the street and had to watch all of this unfold through her rear-view mirrors. The group of protesters, now equipped with their signage, huddled tightly together, Willow in the center of it all. Arielle couldn't hear anything from her distance, but once the huddle broke apart with a raucous cheer, everyone started marching back and forth on the sidewalk, chanting, "We. Want. Clean.

Water."

The chant was slow and emphasized each word as if they had a special meaning. A hand-holding couple passed by in front of Arielle's car, prompting her to slouch in her seat. They paid her no attention as they hurried across the street to join the fun.

Willow impressed Arielle. After tailing her all week, she had somehow organized this protest without anyone else knowing about it. And this wasn't a publicity stunt like the protests outside of Miracle Park, where every visitor could see them. No, this was in the heart of Hilburn on a Friday morning when most residents were at work. This protest didn't need to attract new followers and garner the attention of a curious public—they directed it to the water department and no one else.

Willow confirmed as much, having been handed a megaphone, which she pointed toward the water building and shouted. "How many people have to get sick before Hilburn addresses the water crisis? Are you really going to stand by and let our city die? Every single person relies on this town's water. Our children. Our elderly. Our farmers. We demand answers. And we demand change. Terrance Copeland must be removed as president so we can have someone who actually cares about our drinking water."

The group shouted in unison, "Fire Copeland! Fire Copeland! Fire Copeland!"

The protest had started off quietly enough, but the energy had ramped up since Willow got on the megaphone. They all kept chanting to fire Copeland, waving their signs in the air, many of which read the same thing they were chanting.

A police car crept down the street, but never stopped. The

officer had his window rolled down and studied the protest, but continued one more block before parking in front of the police station.

From the second-floor window overlooking the sidewalk, Arielle saw Terrance Copeland standing with his arms crossed, shaking his head. He wore a suit, as did the two other men standing by his side. They gawked and pointed, and one even laughed while they did so.

Willow saw them watching and pointed up to the window, pressing the megaphone back to her lips. "Why don't you come out of your tower and talk to us, Copeland? We just want an explanation. Don't be a coward!"

Copeland remained stone-faced in the window before eventually turning around and disappearing from sight. The protesters showered the building with boos before returning to their chants. The energy surrounding them bumped up a level—Arielle could sense as much from the car. Their chanting grew so loud it drowned out whatever Willow was barking into the megaphone.

Cars drove by, curiosity slowing them to a crawl as they tried to figure out what was going on. A group of five police officers were making their way over on foot from the station one block down.

Dread swirled throughout Arielle. The last thing they needed was an altercation with the police department, which was allegedly owned by Carter. She understood the frustration Willow had fighting for her cause. If the police could stomp a simple protest out—via the man she was protesting—how would she ever make progress?

But the officers arrived with no sign they were doing anything besides keeping the peace. They stood together twenty feet away from the marching protesters, arms either crossed or hands gripping their collars in that typical cop stance. Two of them leaned against the building and sipped from their cups of coffee.

When the chanting suddenly stopped and shifted to another storm of booing, Arielle stepped out of her car for a better view.

The jeering was directed at Copeland. To Arielle's bewilderment, the water department's president had actually stepped out of the office building, hands raised to quiet the rowdy crowd.

They didn't stop for thirty seconds, Copeland nodding along as if he expected the vile reception.

"Let him speak!" Willow repeatedly pleaded into the megaphone. The crowd finally fell quiet, and Willow waved Copeland to join her in the middle of the circle. He kept his hands elevated and spoke with the conviction of a minister delivering an impassioned sermon.

"Residents of Hilburn," he said. "We see you. We hear you. Our team has investigated your complaints about the drinking water and has found nothing. Please take your energy elsewhere—we have done what we can. But without an actual issue, there is nothing for us to address."

"LIAR!" someone from the crowd shouted, prompting others to copycat.

"You're in bed with Alex Carter!" another screamed, earning a round of cheers and laughter.

Willow lowered her megaphone and addressed her group directly. "We don't act like this. We wanted to speak with Mr. Copeland, and he has kindly come outside for us. No name calling or accusations—stick to the facts."

Murmurs spread through the crowd, many of the protesters shaking their heads at the news they needed to behave themselves.

"Thank you, Ms. West," Copeland said, finally lowering his hands and clasping them in front of his chest. "I want everyone to rest assured we take all complaints regarding the town's drinking water seriously. We are aware of the increasing illnesses hitting Hilburn over these past couple of months, but our team has not found any issues tying it to the water."

A tall man with a blond ponytail stepped forward, pushing his sunglasses up the bridge of his nose. "With all due respect, Mr. Copeland, that doesn't check out. Our own doctors in Hilburn believe tainted drinking water is the cause. We've accrued a list of their signatures on this petition." The man held up a clipboard.

"I see," Copeland said. "And what is the petition, exactly?"

"It's them agreeing the issues our residents have been facing are tied to bad water. We trust their expertise and hope you can, too."

"The doctors are more than welcome to join us in the lab to examine our water," Copeland said. "I will re-open the investigation, but I can't make any promises. I've had no issues with the tap water, and my family drinks it every day. While we'll do what we can, I must urge you to look for other causes behind the illnesses. That is all I have time to address today. Thank you."

Copeland waved at the crowd, who promptly returned to booing him. He started back toward the office building when Willow chased him down, forcing herself between him and the door. Arielle was too far to know what was being said, but Willow spoke with conviction. She held out an open palm and kept jabbing her finger into it, emphasizing whatever point she was making. Copeland nodded along and said a few words back before patting Willow on the shoulder and shuffling around her to get inside the safety of the building.

The police officers turned and left. Willow only stared at the spot on her shoulder Copeland had just touched, disgusted.

# Chapter 27

Later that evening, Felix sat in his car across the street from Copeland's house. He plugged his pair of headphones into the receiver and cranked the volume full blast so he could hear the live feed without having to put them over his head. The clunky vintage headphones rested on his lap, and he fidgeted with them while waiting for Copeland to arrive home.

Each time a car drove by or a neighbor sauntered past his car, Felix had to fight his heart from leaping out of his throat. They trained him in every aspect of stealth, yet none of that helped him sit in his car in the middle of broad daylight. It would be different had it been a bigger neighborhood, but this particular block—West Camino Street—appeared to have neighbors who all knew each other. They were the rich and elite of the small town of Hilburn, and Felix had never felt more out-of-place while on a mission.

The rest of the Copelands were home. Around the side of the house, he saw the two kids kicking a ball in the backyard. Felix had bugged nearly every room in the house and now listened as Mrs. Copeland hummed along to "Three Times A Lady" by the Commodores blasting through the radio while tending to three different pots on the kitchen stove.

*Mrs. Copeland is looking for some lovin' tonight,* Felix thought, checking his watch. It was 5:15 and Terrance was nowhere to be seen. *Is he not coming straight home?*

Copeland had been home no later than 5:15 every night this week, and Felix didn't understand what could hold him up later on a Friday evening. Maybe Willow had really gotten to him, and he needed to blow off steam at a bar. He ran through every possibility his mind allowed, including slashed tires by the hands of a disorderly protester.

After Arielle had filled him on the happenings at the water department earlier in the morning, Felix was convinced tonight was the night Copeland would finally discuss the matter of his scheme with his wife.

After Felix had grown uncomfortably antsy, Copeland's cherry-red convertible Mercedes turned onto the block. It was another hot day, so naturally, he drove with the top down, taking his sweet time pulling into the garage.

Felix's panic waned, allowing his focus to kick back into gear. The rest of the world fell into the background as he narrowed his attention on the sound coming from the headphones.

A door creaked open and slammed shut, followed by the hollow thud of footsteps.

"Hey, honey!" Mrs. Copeland cried out. "How was your day?"

Felix shifted upright in his seat, nearly salivating for Copeland's response.

They exchanged a kiss before Terrance replied. "Oh, I've had better."

*Yes, he's going to talk about what happened.*

"Rough day?" Mrs. Copeland asked.

Terrance sighed, and Felix could only imagine him rubbing his forehead in frustration. "I wish it was only a rough day, Glo."

*Glo?* Felix wondered. *Gloria?*

"Don't tell me it was Mr. Carter," Mrs. Copeland said. "What did he do now?"

"I wish. At least I know how to handle him—by ignoring whatever he says. I'm afraid not, though. It was that Willow girl. She organized a protest outside of the office this morning. I counted thirty-eight people from my office window. It was big."

Mrs. Copeland smacked her lips. "Oh, Terry, don't pay any attention to that little girl—"

"She knows," Terrance cut off his wife. "She has proof."

"Proof?! What kind of proof?"

"I don't know about physical proof, but she told me everything only Carter has told me before. Said she knows the people at Miracle Park are burning the trash and dumping the ashes into the river. She even described how they take the barrels full of ash to the lake using four-wheelers. She claims to have pictures of this but didn't show me any."

"And you're sure that's the truth? She wasn't bluffing to get a reaction from you?"

Felix could hear the trepidation increasing in Mrs. Copeland's voice, suggesting she knew all the dirty work her husband had been involved with.

"I don't think it's a bluff, Glo," Terrance said, deflated. "Those details were too specific. Had she just said the park was dumping trash in the river, then okay, that could just be an obvious guess to fit her cause. But the burning of it and dumping the ashes—that's all true. She *knows*."

"So, what are we supposed to do? Can she turn you in? Does it even matter? Carter has everyone in town paid off. Right?" Mrs. Copeland sounded like she had just been punched in the gut.

Felix saw Terrance through the front window, his back facing the world outside.

"Slow down, Glo," Terrance said in a rather calm tone. "There are so many moving parts to this thing, even if Willow turned me in to the police department, it won't get very far."

"Oh, is that right?" Mrs. Copeland's voice shifted from dread to fury in a split second. Felix could picture her crossing her arms, giving Terrance a look of death. "Just like you said there was no way they could even find any of this out?"

Terrance sighed. "Look, it was all supposed to be a secret. I have no idea how Willow found out these details. That's not even important right now. Mr. Carter has checks and balances in place to make sure nothing gets pinned on us."

"Ha!" Mrs. Copeland let out a sarcastic laugh. "Not important right now? I beg your pardon. You know damn well it's important. If it was supposed to be so impossible for her to find out, then how did she do it? Is she following you? Does she sit outside of Carter's castle and wait to follow him?"

"Gloreen, that's enough," Terrance said, frustration touching his words. Felix jotted down Gloreen as Mrs. Copeland's actual name. "You're jumping to conclusions, and it's not helping."

"The hell it isn't!" Gloreen shouted. She lowered her tone, as if not wanting the kids out back to hear. "I warned you at the beginning that none of this would be worth it. Alexander Carter is a *thug*. A mobster. Don't stand there and act like he isn't. He's paid off anyone of importance in this town."

"Exactly, Glo," Terrance pleaded. "Can't you see? That's *why* everything is going to be okay."

"It's never okay, Terry. Dammit, can't *you* see? Yes, rich people get away with all the bad things they do. But they never truly escape it. It all catches up with them, eventually. It just takes one person in this city to turn their back on him, and his time is up. And I know it will happen, because people in Hilburn are *good*. And honest. It might be hard to remember that after all the corruption this man has brought upon us, but it's still true."

"What do you want from me?" Terrance asked, his voice suggesting he was fed up with this discussion. "What can make you feel better about all of this?"

Silence hung between them for half a minute before Gloreen replied. "Call him and tell him you're out. He can stop his monthly payments and leave our family in peace."

"We can't do that, Glo. Without that money, we can't live here. We'd have to sell both cars and downgrade to something different."

"Yes, Terry, I'm aware of that. It's called owning you. Mr. Carter *owns* you. He gave you the life of your dreams and knows how hard it would be to walk away from it. Sometimes you have to leave behind what's easy to do what is right. You are at that crossroads now, and I hope you choose correctly. Because me and the kids won't visit you in prison when it all comes crashing down."

Terrance laughed. "Prison? Glo, you're really overreacting right now. No one is going to prison."

Gloreen sighed. "You may be right, but this whole situation will collapse. You watch. And even if you don't end up in jail, you'll still be in your own prison. You want to run for mayor one day still, right?"

"Of course."

"How will you ever do that if it's forever known about the illegal activities you did for Mr. Carter? This town will return to its honorable ways, and you won't win a single vote. Not even mine."

"You don't mean that."

Gloreen laughed. "Test me and find out. I don't even know who you are anymore. What happened to the man I fell in love with? The old Terrance would have been fine living in a small house, driving a basic car. Because he believed in the strength of his family. As long as we're together, we can get through anything. Remember telling me that after I lost my job at the cleaners?"

"I'm still that way, Glo," Terrance said, shame smothering every word.

"Haaaaa! That man is dead. Replaced by another mindless, greedy fool. You fell in love with all that money and never looked back. You don't even know the pain and suffering you've put me through, do you? Early mornings and late nights. Whenever we talk, you only want to discuss Mr. Carter's problems and all the money he pays you. 'Glo, I made another fifteen K from those investments last week. Glo, can you take the Benz in for an oil change? Get the *premium* oil so the car runs as smooth as she always has.' Who the fuck talks like that? Do you hear the things you say?! When's the last time we've even discussed *our* children?"

Gloreen's anger gave way to crying. Felix sat frozen in the car, holding his breath like he was hiding in the house to eavesdrop on this conversation.

Terrance cleared his throat. "I'm sorry, Glo. But as the man of this house, I have to stand by my word. I'm fully committed to Mr. Carter. He will endorse me for mayor when the time comes. That agreement is already in place. Everything I've done is to improve our lives as a family. I'm sorry if you can't see that, but we're never going back to being poor. We *deserve* this life. Our kids deserve it."

"You won't get away with it forever," Gloreen replied through a groggy throat. "Your job and reputation are at risk. Not only will the choice be made for you to stop your dealings with Mr. Carter, you're going to bring so much shame to our family's name that we'll have no choice but to leave this city. I wanted to raise our kids here—this is a beautiful city that has everything we need. And you can't see past all your greed just how much you're destroying us."

"I love you, Gloreen. And I love our kids. I have faith we'll move beyond this little blip. Stop worrying."

"I'm done with this conversation," Gloreen said harshly. "Go tell the kids it's time to wash up for dinner."

Silence filled the airwaves for the next minute. Eventually, Terrance Copeland strolled out to his backyard to call in the kids. Felix stopped the tapes and drove off.

# Chapter 28

Arielle was the first one awake on Sunday morning. She was hellbent on getting closer to Willow and arrived outside her house by eight o'clock. No movement came from within until 9:30 when three women and a man strolled out of the home, their hair frazzled messes. The man stumbled, shielding his eyes from the sun with his hands, groaning with each pained step he took.

*Hungover, are you?* Arielle thought, noticing a huddle of beer cans on the porch railing. *Must have been one hell of a party.*

The four friends piled into a car parked three spaces in front of Arielle. She remembered college parties and how sloppy they had gotten. Belligerent drunk boys either groping girls or getting in fights with each other thanks to untethered testosterone. Then you had the drunk girls, who either went into bedrooms with the gropers or hung back to gossip and spread rumors about everyone at the party. The whole situation was always toxic and meaningless.

Arielle shook her head, looking back on those times as the moment she started developing a keen sense of observation. Sure, drunk college students were much easier to predict compared to the high-level criminals she now hunted down for work, but everyone has to start somewhere.

Willow apparently had just as much fun the prior night. She didn't step outside of her house until 11:30, leaving Arielle baking in the car as the day warmed up. Willow was more together than her friends from earlier, dressed in a sun hat and red dress covered with sunflowers. Another woman accompanied her as they got into Willow's Beetle and drove four blocks east.

They parked at Dusters, a breakfast and lunch specialty diner that closed at three in the afternoon. The restaurant had windows all around, so Arielle could see inside the entire building at once. She parked toward the back of the lot, waited for Willow and her friend to go inside to be seated, then pulled up to an open spot with a better view.

They settled in a booth toward the back, near the restrooms.

*Okay,* Arielle thought. *The bathroom helps my cause. I got this.*

She stepped out of her car and walked through the diner's entrance, confidence bursting. There was a host stand with no one present, a sign on the front that welcomed Arielle to seat herself, so she took one half of a two-person booth along the window overlooking the parking lot. She had considered sitting closer to Willow's table but didn't want to seem too obvious—or awkward—when she "accidentally" bumped into her.

"Good morning, darling," a waitress shuffled over to Arielle and greeted. "Coffee?"

Arielle read *Lucy* on the server's nametag. She wore a red and white striped apron, a steaming coffee pot in hand.

"Yes, please." Arielle pushed forward the coffee cup that was already on her table and watched as Lucy filled it. She scanned the dining area, about half the tables occupied with families who had clearly just come from church.

"Anything else I can get you before you look at the menu?" Lucy asked. She was soft-spoken and young, and Arielle knew plenty well how to play her cards.

"I just want two eggs, over-easy, with a side of bacon and toast," Arielle said, watching Lucy whip out her notepad to jot down the order. "And I have a question. Do you know anything about those girls sitting over by the bathrooms?"

Lucy looked over her shoulder. "The one in the hat is Willow West, and I'm not sure who she's with."

"Willow West?" Arielle asked. "She looks familiar, but I can't remember from what exactly."

"Willow comes here every Sunday morning for brunch," Lucy explained, putting her hands on her hips. "Otherwise, she leads a ton of protests here in town. She's one of those environmentalists."

Arielle snapped. "That's what it was. I saw her at Miracle Park, leading a protest."

"Not surprising," Lucy said, uninterested. "Her biggest fight is always with that park."

"I see. Well, thanks for clearing that up for me—it was bothering me that I couldn't remember where I knew her from."

"Of course. Your breakfast should be out in ten minutes."

Lucy hurried over to the next table to take their orders. It wasn't much, but Arielle could eliminate Sunday mornings from her calendar for following Willow. And now she had ten minutes to make a move.

Arielle took a sip of her coffee—it was black and disgusting, and a quick reminder why she never drank the stuff—then rose from her seat and wandered across the floor to the bathrooms. She passed directly behind Willow's seat, overhearing their conversation where they regretted having drunk so much last night.

*You're better than this, Willow,* Arielle thought as she slid into the bathroom and washed her hands to kill a few seconds. *If you're somehow not the one responsible for the tragedy, you have a very bright future.*

None of that mattered right now, and Arielle turned around, dried her hands, and pushed open the door with determination. She took three steps out and came to a screeching halt next to Willow's table.

"Willow?!" Arielle gasped, faking her best college-girl tone.

Willow was in the middle of pouring creamer into her coffee cup when she looked up with a confused frown. "Hi," she said, obviously not recognizing Arielle.

Arielle laughed. "I'm sorry. I didn't mean to startle you. We met at your protest at Miracle Park a couple of weeks ago. You told me all about Alex Carter and how he runs this town."

That flicked on the light in Willow's mind, the memory and recognition coming back to her. "Oh, yes! Forgive me, but I meet lots of people. What was your name again?"

"No worries. I'm Arielle."

"Well, it's good to see you, Arielle," Willow said, then gestured to the woman sitting across from her. "This is my friend Bethany."

"Nice to meet you," Arielle said with a wide grin. *This acting business is exhausting.*

"The pleasure is mine," Bethany said, bowing her head to Arielle. She appeared much more hungover than Willow—bloodshot eyes, subtle hiccups, and dried-out lips. The table reeked of marijuana, and Arielle no longer knew the true source of the red eyes.

Arielle returned her attention to Willow. "You know, I've been thinking about everything you told me that day, and I'd really love to get involved with the cause."

"Is that so?" Willow asked, raising an eyebrow and giving Arielle a closer look. "What sort of research have you done on the matter?"

Arielle thought of Felix's frantic explanation about the conversation he had overheard at Copeland's house. Willow knew plenty about what was going on, but Arielle couldn't portray herself at that same level of understanding.

"Well," Arielle said. "For starters, the rising sickness in Hilburn *is* due to contaminated water. It sounds like these issues started after that *park* opened." She was sure to emphasize the word *park* with an obvious distaste. "And the water department claims to look into the issue but finds nothing wrong. Something isn't adding up, and I think it has to do with that Copeland fellow."

"Copeland?" Willow asked with surprise. "You really have done some digging."

Arielle shrugged. "I'm from Colorado, and we have some of the best drinking water in the country. When I moved here, I immediately noticed the quality was nowhere near as good as what I've been drinking my whole life."

"Colorado, huh?" Willow said. "I'd love to move there. I visited once and got to spend a day in Boulder. So much nature, and people who care about protecting that nature. I guess it's my dream place to live one day."

*Of course it is.*

Arielle had connected with Willow on a personal level,

thanks to finding a common interest. The barriers were down, and Arielle was all in. "Why not just move there?" she asked. "The Denver area is growing, but it's not all that expensive yet."

Willow stirred her coffee, nodding. "I'm from Omaha originally and moved here for college. I used to love this city—it's where I became an adult. And I do plan on leaving, but not until Alex Carter is out of town."

Bethany giggled and rolled her eyes. "It's all she talks about," she said. "Get out now before she goes on a rant."

Arielle offered a polite laugh in return.

Willow continued, now stroking her hair while she spoke. "Bethany isn't entirely wrong. Alex Carter is the only reason I'm still here. He ruined everything good about this city with that *fucking* park. Everyone is afraid to stand up to him except for me, so I have no choice but to stay and organize. If I left Hilburn right now, I don't know if I'd ever sleep again. Imagine if everything remained how it is. People will die in the next few years because of how bad the water has gotten. People I know. That would be entirely my fault."

"It's not your *fault*," Bethany moaned, as if they'd had this discussion thousands of times. "You're not the one polluting the water. If you were, then this would be your fault."

"Semantics," Willow said with a shake of her head. "I'm in too deep now to just leave. No one else will step into my place because they're terrified of Alex. So, yes, if anyone dies from the water, it's entirely my fault for not getting the change we need."

Arielle nodded along, unsure what to say. She saw Lucy drop off her breakfast at her table. *Those ten minutes flew.* But the food wasn't important right now. Arielle was inching her way into Willow's circle of trust.

"When is the next protest?" Arielle asked. "I'd like to attend."

Willow sighed. "None scheduled at the moment, unfortunately. Those assholes in the city haven't approved me for anything. They like to play difficult and dumb most of the time. I'm sure they're just another group Alex has in his pocket."

*This is your chance*, Arielle's inner voice screamed. *Go get her.*

"What if I told you there is a way to protest at the park whenever you'd like?"

# Chapter 29

August 9, 1978

Arielle's gamble paid off. She had explained to Willow that because the city of Hilburn owned a small portion of Miracle Park, as long as she didn't block access to the park entrance, Willow could lead protests every single day right outside the park gates if she wanted.

Willow had squealed at this news, jumping up to hug Arielle and insisting she bring her food over to join them at their table. They enjoyed the rest of their meal together, swapping stories of their time in Hilburn (Arielle made up too many things to keep track of, which was a major issue in the eyes of Selena), and making plans for upcoming protests.

Arielle couldn't help but fear what consequences loomed. The original timeline had no other protests between the prior one and the day of the tragedy. Could another unplanned protest have a ripple effect? Only time would tell, and Arielle could only hope it wouldn't make things worse.

None of that mattered the following Wednesday night, however. Arielle pulled up to Willow's house at six o'clock. Willow had invited Arielle to her next private meeting to make plans for a protest at Miracle Park. It was an invite-only event with Willow's closest confidants. When Arielle had asked if she could bring a friend—Felix—her request was denied.

"Sorry, but these are sensitive matters," Willow had explained. "People need to prove themselves trustworthy before I let them into my home. You understand, right?"

Of course Arielle understood, just knowing how much marijuana was consumed within the house warranted discretion from Willow and her roommates, especially in a time and state that viewed the plant as some sort of danger from hell.

She wished Selena could have joined her for the sake of her acting skills—Arielle had nothing in common with this group of people—but they couldn't risk Selena blowing her cover. If someone in Willow's house recognized Selena from Miracle Park, that would pose more questions and potentially put Selena in a position they didn't need. The Angels needed her to remain undisturbed in her role to ensure they had access to the park through the end of the mission.

Arielle had to face the Hilburn hippies on her own and prepared herself as she walked up the pathway and knocked on the front door. The front window overlooking the porch was open, laughter and chatter carrying outside while Arielle swayed side to side with her hands clasped behind her back.

The door swung open, and Bethany appeared. She looked in much better shape compared to the Sunday brunch at Dusters.

"Arielle! Welcome. Come on in." Bethany let her mouth hang open with an exaggerated grin and shuffled aside to let Arielle pass through.

She stepped directly into the living room where two couches formed an L in the corner, not a spare seat on either of them. Two gray cats dashed across the floor and zoomed down a hallway, banging into the walls on their way.

Behind the living room was an archway leading to the kitchen, where more people gathered around a small dining table covered in newspapers and magazines. Willow came out from the kitchen, chomping on a celery stick covered in peanut butter.

"Arielle, how are you?" she asked, throwing her arms around Arielle's neck for a hug. Willow's celery crunched noisily in Arielle's ear before they pulled apart.

"I'm doing great. Thank you so much for inviting me to this. Are all these people on your team?"

Willow giggled. "Just so you know, we don't use words like *team*. That makes us sound like a group of high school soccer players or something. We just...*are*. Do you know what I mean? We're all from different walks of life and have found unity around a common cause. I don't need to label us, because as soon as I put out the call for one of these gatherings, I just know everyone who will show up. Speaking of, make sure you grab the list of phone numbers before you leave today. We like to do phone trees when it's time to spread word for a protest."

The idea seemed outrageous to Arielle, but also a little genius. All these people—and she had done a rough count of at least sixteen crammed into this house—made an obligation to Willow to show up when needed. Willow was their priority, and they would drop anything else to be here.

Willow must have seen Arielle scanning the faces in the room and grabbed her by the wrist. "C'mon, we're just about to start our brainstorming session."

Arielle allowed herself to be tugged deeper into the living room, stepping around people sitting on the floor with their legs crossed. They stopped in front of a man with a two-foot-tall bong standing between his crossed legs.

"Phoenix," Willow said. "This is Arielle. She's going to be joining us."

Phoenix looked up with droopy eyes, his sandy hair a shaggy mess that flowed behind his head. A matching beard covered nearly the entire bottom half of his face, all but for a sliver of white from his teeth when he cracked his lips into a narrow smile. "Arielle, huh? Your name means 'lion of God.' Did you know that?"

Willow laughed, brushing her fingers through Phoenix's hair with the same playfulness she might if he were a dog. "Phoenix knows the most random shit."

Phoenix nodded, as if this statement had been true his whole life. "My brain is a sponge. If I hear something one time, it just stays in here forever." He balled a fist and knocked on his head.

Arielle gave a polite laugh, unsure what to say, clueless as to if her name actually meant lion of God. "You said we're having a brainstorming session?" she asked Willow.

"Totally. Sit down." Willow dropped to the floor and sat on her folded legs, patting the open space between her and Phoenix.

"Come on down, Lion," Phoenix said. "Or should I say Lioness?"

*What in the actual fuck is going on?*

"We need to open our minds," Willow said in a flat tone. "Every meeting starts with brainstorming. And how can we do that if our minds are filled with all the stress and worries of everyday life?"

"So, we're going to smoke out of this bong?" Arielle asked, already knowing the answer and trying to stall.

"Well, duh," Phoenix said, packing weed into the bowl with

his thumb and index finger.

"We can't take down the patriarchy without some creative thinking," Willow said, grabbing Arielle by the wrist and pulling her down.

"Yeah," Phoenix agreed. "We can't have any more incidents like that time Willow punched the oil executive in the mouth."

Willow smirked and shrugged. "A little punch in the face was worth it to save the millions of lives that will eventually die because of the oil industry's influence on the world. I'd do it again, too. Sit down already, Arielle. Join us."

*A bit extreme*, Arielle thought. But she obliged and took her seat on the floor, legs crossed, and watched while bongs, pipes, and joints magically appeared around the room. The group on the couch lit up a joint and immediately started passing it around.

"Since you're our new guest," Phoenix said, extending the bong to Arielle. "You get greens. Light her up."

Arielle's heart raced as she reached for the bong. Getting high on a mission was an absolute tragedy in her book, and she was already beating herself up for backing herself into this corner.

*Okay, what can I do? Do I tell them I don't smoke and step outside while they 'brainstorm?' Will they kick me out if I do that, thinking I'm not worthy of being part of this inner circle? I haven't smoked weed since college, and that was only twice.*

"C'mon, Lioness," Phoenix said. "We're all waiting for a turn."

Arielle saw the bong shaking in her hand and steadied her grip on the glass. No one seemed to notice, but their small huddle had now grown with three other people hovering around them, all eyes on Arielle.

"I'm sorry," Arielle said. "I don't do this often."

The house smelled like a skunk had just sprayed every corner of the living room, a smoky cloud filling the space.

"Just take a little hit then," Phoenix said. "No need to be a hero."

*I don't think I'm getting out of this,* Arielle thought. *Not if I want to keep on Willow's good side. Why does she have to be at the top of our suspect list? If she was anyone else, I'd be storming out the door and never looking back.*

Arielle gulped and nodded. "Okay."

Fortunately, she saw the group on the other couch smoking from a different bong and knew what she needed to do. She raised the mouthpiece to her lips, and Phoenix handed her a lighter.

*The tiniest of puffs,* Arielle told herself. *I'll inhale for a quarter of a second. That can't possibly make me stoned out of my mind.*

And while that much was true, Arielle couldn't tame the smoke. She lit the bowl and drew in a gentle inhale to bring the smoke into the chamber, where it gradually filled like a fog machine in a haunted house. The gray cloud suspended there, less than four inches away from her lips. She wasn't fooling anyone—it was obvious she hadn't taken in any of the smoke—so she drew another hasty inhale.

The smoke blasted up the chamber, a bullet train of marijuana bursting through the tunnel of Arielle's mouth.

*Oh, shit,* she thought, immediately coughing at the burning sensation running from her mouth into the depths of her lungs. Her eyes watered, and for a solid twenty seconds, all she could do was cough, gasping for air in between each bout. With each gruff hack, her esophagus burned like a roaring fire.

"Whoa there, Lioness," Phoenix said, pulling back the

bong before Arielle accidentally knocked the damn thing over. "Need some water?"

Arielle nodded, clenching her jaw shut to stop herself from coughing any further. Heat prickled all over her face, and she just knew it was red.

"Help yourself," Willow said with a giggle. "The kitchen is right there, and the fridge is loaded with bottled water—we don't drink tap water, for obvious reasons."

This earned a laugh from the room, which now felt like it had hundreds of people in it. Everything had become so *loud*, yet somehow clear. Arielle could hear every single conversation taking place in the house, even a couple of guys whispering to each other in the corner as they passed a pipe back and forth.

She didn't remember standing up but was now marching toward the kitchen. She needed a quick glance down at her legs to ensure they were indeed moving.

*Okay,* she thought. *That was way more than I intended. What happened? I'm high, aren't I? Like* really *high?*

Arielle snickered to herself as she walked in slow motion to the fridge, pulling it open and fishing out one of at least five dozen bottles of Perrier drinking water. She analyzed it like an ancient relic. *Huh, I didn't even know this brand existed this far back in time.*

"Are you gonna stare at it or drink it?" a woman asked from the kitchen table, causing a round of laughter from the group standing with her.

Arielle closed the fridge and spun around. "Oh. Haha. I'm sorry." Her throat still burned, but she had forgotten all about it.

"Take a chill pill," the woman said. "I'm just messing with you. Are you the new girl Willow has been talking about?"

Arielle looked around, not fully realizing *she* was the one Willow must have been talking about. She pointed at herself and raised an eyebrow. "Me?"

The woman laughed and walked over. "You're funny. I see why Willow likes you. I guess we need that comic relief around here because these guys sure as hell ain't funny." She cocked a thumb to the group she had left at the table, half of them laughing, the other half flipping her the bird. "I'm Hannah. It's nice to meet you."

"I'm Arielle." They shook hands and Hannah seemed like she was speaking from a distant world as Arielle's head spun. She looked her up and down, noting Hannah's sandals and knee-length socks. *Did people really dress like this?*

"Are you okay, hon?" Hannah asked, placing a hand on Arielle's shoulder.

"I'm fine. I might just need to lie down."

The world was moving too fast for Arielle, and she needed to get through this catastrophe in one piece. She couldn't exactly sleep it off, not in a stranger's house, but hoped a few minutes away from the raucous laughter and conversation could allow her to think straight again.

"I totally get it," Hannah said. "Why don't you go to Willow's room? She has a bed and a big comfy chair. Take your pick."

Arielle shook her head. "I can't—that's her room. I don't want to violate her privacy."

As soon as those words left her lips, Arielle realized she *did* want to violate Willow's privacy. A few minutes in her bedroom could go a long way in helping the mission, but her brain had been too slow to process the grand opportunity.

Hannah frowned and shook her head. "It's not a big deal.

People hang out in her room all the time when we have these gatherings. There's not exactly a ton of space in this house, and some of us can feel a little claustrophobic and need some space. Willow's room is where we go. C'mon, let me take you."

Hannah pivoted around and started out of the kitchen, Arielle following. The group huddled around the table all watched her with curious glances as she trailed Hannah down the hallway.

The door at the end of the hall was Willow's room. When Arielle stepped in, the scent of incense rushed her heightened senses and made her queasy.

"This is it," Hannah said, stopping at the foot of a bed covered with at least fifteen pillows. A bundle of incense sticks, two lighters, and three pipes lay scattered on the nightstand next to the bed. A copy of *Be Here Now* by Ram Dass stood along the back, leaning against the wall. "If you choose the bed, you will literally feel like you're floating on a cloud. It's just magical. But don't take it from me—I'll leave you to it. Spend as much time in here as you need."

Hannah left the bedroom without another word and closed the door behind her.

*Is this for real?* Arielle wondered. *I get this chance to snoop around Willow's bedroom, and I'm high as a kite. Focus, Arielle. Focus!*

Something rubbed against her ankle, and she looked down to see one of the cats from earlier. It purred as it walked circles around Arielle's leg, begging to be petted.

"Not today, kitty," Arielle said. She stood at the foot of the bed and examined the rest of the room. The chair Hannah mentioned was more of a miniature couch, wide enough to lie down and let her legs hang over the armrest. The dresser was covered with jewelry and a random ash tray portraying two smiling mushrooms fishing at a lake. Next to that scattered mess stood a row of books.

*Who is Willow West?* Arielle thought as she scanned the titles. *Soul on Ice. We Are Everywhere. The Language of Mechanical Engineering. Stranger in a Strange Land.*

"Wait, what?" Arielle said. "Language of Mechanical Engineering?"

Saying the title aloud nearly slapped her sober. She stood frozen in place, glancing at the door and reminding herself anyone could walk through it. The chatter continued down the hallway and showed no signs of slowing, so she reached out for the book and took it off the shelf.

The edges of the cover were tattered, and Arielle winced at all the creases in the spine. The book must have been borrowed, because the others on the shelf looked to have been treated with the care and respect Arielle expected from any book owner. Sticking out like a bookmark was the corner of a piece of paper. Arielle flipped the book open to the page, which showed diagrams of pulley systems and unfolded the paper.

"No way," she whispered. For a moment, she thought her heart had stopped beating. The sheet of paper showed a blueprint of Time Roller. "It's been you this whole time." Arielle shook her head, sick to her stomach. It almost felt like she was holding a written confession in her hands, rather than what *seemed* an innocuous book and roller coaster blueprints.

Footsteps clopped down the hallway, prompting Arielle to refold the paper and stuff it back into the book, slamming the cover shut and putting it back into place on the dresser. She leapt onto the bed of pillows and lay there moaning just as the door swung open.

Willow strode into her bedroom. "Arielle? Are you okay? Hannah just told me you weren't feeling well."

Arielle moaned again to sell her story. "I think I should head out. I just feel awful, like I ate something bad."

Willow laughed, and Arielle didn't hold it against her—it was hard to keep a straight face with so much weed in your system. "I'm sorry you're feeling sick. Take all the time you need in here and head out when you think it's safe to drive. Can I get you anything else for now?"

Arielle rolled her head from side to side. "Thank you, but I think I'm okay for now."

"If you say so," Willow said, circling the bed to open her closet door. She fished out a blanket and tossed it over Arielle's body. "If you need anything, just shout, okay?"

"Thank you. You're a great host." Being in the same room as Willow now sent gooseflesh across Arielle's body.

Willow gave a caring grin before leaving the room and closing the door again. Arielle sat bolt upright. She needed to get out of this house.

# Chapter 30

August 14, 1978

Arielle had moved all in with her belief Willow West was the culprit behind the tragedy that would befall Time Roller in ten days. Yet Felix and Selena remained adamant about not ruling anyone out. Sure, they agreed the blueprints of the roller coaster being tucked into a book on mechanical engineering were the closest thing to a smoking gun they might find, and they believed this for the remainder of the week and weekend.

On Sunday, however, Selena had witnessed another verbal spat between Joy and Alexander Carter. This time, Carter actually followed Joy out of the office building, his face blazing as he showered Joy with accusations of time clock theft. Selena had been walking toward the tables where she liked to eat her lunch when this incident unfolded and could only see the tears running down Joy's face while she stormed away with a clenched jaw and balled fists.

"It's personal for Joy," Selena had explained to the Angels that night over dinner. "She takes so much shit from that man, I'd be surprised if she *doesn't* snap and get some sort of revenge."

Meanwhile, Arielle continued to keep a close watch on

Willow's house and was grateful not to have exchanged contact information. Willow had no way of reaching her, and Arielle debated if she should bother reaching out again, considering she had seen the proof she needed to justify the environmentalist as their top target. Willow had hosted another gathering on Saturday night, and Arielle recognized many of the same faces from her hiding spot further down the block. The meeting evolved into a weekend rager when a group of college-aged men arrived with two kegs of beer. Arielle turned on her car and left at nine o'clock once she had given up on anything of significance unfolding.

All of that led them to tonight, Monday evening, where Felix and Selena sat in Felix's car down the block and across the street from Terrance Copeland's house. Felix had kept up this routine ever since his first visit and was sure to park in front of a different home each evening to ensure the neighbors didn't catch on to him.

Selena had a rare night off from Miracle Park and was ecstatic to join Felix on his nightly stakeout. She could have gone with Arielle to follow Willow around but wanted to see the upscale neighborhood home to the affluent Hilburn residents.

"This has been a strange mission, don't you think?" Selena asked Felix.

"How do you figure?" Felix said, grateful to have company for once. This mission had seen him spend the most time alone compared to the others they had worked on together. His days consisted of his morning trip to the park to swap out the tapes in the receiver, followed by bringing the recorded tapes back to the house where he listened to them, hoping to find a conversation or phone call that might shed light on what was going on.

The weeks had dragged for Felix, but that would all end tonight.

"Well," Selena said, pulling out a mirror from her purse to check the lipstick she had just applied, "it seems like on other missions we've been scrambling to find even one suspect to follow. And this time we each have our own horse in the race—three suspects and we can't come to an agreement."

"Very true," Felix said, eyes glued to the Copeland house. It was seven o'clock, and they had listened to the family's dinner wrap up. "I think it's just because so many people hate Carter. Hatred like this makes everyone a suspect. But the nature of the crime makes me believe it was done by someone thinking of the big picture. No offense, but I don't think it's Joy *because* of how personal it is. What does she get out of Time Roller breaking down and killing those people? Sure, she might not have to work for Carter anymore. But I'd think she's more apt to shoot him or rob him. That's personal, and while it's not right, it would probably make her feel better compared to harming innocent people on a roller coaster."

Selena nodded along. "I see your point. She's been tough to crack, I'll admit. Shoots down all of my requests to hang out outside of work. She lives alone, and the few times I've driven by her house, there's just nothing going on. I have my doubts about her, too, but I can't ignore how much she deserves to get some sort of payback on Carter. How do you figure Copeland factors into this?"

Felix turned down the volume on the receiver now that the kids were getting rowdy during their nightly routine of preparing for bedtime. "The way I see Copeland, he's backed into a corner. He's been doing the dirty work for Carter for so long now, he can't get out from under his thumb. He recognizes what he's doing is wrong. And while I haven't heard him verbally admit it yet, he knows the water situation is growing dire for Hilburn. We also know he wants to run for mayor, but does he really want to do that as long as Carter is the one actually calling the shots in this town? I've watched Copeland long enough to know he's a good man. He loves his family. He even loves Hilburn. He has some questions to answer about how he came into such money. The town has to be suspicious. His lust for money has gotten the best of him. If Carter were to leave town, Copeland would get his life back. And who wouldn't want that?"

A car turned onto the block and crept along West Camino Street, a rare occurrence after seven o'clock in the secluded neighborhood of Christopher's Cove.

"Who's that?" Selena asked, sitting upright.

"It's a Lincoln Town Car," Felix said, guts twisting into knots. "All black."

"Have you not seen this car before?"

Felix shook his head, unable to look away. "I think I've seen everyone who lives on this block by now. No idea who this is."

Even though this neighborhood was home to all the luxury vehicles in Hilburn, something about the Town Car felt *off*. Out of place. It was driving much too slow, like the driver was lost and debating turning around. But it continued along, stopping in front of Copeland's house and parking along the curb, facing the wrong way.

They saw the figures of a driver and someone else in the backseat. The car idled for two minutes before the driver swung the door open and stepped out. He was a tall man dressed in a dark gray suit, a pair of sunglasses perched above an earnest countenance.

"He looks like he could be part of the Secret Service," Selena said.

The man took one step to open the back door, and out stepped Alexander Carter, a cigar in his mouth that he plucked out to blow smoke in the air. Carter patted his driver on the shoulder before laboring up the walkway to Copeland's front door.

"What the hell is he doing here?" Selena asked, head spinning around to Felix, who didn't have a clue.

"This is the first interaction I've witnessed between the two of them," Felix said. "There haven't been phone calls, in-person meetings, nothing."

Carter wore his typical suit and looked like a door-to-door salesman as he reached out his beefy hand and knocked on the door.

"If he goes in the house, we'll be able to hear what they're saying," Felix said, holding his breath in anxious anticipation.

Copeland opened the door and an immediate expression of shock spread across his face. He looked around the neighborhood as if an escaped convict had arrived on his doorstep and he didn't want anyone to know.

"I'll be right back, Glo!" Copeland shouted behind him. The feed picked up his words clearly, until he stepped all the way out and closed the door.

"Dammit," Felix muttered.

The two men shook hands and faced each other on the doorstep. Carter appeared to have a lot more to say, as he rambled for an entire minute, Copeland only nodding as he crossed his arms and gazed toward the ground.

Selena leaned forward, placing her hands on the dashboard

for a better angle of the conversation they couldn't hear. "Why do you think Carter would make a house call?" she asked. "It's gotta be urgent."

"I know, and it's pissing me off we can't find out."

Something shifted in the conversation. Copeland threw his hands in the air before pointing directly at Carter's face. Carter appeared to let out a laugh before reaching inside his suit jacket. He fumbled around for a few seconds while Copeland continued throwing his hands in every direction while he ranted.

Carter pulled out a gun and pointed it at Copeland, who promptly took two steps backward with his hands raised above his head. Carter grinned and nodded, taking another step closer.

"Holy shit!" Selena cried. "He's going to shoot him!"

"That's enough, Selena," Felix said through gritted teeth. "Keep quiet and stay calm. He's not going to shoot him—that never happened in the original timeline."

Copeland spoke, hands still above his head, as he kept inching toward the door. Felix noticed Carter's driver standing next to the car, hands folded in front of his stomach as he stared down the block, acting like nothing was happening.

"They're going inside!" Selena said.

Carter lowered his gun and stuffed it back into his jacket. Copeland lowered his hands and opened his front door, stepping aside to let Carter enter first. Felix immediately cranked up the volume on the receiver so they could hear.

Copeland spoke first after closing the door. "Gloreen! Mr. Carter is here. We'll be talking in the kitchen for a few minutes. Please don't let the kids interrupt."

She shouted back something inaudible, out of range from

any of the hidden mics Felix had set up around the house. That was fine. He had bugged the kitchen and they'd be able to hear everything.

"Where were we?" Carter asked in a gruff voice, his heavy footsteps knocking along the hardwood floor.

"You were about to shoot me for not letting you into my house," Copeland replied in an accusatory tone.

"Now, now," Carter said. "I asked reasonably first. You refused. We can't have these conversations on your front stoop—that's not how I do business. Why don't you fetch me a glass of water and an ashtray. I'd hate to leave a mess on your table."

"Of course," Copeland said. The conversation fell silent for a couple of minutes while Copeland presumably fulfilled Carter's requests.

Eventually, Carter spoke again. "Thank you, Terrance. Here's the letter I received today. It's from your department and I need to know *why* this is happening. This was not part of our deal."

More silence while Copeland read whatever letter Carter had shown him.

"Son of a bitch," Copeland said, slapping the table. "Mr. Carter, this is not my doing. This is from the county. They're opening an investigation into the water pollution accusations. I'm afraid there's nothing I can do to stop them. Do you not have any contacts at the county?"

"I have a couple I'll be reaching out to tonight. There's gotta be something you can do. You're the goddamned president of the water company. You can't just sit back while the county meddles in our business."

"I won't be sitting back, Mr. Carter. In fact, I'll be nothing but cooperative with them. I have the water analysis reports and will share them with the county. The reports are all doctored to show the water is as clean as it's ever been. The only thing I can't control is if they go take a sample for themselves—nothing I can do to stop them from doing that."

"How did this even happen?" Carter grumbled.

"Someone had to have filed a complaint with the county."

"That hippie bitch," Carter snapped. "She needs to be hung by her neck already. That pot-smoking piece of shit is going to bring down this entire city. Tell me something. Would anyone notice if she went missing?"

"Mr. Carter," Copeland said sternly. "You will not discuss such a matter in front of me. I will not be an accessory to whatever you have planned. Willow West is too well known to fall victim. Take it from me—you need to proceed with caution. If the county starts snooping around the park, the last thing you need is the person who turned you in to go missing. No one will see that as a coincidence."

Carter grumbled, his fingers drumming the kitchen table. "I will do as I see fit to protect my business. Life would be much easier with that tree-hugging lunatic out of the picture. What can you tell me about the county? What can they do?"

Copeland cleared his throat. "Well, they can make your life hell, but only if they can prove the water pollution is a direct result of Miracle Park. The quality reports I have filed will show samples pulled from the Platte River directly behind the park. They'll want to review these first, assuming their suspicion is around the park—which it is, since they sent *you* the letter. I can stall them."

"So they'll think the river water is clean. What does that matter to me if everything comes from the water sanitation plant?"

"That's why we'll have some time. This is a slow-moving process. When the county arrives, they'll start their investigation with the paperwork—mainly the reports I was telling you about. After that, they'll inspect every leg of our sanitation system, at which point they'll find *something* wrong. Is there any chance you can stop dumping into the river until the county leaves town?"

Carter laughed, a gruff, hoarse sound. "And do what with all the trash?"

"I don't care. Just stop putting it in the river. Dig a hole behind the park and toss it in there. At some point, the county is going to realize our equipment is operating fine and the increase of chemicals in the water has to be attributed to something else. That's when they'll start snooping around the city. Fortunately, I've thought this far ahead and fudged the reports to show the water sources from the north side of town are worse than the river. Again, this will only buy us time while they start their own water sampling. That's why I'm suggesting you stop dumping now, so that by the time they pull samples from the river, it just might be clean enough to keep us in the clear."

"How long are we looking at?" Carter asked.

"Well, they didn't provide a date in the letter, so they can show up whenever. From the time they arrive, I'd plan for six months until they're pulling samples from the river."

"Christ! Six months?!" Carter let out a harsh chuckle. "I don't know if I can bury that many months' worth of trash."

Copeland lowered his voice, but Felix and Selena could still hear him. "An idea, at least until the county leaves. Reduce whatever you're paying me to help pay for trash services. It's the safest investment you can make right now. It buys time for the river to cleanse itself and will keep the county off both our backs."

Carter coughed up a guttural laugh. "Terrance, my boy, *you* are my best investment. Do you know what I call you to my friends?"

"No, sir."

"The magician. You make things happen. You make problems disappear, just like magicians do when they put those whores into the small boxes. I've got free water at the park *and* the hotel, thanks to you. I pay half the cost of my electric bill, thanks to some other friends in that department. The trash people won't budge—they want to charge me extra fees for having so much trash. Is that not their fucking job? To pick up trash all day. Those crooks only want to charge me more because they know I have the money. But they must have forgotten I also have principles, so they can shove their extra fees where the sun don't shine. Fuck 'em."

Selena laughed. "*That's* the reason he's refused to work with the trash company?! What a nutjob!"

Felix waved at her to be quiet, keeping his ears focused on the receiver.

"I understand, Mr. Carter," Copeland said in the same cautious tone a parent might use to tiptoe around their child's feelings, hoping to prevent a public tantrum. "It was just a suggestion."

"You're the ace up my sleeve, Terrance," Carter said. "Don't ever forget that. As soon as we get you into the mayor's office, we'll have a majority of the votes combined with the city council. Then we can finally start drilling into all that beautiful oil sitting below Hilburn. And when that day comes, you'll be rewarded even more than you have been.  So let's make sure we keep our eyes on that prize, okay?"

"Of course, sir."

"Very good.  I'm sorry my visit tonight started off on the wrong foot, but you have to understand my panic at receiving that letter."

"Of course, sir."

*Copeland's sounding robotic now,* Felix thought. *Probably just wants this man out of his house already.*

"I'll let you get back to your evening," Carter said, the sound of a chair screeching across the kitchen floor.  "You let me know as soon as these county boys arrive."

"Certainly, Mr. Carter. You'll be the first to know."

# Chapter 31

"So all of this is actually about oil?" Arielle asked, shaking her head while sitting at their kitchen table.

Felix and Selena returned home and shared their findings with Arielle, who had already slipped into her pajamas for the night and was well into her second cup of tea.

"Of course," Selena said, pulling out the seat next to Arielle and plopping herself down. "Isn't it always?"

"Everything makes so much more sense now," Felix added. He leaned against the counter, arms crossed. "At least in terms of Carter and his thirst to run this city. Remember, his father got rich from oil and Carter is a byproduct of that."

Arielle nodded. "Carter and his father used to travel through Hilburn. It wasn't the city they fell in love with—it's what lies beneath."

"I bet Carter's dad couldn't get anything worked out with the city to drill," Felix said. "So Carter grew up and took a different approach."

"But why build Miracle Park?" Selena asked. "He could have just as easily bought out the city's politicians and officials without opening a massive amusement park."

Arielle shrugged. "Who knows? That man has surely

gone through so much psychological damage in his life. It's impossible to know *why* he does anything. He probably never got to go to Disney as a kid, and his grand idea was to build one for himself. A spoiled little kid who didn't get his way grew up to throw money at his problems. Not the first or last time such a thing will happen."

"*Why* Carter does anything has no relevance to our mission," Selena said. "And quite frankly, we should stop talking about the guy. We know he doesn't destroy his own ride."

"But we need to know everyone in his circle," Arielle said. "You're correct, we don't need to understand anything about him personally—we just need to know who wants to see him fail. So far, we have Willow West, Joy Gillespie, and maybe Terrance Copeland—although I'm not sure what to think about him after tonight's developments."

"Copeland is a wild card," Felix added. "We need a deeper understanding of him to know which way he leans with Carter. I think he's a good guy battling with himself to get out of a sticky situation."

"Yes," Selena said. "But Carter is also talking about Copeland becoming mayor—which is what Copeland has already admitted to wanting."

"This could be a case of Stockholm Syndrome," Arielle said, giving a mindless stir to her teacup. "Copeland may not be physically held hostage, but Carter has him by the emotional—and financial—throat. Copeland may have a sense of loyalty toward Carter because of the money he receives, yet he's too blind to realize that's what has happened."

The kitchen fell quiet while everyone considered this.

Selena spoke first after a minute. "So we can't really rule out any of the three."

"I'm afraid not," Arielle said. "In fact, it's worse than we realize. If we're considering Joy Gillespie, we have to consider any other disgruntled employee. If we consider Willow West, we have to be open to the possibility anyone in her little protesting group can be responsible. Same for Copeland—Carter admitted others are helping him save money on his bills, all while he positions himself to drill for oil in the near future. Who are those others, and how do they feel about Carter? And now Carter has mentioned having contacts within the county departments. The list of suspects is growing out of control and we're running out of time to narrow it down."

"Ten days to go," Felix added, nodding to himself. "We have to change our approach."

"And just throw away all the time we've been using to follow these people?" Selena asked, not holding back the frustration in her voice. She balled a fist on the table while Arielle took a long sip of tea.

"It's not throwing away anything," Arielle said calmly. "The work we've done so far has created a sound foundation. Even with all the moving parts, I feel confident our perpetrator is from one of the three we've narrowed it down to. Personally, I'm all in on Willow after finding that engineering book and Time Roller blueprints in her bedroom."

"You've told us to never go 'all in' to avoid being made a fool," Selena said. "Not until the facts paint an obvious picture."

"You're right," Arielle said. "And I'm still open to other possibilities, but that's the beauty of our team—we can each focus on someone else, or different aspects of this mission. Felix, what did you mean by changing our approach?"

Felix cleared his throat and stepped closer to the table, keeping his bulky arms crossed. "Think about it. We're ten days out and there still hasn't been any tampering with Time Roller, right, Selena?"

She nodded silently. "I've only checked a couple times. Can't exactly head underneath the ride every day.

"So," Felix continued. "We know the destruction of the pull cable is going to happen within the next ten days, and from what Yokota told us, all it takes is a few hours and a set of bolt cutters. Let's use some logic. No one is going to hide under Time Roller during the day while the ride is operating. They'd have, what, two minutes at a time to cut away at the cable before the ride takes off again? That's no way to get the job done. It has to happen after hours. Our best bet, with how little time remains, is to hide outside the park after it closes each night. Someone will be sneaking in to start their work on the pull cable, and once we know who that is, we can have another discussion about what to do."

"And you're proposing to be the one who camps out overnight?" Arielle asked, arching an eyebrow as she looked at Felix. "Because I can't follow Willow around all day, then pull an all-nighter. And Selena is already starting her days early in the morning and spending her time at the park."

Felix looked up at the ceiling, his mind figuring matters out. "It'll take some shuffling of my schedule, but I can do it. There aren't any snakes at the park, right?"

They all shared a laugh, reminiscing that time Felix passed out from a snake bite.

"What would your schedule look like, then?" Arielle asked.

Felix pivoted around and returned to his spot, leaning against the counter. "I'll have to sleep during the day, then head to the park a little before eight. Probably will want to park far from the entrance so whoever shows up doesn't feel like they're being watched. Selena, any chance I can use the keys to get into the park?"

Selena bit her bottom lip. "I don't know if that's smart. You can't just stroll into the park without an employee badge."

Felix laughed. "Well, someone is going to *break* into the park to sabotage a roller coaster. I think I'll be fine. You've told us how the security guards patrol. I'll figure out their timing and can base everything on that. Besides, I'd only be going in to follow whoever shows up."

"I think that's a great idea," Arielle said. "It's the whole point in having access to the park, Selena. Besides, if the guards were to actually see Felix, do you think they could catch him in a foot race?"

"I guess that's a fair point," Selena said, shifting in her seat. "You just need to be extra cautious. If anything falls back on me and I lose this job, then we're screwed for the rest of the mission. And I *need* to be there on the twenty-fourth."

"You can trust me," Felix said. "You know I won't take any unnecessary risks. The primary part of my role is breaking into people's homes. An amusement park should hardly be a challenge."

"Okay. When I get home tomorrow, the keys are all yours."

Felix bowed his head in gratitude.

"Glad that settles it," Arielle said. "I actually have a potential opportunity coming up. I overheard one of Willow's friends talk about a music festival in Omaha this weekend. Willow mentioned she was going with all her friends. Now, we don't know who that includes, exactly, but this may be our best shot at an empty house. I'd love to get back in there and poke around some more, considering I was stoned off my ass last time."

Selena and Felix cackled.

"And you always make sure I don't have any fun," Selena said, rolling her eyes. "I'll remember that next time I want to go out."

Arielle shook her head. "You know it's not like that. I've been hard on myself for falling to that peer pressure, but I was in such a juicy position and couldn't mess it up. Trust me, it wasn't fun."

"Do you need me to bug the place?" Felix asked.

Arielle shrugged. "Would you even be able to add that surveillance to your schedule, especially if you're going to be sleeping during the day?"

"I suppose not. And if she's gone all weekend, we're only going to have about three days' worth of listening between her return home and the day of the accident. I doubt this attack on Time Roller was done on a whim—especially if she has that engineering book. It's already planned."

"That's a good point," Arielle said, jumping from her seat. "Which means there is no way anything is going to be done on the roller coaster before this weekend."

"Unless that was her plan all along," Selena chimed in, standing to meet Arielle's excitement. "What if Willow actually cuts the pull cable before she leaves? That way, when the accident happens, she has a legitimate alibi for being nowhere near the park."

"But we know when it happens," Felix said, refusing to move from his spot. "If she's already back in town on the day of the accident, then what's the point of having an alibi?"

"Okay," Arielle said, channeling her authoritative voice.

"We're all making good points but not getting anywhere. Too much speculation only leads to more confusion. We have our plans, so let's stick to them. Selena will continue her business as usual at the park. Starting tomorrow, Felix will go to the park at night to watch for anyone breaking in. And I'll continue following Willow, probably with extended hours for the remainder of the week until she leaves for the music festival this weekend. That's all we can do. Now, let's get some rest and prepare ourselves for the home stretch of this mission."

# Chapter 32



August 16, 1978

Felix's first night camped out on Tuesday passed with much the same thrill as sitting in a Los Angeles traffic jam. No one arrived at Miracle Park between 8 p.m. and 6 a.m.

He spent the downtime listening to the day's recordings. Alexander Carter had yet to reach out to anyone from the county, as he had suggested that evening in Copeland's kitchen.

*Was it a bluff?* Felix wondered. *Or is he making secret phone calls from somewhere besides his home or office?*

Miracle Park had a handful of payphones spread throughout, but it made little sense for the park owner to place sensitive calls amid random strangers. His office provided plenty of privacy. Besides, Felix could piece together Carter's routine simply by the timing of the sound-activated recordings.

Carter woke each morning at 6:30, spent an hour getting ready for the day, and left his penthouse suite at 7:30. From there, Carter was off the grid for the following half hour, but he was only dealing with hotel business, seeing as he'd arrive at his park office by eight o'clock. He spent his next two hours either on the phone yelling at vendors or screaming at staff that he called into his office. By Felix's judgment, the matters that infuriated Carter had no reason to warrant such erratic emotions. It had become clear that Carter used his anger as a tool to get what he wanted. Half the time, Felix wondered if Carter was actually angry or just enjoyed shouting to get his way. Regardless, it usually worked.

After his morning phone calls, Carter played a radio until lunch time and hummed along in his gruff baritone to a mix of jazz, pop, and swing music. He'd leave his office at noon and return to his suite for lunch, where he blasted a news station on his television, before heading back to the office at one, where he'd make more phone calls and have meetings—with his emotions under control—with the executive staff of Miracle Park.

He'd leave the office for the day between four and five, returning home where he rarely made phone calls.

For as much as they were hoping to learn from Alexander Carter, Felix found the business owner boring and attached to his daily routine. If a phone call ever ran long, or an issue arose that needed his attention, Carter would go on one of his famous rants and slander whoever threw off his schedule.

*If I have to listen to these recordings all night, every night, I'm going to lose my mind,* Felix thought after sitting through the painful Tuesday night.

Wednesday night had started out the same, until a pair of headlights turned into the parking lot at 10:30.

All the blood in Felix's body rushed to his stomach while his knees quivered. *This is it,* he thought, watching the headlights draw nearer. As they approached, he recognized the perfectly circular shape of each light. *VW Beetle. She's here.*

Felix slouched as low as he could in the driver's seat in case

Willow drove by his car. She'd need to get out and peer inside if she wanted to see him, but would she actually do that?

The engine hummed by at a steady pace, and once it passed, Felix sat tall to see the taillights disappear toward the park entrance. He immediately grabbed the binoculars that were resting on top of the receiver.

The Beetle stopped four rows back from the front and parked out of sight from any guard potentially looking through the gate.

Felix gulped, his heart hammering in his throat and ears. His fingertips pulsed against the cool leather casing on the binoculars. The red glow from the Beetle's brake lights splashed across the parking lot like a fiery floodlight before cutting off, leaving them under the gentle gleam of the streetlamps spaced out across the lot.

The Beetle's door swung open, and out stepped Willow West, hands on her hips as she drew in a deep breath of the night air, a backpack slung over one shoulder.

"She's alone," Felix said.

Willow looked around the parking lot, and she definitely noticed Felix's car parked all the way at the other end, stopping and staring. Through the binoculars, he saw her squinting. Between the darkness and distance, she had no chance of actually seeing him. She gave up on trying to figure out the mystery vehicle and swiveled around to face the park, scanning the area left and right before starting toward the front gate.

She strolled with too much confidence. "Have you been out here before?" Felix asked the empty car. "Do you already know security's routine and timing?"

If she had this all planned out, then it was likely she had

made these basic preparations. Willow pulled the backpack's second strap over her shoulder as she reached the gate and promptly scaled it like Spiderman racing up the side of a building with ease. "You've definitely been out here before. You can't just hop that fence like you're retrieving a ball from your neighbor's yard. Too easy."

Willow disappeared into the shadows of Miracle Park, and Felix fired up his engine. He couldn't park any closer, or Willow might notice on her way out. Instead, Felix sped out of the lot's exit and turned onto the narrow road that connected to the hotel's parking lot. It would be a shorter walk to cross over from the hotel instead of covering all the space of the park's massive lot. Besides, he knew where Willow was going, so he didn't need to follow her every step.

It was late enough that no one was present outside the Miracle Hotel, so Felix reluctantly drove like an asshole, speeding to the front of the lot and taking the first spot he found next to the row of disabled parking spaces.

He parked, turned off the car, and hopped out in one seamless motion, then broke into a sprint down the walkway toward the park. Arielle and Selena had mentioned a secret path around the back of the park that would take him straight to Time Roller, but they had never sat down to explain how to access it. Something about cutting through the trees in the middle of the walkway?

He took one look at those trees and surrounding foliage and knew he wouldn't take that path. The thought of snakes slithering within that pitch blackness made his skin break into gooseflesh in the middle of this eighty-degree night.

*Not today, Satan,* he thought, and ran even faster.

He reached the park's side entrance and fished Selena's key

out of his pocket. *No fence-hopping necessary. This isn't even breaking and entering. I have a key!*

He jammed the key into the lock, keeping his eyes up and on the lookout for any flashlights or security guards. The coast was clear, so he pushed the gate open, the hinges screaming into the night and making a frog leap into his throat. Adrenaline returned and filled every vein in his body, hands trembling as he struggled to close the gate silently. It slipped from his grip and clanged shut.

*Jesus, Felix, calm down. You're going to give yourself away.*

He assured himself that it wasn't so simple to out himself in this immense park. It wasn't like breaking into a home where someone in their bedroom could hear the front door swing open. Not even close. If the guards were in the security office, they wouldn't have any way of hearing what had just happened. If anything, it might have distracted Willow.

Now inside the park and away from the clatter he had just caused, Felix shuffled toward a trash can and crouched behind it, needing to catch his breath and calm his racing thoughts. He really wouldn't have a problem outrunning a security guard if it came down to that. Felix had been going on runs around the neighborhood during the weekdays to stay in shape and kill time, and had never felt faster.

After a minute, he was ready to continue and stepped out from the confines of the trash can. Miracle Park was silent, except for the crickets and a couple of owls hooting somewhere in the distance. It was a half-moon tonight, and that kept the park mostly under the wraps of an eerie gloom.

Felix knew the exact route to take to Time Roller, thanks to their prior visits. He crouched low as he followed the paths from the entrance, going alongside the office building and cutting through the area of tables where Selena liked to enjoy her lunch breaks.

They left on no lights in the park, surely so Carter could save on his already reduced electric bill. Felix hadn't brought a flashlight and could only navigate one step at a time, his visibility only ten feet ahead thanks to the half-moon. He kept jumping at shadows that resembled human-like figures. A gust of wind rustled the leaves high in the trees, providing a blanket of white noise that was deafening in the silence.

*Relax*, Felix told himself. *No one is hiding in the shadows watching you. Get to Time Roller and stop worrying.*

He moved station to station, hiding behind trash cans, poles, and anything else that could conceal him. The top of the roller coaster came into sight as he ducked behind a lemonade stand and peered around the corner. Willow wasn't in sight.

*What if she's hiding somewhere else, waiting to make her move? What if she saw me and left because I'm following her?*

The angst from the situation was practically choking Felix. He had proceeded toward Time Roller without confirming Willow wasn't camped out somewhere else. He had been so confident she had gone directly to the roller coaster that he never stopped to consider she might have taken a different, more careful approach.

*What if I've just thrown off the past? Willow was supposed to be cutting away at the pull cable right now. And if she left, what does that mean for the accident next week?*

From beneath the roller coaster, a flash of light went off as briefly as a lightning strike, allowing relief to pour over Felix's panicked mind.

*Okay, so she is there. Sneaky.*

If Willow hadn't been the criminal behind such an atrocious

act, Felix would have urged the Angels to recruit her. She had more confidence than Felix breaking into this amusement park and clearly had plenty of stealth in her arsenal.

*A hippie combination of Arielle and Selena.* He chuckled at the thought and remained stuck behind the lemonade stand. Felix couldn't exactly walk up to the roller coaster to investigate what Willow was up to. But the flash of light had come from under the main platform, exactly where one would need to be to cut the pull cable.

*With a pair of bolt cutters in that backpack, she just needs a couple hours of no interruptions to get started.*

Felix shook his head and considered finding a rock or something to throw at the roller coaster. Until he saw the bolt cutters in action, he had nothing to actually report back to Arielle and Selena. *I might have to wait until she leaves, then I can go look at the damage she managed for the night.*

His stomach churned at the thought of sitting behind this lemonade stand for an unknown amount of time, but he had little choice. Fortunately, he was out of sight from the main path the guards patrolled. He'd hear them pass, but they had no reason to check behind the stand.

* * *

Only thirty minutes had passed when the flashlight beneath Time Roller turned back on. A security guard had just passed them by five minutes prior, whistling while his flashlight danced in every direction. Felix nearly had a panic attack, but the guard had no suspicions and kept on his jolly way.

Willow must have seen him, too, considering her timing for turning on her own flashlight. Felix didn't think half an hour was enough time to make any significant progress on cutting the pull cord, especially if Willow planned to leave in two days.

*Maybe she's going to pull an all-nighter tomorrow to finish the job. Or she could slowly chip away. Thirty minutes a night for three or four nights should do the trick.*

He watched the glow from her flashlight bounce around beneath the coaster, illuminating brief glimpses of the white-colored wood.

The light turned off and Felix kept his gaze glued to the platform.

An entire minute passed until her silhouette finally appeared and promptly hurried down the exit lane from Time Roller. Willow couldn't have been as comfortable as Felix had originally thought, considering she broke into a sprint, taking the occasional glance over her shoulder.

He remained frozen until she vanished from sight. Thanks to the timing of the guard's recent passing by, Felix had enough time to check out the scene beneath the roller coaster and escape the park before they came back around.

*Just be fast,* he reminded himself, stepping out from the lemonade stand and jogging with gentle footsteps toward the ride. He skipped the regular line and zoomed down the exit lane, a clear shot to the coaster's main platform.

He hadn't gone beneath the ride on any of their prior trips, and pushed open the maintenance crew's gate, unsure of what to expect. Four quick steps took him to the bottom landing, a level concrete slab running beneath the length of the platform.

Felix looked around, saw a collection of spider webs in one

direction, and promptly turned the other way, finding the pull cable. Without a flashlight, he had to rely on the moonlight clambering through the wooden slats of the platform above.

At first, he couldn't believe what he saw—or at least, what he thought he was seeing. It was dim, sure, but there was just enough light to see the pull cable had zero markings on it.

Felix blinked rapidly, as if that might help his eyes focus. He reached up and ran his fingers along the grooves of the cable.

*Smooth.*

If Willow had started cutting, he would have felt part of it frayed. The amount of cable within reach was a stretch of six feet. Felix ran his fingers gracefully along the cable, feeling the top, bottom, and sides to ensure he covered every angle.

*Nothing. If she didn't cut anything, then what was she doing?*

Felix continued running his fingers back and forth along the pull cord, determined to find *something* that showed Willow had started her sabotage of Time Roller.

*So she came in with a backpack, but used nothing to cut the cord. She could have been studying it, hoping to return later to get the job done.*

Felix gritted his teeth in frustration. Once he had seen Willow turn into the parking lot, he presumed everything would come together. He'd have his proof and they could stop Willow from going any further. *Easy as pie,* as his mother used to say when he and his sisters were young kids.

But this was the past they were dealing with. And it was never as easy as pie. Whatever the hell that meant.

Felix felt the cord one last time before giving up and leaving the park with more questions than he had upon arriving.

# Chapter 33

August 17, 1978

The Angels sat at the dining table the next evening, Selena tending to a glass of wine while Arielle stared mindlessly at the table, jaw clenched as intensely as her fists.

Felix had left a note on the table when he arrived home at six in the morning, expressing a need for a team meeting. Arielle and Selena had gone their separate ways in the morning while Felix slept the day away, bracing for another long night camped outside of Miracle Park.

He had just shared last night's findings—or rather, his lack of concrete evidence.

"If Willow isn't cutting the pull cable, then who is?" Arielle asked in a low tone. She felt the rage boiling within and knew the rest of the room sensed it. This mission was spiraling out of control, and she wanted nothing more than to plant her fist through the wall. When no one answered, she laughed under her breath and shook her head. "This is not fucking happening. One week out and we have nowhere to go."

Felix cleared his throat. "I know you don't want to hear it, but we might have to hide in the park every night until we see who it is."

Arielle crossed her arms, still glaring at the table. "If it was that simple, we wouldn't have wasted these last few weeks. We could have just shown up today and camped outside the park until we figured it out. But that's not how any of this works. The past doesn't allow it to be that simple. You got lucky last night. If you keep going back, I can guarantee something will happen—whether it's security finding you or the perpetrator. And it's nothing to do with your skills. The past doesn't let you take a backseat to watch the show. Trust me, I tried that plenty of times early in my career. It only ensures you end up running away."

"What are we supposed to do, then?" Selena asked, swirling her wine before taking a sip.

"I'm worried," Arielle said. "But not panicking. Not yet, at least. We still have this weekend with Willow out of town. I'm hoping we can find whatever we need to put this matter to rest."

"Let me join you," Selena said. "A fresh pair of eyes is just what we need."

"That's fine. I won't be going over until later at night. The houses are all close together on Willow's block, so we can't risk breaking in during the day. Have there not been any other disputes at the park?"

Selena shook her head. "Not that I've seen or heard about. It's actually been a pretty quiet week."

"Of course it has. And how is Joy?"

Selena shrugged. "I haven't seen her too much. All the high schoolers started class this week, and she's been left to scramble to cover their shifts. I think she's worked doubles every day this week, and I don't see her slowing down."

"And when does the park close for the winter?"

"Not until Halloween."

Felix rummaged through the fridge to grab a bottle of Coke before joining them at the table. "So she's too busy to carry this out?"

"Obviously," Selena said with a roll of her eyes. "She's there before I get in, and there when I leave. I highly doubt when she finishes her twelve-hour shift she wants to hang out even more to cut the pull cable on Time Roller."

"I'll never understand people like her," Arielle said. "She is giving her life to Miracle Park and Alex Carter, whom she despises. Why does she care so much about winning his approval when he's been nothing but abusive toward her—both verbally and physically?"

"I think she sees Miracle Park as a stepping stone to other opportunities," Selena said. "I wouldn't be surprised if she sought a job at Disneyland, just to piss off Carter. Maybe *that* is the revenge she's been chasing all along. It really is hard to see her as a suspect anymore. Lately, she just keeps to herself, puts her head down, and gets to work. She doesn't complain about anything and always puts on a smile in front of the guests. If I didn't know any better, I'd think she genuinely loved her job."

"She's probably just trying to stay out of Carter's way," Felix said. "Only two months to go. Why not avoid the drama? If she works overtime and is getting shit done, what reason does Carter have to shout at her?"

Selena snorted. "How naïve to think Carter won't shout at someone just because they're doing their job. The man is mental. We had a rare all-staff meeting last week to thank the teens for their work over the summer and wish them luck for the new school year. Carter said nothing and made

Grazella, our HR lady, do all the talking. And what do you think Carter did the whole time? He stuffed his face with cake and grumbled under his breath about how kids shouldn't have to deal with school if they already had a job."

"I wish I could say I'm surprised," Arielle said, shaking her head.

"We should check on Copeland," Felix said. "It's been a few days since I've been out to his house. Think one of you can stop by and see if those bolt cutters are still in his shed?"

"I can," Arielle said. "With kids back in school, I'd just need to wait for Mrs. Copeland to leave to drop them off or pick them up. Shouldn't be too difficult."

A knock came from the front door, and all three fell silent, looking at each other with puzzled expressions.

"Who the hell is it?" Selena whispered.

Arielle checked the clock on the wall. It was only 6:30, not late enough to warrant so much suspicion.

"I'll go check," Felix said, and tiptoed away.

Arielle and Selena followed behind and watched Felix peek through the curtains in the living room.

"It's just the neighbors," Felix said. "Linda from across the street, and I'm guessing that's her husband she's with. No one has met him yet, right?"

"No," Arielle said. "He has been gone this entire time I think."

Felix shrugged before opening the door, Arielle and Selena shuffling up behind him.

Linda stood there with a ghastly expression. Her husband, dressed in his Air Force combat uniform, had his beefy arms crossed behind his back, face red, while thick cords stood out on his neck.

"Are you Felix?" the man asked through gritted teeth.

Linda had her eyes glued to Felix, and Arielle could see guilt swimming behind them.

"Uhh, yes," Felix said. "Is everything okay?"

The man reared back a fist and swung it forward.

Fortunately, Arielle had seen everything unfolding and sensed the tension radiating from Linda's husband. If she hadn't stepped forward, Felix's face would have been smashed.

Arielle shoved Felix aside moments before the collision, causing the man to stumble forward into their living room. With his head lowered and face looking down, Arielle dropped an elbow on the back of the man's neck.

"Fuck!" he shouted as he collapsed to the floor.

Arielle didn't trust the man's immense size. His muscles were so large he looked like an inflatable toy soldier who might pop any moment. If he knew how to use those muscles to his advantage was another question, but Arielle wasn't going to wait to find out. She fell on top of him and planted a firm punch on the top of his spine.

"What the fuck, lady!" the man screamed, his face now a deep scarlet.

Arielle grabbed the back of his head and pressed his face into the carpet. "You don't come into our house and attack. Do you understand?"

She spoke with the scolding tone of a pissed-off mother. Linda had backed two steps away, crying for help, while Felix regained his balance and composure after Arielle had knocked him into the door.

When the man didn't respond, Arielle pinched the skin of the man's bald head and pushed harder into the floor. Linda shrieked and started running circles around their front yard.

"Felix," Arielle snapped. "Go shut her up before someone calls the cops." She turned her attention back to the man wriggling beneath her knees. "I asked if you understand."

He nodded, gasping for air and unable to speak.

Arielle felt the tension leave his back and knew he had given up fighting. "Selena. Gun."

Selena nodded and disappeared into the kitchen, returning seconds later with Arielle's pistol. Arielle took it and stood up, brushing off her legs. She pointed the gun at Linda's husband. "On the couch. Now."

The man gulped once he made eye contact with the gun, and climbed slowly to his knees, crawling to the couch like a terrified child. He held his hands up high as he sat down.

Arielle lowered her gun. "Put your hands down. I'm not going to shoot you."

The shrieking from outside stopped, and Arielle saw Linda retreating to her house. Felix stepped back in, eyes bulging at the scene.

"What are—" he started.

"What's this all about?" Arielle snapped, glaring at the man. "You come to our house and try to punch Felix. Explain yourself."

"Who the hell are you people?" he asked, rubbing the back of his neck.

"I'm asking the questions," Arielle seethed, slipping the gun back into her waistband. "And for your own sake, you better answer. Now tell us what you're doing here."

The man gawked at the three Angels surrounding him, oblivious that they had come from forty-five years in the future, and knew he had no chance of escaping. "Okay. Maybe

I came at this the wrong way."

He reached for his breast pocket, prompting Arielle to whip her gun back up. "Easy," she said.

"You take it easy, lady," the man said, reaching into the pocket and pulling out a stack of photographs. He tossed them on the coffee table. "I found these in my wife's dresser and wanted an explanation."

The three Angels stepped forward in unison, looking at the top photo that showed Felix running down the sidewalk, topless and sweaty.

Felix frowned and reached down to spread the stack of pictures across the table. All the photos were of him. Candid shots of him running around the neighborhood. Some of him doing yardwork.

"Um," Felix said, never appearing more perplexed than this moment. "I think I'm the one who needs an explanation. Why do *you* have pictures of *me*?"

The man laughed and rubbed his forehead, his face turning red again, but not from asphyxiation like last time. "I'm sorry, guys. I saw these pictures in Linda's dresser and assumed the worst. She had told me about the new neighbors, and when I found these, I made up my own story. All the way up to when I knocked on your door. Clearly, you have better things going on with these two." He nodded to Arielle and Selena.

"That's not at all what's happening," Selena said, balling a fist and stepping toward the man. Arielle pulled her back. "You fucking sicko. We're cousins."

"Cousins?" the man asked, raising an eyebrow. "So you *are* fucking my wife?"

"What?!" Felix gasped. "We met your wife the day we moved in and haven't seen her since. We're busy with work and school. Clearly, she's the one sneaking around because I've never seen these pictures."

The man giggled, and Arielle wished she could blast her fist through his face. Give him a reason to laugh. But she knew better, and asked, "What's your name?"

The man fell silent and appeared to debate answering the question, but finally gave in. "Eddie."

"Okay, Eddie," Arielle continued. "I understand you spend a lot of time on the road for work—and we thank you for your service—but you've created a story in your head that is completely off base. Like Felix said, we're in Hilburn for school and work. We have little free time, and when we get some, the last thing anyone wants is to have an affair with a neighbor."

"Then why does my wife have pictures of this guy?" Eddie asked, as if Felix was no longer standing three feet in front of him. "What else am I supposed to think?"

Arielle tossed up her hands. "C'mon, man. Don't put this on us. Obviously, Linda is going through something. Do these pictures look like Felix is even aware they're being taken? Half of them are from behind. Your wife is the one you should be questioning."

Eddie rubbed the back of his neck, where a welt formed in the outline of Arielle's fist. "I don't know who to believe. Linda says Felix came on to her and takes his shirt off on purpose so she can take the pictures."

"Bullshit!" Felix cried.

Arielle raised a hand for him to keep quiet. "Eddie, that is a complete lie. Now, if you can't see that for yourself, I don't know what to tell you. What I can say is that you need to leave our house and never show your face here again. You or Linda, for that matter. Because next time, I won't be so generous with the consequences."

Eddie pursed his lips and nodded. He raised his hands as he stood from the couch, and Arielle's hand slid back to the gun she had tucked into her waist band.

"Okay," he said, keeping his hands elevated as he shuffled to the door. He pulled open the door and looked over his shoulder and directed his words to Arielle. "If you ever need to put that sweet mouth of yours to use on a real man, you know where to find me."

Eddie stepped out and slammed the door behind him. If Arielle thought she could get away with it, she just might have chased him down and shot him in the back of the head. People like Eddie had no place in a healthy society.

"What the *fuck* was that?" Selena asked, eyes still wide from the confrontation.

Arielle locked the door and leaned on it. "We're getting close. That was definitely the past pushing back at us."

# Chapter 34



August 18, 1978

Friday night brought an unforgiving thunderstorm over the small town of Hilburn, Nebraska. The first few raindrops had started shortly after seven o'clock when the Angels were finishing dinner. Felix was prepared to head to Miracle Park, but the weather canceled those plans. The park closed down, and they agreed it was highly unlikely anyone would try to sneak in amid a torrential downpour.

Not having the luxury of checking the forecast on a smart phone, they had to watch the evening news through a scrambled feed that gave out each time lightning struck in the area. Eventually, they reached the weather segment where the meteorologist explained the rain would continue well into the following morning.

"I suppose we can all go together now," Arielle said, thrilled to have her entire team to help snoop around Willow's house. She had driven by a few times earlier in the day, and the home appeared to be empty.

Felix laughed. "Yes, I probably should go. Would hate to be accused of banging the neighbor while sitting around the house on such a gloomy night."

The mood had lightened after the events of last night, and Arielle explained if the past was already playing dirty, they'd need to be on their toes for the rest of the mission. As they drove to Willow's house, the wiper blades blasting frantically back and forth on the windshield, Arielle said, "I suspect more fireworks tonight once we get into Willow's house. Stay focused, but be ready for anything."

Once they parked in front of Willow's house, the rain intensified. They could barely see the homes across the street through the sheet of water pouring from the skies.

"I've never seen rain this heavy," Selena said from the backseat. "Are we in any danger of a flood?"

Felix shook his head. "The land is too flat here. It would have to rain for at least three days straight for there to be any risk. Doubtful, unless we think the rain is part of the past pushing back?"

Arielle shook her head. "If anything, the rain is helping us. We might as well head in—no point in waiting for the rain to lighten up. Straight around the house to the back door. She keeps it unlocked. Just make sure her cats don't get out."

"She's a cat lady?" Selena asked, rolling her eyes. "Yeah, she's definitely guilty."

"Let's go," Arielle said, swinging her door open and jumping out. The other two followed, splashing in the muddy puddles as they dashed across the front yard to hurry along the side of the house. Selena screamed in fright when her foot sunk into a mudhole up to her ankle. Felix was running behind Selena and pulled her along without missing a beat. The rain was so heavy, by the time they reached the back door ten steps later, Selena's shoes looked brand new.

"This is so nasty," Selena whined as Arielle pushed open

the back door.

Felix and Selena piled in behind her, shaking off like wet dogs.

"Dry off," Arielle said, dragging her shoes aggressively on the rug.

After a minute, they continued through the kitchen, hair plastered to their foreheads, shirts clinging to their skin.

"Hello!" Arielle shouted, receiving only her echo in response. She marched forward and looked over her shoulder. "We're clear. Just wanted to be safe."

They entered the living room, where the coffee table had a metropolis of bongs standing like skyscrapers. Ash trays with half-smoked joints decorated each corner of the table.

"So, this is where you had all that fun without us," Selena said sarcastically. "He may just be a little kid in 1978, but these guys would definitely make Snoop Dogg proud."

Felix laughed. "Don't act so young. These guys have Cheech and Chong, and Willie Nelson for their stoner idols. Tell me you at least know who those guys are."

Selena shrugged. "I've heard the names but couldn't pick them out of a lineup."

Felix threw his hands in the air. "Can you believe this, Arielle? Do you see what they give us to work with?"

Selena pinched her lips tight and punched Felix on the arm. "That's for Eddie."

Even Arielle couldn't help but break into howling laughter at the banter as Felix rubbed his arm, shaking his head.

"Enough, you two," Arielle said when they calmed back down. "I'm going to check out Willow's bedroom."

"We'll join you," Felix said, following Arielle down the hallway.

Willow's bedroom door was open, and the two cats were lying curled up on the bed, purring as they studied the three people from the future trickling in.

"Do they attack?" Selena asked.

"Attack?" Arielle replied with a laugh. "They're lazy house cats. What exactly do you think they're going to do?"

"Hey, I've had my share of encounters with cats," Selena snapped. "I don't trust those things."

"Can you forget about the cats and get to work?" Felix said, examining the books on top of Willow's dresser.

Selena rolled her eyes. "Yes, sir, on it."

Arielle knew Selena was in a mood thanks to being the only one who stepped into mounds of mud. Her shoes still made a squishing sound with each step she took.

"I don't see the engineering book," Felix said. "Didn't you say it's in here?"

"Yes," Arielle said, hurrying to join Felix at the dresser. She scanned the row of books, running her fingers along the tops as she slowed down to read the title on each spine. "I don't understand. It was right here last time. Piece of paper sticking out the top with the blueprints for the roller coaster. We need to find that book."

Felix slid over to the second dresser and started pulling open the drawers. Arielle did the same for the dresser she was standing at, and Selena strolled around the bed to search through the nightstand.

"Why would that book be gone?" Arielle asked. "It doesn't make sense." She flipped through clothes in each drawer, patting the walls in case the book was hidden.

"Or does it?" Felix asked. "Think about it. If she's the one behind this, would she not be making final preparations?

She spent the other night at the park to get a closeup view of the coaster. And now she's away for the weekend with her engineering book and blueprint planning exactly what to do."

"But to do that so openly?" Arielle said. "She's at a music festival with friends. They're probably all crammed into a tent together. Is she really going to open a mechanical engineering book while they're passing around a bong? Are you finding anything in there?"

Felix shook his head. "Clothes and jewelry. Nothing else."

"I don't have the book," Selena said from the nightstand, "but I found something else."

Arielle and Felix spun around. Selena held up a manila envelope and pulled out a set of photographs. She dropped them on the bed and splayed them out.

"Holy shit," Arielle whispered, touching her hand to her lips as she stepped closer.

The photos were all eight by ten, and each showed either Alexander Carter or Time Roller. The pictures of Carter were candid and from a distance. One showed him getting into his car. Another showed him walking along the path that connected the park to the hotel. One even had him standing at the window in his penthouse suite.

"This is...wrong," Selena said. "She's been following him. Has pictures of him where he lives and works. Do we have any more doubt about who is behind this attack?"

Felix stepped forward and looked over their shoulders. "This is something an insane person does. If Willow's crazy enough to do this, then she's definitely capable of sabotaging the coaster."

"Willow does photography on the side," Arielle said. "That's a random thing I learned from following her. She's capable of taking these kinds of pictures from a distance. I agree—she's the one we're after."

"What about the book?" Selena asked.

Arielle shook her head. "I don't know. But seeing these pictures, does it even matter at this point? We have enough to tie it all to Willow. Let's look around some more and see what else we can find, then we can head out and plan our next move."

From down the hall, the sound of the back door creaking open froze them each in place.

# Chapter 35

Arielle immediately shot up a finger to her lips to tell them to remain silent.

Felix turned white as snow while Selena stuffed the photos back into the envelope.

"Put them back," Arielle whispered.

"Hello?" a woman's voice called from the kitchen. "Is someone here?"

*Dammit all,* Arielle thought. *Is it a coincidence this is happening* seconds *after we found those pictures in the nightstand?*

"Get under the bed," Arielle whispered, pointing to the floor. "I got this."

"Hello?" the woman shouted again. "I see wet footprints. I know someone is here."

"I'm in the bedroom!" Arielle hollered. Selena and Felix dropped to the floor in unison and squirmed their way under the bed.

Once they were out of sight, Arielle hurried out of the room. A petite woman stood at the end of the hallway, a chef's knife in hand. Arielle recognized her face from the day she had come to the meeting but didn't recall actually meeting her.

"Hi," Arielle said, offering a friendly wave.

"Hi?" the woman replied, lowering the knife. She noticed Arielle staring at it. "I may have overreacted, but I wasn't expecting anyone here. Are you a friend of Willow?"

"Yes," Arielle said with full confidence. "Willow asked if I'd stop by to feed her cats over the weekend while she's out of town. I was just looking for them—they were sleeping on her bed."

The woman let out a sigh of relief, then started laughing. "Well, it appears we've been double booked. Willow asked *me* to feed her cats this weekend, too."

"Oh?" Arielle crossed her arms and rubbed them for warmth. The heater wasn't running during the summer, and the thunderstorm had dropped the temperatures well below her comfort level. "Classic Willow, right? Can't remember who she asked for a favor. I'll bet she forgot she asked you, because she just called me last night to ask if I'd swing by twice a day to check on the cats."

The woman giggled. "This is awkward. Sorry if I startled you—I'm sure you weren't expecting anyone to just barge in through the back door. I'm Sarah."

Sarah took a step back to place the knife on the coffee table before extending a hand to Arielle.

"I'm Arielle. Nice to meet you."

Sarah couldn't have been any more than five feet tall. Her jet-black hair was pulled into a sopping wet ponytail. She had droopy eyes that reminded Arielle of Eeyore from Winnie the Pooh, yet her smile swarmed the room with charm. "Have we met before?" Sarah asked, cocking her head like she was studying an animal in the zoo. "You look kind of familiar, but I can't remember from where."

"I was here last week for the meeting. I met a ton of people that night, so maybe we met then?"

Sarah's eyes lit up, and she pointed a finger at Arielle. "Yes! I was here, too."

Arielle couldn't tell her she had gotten high and paranoid that night and remembered little beyond finding the engineering book in Willow's bedroom. But as long as Sarah remembered the encounter, that was all that mattered for their sake right now. She just needed to get her out of the house so they could get back to business.

"So, what do you want to do?" Arielle asked. "I'm happy to let you finish the weekend of feeding the cats, since I'm assuming Willow asked you first."

Sarah nodded. "Sure. She asked me a couple of weeks ago. Like you said, must have slipped her mind. I only live one block over, so it's really not a hassle for me."

"That's great. I appreciate that." Arielle gave a warm smile. "I can wrap things up here tonight if you want to head out. Then it's all yours for the rest of the weekend."

"Great," Sarah said. "It was so good to see you again. Will you be at the next protest?"

Arielle had been dodging Willow ever since she found the engineering book in her room last week and hadn't caught wind of any upcoming protest.

"I'm not sure. When is it?" Arielle asked.

Sarah looked up at the ceiling like her calendar was kept there. "Oh, it's next Saturday, the twenty-sixth."

* * *

Sarah finally left fifteen minutes later. The girl could talk and kept going on about past protests and hopes for the future. After their extended conversation, Arielle decided Sarah was quite similar to Willow, just less aggressive. They carried the same passion for making the world a better and fair place, but Sarah lacked Willow's leadership qualities.

By the time Arielle returned to the bedroom, Felix and Selena were already out from under the bed, studying the candid portraits of Alexander Carter and Time Roller.

"Did you guys hear that?" Arielle asked, paying no attention to what they were doing. Her mind had been wandering ever since Sarah informed her about the next planned protest.

"Which part?" Selena asked with a chuckle. "About her first protest, or her twenty-seventh?"

Felix joined the laughter, but Arielle only looked at them. "No," she said firmly. "About the protest next Saturday. Why would she have a protest planned so close to sabotaging the park? She must know there will be investigators and press covering the accident. Why put the spotlight on herself as a potential suspect?"

"You're thinking too much into it," Felix said. "Remember how Yokota explained it? The pull cable only has to be frayed. The ride operating constantly is what eventually snaps the cord and causes the accident. Willow has no way of knowing when the cord will snap. Was anything mentioned about this next protest in the pre-mission reports? I don't remember reading about it."

Arielle shook her head. "Not that I can recall."

"See," Felix said, raising his brow. "I'll bet they had the protest scheduled and called it off after the accident. The real question is, who else knows about Time Roller?"

"We have no way of knowing," Arielle said. "Willow has made it impossible to know who she trusts the most. I've observed her plenty on this mission, and she rarely spends time with the same person. I suppose, by default, her roommates are the ones she's closest to. They *did* go with her to this music festival, after all."

"Let's go check out their bedrooms then."

"Fine, but we need to make it fast. I don't like how this Sarah girl just showed up out of the blue. Too many roadblocks these past couple days—they're only going to get worse."

They filed out of Willow's bedroom without another word. Arielle waited a moment to look over the room one more time, the missing book still weighing heavily on her mind. Something about that detail sowed the faintest amount of doubt for Arielle. Willow had to have *someone* she trusted with the secrets of her plan to destroy Time Roller. But who?

She ventured out to the hallway and turned into the second bedroom, where Willow's two roommates shared a space—twin beds pushed against opposite walls, with a narrow dresser at the foot of each. With the cramped area, the Angels had little to search through.

Felix and Selena each took a dresser and rummaged through the drawers. Only one bed had a complementing nightstand, and Arielle pulled open its top drawer.

"Whoa!" she cried out, reaching in and pulling out a silver pistol.

"Never expected to find a gun in a house full of hippies," Selena said, slamming the drawers shut in frustration and joining Arielle. "What do you think they have it for?"

"Protection," Felix said, closing his drawers and spinning around. "Obviously. This group is always out leading protests.

They deal with dangerous men like Carter. Why wouldn't they have a gun? Can you imagine if Carter ever made a house call here? How threatening that might feel. You can't take any chances."

Arielle put the gun back in the nightstand drawer and crossed her arms as she glared at it. "It still doesn't add up. I get what you're saying, but I've seen these people in action. They catch bugs in the house and carry them outside to 'return to their natural environment.' I can't see those same people carrying a gun for any reason."

"I wonder if Willow knows there's a gun in her house," Selena said. "Seems like something they could be hiding from her."

The nightstand had two drawers, so Arielle crouched down to open the lower one.

"Guys," she said, voice shaking like she had just witnessed a murder. "Never mind the gun. Look what we have here."

She reached into the drawer and pulled out a small pair of bolt cutters.

# Chapter 36

The bolt cutters lay on the kitchen counter as the Angels argued in their kitchen.

"We shouldn't have taken them out of Willow's house," Arielle said, pacing back and forth. If the kitchen was any bigger, she might have broken into sprints. The possibilities of what could happen because of the stolen bolt cutters tormented her.

"Slow down," Felix said. "We discussed this over there. We have no proof these are *the* bolt cutters used to fray the pull cable. All we did was remove a possibility from the equation."

"A *likely* possibility," Arielle snapped. "Very likely. Who the hell keeps bolt cutters in their nightstand? Dammit, guys—we've made a mistake."

"No mistake," Selena said. "You agreed taking them out of the house can throw a wrench into their plans. Granted, not a major wrench, because they can just go get another set."

"I know," Arielle said through gritted teeth. In a rare instance, Arielle feared the consequences of her actions. If not Willow, someone in Willow's house was responsible for cutting Time Roller's pull cord. They'd arrive home in a couple of days to finish their plan of destroying the ride and Alexander Carter. But when would they notice the bolt cutters were missing? "We don't know what this will do to the timeline of events, and that concerns me the most. We may have just completely fucked our chances on this mission."

Arielle stopped in front of the bolt cutters and punched the countertop.

"I don't understand why you're so upset," Felix said calmly. "We did the right thing."

Arielle jerked her head from side to side. "We may have done what seemed like a *good* thing, but it was far from the right decision. Our mission centers on the date of the tragedy—August 24, 1978." They kept a calendar tacked to the wall above the trash can. Arielle strolled right up to it and jammed a finger on the date. "*Everything* has been based on this date. By taking these bolt cutters, we may have moved the date. Say they get home Monday morning. Do you really think the roommate is going to head straight in and make sure the bolt cutters are stored safely in the nightstand? No. Why would anyone have reason to think *bolt cutters* were stolen from a *nightstand*? If they don't check until whatever night they plan on sneaking into the park, they're going to find quite the surprise. Everything closes early in this town, and we know this crime happens overnight. They won't be able to walk into a hardware store and get a new set—they'll have to wait until the next day. And that's what changes everything. It can push the accident back by a day. Maybe they wait even longer. Maybe they decide not to even go through with it."

"Is that not what we want?" Selena asked, frowning at Arielle like she was making a big deal out of nothing.

"Dammit, Selena, that's not the point!" Arielle stepped away from the calendar, arms shaking with rage. "Of course, that's what we want, but we'll have no way of knowing. They could end up delaying it for two weeks. We'll be long gone, and we won't find out until reading the Futures Report. I like to know for certain how the mission turns out—no matter the outcome. Do you know who leaves things to chance and hopes everything turns out fine on the Futures Report?"

Arielle put her hands on her hips and jutted her chin towards her team, demanding an answer with a glare from hell.

Felix held a grave expression and shook his head.

Arielle stood tall and folded her hands in front of her thighs. "Angels who rank near the bottom leave everything up to chance. New, inexperienced Angels. We are the top-ranked team. We cannot, and do not, work like this. Do we really want to risk our status as the top team and lose all the perks that come with that? We've come so far in such a short amount of time—we should only lose our ranking when we're ready for that to happen."

"We're not in danger of dropping," Felix said calmly. "Even if we completely failed this mission. We have a cushion in the rankings that would take multiple failures to lose."

"I'm not risking it," Arielle said. "We're already so close to the truth. We found the bolt cutters in Willow's house. She has pictures of Carter and the roller coaster *in* her nightstand. And somewhere is that goddamned book on mechanical engineering. I'm taking the bolt cutters back, and we'll make plans to stop Willow next week."

Selena opened her mouth to speak but was immediately interrupted by Arielle. "And that's final. No discussion."

* * *

Fifteen minutes later, Arielle was back inside Willow's house, knowing Sarah wouldn't be back until the morning. After Arielle put the bolt cutters back in the nightstand drawer, she returned to Willow's room for one last check for the engineering book.

*I saw it, right?* Arielle wondered. She had consumed far too much marijuana that day she found the book and was doubting if it had been some sort of illusion. What bothered her the most was the order of the books on top of Willow's dresser. If the book was gone for the weekend, shouldn't there be a gap where it had been? All the books were pushed tightly together as if there had never been a thick textbook among them.

Arielle took pride in her personal bookshelf back home. They all had to be presented in a particular order on the shelf. She sorted by genre, then by alphabetical order of the titles. When she removed a book, she never pressed the remaining ones together. There would be a gap to return the book to its proper place once she finished reading. Closing that gap seemed like utter madness.

*But Willow is crazy, right? If she sabotaged a ride knowing it would kill innocent people, that is the definition of utter madness. And why is she okay with letting people die? Sure, she wants to take down Carter, but the action doesn't match her personality.*

"Maybe it's not her," Arielle said aloud, the pounding of raindrops reverberating throughout the house. She let out a nervous laugh. It was still a possibility, albeit a slim one, that everything they had found so far was entirely coincidental. Willow could have come up with the idea in the heat of the moment, then dismissed it as too extreme. But one of her followers might have liked the idea and wanted to see it through.

Wasn't it always some crazed follower who went rogue and pushed matters beyond the limit? Willow had dozens of people cycling through her home, and she clearly didn't care if any of them needed to lie down or have quiet time in her own bedroom. Anyone could have swiped that mechanical engineering book if they knew it existed on Willow's bookshelf. They could have snuck in yesterday and taken it, then rearranged the books to look like nothing was missing. The price of leaving your back door unlocked.

Willow's carelessness and blind trust of those close to her just might lead to her downfall. But she was too smart. If this had all been Willow's idea originally, she actually got away with it. No one even suspected the roller coaster collapsed on purpose. They just accepted that the pull cable snapped.

Faulty equipment. Poor workmanship. These were phrases thrown around by investigators during the original timeline of events. When a pull cable snapped or got caught in the gears, it frayed on the ends just the same as destroying it with bolt cutters. In a sense, it was the perfect crime for the times. The actual cause was masked by other possibilities. The small town of Hilburn was too naïve to consider something so horrific might have happened intentionally. People hated Alexander Carter, sure, but no one would stoop so low to kill innocent people. Not in Hilburn, where a murder hadn't been committed since the early 1960s.

Arielle stormed out of the bedroom, the cats still on the bed and watching her curiously. If only she could talk to them. They would know what happened to that book. Despite her disgust with being unable to find it, Arielle already felt relief for putting the bolt cutters back into place.

She hurried down the hallway, through the kitchen, and out

the back door.

*Six more days.*

# Chapter 37

August 22, 1978

Arielle spent the rest of her weekend trying to relax. With no one to follow, she grew antsy from having to wait for Willow to return. She headed to the Copeland residence on Sunday while the family was at church and took her time exploring the water department president's tool shed. The bolt cutters they had discovered earlier lay in the same place. She was ready to dismiss Copeland as a suspect but had to leave the door open. There were still two days until Time Roller was supposed to come crashing down, yet zero progress had been made on the roller coaster's pull cable.

Felix camped in the parking lot on both Sunday and Monday night and watched as the staff filed out shortly after eight o'clock each night and cleared out.

Willow arrived home on Monday afternoon. Arielle had driven by every couple of hours until she saw the lights inside turned on, and figures moving throughout the house. Willow's Beetle was parked in its usual spot along the sidewalk, and seeing it there helped Arielle fall back into the mission. No more failed attempts at watching TV or reading books—she could again focus on Willow and resolving this mission.

Willow needed little time to settle back home before inviting over people. Arielle parked two houses away and watched as several cars gradually filled the block, everyone filing into Willow's house.

Arielle recognized plenty of familiar faces from the last meeting, but there were plenty of new ones, too.

*Do I go in?* she debated. *I can always say I heard about the meeting from someone else and thought I should show up.*

Arielle hadn't spoken to Willow since the last time she was over. Avoiding people was much simpler in 1978. Willow didn't have Arielle's phone number or address, leaving her with no way of getting in touch.

"Fuck it," Arielle said, pushing her door open and stepping out of her car. The probability of Time Roller coming up in discussion during this meeting was too high for her to sit around.

"Lioness?" a familiar voice called from behind, dread instantly settling into Arielle's stomach.

She spun around to see Phoenix, eyes already bloodshot, as he took his sweet time strolling down the sidewalk.

"Phoenix!" Arielle cried, putting on a fake smile. "How are you?"

"Oh, you know, hanging in there," Phoenix replied in a lazy monotone. "It's been too long since I saw you last. How have you been?"

Phoenix finally reached Arielle on the sidewalk, and they continued toward Willow's house.

"I've been busy with work," Arielle said, keeping her gaze on the concrete below, where some cracks were just wide enough to cause a stumble if you weren't paying attention. "School, work, school, work. Some days I just feel like a robot."

Phoenix let out a hearty laugh while sticking his pinky finger deep into his ear to scratch an itch that didn't seem to give up. "Don't work yourself too hard, Lioness. You only get one life on this beautiful planet. You shouldn't spend it all under a pile of work."

*Easy to say when you live with your rich parents and smoke weed in the basement all day.*

"Of course," Arielle said. "I wouldn't dare. I still have some fun."

Arielle was grateful to reach Willow's door, ending the impromptu conversation with Phoenix.

"Ladies first," he said, pulling open the screen door and gesturing for Arielle to enter.

The main door was already open, so Arielle shuffled into the crowd, finding a dozen people gathered between the living room and kitchen.

She hadn't spotted Willow but noticed a few pairs of eyeballs watching her closely from the kitchen. Sarah was sitting on the couch and frowned when she saw Arielle.

*Why is everyone looking at me?* she wondered, Phoenix slipping by her and heading straight to the bongs on the coffee table.

The wandering eyes put Arielle on edge. Something was going on, and she sensed it immediately. She considered leaving, but she had already come this far and needed to know what was being discussed only two days before the biggest tragedy that would ever strike Hilburn, Nebraska.

Someone tapped Arielle's shoulder, and she turned around to see Willow with her arms crossed and brows furrowed above an intense glare.

"Well, well, well," Willow said. "If it isn't little miss Arielle. Did you have a good weekend?"

The house fell silent. Now, all eyes *were* on Arielle as the walls of the unknown closed around her.

*Does she know?* Arielle thought, eyes jumping to Sarah on the couch, who watched with a flat expression.

"Hey, Willow," Arielle said, trying to sound calm despite her heart jackhammering in her chest. "How is everything?"

Willow's stern countenance softened into a tight-lipped grin, but Arielle knew it wasn't for a positive reason. "Maybe we should talk outside." She turned to the silent crowd. "Everyone carry on. I'll be right back."

Willow took a step back and held up her hand to the door while everyone resumed tense chatter. Arielle's stomach sunk to her knees. *Sarah told her I was here. I've been caught red-handed.*

Arielle pushed open the creaky screen door and took slow steps on her way out. She had options.

*I can start the conversation. Beat her to the punch and make up some reason I was here. Or I can run. Sprint to my car and speed off. She doesn't know where I live—she'll have no way of tracking me down.*

She felt Willow's stare burning a hole into her back and decided running now would only be a waste of their efforts on this mission. She needed to get back in that house, and running was the only option that guaranteed it would *not* happen. Trying to talk her way back in was her only option, but Willow didn't give her the chance to speak first.

"Why were you in my house on Friday night?" Willow asked, accusation swimming behind each word.

Arielle reached the front of the porch and turned around.

"I was here taking care of your cats. I heard you were out of town, and I was in the neighborhood. Thought I'd stop by and check on them—they're just too cute."

"Oh, really?" Willow asked, putting her hands on her hips. "What are their names?"

Running didn't sound so bad after all. Arielle looked up, then down, licking and pursing her lips while beads of sweat ran down her back. "I can't say I've ever gotten their names."

"Well, you must love them a ton, because their names dangle from their collars. Spent some good quality time with them, did you?"

"Well, I—"

"Save it," Willow said, sticking up her hand like a stop sign. "Truth is the only way to an honest life. Just tell me what you were doing here, so we can get back on with our lives."

Arielle gazed firmly at Willow. She knew how to eliminate the common tells of lying, minus the sweat now making her shirt cling to her back.

"I lost something, and have been retracing my steps to find it," Arielle said.

Willow laughed, her shoulders shaking uncontrollably as she shot a hand to her mouth. "Do you really expect me to believe that? You lost something? If you lost something, you could have come by anytime. But you waited until I was gone. You knew the house would be empty and wanted to take your time inside. Thank goodness for real friends like Sarah. She told me about your encounter. You thought you could play me for an idiot? I don't forget things, especially like who I ask to watch my house while I'm away. I may look like some dumb blonde to you, but my mind is a steel trap."

"Willow, it's not what you think," Arielle pleaded. "I can't tell you exactly what I was doing, but you need to trust that I wasn't doing anything to harm you or your home. I care about you a ton."

Now Willow threw her head back and howled laughter to the sky. Her eyelids fluttered as she refocused her attention on Arielle. "You should know something. I investigate everyone who comes into my life. I know that sounds extreme, but I don't have a choice. Too many people in the past have hurt me and the causes I fight for, so I have people who dig."

*You're caught. Turn around and run! There's no coming back from this.*

"I'm sorry," Arielle said, brushing back strands of hair that had fallen over her face. "You've been investigating me?"

"Sure have," Willow said. "And you know what I've found?"

*That I'm a time traveler from the future sent here to destroy you? She can't actually know that, unless she somehow knows another time traveler. This era is swarming with old Revolters who enjoyed nothing more than killing Road Runners.*

Arielle only stared at Willow, clueless what she could say to get out of this mess.

"Nothing," Willow said, re-crossing her arms and shifting her weight to lean back on one leg. "Not a single thing about Arielle Lucila, if that's even your real name. You told me you were out here for school. The school has no records of your registration, and I know my sources there are some of the best. The city has no record of your name tied to any property. As far as anyone knows, you're homeless. How do you stay off the grid so well? I'm genuinely curious."

Willow waited for a response, beaming sarcastically at Arielle, who only shook her head. "I don't know what you want me to say," Arielle replied. "Again, none of this is what you think."

"Oh, I'm pretty sure it's exactly what I'm thinking." Willow wiped away her fake smile and took a step toward Arielle, jamming a finger into her chest. "I've dealt with people like you before. You come into town with your made-up story about why you're here, then you raise hell for everyone you come into contact with. I will not fall victim to these games again. I've learned from my past mistakes."

Arielle raised her hands to show she had no intention of fighting. She had no desire to humiliate Willow in her own front yard with a house full of friends watching through the blinds. "Maybe we should just take a step back and start over."

Willow laughed as she inched her face even closer to Arielle. The mixed stench of weed and iced tea from Willow's breath made Arielle nauseous. "Start over? I think maybe you should leave and never show your face here again. If you do, I have a house full of people ready to do anything to defend our cause. All I have to do is tell them you're a threat, and you'll be dealt with."

It had become crystal clear over the past five minutes that Willow would not be inviting Arielle back into her home for any reason.

"Oh, is that right?" Arielle asked, jutting her face out to get closer to Willow. They looked like a baseball coach and umpire having a shouting match mere inches apart. "Is that how you deal with things, Willow? If something is going against you, do you just make it disappear?"

It took every ounce of discipline in Arielle's body not to throw all the facts about Alexander Carter and Time Roller in Willow's face. Doing so would definitely throw off the rest of the mission.

"As a matter of fact," Willow said, taking a step back, "it is. I know who you are and what you're doing here, and you can't stop me. You're not as good as you think, by the way. Maybe you dress the part of a local, but something about you is just off. You're not from here, and anyone who pays attention in this town can tell that right away."

Arielle felt all the blood drain from her chest. *How does she know who I am?*

Willow continued. "I know you're working for that greasy thug, Alex Carter. Thought you could infiltrate my group to find out what we're up to? Well, I have news for you both, if you'd like to share with that fat *thug.* I have insiders, too. And he has no way of finding out who they are. Does little Alex think just because he's so rich, he can get away with playing these games? You don't need money to buy people, you just need a purpose people can get behind. Does he think he's the only one with connections inside the government? Two can play his corrupt games, but only one of us is on the wrong side of history."

Arielle wanted to throw her arms around Willow and thank her for sharing so much information. She wanted to ask her to keep spilling the details, maybe offer some names. But with Willow believing Arielle worked for Carter, there was no chance she'd do such a thing.

"You have people in city hall?" Arielle asked, genuinely curious.

Willow chuckled. "I have connections where I need them, and that's all you need to know. Now, why don't you get off my property before I call the police and turn you in for trespassing."

# Chapter 38

August 23, 1978

For most of the Wednesday following Willow kicking Arielle off her front lawn, Arielle took a list of names of Willow's known associates and drove around Hilburn, tracking them down.

While the task took up her time—and she was grateful it had—it proved worthless by the end of the day.

Arielle was spiraling.

The mission felt closer to failure than success on the eve of Time Roller's collapse. She couldn't risk following Willow, not after they found that gun in her house. The environmentalist who had created a peaceful image of herself was no less crooked than Alexander Carter. Regardless of who the gun in Willow's house belonged to, Arielle was certain they had it for anyone who disrupted their causes and protests. She couldn't put herself or her team anywhere near that type of danger.

Knowing how desperate Willow was to defeat Alexander Carter, Arielle doubted their other options. It wasn't Terrance Copeland or Joy Gillespie behind the accident. Not any of Willow's blind followers. It was her. She and Carter were playing a game of chess, with neither entirely knowing what the other had up their sleeve.

When the sun set on Wednesday night, the three Angels packed into Arielle's car and drove to Miracle Park.

"We need to prepare for different scenarios," Felix said, pulling out a notepad and pen. "There are a few possibilities tonight. We might see the suspect break in. We can either follow them all the way to Time Roller and stop them, or we can simply observe and confirm who they are. Our confrontation can happen at any time. We can even wait for them to come back out of the park and put the pressure on them. This mission is getting messy. Do you think we should even bother interjecting or just call the police to report what happened?"

Arielle had no control over the laugh that slipped out of her mouth. "We did not come this far to hand it over to the police. I understand where you're coming from, but we'll see this all the way through. We don't have much of a choice. The way things are going, I wouldn't be surprised if *nothing* happens tonight." She rubbed her forehead as they pulled up to a red light. "This last week has felt like an uphill battle. How else do you make sense of what has happened? The past may have beat us on this one, guys, and I'm not sure how to explain that to the commander when we get home."

"You're getting ahead of yourself," Selena said from the backseat. "You always tell us not to assume anything, and here you are, assuming this mission is done for. Do we not have all of tonight and tomorrow to finish the job?"

Arielle hated having her own words thrown back in her face. "You're right. I'm sorry, guys. This has just been difficult. I really feel like the past has been toying with us. Teasing us. Think about it. The bolt cutters at Copeland's house led to nowhere. Carter's arguments with Joy were just one-sided shouting matches—she doesn't even have the time to carry out this attack on the roller coaster. We were getting close with Willow—the bolt cutters in the second bedroom, the creepy pictures of Carter and Time Roller, and that *fucking* engineering book that just vanished."

"Don't you see, Arielle?" Selena said. "You're right about all that, but we know it has to be Willow, or at the very least, someone in her circle. We've narrowed it down. Now we just need the proof."

Arielle's frustration had boiled over to anger, but she couldn't show that in front of her team. She was supposed to be the calming presence they needed during difficult times. *What have I created? These two sound just like me. Felix focused on the work, Selena keeping a cool head. And I'm the one acting like a spoiled brat who didn't get their way.*

"We've needed the proof this whole time," Arielle said. "I guess if it comes to it, we'll treat this as observational tomorrow night. Stopping the accident was always optional—let's not forget that. All we need to do is find out who is responsible and make sure they get justice. It's always nice to save lives, but sometimes there's nothing we can do about it on these missions."

Arielle turned into the Miracle Park entrance and rolled through the parking lot.

"Don't park close," Felix said. "If someone wants to break in tonight, they could turn away if they see a random car parked close to the gate."

"Shouldn't there be a few cars here?" Arielle asked. "There is a security team inside overnight, and I'd assume anyone breaking into the park would know that."

"Carter makes all staff park at the hotel," Selena said.

"Regardless of their shift times. He really makes the graveyard team bypass this big, empty lot so they can walk over from the hotel."

Arielle shook her head. "So ridiculous."

"I've asked about that policy," Selena continued. "Park employees used to park at the back of the lot. It's actually a longer walk than coming from the hotel, so someone asked Carter if they could park at the hotel instead. Apparently, he fell in love with how busy the hotel's parking lot always looked because of it, and made that the policy. No exceptions."

"What about people with disabilities?" Felix asked. "They have to park closer."

Selena let out an exaggerated laugh. "Like Carter would ever hire someone with a disability."

Arielle stopped the car close to where Felix had parked the night he followed Willow into the amusement park. "Does this work?"

Felix pulled out his binoculars and looked toward the main gates. "Yep. Can see everything just fine from here. Now, we wait."

# Chapter 39

Selena had packed snacks for their overnight stakeout. When the clock struck midnight, Arielle poured the last of the almonds into her mouth after stress-eating them for the past hour.

During their four hours in the lot, only one other car had appeared—a high school couple looking for privacy as they settled into the backseat for a few minutes of fun. They had left after half an hour, windows fogged with passion, and that's when Arielle had started shoveling almonds by the handful.

"Do I need to go in there and cut the cord myself?" Arielle joked, frustration lying dormant behind her words. Despite making no progress on the mission, they had bonded in the car, swapping more stories from their lives and getting to know each other even better.

"Should we have split up tonight?" Selena asked, lying across the backseat with a lollipop between her lips. "One of us could have followed Willow around, and another followed Copeland."

"This scenario we're in doesn't require any more following," Arielle said. "And you're sure nothing was done to the roller coaster today?"

"I stopped by it around three o'clock and waited for the employees to have their backs turned so I could sneak underneath the platform. I waited for three rides to complete and examined the cord the whole time. Nothing."

Arielle sighed. She already knew this but needed to hear it one more time. "We're running out of time. Soon, it will be physically impossible to cut that cord in order to snap tomorrow night. If no one shows up in the next four hours, I'm not sure what we're supposed to do."

"Four hours is a long time," Felix said. "We've been here that long, and not a second of it has felt quick. If no one shows up, we'll just have to come back tomorrow and try again. The biggest decision will be how many nights do we want to keep doing this? At some point, we'll have to assume we prevented it from ever happening. Maybe the argument between Arielle and Willow threw something off."

"I highly doubt the past would allow that," Arielle said, leaning her head on the window. She looked at the vast parking lot in front of them and thought back through all the prior missions she had worked. Not once had a crime been stopped by coincidence. She had always forced the matter and could pinpoint which exact moment in the mission had caused the past's plans to unravel. "You can't accidentally defeat the past. If that were the case, we'd have no rankings or special teams. Everything would just be left to chance."

"Isn't everything left to chance?" Felix asked. "I'm talking about in our Present Time—not the past."

Arielle shook her head. "People like to think life is random, but we know better. It's only the not knowing what comes next that makes it seem random to regular people. We could choose any person in the world, jump forward a few days and follow them for years. We'd know everything that person will do and could return to the present to follow them and watch the same things happen."

"Have either of you ever done that?" Felix asked in a soft tone. "Traveled into the future to see how your life turns out?"

"That's not allowed," Arielle quickly replied. "Don't tell me you've done that."

"First off," Felix said with a crooked grin, "there isn't an actual rule against doing it. I've read through the Bylaws and it's mentioned nowhere. It's one of those things that's more frowned upon and discouraged, rather than illegal."

"So you've done it?!" Selena jolted upright and scooted to the edge of her seat. "Tell us everything."

Felix maintained his grin, but only shook his head. "I never said I did it."

Selena whacked the back of his seat. "Please. You're the worst liar on this team. Obviously you've done it. Now give us the details. Your secret won't leave this car."

Felix chuckled. He *was* the worst liar in the group, and everyone knew it. "I have nothing to say. Perhaps we can discuss this matter another time. But as long as I've admitted nothing, I can't be turned in by the great Arielle Lucila."

Arielle gasped. "Excuse you! You think I'm a snitch? I would never."

Selena wrapped her arms around both head rests and pressed her face forward in the gap between the front seats. "I don't know about you two, but I never trust a person who memorizes a rule book from cover to cover."

Arielle spun around in her seat to meet Selena's accusing grin. "I'll have you know that people who study rule books do it so they understand exactly how to bend the rules in their favor."

"You've never broken a rule in your time as an Angel," Felix said. "I guarantee it."

Arielle snickered. "I said bend, not break. Keep up with the conversation. Any Angel ranked in the top twenty-five has to bend rules to get there. The Road Runners have too many parameters in place for us to effectively do our job. If we followed every rule by the book, nothing would ever get done."

"Does the Council know their precious Bylaws are being broken by their most revered members?" Felix asked.

"You mean *bent*," Arielle said through gritted teeth, earning a raucous laugh from the backseat. "And yes, they are aware. Why do you think they've never made changes to the rules to make them clearer? They understand we walk a fine line between judge and executioner. They also know how invested we are in our missions, that some simple rule changes won't alter how we approach our work. At least not drastically. See, in our line of work, we have to think like criminals to succeed. And doing such only opens the doors for us to find loopholes within our own guidelines."

Selena slow-clapped from the back. "There you have it, folks. Arielle Lucila, an outlaw on the run."

Arielle laughed. "I've been called a lot of things, but an outlaw...come on now."

Silence lingered in the car. The clock ticked toward 12:30, and still nothing.

"Do you guys feel it?" Selena finally asked, her tone bordering on sorrow.

"Feel what?" Felix asked.

"Nothing is going to happen tonight. I know we're not

supposed to trust our instincts, but I do. And I can always sense things. Everything about this night feels completely... normal. No one's coming through this parking lot tonight. Don't ask me how, but I just know it."

"I'm sure I'm just being pessimistic because everything seems to be going wrong," Arielle said. "But I sense it, too. We need to be ready to pivot. If the timeline of events isn't unfolding how it should, then we're completely on the defensive."

Felix shifted in his seat. "If the past tries to preserve itself, won't there still be some sort of accident tomorrow night? We can't exactly walk around the park and wait for something to happen. But I guess the bigger question we need to ask is which event is the past wanting to preserve? The deaths on Time Roller or the closure of Miracle Park? The two are connected, but they both can happen independently of each other."

Arielle nodded. "That's a really deep way of thinking about the past. I haven't even considered it. From what I've seen, the past will protect the events that affected the most people. The ones that cast a wider net, if you will."

"Obviously, the deaths had more of an effect," Selena said. "The park closing down only hurts Carter."

"That's where you're wrong," Arielle said. "We're not talking about harm—it's about overall effect. If the park remains open, how many families will vacation here over the next thirty years? Fifty years? Millions of families in the future will base their entire summer plans around Miracle Park if it stays open. The deaths in the Time Roller accident are tragic, and the families will certainly suffer, but the reach is limited to those who knew the victims. Think about it. There are people not even born yet who will someday make plans to come to Miracle Park. That's a much wider reach."

Felix rubbed his forehead. "That's what I was afraid of. I think we all agree this park shutting down is for the best. Carter doesn't deserve an ounce of the glory he's received."

"Whoa," Selena said with a chuckle. "Look at Felix, sharing his feelings about the mean businessman."

"I'm serious," Felix replied sternly. "And Arielle is right—the park closing down has the widest reach. It's going to happen with or without Time Roller breaking. I just hate seeing innocent people get hurt. A park can close for any reason—deaths from a seemingly malfunctioning ride is probably the easiest way—but it can be something as simple as a failed report from the health department."

"I'm sure Carter has them paid off," Selena said.

"That was just an example. I'm just saying something as simple as clerical work can shut this place down. We don't necessarily have to look for tragedy."

"So, what are you proposing?" Arielle asked, hearing a looming idea in Felix's voice.

"I've been thinking," he replied. "I've had a lot of time to do that sitting in this parking lot every night. Our best bet is to keep people from going into the park. And I know it won't really work, but it will cause a scene, stir up some trouble. What do you think of leading a protest tomorrow?"

# Chapter 40

August 24, 1978

The prior night played out how they had imagined. No one showed up by four o'clock, and the Angels left at five. Three hours remained between their departure and the park opening at eight, leaving no time for someone to cut the pull cord.

Selena had asked to work the later shift on the day of the tragedy, but they had denied her request. They saddled her with the eight o'clock start time, and thanks to the late night out, she called in to let them know she would be in at nine o'clock.

She didn't shower or eat breakfast, needing every second for sleep. She arrived at work with heavy bags under her eyes, her hair done in a sloppy bun that hung on for dear life on the back of her head.

Selena entered the park office and clocked in at 9:01, stopping in the bathroom to gather herself after driving over in a complete mental haze.

She looked in the mirror and splashed water on her face. Her brain burned with fatigue, and she doubted her ability to make it through the end of the day. Arielle demanded they all hang around until the park closed at eight o'clock.

*Eleven hours. I can do this.*

Just thinking about the eleven hours waiting between her and sleep made her stomach sink. Lightheadedness had already taken over, and her stomach grumbled with hunger.

"Hungover without any of the fun last night," she said to the mirror, reaching into her backpack to grab a Miracle Park ball cap to slip over the embarrassment that was her hair. "Last day. Let's do this."

Arielle and Felix planned to arrive at the park shortly before noon to start their impromptu protest outside the front gate. The two had bickered over the idea. Arielle suggested the protests didn't actually keep people out of the park. Most guests came from out of town and wouldn't change their vacation plans over some accusations of dirty drinking water in the town of Hilburn. All the protests might achieve were a boost in bottled water sales inside the park, where Carter jacked up the prices.

Felix agreed with the points Arielle brought up, but argued their goal was to throw off the park guests' plans for the day, even if for thirty seconds. People *did* stop to see what the protest was about, he said. And if those few seconds altered their time in the park, no matter how minuscule, it was worth a try.

Selena stepped out of the restroom to find the park already bustling with a crowd. It was the last week of summer break for the Hilburn high school and college students, and the teenagers were sure to get their fix at Miracle Park before returning to the grind of classrooms and homework.

The sun blared, shooting pain to the back of Selena's brain as she held up a hand as a shield. The smell of hot dogs on the grill so early in the morning made her queasy.

A group of teens strolled by, looking Selena up and down.

*Do I really look that bad?* she wondered. *I need to get to Time Roller before the day gets away from me. One last look before we give up and brace for something else to happen.*

Selena was supposed to check in with Joy upon arriving each day for work, and according to the schedule, Joy was working in Kiddie Land until her lunch break at noon. This gave Selena a window of opportunity to stop by Time Roller, sneak past whoever was working the roller coaster, and check out the pull cable beneath the platform.

She circled around the bathroom and took the path rarely used by the park's visitors—the same one that led to the secret exit behind Time Roller. Five minutes later, she arrived at Time Roller, the coaster zooming along the tracks, vibrating the world around them.

Unfortunately, there was no back way to access the ride's platform, thanks to the fencing that separated the pathway from the coaster. She had to walk against traffic in the exit lane. Before doing that, she stopped in front of the ride's main entrance and looked up at the towering hill. Would tragedy still strike today? Selena could only speculate.

With gooseflesh breaking across her arms, Selena started up the exit path. The ride had just ended, and she stood along the railing while everyone shuffled by. She hurried along once the pathway had cleared. Having done this same maneuver before, Selena knew her best chance to sneak by her colleagues was to wait for them to check the seat belts for each new rider. This left their backs turned to the exit gate where Selena could slip through undetected.

Her pace slowed as she reached the gate and saw Joy working Time Roller. While all the entry-level staff wore black or blue polos, Joy stood out in her fiery red shirt.

*Didn't she wear that same color yesterday?* Selena wondered, knowing Joy hadn't violated such a fashion rule all summer.

Joy must have felt Selena staring at her because she looked over her shoulder after strapping in a young girl. She pointed toward the panel for Selena to meet her there.

*Shit,* Selena thought, wishing she had waited to do this later in the day. But Joy wasn't supposed to be here, according to the schedule. *Is the past already getting to work?*

Joy wished the riders a miraculous time before the ride took off. A scrawny, skittish boy was working the panel. Joy paid him no attention as she hopped over the tracks and started straight for Selena. "Where the hell have you been?"

She had never spoken to Selena in such a harsh tone, and Selena's mind wasn't sharp enough right now for such a confrontation.

"I-I'm sorry," Selena said, nerves filling up within her chest. Life in the amusement park moved at a brisk pace, and all Selena could think about was finding a shaded bench to take a nap on. "I called in to let them know I was running a little behind."

Joy gritted her teeth and shook her head. "I *know* that. What the hell was so important that you couldn't be here on time? We're getting eaten alive this morning. Four people called out before I received your message. Did I do something to the universe? Because it sure seems pissed off at me today."

Selena placed her fingers to her mouth to feign surprise, not particularly caring about who had called out, but sensing it was about to be her problem. "I'm so sorry, Joy. You know I've never done anything like this before. I just had a terrible time sleeping last night. Only ended up with about three hours total."

"Well, that explains why you look like a mess," Joy said, crossing her arms as she looked Selena up and down.

*Please ask me to stay here and work Time Roller. That would be a pleasant gift from the past.*

"I can go clean up a bit more in the bath—"

Joy jerked her head from side to side. "No time for that. Come with me." She turned her attention to the boy at the panel. "Andy, you're good here on your own for a bit. Okay?"

It was half statement, half question, and the poor boy named Andy could only offer a nervous thumbs up.

Joy spun around and rushed through the exit gate, Selena having to jog to keep up. "I'm so sick of this fucking place," Joy muttered loud enough for Selena to hear. She stopped when they reached the end of the exit lane, standing just outside Time Roller. "That Andy has zero confidence. This job is not that hard. You check the seat belts, then push a button to start the ride. A fucking six-year-old could figure it out."

Rage radiated from Joy, and Selena needed to calm her immediately. "Look, Joy, I'm sorry I was late. It won't happen again. What do you need from me?"

Joy let out a maniacal laugh . "Everything is falling apart. Kiddie Land is a mess. We have workers hopping back and forth to run different rides, and the lines won't stop growing. Once lunch breaks start, we're going to have the same issue in the rest of the park. Today feels like a game of Whack-A-Mole. Whenever I fix one issue, the next one pops its dirty fucking head up. And it's not even 9:30 yet. Christ!"

Joy rubbed her forehead before burying her face into her palms. Her shoulders shook as she sobbed. Selena placed a hand on Joy's shoulder. "You need a day off," she whispered.

"When's the last time you've even had one? I know you're working every day of the week. I just don't understand why."

Joy looked up, tears welling in her eyes. Her lips quivered while she shook her head. "I don't understand, either. I hope it's all worth it. It's been a long summer, and I'm not sure how much more of it I can take."

She wiped the tears away and straightened up, tugging on her polo shirt collar as if it were a magical reset button.

"You okay?" Selena asked, releasing her hand from Joy's shoulder.

"I'm fine. Just a few more days until things die down. Labor Day weekend is our last rush for the year. Then finally I should be able to take a day off."

"Seriously," Selena said in a hushed tone. "When's the last time you had a day off?"

Joy looked around in thought, then shrugged. "I honestly don't know. I would guess in April or May."

Selena's eyes bulged. "You didn't have a single day off the entire summer?! Joy, that's...reckless. And might even be illegal. You can report Carter for forcing you to work that much. Clearly, it's taken a toll on you. No one should cry in the middle of their workplace."

Joy nodded. "I know. And it would be illegal if I hadn't volunteered myself for all that extra overtime. Mr. Carter never forced me, or even asked me, to work all that extra time. I did it on my own."

"Why in the world would you do that to yourself?"

Joy laughed. "I don't know. I thought if I positioned myself as an employee who gave their all, my job would never be at risk."

Selena frowned, took a step back, and crossed her arms.

"Hold on. So you worked around sixty hours each week to *not* get fired? Do you realize how absurd that sounds?"

"Absurd, yes. But it worked. I'm going on two years here and have only been fired twice." She laughed as she said this. Most employees at the management level had often been told they'd been fired, only to ignore Carter's request.

Selena shook her head. "Okay, you made it this long, but do you still really think Carter won't fire you if you make a simple mistake? Not like it takes a ton to set him off."

"Honestly, I don't care. I've saved a ton of cash from working all these hours. After the summer, I think I'm going to take all that money and leave town. I need a change of scenery. I'm tired of working here, tired of eating at the same restaurants, tired of my friends."

"I know what you mean," Selena said. "That's why I left Denver to come here. Sometimes you just need to shake things up."

Joy grinned. "You're a good person, Selena. I'm sorry we couldn't have more of a friendship. I had no social life this summer."

*You're telling me*, Selena thought, pissed that she could have grown closer to Joy during this mission if she hadn't sold her soul to the devil that was Alexander Carter.

"Don't worry about it," Selena said. "We're all just doing what we need to get through life, right?"

Joy swallowed hard, giving some deeper thought to this. "I guess that's true. We do what we need, even though no one makes it out of here alive. We're all just mindless cogs in the machine that keep the world turning." She checked her watch. "Shit, we've been standing here too long. Let's go—I wanted to take you to Kiddie Land to check on a couple of things."

They started away from Time Roller, and Selena could only look over her shoulder, hoping to come back later to check on the pull cord.

As they passed the lemonade stand, a deep, angry voice called out from behind. "You two, stop right there!"

# Chapter 41

Selena stopped and spun around to see Alexander Carter barreling toward them, a fat cigar pinched between his gritted teeth. He wore his usual three-piece suit, a horrible decision for how hot the day was, in Selena's opinion.

When Carter reached them, he plucked the cigar out of his mouth and pointed it at Selena. "You. Are you the one who came in late this morning?"

Selena looked at Joy, who had taken a step back as all color left her face. She looked back at Carter, heart thumping. "Yes, sir, that was me."

"I hope you have a damned good reason for hanging us out to dry this morning," Carter snarled. "Of all the days. Let's hear it."

"Mr. Carter," Joy interrupted. "Shouldn't you do this in the office? Our guests are here."

Carter cracked a slit of a grin. "Don't you have something you should be doing, Joy? Do I pay you to defend the staff who refuse to work as hard as you?"

"No, sir, I just—"

Carter shot up his hand and snapped his chubby fingers. "You just nothing. Now tell me, *Selena*, what was so important that you couldn't arrive on time for your shift this morning?"

Selena gulped. *He knows my name?!* "Well, sir, I had a rough time sleeping last night. Barely got three hours of—"

"Sleep?!" Carter gasped. "Well then, in that case, maybe you should go home and take a nap. Get nice and refreshed. Would you be able to join us in the afternoon then, princess?"

Selena knew Carter wasn't being serious, steaming rage clinging to every word that came out of his lips. "No, sir. I'm here and ready to work."

Carter threw his head back. "Ha! Ready to work, you say. I'd believe that if you were here at 7:55. Not this 9:01 business. Go clean out your locker. You no longer work here."

The past delivered its ultimate punch in style. On the one day they actually needed access to the park, Selena had just been fired. And it was a result of the wasted time parked outside the night before. She should have just stayed at the hotel to walk over first thing in the morning. *Fuck!*

"Mr. Carter," Joy said, stepping forward. "Wait a minute. I think this can be worked out."

Carter let out a laugh that sounded more like a squeak. "Worked out? You're correct! If Selena here wanted things worked out, she should have been here on time."

"Mr. Carter, please," Joy begged. "This is not the time to send another body away. Selena is here and ready to work now. We need her, or today is going to get even worse. Please reconsider. She's been nothing but a stellar worker since she started. This is only her first infraction."

Carter popped the cigar back into his mouth and placed his hands on his hips as he stared at his two employees. Selena thought he was actually considering letting her stay. He removed the cigar, blew a thick cloud of smoke into the air, and pointed the cigar at Joy. "The only thing I will consider is having Ms. Nicole here escorted from the park."

"It's fine," Selena said, waving her hands at Joy. "No need for you to get in trouble on my behalf. I'll see myself out."

Joy dashed away to a nearby trash can and vomited. She snatched a handful of napkins from the lemonade stand to clean herself.

"Very good," Mr. Carter said, looking disgustedly at Joy, before returning his attention to Selena with a crooked grin of tobacco-stained teeth. "You have five minutes to clear out your locker. Leave your badge at the front desk. Thank you for being another waste of time here at Miracle Park."

He snorted before taking another drag from his cigar.

"Oh, you think *I'm* the waste of time?" Selena replied, fists balled at her sides. It was going to take every ounce of self-control not to kill this pathetic excuse for a human being. But they were in the middle of an amusement park, where wandering eyes were already watching the scene unfold. "You, *sir*, are a waste of time, space, and energy. Do you really think you can compete with Disneyland? Have you even *been* to Disneyland? That place is actually *fun*. And pleasant. Do you know why that is? Because they treat their employees like people who matter. They pay them well and take care of them. Those employees show up every day with a smile on their face, and that kindness radiates until all the guests are smiling right along with them. But that can never happen here, because a theme park is only as good as the person running it. And you're a miserable joke."

"What the fuck?!" Carter shouted, biting a dent into his cigar, flakes of tobacco sticking to his sweaty chin.

"What's the matter?" Selena taunted. "No one ever speaks

back to you? I'm not afraid of you or all your connections with the city. There are plenty of men just like you where I come from, and you're all the same. You would chase a dollar bill off a cliff if it meant padding your bank account just a little more. You're driven by greed, and it will always be your downfall. One day you're going to find yourself alone and broke. No one will remember Alex Carter or his failed Miracle Park. This place will stand in ruins like a forgotten blemish on the past. And you'll be in hiding, wondering where it all went wrong."

Carter's face had turned as red as a tomato. He threw his cigar aside, teeth gritted like an attack dog ready to pounce. "One more word out of your mouth and I'll have you in jail by the end of the hour."

Selena giggled and was about to reply when Miracle Park's receptionist, Mary Pickett, ran up to them, panting for breath.

"Mr. Carter," she said, hands on her knees while she gathered herself.

"Mary?" Carter said, rage still lingering on his face. "What the hell is going on? I'm in the middle of something."

"Sorry, Mr. Carter," Mary said in a normal tone, standing back upright. "You told me to inform you whenever a protest is forming outside the front gate."

"WHAT?!" Carter snarled, spit flying every direction from his lips. "A protest? Right now?"

Mary nodded. "Yes, sir. They just arrived and have signs."

Carter pointed at Selena. "I mean it, girl. Five minutes and I never want to see your face in here again."

He stormed off, stomping on the cigar he had tossed moments ago, Mary chasing after him.

Joy stood with her mouth hanging open and returned from the trash bin where she had watched the rest of the encounter.

"What just happened?"

"I could ask you the same," Selena said, frowning with concern. "Are you okay?"

Joy licked her lips. "I'm fine. I suppose I *am* sick. Exhaustion, heat, and now more stress added to my plate. My body must *hate* me."

"You need a day off. Seriously."

"Soon enough," Joy replied with a shrug. "Did you really say all that to Carter, or was I dreaming?"

Selena grinned. "What can I say—some men need to be put in their place. Don't get all excited. It's not going to change anything here at Miracle Park. I said all that stuff for you and everyone who hasn't been able to stand up for themselves."

Joy shook her head. "You're really not from here. I've never seen someone so much as roll their eyes at Carter. And here you are. Telling him off like you have nothing to lose."

Selena shrugged. "Well, I really don't have anything to lose. He fired me, and I'll probably leave Hilburn, too. Fuck this place."

Joy slapped a hand to her mouth as she squealed with laughter.

"I suppose this is goodbye," Selena said, extending her arms for a hug. "I want to go check out this protest. Who knows, I might even join them."

Joy laughed one final time. "You can apparently do whatever you want. I'll never forget today for as long as I live."

# Chapter 42

Arielle and Felix arrived at Miracle Park and immediately got to work. Felix had spent the morning making the signs they would parade around, while Arielle called the handful of numbers she had obtained from Willow's group of protesters to round up as many bodies to join them.

The group had a phone tree set up, so once Arielle placed her initial five phone calls, the word spread within a matter of minutes. Only two of the five people she had called hung up once she identified herself. There was still plenty of bad blood between Arielle and Willow, and some were happy to choose sides in the dispute.

Despite that, sixteen people showed up at Miracle Park ready to protest by 9:30, including Arielle's favorite stoner, Phoenix. Arielle and Felix made brief introductions with everyone as they handed out signs well ahead of their originally planned schedule.

Felix took a ninety-minute nap upon arriving home last night before getting a start on the signs and multiple pots of coffee. "The more people we can sway today, the better," he had said. "People will get there when the park opens and plan to stay until it closes."

The exhaustion had made Arielle lightheaded through the first part of the morning, and she had no energy to argue with Felix. As far as they were concerned, Time Roller was fine, and they didn't need to focus so much on the roller coaster. Selena would confirm that upon her arrival at the park.

But Selena never called them, and Arielle planned to buy a ticket to go into the park to track her down for an update. When she saw Selena walking out of the park gates with a paper bag at her side, she knew immediately something was off.

Phoenix had brought a megaphone and was shouting into it about the dangers of polluted water.

"Selena?" Arielle said as she walked up to her friend.

Selena drew a deep breath while keeping her lips pinched tightly together. "He just fired me."

"He *what*?!" Arielle gasped. "Why? How? Today?"

Selena shook her head. "All because I didn't arrive on time. *Fired* for doing one thing wrong the whole time we've been here. I wish I could say I'm surprised, but it looks like the past wins another one."

Arielle rubbed her temples, her brain throbbing with fatigue as she digested the latest setback on the mission.

"What happened to getting here at noon?" Selena asked, nodding to the crowd of protesters marching in a circle around Phoenix, waving their signs about Miracle Park's role in polluting the town's water supply.

"Felix was up early, and I couldn't sleep in with the smell of coffee oozing throughout the house. But who cares about that, what the hell are we going to do? Did you even get to check out Time Roller to confirm?"

Selena shook her head. "I was about to when Joy stopped

me. She's been having a rough time and took it out on me for being late, too. Once I got her calmed down, we were about to start working when Carter tracked me down and fired me right in the middle of the park."

The heat was far too much for Arielle to handle this early in the morning, and she had to make a conscious effort to focus on every word leaving Selena's mouth. "He fired you in the middle of the park? In front of the guests?"

"Sure did. He really is as savage as everyone makes him out to be." Selena laughed through her nose. "I've gone this entire time without having a confrontation with him, and it didn't matter. Shit, I didn't think he even knew who I was—that's how well I've blended in. But he knew exactly who he was looking for when he came to find me. I'm sorry, Arielle. I should have just powered through and been here at eight."

Arielle shook her head. "We're already pushing our limits. The last thing I would do is force you to be here all day and night on only three hours of sleep."

Selena laughed, a sound that seemed just out of her control. "I'm sorry. I don't know why I'm laughing."

"You're slaphappy. Go home and sleep as long as you can. Me and Felix are already running on fumes. Maybe if we have at least one rested mind, someone can think straight. We can't have the blind leading the blind—not tonight."

"So you think a tragedy will still happen at the same time?" Selena asked with a confused frown.

"Honestly, I don't know what to think. Who's to say the cord still won't snap on Time Roller? The past doesn't owe anyone an explanation. It just preserves itself and keeps moving forward. If I had any clue of where to even look inside the park, I wouldn't be standing out here trying to keep people out."

Selena looked past Arielle. "Well, your next challenge is about to arrive."

Arielle spun around to see Carter barreling through the gates. "You better leave. Go sleep, come back when you wake up later this afternoon, ready to be the brains for all of us."

Selena nodded, then dashed out of sight before Carter could get close enough to realize it was her.

Arielle was surprised at how quickly Carter moved in his oversized suit. She braced for impact, noticing his forehead and neck were equal shades of red.

Carter pushed through the circle of protesters and stormed up to Phoenix, grabbing the megaphone and throwing it to the ground. Shards of plastic flew in every direction as the megaphone screeched, a disturbing feedback sound that grabbed everyone's attention.

"Hey man!" Phoenix said, throwing his hands in the air. "What the hell was that for?"

"Get the fuck off my property!" Carter shouted, pointing his fat finger in Phoenix's face. "The police are on their way and will arrest anyone who is still here."

"Not cool, man," Phoenix said. "We have the right to protest."

"And I have the right to call the police for trespassing. Now scram, you dirty fucking hippies!"

Arielle hurried toward Phoenix, who had fallen to his knees to gather the broken pieces of his megaphone. "Are you okay?"

"I'm fine," he replied lazily. "Fuck this guy."

Carter stood with his hands on his hips, a satisfied grin

spreading from cheek to cheek.

"You can't do this, Mr. Carter," Arielle said in her most polite tone. Deep down, she wanted nothing more than to strangle him in front of all these people.

"And who might you be?" he asked, pulling a handkerchief out of his suit pocket and patting the sweat off his forehead. "Another friend of Willow West?"

"On the contrary, Willow West hates me."

Carter's eyes lit up. "Ahhh, so you're here to help me? It's about damn time someone counterprotests on my behalf."

"Not exactly. We're here to protest the same thing as Willow, and you better be careful before we take you down."

Carter looked around at the group of protesters now huddled around Phoenix, then threw his head back and laughed. "Take me down? You must be new around here, sweetheart. So much ambition."

"I know things that can bury you. Unlike Willow, I actually got to the bottom of this mess you've caused the town."

Carter chuckled. "You know things? Let's hear it." He crossed his arms and nodded for her to continue, seeming to rather enjoy this game.

The weight of destiny hovered over Arielle. So many prior missions ultimately came down to a tough decision. Pull the trigger, or not? Throw that knife, or not? Now, she had to decide in a matter of seconds if telling Carter everything they had learned was worth it. Did his knowing that other people were aware of exactly what he was doing alter the past's plans? Ultimately, Carter didn't have a direct involvement with the tragedy that was supposed to play out.

The mission hung in limbo, and it seemed as if the world around Arielle was paused while she decided.

"Okay," she said, staring Carter straight in his despicable eyes. "For starters, I know the city of Hilburn still owns a small percentage of Miracle Park. That makes it public property and gives us the right to assemble and protest. We cannot be charged with trespassing, especially since we are not entering the actual park."

"Horse shit!" Carter cried. "You have no proof of such a wild claim!"

Arielle pointed at him. "Don't worry about what I have. These facts can be backed up, and that's all you need to know. Shall I keep going? Let's see. I know you incinerate the park's and hotel's trash in that little hidden building behind all the trees. Then you have your little goons dump the ashes into the river. And where does that river go? Straight into the town's water supply. But it doesn't stop there." Arielle turned to the rest of the crowd, Carter's face somehow turning an even deeper shade of red. "What's worse is the town knows all of this, but Carter has paid off Terrance Copeland, the president of the water department, to make sure no one ever looks into the matter. He's also paid off and threatened Dustin Nash, Hilburn's city clerk, to make it more difficult for you to get the permits needed for protesting."

The crowd, which had added another handful of people, showered Carter with an intense round of booing. Arielle turned back around to see the redness had completely vanished from Carter's face, replaced by a sheet of white.

*Got him,* she thought. She had given too many details he considered impossible for anyone to know. Maybe her speech would be enough to drive him out of town, but that wasn't something that could happen tonight. They still had to be ready for tragedy to strike at any moment.

"This is slander!" Carter grumbled. "I'm calling my lawyer, and the police should be here any minute."

He stomped away, earning a raucous cheer from the protesters. Arielle watched Carter disappear back into the park and could only brace for the unknown.

# Chapter 43

They continued protesting and enjoyed a noticeable increase in energy after Arielle sent Carter away with his tail between his legs. While everyone else loosened up, Felix remained on high alert.

Carter was too unpredictable for his liking. He could return with a gun and really crank up the heat. Alexander Carter was like a hippopotamus. Fine to look at in the zoo, but not something to be provoked in the wild. And Arielle had just poked the hippo with a stick.

Felix looked toward the park gates every ten seconds, waiting to see Carter storming back with a heart full of vengeance. But he never returned, and after fifteen minutes, two cop cars rolled into the parking lot and pulled up to the curb.

One officer stepped out of each vehicle and watched the protest with a lackadaisical approach. The two men stood next to each other, arms crossed as they exchanged words from a distance.

Judging by their body language, they must have been called to Miracle Park each time there was a protest. This was routine for them. One officer even waved at someone in the crowd. The protest continued, even with a few side-eyed glances toward the two officers. Felix kept marching in the circular formation, watching the cops and the gate. After two minutes, both officers strolled up directly to the group, the taller of the two calling out, "Okay, who organized this?"

Half the group stopped and fell silent, while the other half continued half-heartedly.

Arielle stepped forward, and Felix pushed his way to get right behind her.

"I did, officers," she said, confidence not wavering. As always.

"And you are?" the officer asked. Felix saw his name badge as *Meadows*.

"My name is Arielle Lucila, sir," she replied calmly.

Officer Meadows frowned and looked at his partner, Officer Milligen. The two cops had similar builds. Small beer bellies under their blue uniforms, thick mustaches, and both had sandy hair with specks of gray. Officer Milligen shrugged.

"You live here in Hilburn?" Officer Meadows asked, eyes boring into Arielle.

"Yes, sir. North side of town."

Felix's heart raced. The three Angels each had a fake ID for the times, showing their home address in Hilburn. It was a detail always covered before the start of each mission, but not one they'd ever needed to use.

"You connected with Willow West?" Officer Milligen asked with a subtle roll of his eyes.

"I know her," Arielle said. "But I wouldn't call us friends. Many of the people here are part of her group, but I'm not personally."

"What does that even mean?" Officer Meadows asked. Then he raised a hand like a stop sign. "Never mind. I don't really wanna know. Girl issues, I'm sure."

Officer Milligen nodded in agreement.

"I'm sorry, officer," Arielle said. "Is there a problem? We haven't done anything wrong. We're not causing a disturbance to any of the guests inside the park."

Officer Meadows shrugged. "Look, we're not here to cause anyone trouble. If everyone agrees, we can all go home and have nothing to report."

Arielle replied, "I don't agree with that, officer. I'd like to know what we've done that's warranted your presence here."

Officer Milligen chuckled. "We've got a future lawyer on our hands. You must go to the college." He shook his head before speaking to himself. "North side of town."

"I'm not a lawyer," Arielle said. "But I've studied the law enough to know we have the right to peacefully protest in this exact spot. If we *are* violating a law, I'd like to know which one. That's all."

Officer Milligen's face soured into frustration. "We got a call for trespassing. And by the looks of it, you're not the owner of Miracle Park. So, unless you're buying a ticket to enter the park and enjoy the day, you have no right to be here."

Officer Meadows looked down and kicked a rock with his boot. They clearly had a good cop/bad cop routine. Or maybe Officer Milligen was just an asshole.

Felix's heart was nearly jumping out of his throat. The tension had shifted, and he wasn't sure Arielle should continue with whatever she had up her sleeve.

She must have sensed it, too, because she took a step back, nearly stepping on Felix's toe. But that didn't stop her from saying exactly what was on her mind. "This park is partially owned by the city, making it public property. And in the town of Hilburn, you only need a permit to protest if traffic will be impeded. That's not the case here." She shifted her weight to one leg and placed her hands on her hips. "I don't know if the judges in this town are also paid off by Mr. Carter, but I'll trust my faith in humanity and say they're not. If that's the case, then arresting any of us is only a waste of time and taxpayer money. Sure, you'll score brownie points with Mr. Carter and the police chief, but ultimately, we'll walk free."

Officer Milligen took a sharp step forward. "What the fuck did you say, girl?"

Felix saw the cop's hand slide to the handle of his gun. *Please don't let these cops try anything on Arielle. They'll be toast.*

"Ed," Officer Meadows said. "Let's calm down."

Milligen looked over his shoulder. "The fuck I will. Are you not hearing how she's talking to us? Kids these days have no goddamned respect for their elders. Or authority. Maybe we need to teach them a lesson. Fucking hippies running all over this town."

"Ed," Officer Meadows said through gritted teeth with a lot more conviction. "Enough."

If it wasn't for the cool head of Officer Meadows, Milligen just might have started shooting at everyone in the crowd.

Milligen looked Arielle up and down, then spat at her feet before returning to Meadows' side. "Fuck you, girl. This ain't over."

Meadows pursed his lips. "Okay, I think we've had enough. Let's just break it up, everyone. Go your separate ways and we'll see you at the next protest."

"Do it," Felix whispered behind Arielle. "Take the deal."

Felix rarely listened to his gut, but everything in his body was urging him to get out of this situation as quickly as possible.  Neither Officer Milligen nor the past were to be fucked with. Not today.

"Very good," Arielle said, pivoting to face the group of protesters. "You heard the officers. Let's clear out."

Moans bounced around the group as they tossed their signs into a pile, grabbed their water bottles, and dispersed from the area.

The two cops waited until nearly everyone was gone, as had Arielle and Felix.

Officer Milligen glared at Arielle, refusing to break his stare. Meadows remained in control of himself and spoke. "Thank you," he said.  "I know there's a lot of gray area around protesting in this city, especially here. We can't stop you from coming back, but I strongly urge you to stay away.  We've thrown Willow in jail multiple times, and we can do the same to you.  Sure, you'll get out, but sometimes we have to set an example. Don't let yourself become that example. Are we clear?"

Arielle gulped, and Felix knew she was holding back everything she wished she could throw in their faces. "Yes, sir."

A grin touched the lips of Officer Meadows.  "Thank you. Now, get out of here and have a good rest of your day."

# Chapter 44

Selena stirred out of her sleep at four o'clock in the afternoon. Her mind was no longer foggy. In fact, it was a freshly sharpened knife.

Silence blanketed the house. She didn't know where Arielle and Felix were—presumably still at the park. But were they still protesting this late into the day? Arielle had mentioned wanting to get a ticket to enter the park as a guest. They'd stroll around like unofficial security guards sent from the future, ready to protect whenever tragedy struck.

The entire morning seemed like another lifetime. Even a little dreamlike. She was certainly tired enough for that cloudy feeling to have lingered over her memory of the morning's events. Carter really had fired her. And Joy really had a nervous breakdown that ended with her puking in the middle of Miracle Park.

The details might as well have been tossed in the river with the trash during those early hours at the park, but now, with a focused mind, everything was coming back to Selena.

*Joy was wearing the same outfit as yesterday,* she thought. The park had a uniform requirement of solid black, blue, or khaki pants along with a Miracle Park polo shirt for team members who interacted with the guests. The shirts were offered in nearly every color. While many team members owned several polo shirts of the same color—typically black or blue—Joy had never worn the same thing on consecutive days, as far as Selena knew.

*It doesn't mean anything. Joy is clearly at her wit's end. Judging by her emotions today at work, she just might have slept in her work uniform and woke up to do it all over again today.*

Selena shook her head. That was a logical explanation, but it didn't add up. Joy had to have been in this frantic state of mind all summer, yet she always put care into her appearance. A light powder of makeup, lipstick, and eyeliner were part of her daily routine. Someone who cared so deeply about their appearance wouldn't be caught dead in the same outfit for two days in a row.

"Why did you do it?" Selena asked her bedroom. She had gradually started packing her belongings during the past week, just in case they needed to grab their suitcases and flee 1978 tonight. Her bedroom remained barren, minus a couple of skin and hair care products scattered across the top of her dresser.

A twisting knot formed in Selena's gut, an early sign her body was urging her to listen to her instincts. She had long thought Joy might have involvement in the destruction of Time Roller, but they had zero clues tying her to any of it. Joy practically lived at Miracle Park, and never had time to make such an evil plan on her free time. Plus, Joy and Willow had no connection, and Willow was most definitely involved.

"Why did you nearly kill yourself working there all summer?" Selena asked, jumping off her bed and staring at herself in the mirror attached to the back of the dresser.

*Didn't she say something about leaving town and having so much money saved? She didn't need the money, so why work so many hours? And she said she's sick of her friends. That was strange because we've never seen her have a social life.*

Selena grabbed her keys out of her purse that had been tossed on the floor during her exhausted climb into bed earlier, raced to the garage, and climbed into her car.

She needed to go to Joy's house.

# Chapter 45

Joy lived in a small ranch-style house of only 700 square feet. And it was directly across the highway from Miracle Park, less than a five-minute drive for her to get to work.

The house stood on the corner of Sixth and Thirtieth Street, so Selena parked along the side, where a sidewalk separated a strip of grass from Joy's open backyard. None of the houses in the neighborhood had fences, and this immediately made Selena uneasy. For Selena to break in through the back door, it would expose her to anyone potentially driving by.

*I can't even wait for nightfall—it'll be too late.*

A pickup truck drove in Selena's direction, smoke puttering from the exhaust pipe. The driver was an older man with his arm slung out the window, cigarette in his mouth as he waved at Selena.

*Fuck,* she thought, adrenaline filling her limbs. But the truck kept going, soon disappearing from sight in Selena's rear-view mirror.

"Okay, you can do this," she said to herself, checking all mirrors and looking in every direction. There were no cars, no pedestrians. Just Selena and the destiny that awaited. She stepped out of the car and cut across the backyard, rushing to

Joy's back door as she fidgeted with one of Felix's lockpicks between her fingers. He had taught them how to use the tool in case they ever needed, and she hoped she had retained enough of the information.

Selena jammed the tension wrench into the lock. *Apply a little pressure. Insert the pick. Apply torque. And repeat five or six times.*

She had to mentally talk herself through this process, and keeping her attention on the lock proved incredibly difficult. Another car drove by but went in the opposite direction of the truck from moments earlier. They wouldn't have seen Selena standing at the back door unless they specifically looked behind them.

She heard faint clicks coming from within the lock and had no idea if the sounds meant success or failure. Her hand guided the pick in and out as she twisted. After the sixth time, the tension vanished in a split second as the door jerked within the frame.

*Holy shit, I think I did it!*

Selena turned the knob and let relief consume her as the door swung open. She stepped into the kitchen and closed the door behind her.

The house was plenty cramped. The kitchen had a stove, sink, and a narrow refrigerator. It opened to a living room/-foyer combination space that had a coat rack standing next to a single lawn chair parked beneath the window overlooking the weed-infested front yard. To the left was the bathroom, and to the right was Joy's bedroom.

"That's it?" Selena asked, staring at the open doorway that led into the bedroom. Joy lived by herself and needed little space, but Selena imagined she wasn't exactly hosting events in such a cramped space.

*I'm sick of my friends...*

That line kept repeating itself in Selena's mind. Why had Joy said that? From everything Selena could gather, Joy didn't have friends to be sick of.

She entered the bedroom, the biggest room in the house, and it looked like it belonged to someone who was never home. Two piles of laundry stood at the foot of the unmade bed. A basket of laundry was in front of the closet doors, socks and underwear hanging over the edges. *She must be living out of the laundry basket.*

To confirm, Selena rummaged through the lone dresser, finding the drawers mostly barren, except for a few long-sleeved Miracle Park polos. Joy had no nightstand, just a lamp on the floor next to the twin-sized bed.

Even with all of Joy's clothes and few belongings present, it didn't much feel like someone actually lived here.

Selena wasn't sure where to start, so she dropped to look under the bed. Somehow there were even more clothes, a couple of empty soda cups with the Miracle Park branding on the sides, and a bottle of pills. *Valium,* Selena read on the bottle. *That's for anxiety. And sleep disorders.*

There was no questioning why Joy was taking the decade's most prescribed happy pills. She worked beyond the limits of reason and worked for perhaps the most demanding man in all the Midwest. *I wonder if she lost these pills, and that's why she snapped this morning.*

Selena examined the pill bottle closer, and the world seemed to stop when she realized the name on the label.

*Willow West.*

Her mind spun, heart sinking as she uncovered yet a new

piece to this puzzle.

"What in the actual fuck?" Selena whispered, glaring at the label for another minute, as if it was a mistake. "So Joy and Willow *do* have a connection."

She placed the pill bottle back where she had found it and rubbed her temples. Selena had wanted to come to Joy's house based on a hunch. Something—and she couldn't pinpoint what, exactly—had felt off during her last conversation with Joy. Now that she found Willow's anxiety meds under Joy's bed, there was only more to discover.

Selena stood up from the bed and scanned the room. There was nowhere else to look besides the closet, so she pushed the piles of clothes aside with her foot and pulled the creaky double doors open.

A hamper overflowed with more clothes, beneath a rack of hanging shirts and pants. *Does she even do laundry?* Selena wondered. It seemed like there were at least two months' worth of dirty clothes, another sign Joy rarely had a moment to herself. The closet had a shelf above the rack, a dozen hoodies folded in neat piles on it. A stack of hats and visors stood next to the hoodies.

Selena wished she had brought a pair of rubber gloves to sift through this mess. But now wasn't the time to get picky, so she continued using her foot to move aside the heaps of dirty laundry on the floor. She kicked something solid and squatted down to find it was an old, dirty suitcase tucked along the closet's back wall.

She pulled the suitcase out of the closet and placed it on Joy's bed, running her hands along the brown leather exterior. It felt nearly empty, but something thumped around inside.

Selena unzipped the suitcase and flung the top open, finding a pair of bolt cutters, a copy of *The Language of Mechanical Engineering,* and a white envelope.

"Oh my God!" Selena gasped, recoiling back like she had just revealed a venomous snake. "It's all here."

She touched her lips with trembling fingers, staring at the book and bolt cutters. Selena reached around the two objects and grabbed the envelope.

She flipped it open and pulled out a written letter dated August tenth:

*Joy to the world,*

*This is the last letter I will send. Thank you so much for your hard work this summer at the park. Everything is falling into place perfectly for our plan. I was hoping to get you out of town sooner, but we ran into delays meeting with our engineering friend.*

*The book has been marked up and highlighted to show exactly what you need to do. Everything has been tested out. We went through four different sets of bolt cutters to find the perfect ones. I spent plenty of nights underneath the roller coaster to take pictures and relay information back to my engineer friend. Even though everything is laid out for you, I'll give you a couple weeks to study and get familiar with it. Our engineer friend visited the park yesterday and made calculations. He believes if you complete these actions on the night of August 23, the "accident" will happen on the following day. If it doesn't for some reason, it definitely should on the day after that.*

*We chose you for this because of your attention to detail. I know you'll do great. Again, take your time getting familiar with how you're supposed to cut the cord. If you cut too much, the ride might not even get off the ground. If you cut too little, it could take weeks or months to snap. Our friend supplied a picture of what the cord should look like once you've cut it precisely to the calculations he worked out.*

*Hide the book and bolt cutters in your bedroom closet and destroy this letter. We'll come clean up as soon as everything is finished. Thank you again for living through these two summers of hell for this wonderful cause. The town of Hilburn will never know it, but you're a hero. I know it's been lonely and challenging, but surviving at a job under AC for two years shows exactly how dedicated you are. The attached envelope has your cash and new house keys. I hope you'll enjoy California.*

*I wish you the best of luck wherever life takes you after this. My only hope is you can look back one day and be proud of what you accomplished. If you're ever back in Hilburn, don't be a stranger.*

*XOXO*

*WW*

Selena folded up the letter and stuffed it back into the envelope, dropping it into the suitcase. "Well, she never destroyed the letter," she said nervously. She zipped up the suitcase and put it back where she had found it, stuffing all the dirty clothes back on top to bury it.

*Okay, so Willow has been the brains all along and had Joy planted as an insider at the park for the last two years. No wonder Joy has been doing everything possible to never get fired. She needed to be there. This isn't even her house, either. Not if she's planning on vanishing in the middle of the night.*

Selena's head felt like it might explode with all the new information. She checked her watch to see it was almost 5:30. A cloud rolled through the sky and made the world outside gloomy. They still didn't have proof the pull cord had been cut, but Selena didn't need to see it with her own eyes. Not anymore.

It became obvious what was going on, and there was no reason to think Willow's plan had been thrown off by anything—including the Angels' interference. *Joy must have stayed at the park after closing and took her time cutting the cord. Then she slept in the park overnight. That's why she was wearing the same outfit.*

Selena scanned the room one more time, but knew she had already found what she needed. Satisfied, she hurried out of the house and hopped into her car, driving straight to Miracle Park.

# Chapter 46

Selena arrived at the front gates of Miracle Park ten minutes later after catching all four red lights on the short drive from Joy's house.

Not having a cell phone was proving highly inconvenient. She had no way of tracking down Arielle and Felix.

There were no longer any protesters outside the park, so she figured Carter had succeeded in breaking up the fun.

*I just need to get in there. Arielle and Felix have to be inside.*

It was the day of the tragedy, and Arielle wouldn't dare leave the site until their work was done. Selena considered sneaking into the park but opted to buy a ticket like a regular person. The skies remained gray and suggested rain. But she knew that would never happen. Rain would only close the park, which meant no guests on Time Roller when it was time to collapse.

There was no line to buy tickets, and Selena strolled through the park gates two minutes later, keeping her head down to avoid any of her old coworkers. Word might have not even spread about her firing, but she couldn't risk them seeing her just in case.

She grabbed a map and opened it up all the way to use it

as cover, looking over the top as she maneuvered past the carousel spinning with gleeful children.

"Okay," she whispered. "If I was Arielle, where would I be?"

The map proved a helpful visual. Knowing both Arielle and Felix were in the park, one of them had to be posted near Time Roller. It seemed as good a place as any to start her search, so she started down the pathway in that direction.

All lunch breaks for staff were completed by now, leaving the park mostly free of wandering employees. She took the back way to Time Roller and remained opposite the roller coaster, ducking behind a wooden post with various arrow-shaped signs pointing in the directions of the park's attractions.

No one paid her any attention, families and groups of friends gawking at Time Roller like they had just stepped foot on the base of Mount Everest. A mother dragged her teenaged son past Selena, muttering with disdain, "That's enough, Bobby Tanner. If you ask for a funnel cake one more time, we're going back to the hotel. I don't care if you haven't ridden your precious Time Roller yet!"

Selena looked around and saw a long line at the lemonade stand. Leaning on the side wall of the stand was Felix, arms crossed as he sipped from a cup of lemonade, sunglasses concealing his eyes that were certainly wandering.

Selena made a direct line for him, watching his face brighten up once he realized it was his friend and teammate. She stood next to him and assumed the same position, only holding the map up to keep them both out of sight.

"Good morning," Felix said sarcastically. "Nice of you to join us, Sleeping Beauty."

"Shut up," Selena snapped. "I just found out a ton. Where's Arielle?"

Felix shrugged. "We've been taking turns. One of us stays here at Time Roller while the other does a lap around the park."

"And nothing yet?"

Felix lowered his sunglasses and glared at Selena. "Do you think if something happened, my exhausted self would be standing here sipping a lemonade without a care in the world? Today has been brutal. We had the cops break up the protest after Carter came out screaming at everyone. And we've been doing our laps around the park for almost five hours. Only reason I'm not sitting on a bench is because I'd definitely tip over and fall asleep. I can't remember ever being so tired in my life."

On cue, Felix opened wide and yawned like an old cat after waking from a nap.

Arielle was right to send Selena home to sleep. Felix seemed nearly useless, and if Arielle was in similar shape, then Selena really was the only one of them with a fully functioning mind.

"What did you find?" Felix asked.

"Time Roller is still going to break. I found the engineering book and bolt cutters at Joy's house, plus a letter from Willow to Joy about their plans to carry this out. This has been two years in the making—at least that's how long Joy has worked here. I'm still not entirely clear on those specifics, but I know Joy hid in the park after it closed last night and took her time on the pull cord. Have you seen her at all?"

Felix nodded. "She's been working Time Roller all day. Still there." He nodded toward the roller coaster, and Selena squinted for a better view of the platform. Sure enough, Joy was running up and down to check on riders' seat belts.

"Damn," Selena muttered. "She's probably been working it all day to keep a close eye on things. That's gross. Why would she want to have a front row view of the accident?"

But Selena knew. All Joy wanted was to leave Hilburn behind. The friends she claimed to be sick of were nothing more than Willow and whoever else was involved with sabotaging the roller coaster. The sooner she saw the destruction, the quicker she'd be on the road, vanishing in the night like she had never existed inside the confines of Miracle Park.

Arielle strolled up to them, eyes narrowed on Selena while a small grin touched her lips. She seemed plenty more focused compared to Felix. "You're back! How are things?"

Selena informed Arielle of everything she had found at Joy's house.

"But we still don't know for sure if the pull cord was cut?" Arielle asked.

"We haven't visually seen it," Selena said. "And we're not going to have a chance, either. Joy won't leave Time Roller. But that's how I *know* the cord has been cut."

"How do you figure?"

"I've worked with Joy long enough to learn her routines," Selena explained. "Even though her employment has been a sham, she still had to make the best of her time here. And for her, that means not staying at the same ride for too long. She hates it—claims it makes her feel like a regular employee instead of a team lead. Why else would she be at Time Roller since she got here this morning? Of all the days, too. We may not have the exact proof you're looking for, but everything is adding up."

Arielle rubbed her forehead. "I know it makes sense, but we

can't exactly start shouting that the roller coaster is in danger without knowing for sure. We run a lot of risks doing that."

"Let's stop people from getting in line," Felix said. "Create a distraction or something."

Arielle glanced over at Time Roller, where the line had at least one hundred people waiting anxiously for their turn. "Stop people? Good luck. Anyone from out of town is at this park for that ride specifically."

"Do either of you know how to make yourself throw up?" Selena asked. "If we can get someone to sit down on the ride and puke, they'll have to at least shut it down for a bit."

"I'm not sitting on that ride," Felix snapped.

Arielle laughed. "I'd guess you'd be the one who can vomit on demand, Selena."

"I can cry on demand, but throwing up is not in my repertoire," Selena said. "I can sit down and fake a heart attack. That's actually something I've studied a bit."

Felix shook his head. "Let's just admit we've been beat. We need to either go all in and trust the pull cord has been cut, or we wait around for the ride to—"

A piercing shriek was the first that echoed throughout the park, and it came from Time Roller. Arielle's eyes bulged as she realized what was happening. Selena threw her map aside. Felix dropped his lemonade as the three Angels darted from the side of the drink stand, gawking at the train that had nearly reached the peak on the roller coaster where it remained stuck for a brief three seconds.

For a moment, Selena thought the ride would remain fixed in place, but that hope vanished when a sharp *crack!* reverberated around them. The cars started rolling backwards and gained an intense speed as they reached the platform.

Selena noticed Joy dive out of the way, then turned her head when the front three cars whipped violently off the track and became missiles of death to the park guests below.

Two bodies flew out of the front car and crashed into a crate of glass milk bottles being used for the ring toss game.

Screams rang throughout the area as everyone who had been standing in line for Time Roller stampeded toward the exit.  People tripped and were trampled by the panicking masses. The train of cars was completely flipped over, only one even remaining near the track. The ride itself had taken a blow from a flying car, splinters of wood shooting in every direction like an exploding grenade.

At some point, Arielle had tackled Selena and Felix to the ground next to the lemonade stand, all three of them shielding their heads.

"It fucking happened!" Arielle cried, rising back to her feet now that the flying debris had finally stopped. "Jesus Christ!"

Selena and Felix forced themselves up and scanned the area with their leader. Shards of wood and plastic from the roller coaster littered the walkway. Bodies lay scattered across the ground, some moving, some not. Streaks of blood weaved in every direction along the pavement.

One man limped away from the Time Roller exit, both hands squeezing his thigh that had blood gushing from between his fingers.

A teenage girl followed behind the man, walking in a daze as she looked from left to right, struggling to balance with each step she took. After six wobbly steps, she spun around on one leg and collapsed to the ground.

A siren blared through the park intercom system, adding to the chaos.

"This is not a test," a shaky voice announced. "Please exit the park immediately. I repeat, this is not a test. All guests must exit the park immediately."

There were still at least sixty people making their way from Time Roller, some dazed, some shocked, others breaking into sprints toward the exits.

"Where is she?!" Arielle screamed, going against the wave of people. Others were doing the same—looking for their loved ones.

"C'mon," Selena said, grabbing Felix's arm and pulling him to follow Arielle.

His legs must have been locked up because he tripped over himself four times before finding his stride.

Selena had last seen Joy diving on the platform, but she was nowhere to be seen now. "Arielle! I know where she went. Let's go!"

They had to cut diagonally through the herd of people fleeing the scene. They could already see the end of the line for those leaving Time Roller. Joy wasn't there, and Selena knew she only had one other way to go.

Arielle stopped and let Selena pass her to lead the way. Once they broke free of the crowd, they hurried on the pathway along the rear of the park. "She's going to slip out the back!" Selena called over her shoulder.

Joy had at least a ninety-second head start on them.

They reached the gate and found it still open, racing through it like a SWAT team ready to attack.

"There she is!" Felix gasped, his long arm pointing to the right. Halfway between them and the hidden shed where Carter had been burning trash, was Joy Gillespie, not quite running, but moving at the pace of a challenging power walk.

"I can catch her."

Despite his preference to stay inside all day and solve missions from his computer, Felix kept in incredible shape. He broke into a sprint comparable to a track star making their last dash to win Olympic gold.

Arielle and Selena had no chance of keeping up with him, but ran at their full speeds, anyway. Felix had separated from them by ten paces, moving like a starved cheetah hunting a gazelle. Joy looked over her shoulder and screamed at the sight of the three people chasing her.

She tried breaking into a run, but couldn't move much faster than she already was. Selena noticed the slightest limp in Joy's strides and knew she had no actual shot at escaping.

Felix closed the gap and leapt forward, arms outstretched toward Joy, while his legs flew behind him. He threw his arms around Joy's thighs and squeezed until she lost her footing and tumbled to the ground. Felix's body rolled in the opposite direction, causing him to climb to his feet.

Arielle and Selena caught up, Joy attempting feebly to crawl away.

Tears filled Joy's eyes as Arielle stomped toward her, grabbed her by the shirt collar, and yanked her up to her feet. "You thought you could get away with it?!" Arielle shouted into Joy's face. "Do you have any idea what you've just done?!"

Joy blubbered, mucus dripping from the tip of her nose, tears spilling down her cheeks. "I didn't mean to," she cried. "Oh, please God, I didn't want to kill anyone."

"What the hell did you think would happen?!" Arielle shouted, shaking Joy like a rag doll. "You snapped the pull cord for a roller coaster. What were you hoping to do?"

"I don't know," Joy pleaded. "It was supposed to be a little accident. Maybe some whiplash for the riders, but not all *this.*"

Joy fell back to her knees, and vomited on the ground. Selena didn't know whether to extend a hand of sympathy or kick Joy in the face while she was crouched on all fours.

"You're going to jail for a very long time," Selena said. "I'll see it through myself if I need to."

"Selena?" Joy asked, gawking around the group of Angels. "What are you—"

Joy whipped her head back and forth between the three of them.

"Calm down," Selena said as Joy broke into bouts of hyperventilation. "I've been working undercover at the park to figure out what was going on."

"Undercover?" Joy asked, frowning. "Aren't you just a college student?"

Selena shook her head. "I'm afraid that's not true, either. It appears I wasn't the only one living a double life. I'll admit, you had me fooled. We all dismissed you as a suspect early on because of how tirelessly you worked. But now it all makes sense. I gotta know something. Did Willow pay you to trade in these last two years of your life?"

"That bitch!" Joy said through gritted teeth. "She better be going down with me. This was all her idea. She's the one who said it would only be whiplash! Enough lawsuits to close down the park and send Carter packing!"

"Don't worry about that," Arielle said, stepping forward and pulling Joy back up to her feet. "We have all we need to pin this on both of you. You did the right thing by never destroying that last letter Willow sent you. She won't get as much time as you, but she'll get what she deserves, too.

"You had no right to go into my house!" Joy shouted. She kicked Arielle in the knee, giving a brief moment to spin around and dash away. But Selena stopped her before she could get any further, once more tackling Joy.

Arielle pulled out a couple of zip ties she kept in the utility belt under her shirt. She hadn't brought any lethal weapons into the park, not wanting to put innocent families at risk. She dropped to one knee, grabbed Joy by the arm and twisted it so she would turn face down.

"Where are we going to leave her?" Selena asked.

Arielle forced Joy's two wrists together and fastened them with a zip tie. "Let's take her back to the gate. We'll tie her to the fence and let them find her. I don't think we should exit through the park right now, so we'll come back this way and cut through the trees by the shed. That'll put us back on the pathway where I'm sure there is a big crowd by now. Then we'll drive to the house, grab our things, and get the hell out of here. Right before we leave, one of us needs to call the police station and leave an anonymous tip about what's waiting inside Joy's closet."

Joy groaned beneath Arielle's forceful grip. "I'm going to tell them all about you. How you broke into my house. You can't just get away with it."

Selena laughed. "We're not the ones in the wrong here, Joy. We didn't just destroy a roller coaster and leave a trail of dead bodies behind. Besides, we'll be out of town before they even find you tied to the back gate. Have a good rest of your life in prison."

As sirens wailed in the distance, the three Angels led Joy to the park's not-so-secret back gate and tied her to the fence.

# Chapter 47



*Present Day*

Arielle, Felix, and Selena had jumped back into the present day within thirty minutes of leaving Miracle Park behind.

They had watched the news that was covering a developing story about a tragic accident at the park that left ten people dead and dozens injured.

"More casualties than the original event," Felix had said before calling the police station to inform them about Joy Gillespie and her ties to the "accident."

"We can't control that," Arielle had assured him. "I know it hurts to hear more people died, but this time around, Joy doesn't get to start a new life in California. She'll be staring at a concrete floor the rest of her days. And Willow will get some justice, too. In the long run, we helped remove two bad people from society."

When they arrived in the present, they stopped at a convenience store to buy an ice pack for Arielle's knee. Joy had gotten in a solid shot, causing some light swelling around the kneecap. They were still on the north side of town, a now booming community that had developed in the land between their former neighborhood and the college campus. Signs in the store window supported the new North Hilburn High School.

The clerk behind the counter was a middle-aged man with a thick gray beard. Arielle put the ice pack on the counter along with three bottles of water.

"Good evening, folks," the clerk greeted. "Is this all you'll need today?"

"Yes," Arielle said. She looked around the store and saw other patrons all wearing their North Hilburn High gear. *STOMP THE SOUTH!* one shirt read. *WE ARE THE NORTH!* read another. "Can I ask you a question?"

"Of course, young lady," the man replied, popping a toothpick into his mouth. "Shoot."

"I used to have family in Hilburn a long time ago. They've all moved away since. But I've heard stories about the accident at Miracle Park. Whatever happened with that?"

This caught the clerk's attention as a look of seriousness swept over his face. "Wow," he said, taken aback. "I haven't heard the words *Miracle Park* in quite some time. Your family must have lived here in the Seventies. I was just a little boy when that happened, but I remember it clearly."

Felix and Selena shuffled to stand next to Arielle.

"All they ever said was that it was such a nightmare," Arielle said.

The man nodded. "That it was. God bless those souls we lost that night. Easily the darkest day in Hilburn's history. But what is the light without darkness, right? Everything in town changed after that day. The park closed down because the owner had to pay out a ton of money to all the victims. That alone did him in, but then a scandal came out about the owner dumping trash into the town's water supply. Can you believe that? He had fines and jail time coming at him from every angle. It's kind of funny looking back all these years later. There were two girls behind the crime that killed all those innocent people. And they had only done it to try to close the park down and send that owner out of town."

"Wait," Arielle said, playing dumb. "So it wasn't an accident?"

The man shook his head. "No, young lady, it was very much on purpose. Those two girls made a plan to cut the pull cord on the roller coaster to get back at the owner. See, they knew about the polluted water, and I guess they wanted to take matters into their own hands. Anyway, once those two were arrested, they spilled all the info they had on the park's owner. What *was* his name?"

"Alexander Carter," Arielle said. "I've heard it plenty of times."

The man snapped and pointed at Arielle with a wide grin. "That's it. Alexander Carter. So these girls tell everything Alexander had done, and the state investigated it. It was all true. I think he's dead by now. Not too sure what happened to him. There were a lot of rumors."

"So, how did Hilburn become so different? My family always talked about it being a small town, but it doesn't seem like that anymore."

"Now, that's what I was talking about the light meaning nothing without the darkness. Millions of dollars were paid out to the survivors and the families of the deceased. A couple of families pooled their money together and bought the land where Miracle Park used to be. Now it's home to the largest water park in the Midwest. They expanded the hotel and made a whole resort out of it. This was in the early 2000s. Business was booming, and these two families continued to expand their empire. They opened a golf course next to the water park, along with many other businesses in town. But what they did was make Hilburn a popular tourist attraction. The entire economy skyrocketed, and suddenly, people started moving here from Omaha and Lincoln. Shoot, even as far as Des Moines and Kansas City. We're still small compared to those cities, but we're carving out our own place in this big world."

A tear ran down Arielle's cheek, and she wiped it away before the clerk could see. "Thank you for sharing that story. It really is incredible."

"And beautiful," Selena added.

The clerk nodded with satisfaction, paying no attention to the line of customers forming behind the three Angels. "That it is. We don't talk about it much anymore. I suppose because most of the adults from back then are long gone. And half the town isn't from here originally. But you'll never find a Hilburn native who doesn't credit that horrific night to changing this city for the better. If I can leave you with one bit of advice—I need to get back to ringing up all these fine people behind you. Never let a tragedy define you. Look for the good, no matter how impossible it seems."

The three of them nodded and thanked the clerk one final time before stepping out of the store.

"I feel like that guy was staring into my soul and speaking directly to it," Arielle said once the door closed behind them.

Selena slung an arm over each of them. "He's right, though. We were so worried about there being more deaths. And yes, we'll carry those victims on our conscience forever, but look at what came out of it. Our work made an entire city better.

Talk about improving lives for generations of strangers we'll never meet."

"I know it was random luck," Felix said, "but I'm glad we went into this store. I needed to hear all of that. There's always more to a story than meets the eye. Hopefully, I won't be so hard on myself on future missions."

"Hey, we're all just learning along the way," Arielle said.

Selena pulled them in tighter. "And I wouldn't want to do this with anyone else. Now, let's go see what kind of margaritas this new Hilburn has to offer."

# READ THE FUTURES REPORT!

Just because Arielle Lucila doesn't want to look at the Futures Report to find out what happened after the mission, doesn't mean you can't!

Enjoy an exclusive look at the official Futures Report for the Miracle Park mission that is prepared for the Commander's office following each mission.

All you need to do is join my e-mail Reader Club by signing up at https://BookHip.com/THQRRTT

# Want more Arielle?

Have you read the other Arielle Lucila books?  This series does not need to be read in any particular order, though I recommend at least reading the first book before the others, as it establishes most of the "rules" of the universe.

Arielle Lucila Series:
- Book 1 - Angel Assassin
- Book 2 - Secrets in the Vault
- Book 3 - Dirty Money
- Book 4 - Time Roller <—you are here!

# Author's Note

Thank you for reading Time Roller. I hope you enjoyed the book! I read a book called Joyland by Stephen King several years ago, and loved the idea of a story taking place in an amusement park. There's something nostalgic about going into a theme park, no matter your age. It can make you feel like a kid again.

Here in Denver, we have Elitch Gardens, which still has one of those old wooden roller coasters. I've been to several theme parks and have ridden dozens, maybe hundreds, of different rides over the years. But for me, there is something special about the charm surrounding our old wooden roller coaster. It rumbles and rattles when you ride it. The vibrations are constant. And I'm convinced there's a split second on the ride where the train comes off the track. Now, I know that's highly unlikely, but what a rush to think of it being true. There's also a point where you're speeding down a steep hill with a completely dark tunnel at the bottom. The angle tricks the eye, and makes you think your head is going to come right off before you hit that tunnel. Fortunately, that doesn't happen, or else I'd had never gotten the chance to write this book!

Okay, that was all macabre. Apologies, but I'm forever a horror lover first, and appreciate a good scare.

When I was brainstorming for this fourth installment in the Arielle Lucila series, I came across a story of a ride malfunctioning at a small theme park that killed three people. It was tragic and sickening to read about it, but being a writer, it naturally sparked my creative juices.

What if someone sabotaged the ride? What reason would they have to do that? And that's how this story came to do. I started with a simple tragedy, and let it unfold from there, bringing in different characters with their own agendas, so much so that you have to figure out who is being the most selfish.

I've equally always loved stories with "heroes" who are really villains. Willow West in this book. She has good intentions and wants to make the world a better place. She has a big circle of friends who believe in her. But her approach is so ruthless, and her thirst for justice clouds her basic reasoning skills. Bring in Joy, and Willow has her puppet to make things happen within the park. It's briefly mentioned, but we understand Willow has bribed Joy with money and housing in California. I toyed with the idea of blackmail, but felt that would have put Willow too far into the villain category, and perhaps a little too similar to Alexander Carter, a villain in his own right. Greed is definitely a driving force in this story. Whether that was for money or justice, I wanted to portray the characters as having tunnel vision for their ultimate goals.

And as always, I hope you could connect with Arielle, Felix, and Selena on some level. They're the true heroes, just going about their business to save lives of innocent bystanders. They still have so much depth to explore, it's impossible to cover it all in a single book.

The next one will be a lot of fun, as the three Angels will jump through different eras to catch a time traveling serial killer.

Until then, I want to thank the team at 100Covers for another beautiful book cover. Melissa Prideaux for lending her hawk eye as an editor and tightening up this story. And of course to my wife, Natasha, and our kids, for keeping the fire burning within me.

# Enjoy this book?

You can make a difference!

Reviews are the most helpful tools in getting new readers for any books.  I don't have the financial backing of a New York publishing house and can't afford to blast my book on billboards or bus stops.

(Not yet!)

That said, your honest review can go a long way in helping me reach new readers. If you've enjoyed this book, I'd be forever grateful if you could spend a couple minutes leaving it a review (it can be as short as you like) on the site where you purchased this book.

Thank you so much!

# Also by Andre Gonzalez

**Arielle Lucila Series:**
Time Roller (#4)
Dirty Money (#3)
Secrets in the Vault (#2)
Angel Assassin (#1)

**Wealth of Time Series:**
Time of Fate (#6)
Zero Hour (#5)
Keeper of Time (#4)
Bad Faith (#3)
Warm Souls (#2)
Wealth of Time (#1)
Road Runners (Short Story)
Revolution (Short Story)

**Amelia Doss Series:**
Salvation (#3)
Nightfall (#2)
Resurrection (#1)

**Insanity Series:**
The Insanity Series (Books 1-3)
Replicate (#3)

The Burden (#2)
Insanity (#1)
Erased (Prequel Short Story)

**The Exalls Attacks:**
Followed Away (#3)
Followed East (#2)
Followed Home (#1)
A Poisoned Mind (Short Story)

**Standalone books:**
Snowball: A Christmas Horror Story

# About the Author

Born in Denver, CO, Andre Gonzalez has always had a fascination with horror and the supernatural starting at a young age. He spent many nights wide-eyed and awake, his mind racing with the many images of terror he witnessed in books and movies. Ideas of his own morphed out of movies like *Halloween* and books such as *Pet Sematary* by Stephen King. These thoughts eventually made their way to paper, as he always wrote dark stories for school assignments or just for fun. Followed Home is his debut novel based off of a terrifying dream he had many years ago at the age of 12. His reading and writing of horror stories evolved into a pursuit of a career as an author, where Andre hopes to keep others awake at night with his frightening tales. The world we live in today is filled with horror stories, and he looks forward to capturing the raw emotion of these events, twisting them into new tales, and preserving a legacy in between the crisp bindings of novels.

Andre graduated from Metropolitan State University of Denver with a degree in business in 2011. During his free time, he enjoys baseball, poker, golf, and traveling the world with his family. He believes that seeing the world is the only true way to stretch the imagination by experiencing new cultures and meeting new people.

Andre still lives in Denver with his wife, Natasha, and their three kids.